FISHHEAD

The Darker Tales
of
IRVIN S. COBB

Fishhead, *illustrated by Jim Pitts*

FISHHEAD

The Darker Tales
of
IRVIN S. COBB

Selected by David A. Riley

Parallel Universe Publications

CONTENTS

INTRODUCTION

by Linden Riley

Irvin S. Cobb

June 23rd, 1876 – March 11th, 1944

During his lifetime Irvin S. Cobb was one of the most celebrated writers in American literature, though nowadays he is almost forgotten, apart perhaps from his Lovecraft connection.

Irvin Shrewsbury Cobb was born in Paducah, Kentucky on the 23rd June, 1876. His father, unable to cope with the death of his own father, succumbed to alcoholism when Cobb was only sixteen. As a result, Cobb's education came to an

end and he started work, first on the *Paducah Daily News*, then the *Louisville Evening Post*. By 1904 Cobb's career in journalism was doing so well that he moved to New York, where he would go on to spend the rest of his life, starting work at the *Evening Sun*, though it wasn't long before an assignment to cover the Russian-Japanese peace conference in Portsmouth, New Hampshire so impressed Joseph Pulitzer that he offered Cobb a job at the *New York World*, where he became the highest-paid staff reporter in the United States. In 1911 Cobb moved to the

Saturday Evening Post. Three years later he was asked to cover the Great War. Amongst the many stories he wrote while there were the exploits of the Harlem Hellfighters, a unit of black American soldiers who had gone on to earn distinction for their courage and discipline, which Cobb celebrated in his book *The Glory of the Coming*.

Besides his prolific work as a journalist, Cobb's fame largely came from his humorous stories, which were published in the leading magazines of his day, and collected in numerous books during his lifetime. But, though he was best known as a humourist, he did have a darker side, exemplified by the tales collected in this volume. Two of the most famous succeeded in catching the attention of H. P. Lovecraft. It is claimed that *Fishhead* influenced Lovecraft's *The Shadow Over Innsmouth*. And there is certainly no doubt that Lovecraft was favourably impressed with this tale. In his groundbreaking essay, *Supernatural Horror in Literature*, Lovecraft wrote: "Still further carrying spectral tradition is the gifted and versatile humourist Irvin S. Cobb, whose work both early and recent contains some finely weird specimens. *Fishhead*, an early achievement, is banefully effective in its portrayal of unnatural affinities between a hybrid idiot and the strange fish of an isolated lake, which at the last avenge their biped kinsman's murder." *The Unbroken Chain* gave Lovecraft the key idea behind *The Rats in the Walls*, though in all other respects the two tales are totally different.

Besides writing and journalism, Cobb's career extended to Hollywood, where legendary director, John Ford, made two films based on his books: *Judge Priest* (1934) and *The Sun Shines Bright* (1953). Other films included *Peck's Bad Boy* (1921), starring Jackie Coogan, and *The Woman Accused* (1933), with a young Cary Grant. Cobb also did a stint at acting himself, appearing in ten movies altogether, including *Pepper, Everybody's Old Man* (1936), *Steamboat Round the Bend* (1935) and *Hawaii Calls* (1938). It's a sign of the prominence he had achieved that in 1935 he was invited to host the 7th Academy Awards.

Other than the tales that inspired Lovecraft, Cobb also wrote some brilliantly dark stories that culminate in a kind of sadistic irony. They are some of the finest *conte cruel* ever written. Amongst the best of these is the final story in this collection: *Faith, Hope, and Charity*, whose protagonists, as is often the case

Hosting the Academy Awards 1935

in Cobb's stories, struggle against fates that are not only pre-ordained but are horrendously appropriate! It must be added his hapless victims are far from blameless. What fates await them under Cobb's pen have most definitely been brought upon them by themselves! Through most of the tales there is a wry sense of humour, so wry, in fact, that it never detracts from the impact at the end; indeed, it often adds to and embellishes it!

I hope you enjoy reading these stories as much as I did and share with me the conviction that it is high time they were revived.

As Captain Eli in *Steamboat Round the Bend* (1935)

BIBLIOGRAPHY

A Little Town Called Montignies St. Christophe – 1907 story
Funabashi – 1907 musical comedy
Mr. Busybody – 1908 musical comedy
Talks with the Fat Chauffeur – 1909 collection
The Escape of Mr. Trimm – 1910 story
The Exit of Anse Dugmore – 1911 story
Cobb's Anatomy – 1912 book
Words and Music – 1912 story
Back Home: Being the Narrative of Judge Priest and His People – 1912 collection
The Escape of Mr. Trimm: His Plight and Other Plights – 1913 collection
Cobb's Bill of Fare – 1913 book
Fishhead – 1913 story
Roughing It Deluxe – 1914 book
Europe Revised – 1914 book
Irvin Cobb at his Best – 1915 collection
Back Home – 1912, produced as a comedy, 1915
Paths of Glory: Impressions of War Written at and Near the Front (expanded as The Red Glutton) – 1915 book
Speaking of Operations – 1915 book
Old Judge Priest – 1916 collection
Fibble, D.D. – 1916 collection
Local Color – 1916 collection
Speaking of Prussians – 1917 book
The Lost Tribes of the Irish in the South – 1917 booklet
Those Times and These – 1917 collection
The Great Auk – 1917 story
The Thunders of Silence – 1918 book
Boys Will be Boys – 1918 story
The Glory of the Coming: What Mine Eyes Have Seen of Americans in Action in This Year of Grace and Allied Endeavor – 1919 book
Eating in Two or Three Languages – 1919 book
The Life of the Party – 1919 book
The Works of Irvin S. Cobb (14 volumes) – 1912-20 collections
From Place to Place – 1920 collection
Oh, Well, You Know How Women Are! – published in one

volume with Isn't That Just Like a Man! by Mary Roberts
Rinehart – 1920 book
The Abandoned Farmers – 1920 collection
A Plea for Old Cap Collier – 1921 book
Darkness – 1921 story
One Third Off – 1921 book
Sundry Accounts – 1922 collection
J. Poindexter, Colored – 1922 book
Myself to Date – 1923 book (Stickfuls: Compositions of a
Newspaper Minion)
A Laugh a Day Keeps the Doctor Away: His Favorite Stories as
Told by Irvin S. Cobb – 1923 collection
The Snake Doctor – 1923 story
Snake Doctor and Other Stories – 1923 collection
Goin' on Fourteen: Being Cross-sections Out of a Year in the Life
of an Average Boy – 1924 book
Indiana: Cobb's America Guyed Books – 1924 book
Kansas: Cobb's America Guyed Books – 1924 book
Kentucky: Cobb's America Guyed Books – 1924 book
Maine: Cobb's America Guyed Books – 1924 book
New York: Cobb's America Guyed Books – 1924 book
The Chocolate Hyena – 1924 story
North Carolina: Cobb's America Guyed Books – 1924 book
Alias Ben Alibi – 1925 book
A Bull Called Emily – 1925 story
One Block From Fifth Avenue – 1925 story
Many Laughs for Many Days: Another Year's Supply of His
Favorite Stories as Told by Irvin S. Cobb – 1925 collection
"Here Comes the Bride –," and So Forth – 1925 book
On an Island That Cost $24.00 – 1926 book
Prose and Cons – 1926 book
Some United States: A Series of Stops in Various Part of This
Nation with One Excursion Across the Line – 1926 book
All Aboard: A Saga of the Romantic River – 1927 book
Ladies and Gentlemen – 1927 book
Chivalry Peak – 1927 book
This Man's World – 1929 story
Red Likker – 1929 book
This Man's World – 1929 collection
At the Feet of the Enemy – 1929 story

Both Sides of the Street – 1930 collection
To Be Taken Before Sailing – 1930 book
The Belled Buzzard – 1930 story
Three Wise Men on the East Side – 1930 story
Incredible Truth – 1931 collection
Down Yonder with Judge Priest and Irvin S. Cobb – 1932 collection
A Colonel of Kentucky – 1932 story
Murder Day by Day – 1933 book
One Way to Stop a Panic – 1933 book
"Who's Who" Plus "Here's How!" – 1934 book
Faith, Hope, and Charity – 1934 story
Faith, Hope, and Charity – 1934 collection
Irvin S. Cobb's Own Recipe Book – 1936 book
Judge Priest Turns Detective – 1936 book
Azam: The Story of An Arabian Colt and His Friends – 1937 children's book
Four Useful Pups – 1940 children's book
Favorite Humorous Stories of Irvin S. Cobb – 1940 collection
Exit Laughing – 1941 book
Glory, Glory, Hallelujah – 1941 book
Roll Call – 1942 collection
Cobb's Cavalcade – 1944 collection
The Governors of Kentucky – 1947 book
Piano Jim and the Impotent Pumpkin Vine – 1950 book

FISHHEAD

It goes past the powers of my pen to try to describe Reelfoot Lake for you so that you, reading this, will get the picture of it in your mind as I have it in mine. For Reelfoot Lake is like no other lake that I know anything about. It is an afterthought of Creation.

The rest of this continent was made and had dried in the sun for thousands of years — for millions of years for all I know — before Reelfoot came to be. It's the newest big thing in nature on this hemisphere probably, for it was formed by the great earthquake of 1811, just a little more than a hundred years ago. That earthquake of 1811 surely altered the face of the earth on the then far frontier of this country. It changed the course of rivers, it converted hills into what are now the sunk lands of three states, and it turned the solid ground to jelly and made it roll in waves like the sea. And in the midst of the retching of the land and the vomiting of the waters it depressed to varying depths a section of the earth crust sixty miles long, taking it down — trees, hills, hollows and all; and a crack broke through to the Mississippi River so that for three days the river ran up stream, filling the hole.

The result was the largest lake south of the Ohio, lying mostly in Tennessee, but extending up across what is now the Kentucky line, and taking its name from a fancied resemblance in its outline to the splay, reeled foot of a cornfield negro. Niggerwool Swamp, not so far away, may have got its name from the same man who christened Reelfoot; at least so it sounds.

Reelfoot is, and has always been, a lake of mystery. In places it is bottomless. Other places the skeletons of the cypress trees that went down when the earth sank still stand upright, so that if the sun shines from the right quarter and the water is less muddy than common, a man peering face downward into its depths sees, or thinks he sees, down below him the bare top-limbs upstretching like drowned men's fingers, all coated with the mud of years and bandaged with pennons of the green lake slime. In still other places the lake is shallow for long stretches, no deeper than breast deep to a man, but dangerous because of the weed

13

growths and the sunken drifts which entangle a swimmer's limbs. Its banks are mainly mud, its waters are muddied too, being a rich coffee color in the spring and a copperish yellow in the summer, and the trees along its shore are mud colored clear up to their lower limbs after the spring floods, when the dried sediment covers their trunks with a thick, scrofulous-looking coat.

There are stretches of unbroken woodland around it and slashes where the cypress knees rise countlessly like headstones and footstones for the dead snags that rot in the soft ooze. There are deadenings with the lowland corn growing high and rank below and the bleached, fire-blackened girdled trees rising above, barren of leaf and limb. There are long, dismal flats where in the spring the clotted frog-spawn clings like patches of white mucus among the weed stalks and at night the turtles crawl out to lay clutches of perfectly round, white eggs with tough, rubbery shells in the sand. There are bayous leading off to nowhere and sloughs that wind aimlessly, like great, blind worms, to finally join the big river that rolls its semi-liquid torrents a few miles to the westward.

So Reelfoot lies there, flat in the bottoms, freezing lightly in the winter, steaming torridly in the summer, swollen in the spring when the woods have turned a vivid green and the buffalo gnats by the million and the billion fill the flooded hollows with their pestilential buzzing, and in the fall ringed about gloriously with all the colors which the first frost brings — gold of hickory, yellow-russet of sycamore, red of dogwood and ash and purple-black of sweet-gum.

But the Reelfoot country has its uses. It is the best game and fish country, natural or artificial, that is left in the South today. In their appointed seasons the duck and the geese flock in, and even semi-tropical birds, like the brown pelican and the Florida snake-bird, have been known to come there to nest. Pigs, gone back to wildness, range the ridges, each razor-backed drove captained by a gaunt, savage, slab-sided old boar. By night the bull frogs, inconceivably big and tremendously vocal, bellow under the banks.

It is a wonderful place for fish — bass and crappie and perch and the snouted buffalo fish. How these edible sorts live to spawn and how their spawn in turn live to spawn again is a marvel, seeing how many of the big fish-eating cannibal fish there are in Reelfoot. Here, bigger than anywhere else, you find the garfish, all bones and appetite and horny plates, with a snout like an alligator, the nearest link, naturalists say, between the animal life of today and the animal life of the Reptilian Period. The shovel-nose cat, really a deformed kind of freshwater sturgeon, with a great fan-shaped membranous plate jutting out from his nose like a bowsprit, jumps all day in the quiet places with mighty splashing sounds, as though a horse had fallen into the water. On every stranded log the huge snapping turtles lie on sunny days in groups of four and six, baking their shells black in the sun, with their little snaky heads raised watchfully, ready to slip noiselessly off at the first sound of oars grating in the row-locks.

But the biggest of them all are the catfish. These are monstrous creatures, these catfish of Reelfoot—scaleless, slick things, with corpsy, dead eyes and poisonous fins like javelins and long whiskers dangling from the sides of their cavernous heads. Six and seven feet long they grow to be and to weigh two hundred pounds or more, and they have mouths wide enough to take in a man's foot or a man's fist and strong enough to break any hook save the strongest and greedy enough to eat anything, living or dead or putrid, that the horny jaws can master. Oh, but they are wicked things, and they tell wicked tales of them down there. They call them man-eaters and compare them, in certain of their habits, to sharks.

Fishhead was of a piece with this setting. He fitted into it as an acorn fits its cup. All his life he had lived on Reelfoot, always in the one place, at the mouth of a certain slough. He had been born there, of a negro father and a half-breed Indian mother, both of them now dead, and the story was that before his birth his mother was frightened by one of the big fish, so that the child came into the world most hideously marked. Anyhow, Fishhead was a human monstrosity, the veritable embodiment of nightmare. He had the body of a man — a short, stocky, sinewy body — but his face was as near to being the face of a great fish as any face could be and yet retain some trace of human aspect. His skull sloped back so abruptly that he could hardly be said to have a forehead at all; his chin slanted off right into nothing. His eyes were small and round with shallow, glazed, pale-yellow

15

pupils, and they were set wide apart in his head and they were unwinking and staring, like a fish's eyes. His nose was no more than a pair of tiny slits in the middle of the yellow mask. His mouth was the worst of all. It was the awful mouth of a catfish, lipless and almost inconceivably wide, stretching from side to side. Also when Fishhead became a man grown his likeness to a fish increased, for the hair upon his face grew out into two tightly kinked, slender pendants that drooped down either side of the mouth like the beards of a fish.

If he had any other name than Fishhead, none excepting he knew it. As Fishhead he was known and as Fishhead he answered. Because he knew the waters and the woods of Reelfoot better than any other man there, he was valued as a guide by the city men who came every year to hunt or fish; but there were few such jobs that Fishhead would take. Mainly he kept to himself, tending his corn patch, netting the lake, trapping a little and in season pot hunting for the city markets. His neighbors, ague-bitten whites and malaria-proof negroes alike, left him to himself. Indeed for the most part they had a superstitious fear of him. So he lived alone, with no kith nor kin, nor even a friend, shunning his kind and shunned by them.

His cabin stood just below the state line, where Mud Slough runs into the lake. It was a shack of logs, the only human habitation for four miles up or down. Behind it the thick timber came shouldering right up to the edge of Fishhead's small truck patch, enclosing it in thick shade except when the sun stood just overhead. He cooked his food in a primitive fashion, outdoors, over a hole in the soggy earth or upon the rusted red ruin of an old cook stove, and he drank the saffron water of the lake out of a dipper made of a gourd, faring and fending for himself, a master hand at skiff and net, competent with duck gun and fish spear, yet a creature of affliction and loneliness, part savage, almost amphibious, set apart from his fellows, silent and suspicious.

In front of his cabin jutted out a long fallen cottonwood trunk, lying half in and half out of the water, its top side burnt by the sun and worn by the friction of Fishhead's bare feet until it showed countless patterns of tiny scrolled lines, its under side black and rotted and lapped at unceasingly by little waves like tiny licking tongues. Its farther end reached deep water. And it

16

was a part of Fishhead, for no matter how far his fishing and trapping might take him in the daytime, sunset would find him back there, his boat drawn up on the bank and he on the outer end of this log. From a distance men had seen him there many times, sometimes squatted, motionless as the big turtles that would crawl upon its dipping tip in his absence, sometimes erect and vigilant like a creek crane, his misshapen yellow form outlined against the yellow sun, the yellow water, the yellow banks — all of them yellow together.

If the Reelfooters shunned Fishhead by day they feared him by night and avoided him as a plague, dreading even the chance of a casual meeting. For there were ugly stories about Fishhead — stories which all the negroes and some of the whites believed. They said that a cry which had been heard just before dusk and just after, skittering across the darkened waters, was his calling cry to the big cats, and at his bidding they came trooping in, and that in their company he swam in the lake on moonlight nights, sporting with them, diving with them, even feeding with them on what manner of unclean things they fed. The cry had been heard many times, that much was certain, and it was certain also that the big fish were noticeably thick at the mouth of Fishhead's slough. No native Reelfooter, white or black, would willingly wet a leg or an arm there.

Here Fishhead had lived and here he was going to die. The Baxters were going to kill him, and this day in mid-summer was to be the time of the killing. The two Baxters — Jake and Joel — were coming in their dugout to do it. This murder had been a long time in the making. The Baxters had to brew their hate over a slow fire for months before it reached the pitch of action. They were poor whites, poor in everything — repute and worldly goods and standing — a pair of fever-ridden squatters who lived on whisky and tobacco when they could get it, and on fish and cornbread when they couldn't.

The feud itself was of months' standing. Meeting Fishhead one day in the spring on the spindly scaffolding of the skiff landing at Walnut Log, and being themselves far overtaken in liquor and vainglorious with a bogus alcoholic substitute for courage, the brothers had accused him, wantonly and without proof, of running their trot-line and stripping it of the hooked catch — an unforgivable sin among the water dwellers and the

17

shanty boaters of the South. Seeing that he bore this accusation in silence, only eyeing them steadfastly, they had been emboldened then to slap his face, whereupon he turned and gave them both the beating of their lives — bloodying their noses and bruising their lips with hard blows against their front teeth, and finally leaving them, mauled and prone, in the dirt. Moreover, in the onlookers a sense of the everlasting fitness of things had triumphed over race prejudice and allowed them — two freeborn, sovereign whites — to be licked by a nigger.

Therefore, they were going to get the nigger. The whole thing had been planned out amply. They were going to kill him on his log at sundown. There would be no witnesses to see it, no retribution to follow after it. The very ease of the undertaking made them forget even their inborn fear of the place of Fishhead's habitation.

For more than an hour now they had been coming from their shack across a deeply indented arm of the lake. Their dugout, fashioned by fire and adz and draw-knife from the bole of a gum tree, moved through the water as noiselessly as a swimming mallard, leaving behind it a long, wavy trail on the stilled waters. Jake, the better oarsman, sat flat in the stern of the round-bottomed craft, paddling with quick, splashless strokes. Joel, the better shot, was squatted forward. There was a heavy, rusted duck gun between his knees.

Though their spying upon the victim had made them certain sure he would not be about the shore for hours, a doubled sense of caution led them to hug closely the weedy banks. They slid along the shore like shadows, moving so swiftly and in such silence that the watchful mud turtles barely turned their snaky heads as they passed. So, a full hour before the time, they came slipping around the mouth of the slough and made for a natural ambuscade which the mixed breed had left within a stone's jerk of his cabin to his own undoing.

Where the slough's flow joined deeper water a partly uprooted tree was stretched, prone from shore, at the top still thick and green with leaves that drew nourishment from the earth in which the half-uncovered roots yet held, and twined about with an exuberance of trumpet vines and wild fox-grapes. All about was a huddle of drift — last year's cornstalks, shreddy strips of bark, chunks of rotted weed, all the riffle and dunnage of a quiet eddy. Straight into this green clump glided the dugout and swung, broadside on, against the protecting trunk of the tree, hidden from the inner side by the intervening curtains of rank growth, just as the Baxters had intended it should be hidden, when days before in their scouting they marked this masked place of waiting and included it, then and there, in the scope of their plans.

There had been no hitch or mishap. No one had been abroad in the late afternoon to mark their movements — and in a little while Fishhead ought to be due. Jake's woodman's eye followed the downward swing of the sun speculatively. The shadows, thrown shoreward, lengthened and slithered on the small ripples. The small noises of the day died out; the small noises of the coming night began to multiply. The green-bodied flies went away and big mosquitoes, with speckled gray legs, came to take the places of the flies. The sleepy lake sucked at the mud banks with small mouthing sounds as though it found the taste of the raw mud agreeable. A monster crawfish, big as a chicken lobster, crawled out of the top of his dried mud chimney and perched himself there, an armored sentinel on the watchtower. Bull bats began to flitter back and forth above the tops of the trees. A pudgy muskrat, swimming with head up, was moved to sidle off briskly as he met a cotton-mouth moccasin snake, so fat and swollen with summer poison that it looked almost like a legless lizard as it moved along the surface of the water in a series of slow torpid s's. Directly above the head of either of the waiting assassins a compact little swarm of midges hung, holding to a sort of kite-shaped formation.

A little more time passed and Fishhead came out of the woods at the back, walking swiftly, with a sack over his shoulder. For a few seconds his deformities showed in the clearing, then the black inside of the cabin swallowed him up. By now the sun was almost down. Only the red nub of it showed above the timber line across the lake, and the shadows lay inland a long way. Out beyond, the big cats were stirring, and the great smacking sounds as their twisting bodies leaped clear and fell back in the water came shoreward in a chorus.

But the two brothers in their green covert gave heed to nothing except the one thing upon which their hearts were set and their nerves tensed. Joel gently shoved his gun-barrels across the log, cuddling the stock to his shoulder and slipping two fingers caressingly back and forth upon the triggers. Jake held the narrow dugout steady by a grip upon a fox-grape tendril.

A little wait and then the finish came. Fishhead emerged from the cabin door and came down the narrow footpath to the water and out upon the water on his log. He was barefooted and bareheaded, his cotton shirt open down the front to show his yellow neck and breast, his dungaree trousers held about his waist by a twisted tow string. His broad splay feet, with the prehensile toes outspread, gripped the polished curve of the log as he moved along its swaying, dipping surface until he came to its outer end and stood there erect, his chest filling, his chinless face lifted up and something of mastership and dominion in his poise. And then — his eye caught what another's eyes might have missed — the round, twin ends of the gun barrels, the fixed gleams of Joel's eyes, aimed at him through the green tracery.

In that swift passage of time, too swift almost to be measured by seconds, realization flashed all through him, and he threw his head still higher and opened wide his shapeless trap of a mouth, and out across the lake he sent skittering and rolling his cry. And in his cry was the laugh of a loon, and the croaking bellow of a frog, and the bay of a hound, all the compounded night noises of the lake. And in it, too, was a farewell and a defiance and an appeal. The heavy roar of the duck gun came.

At twenty yards the double charge tore the throat out of him. He came down, face forward, upon the log and clung there, his trunk twisting distortedly, his legs twitching and kicking like the legs of a speared frog, his shoulders hunching and lifting spasmodically as the life ran out of him all in one swift coursing flow. His head canted up between the heaving shoulders, his eyes looked full on the staring face of his murderer, and then the blood came out of his mouth and Fishhead, in death still as much fish as man, slid flopping, head first, off the end of the log and sank, face downward, slowly, his limbs all extended out. One after another a string of big bubbles came up to burst in the middle of a widening reddish stain on the coffee-colored water.

The brothers watched this, held by the horror of the thing they had done, and the cranky dugout, tipped far over by the recoil of the gun, took water steadily across its gunwale; and now there was a sudden stroke from below upon its careening bottom

20

and it went over and they were in the lake. But shore was only twenty feet away, the trunk of the uprooted tree only five. Joel, still holding fast to his hot gun, made for the log, gaining it with one stroke. He threw his free arm over it and clung there, treading water, as he shook his eyes free. Something gripped him — some great, sinewy, unseen thing gripped him fast by the thigh, crushing down on his flesh.

He uttered no cry, but his eyes popped out and his mouth set in a square shape of agony, and his fingers gripped into the bark of the tree like grapples. He was pulled down and down, by steady jerks, not rapidly but steadily, so steadily, and as he went his fingernails tore four little white strips in the tree bark. His mouth went under, next his popping eyes, then his erect hair, and finally his clawing, clutching hand, and that was the end of him.

Jake's fate was harder still, for he lived longer — long enough to see Joel's finish. He saw it through the water that ran down his face, and with a great surge of his whole body he literally flung himself across the log and jerked his legs up high into the air to save them. He flung himself too far, though, for his face and chest hit the water on the far side. And out of this water rose the head of a great fish, with the lake slime of years on its flat, black head, its whiskers bristling, its corpsy eyes alight. Its horny jaws closed and clamped in the front of Jake's flannel shirt. His hand struck out wildly and was speared on a poisoned fin, and unlike Joel, he went from sight with a great yell and a whirling and a churning of the water that made the cornstalks circle on the edges of a small whirlpool.

But the whirlpool soon thinned away into widening rings of ripples and the cornstalks quit circling and became still again, and only the multiplying night noises sounded about the mouth of the slough.

The bodies of all three came ashore on the same day near the same place. Except for the gaping gunshot wound where the neck met the chest, Fishhead's body was unmarked. But the bodies of the two Baxters were so marred and mauled that the Reelfooters buried them together on the bank without ever knowing which might be Jake's and which might be Joel's.

21

THE ESCAPE OF MR. TRIMM

Mr. Trimm, recently president of the late Thirteenth National Bank, was taking a trip which was different in a number of ways from any he had ever taken. To begin with, he was used to parlor cars and Pullmans and even luxurious private cars when he went anywhere; whereas now he rode with a most mixed company in a dusty, smelly day coach. In the second place, his traveling companion was not such a one as Mr. Trimm would have chosen had the choice been left to him, being a stupid-looking German-American with a drooping, yellow moustache. And in the third place, Mr. Trimm's plump white hands were folded in his lap, held in a close and enforced companionship by a new and shiny pair of Bean's Latest Model Little Giant handcuffs. Mr. Trimm was on his way to the Federal penitentiary to serve twelve years at hard labor for breaking, one way or another, about all the laws that are presumed to govern national banks.

All the time Mr. Trimm was in the Tombs, fighting for a new trial, a certain question had lain in his mind unasked and unanswered. Through the seven months of his stay in the jail that question had been always at the back part of his head, ticking away there like a little watch that never needed winding. A dozen times a day it would pop into his thoughts and then go away, only to come back again.

When Copley was taken to the penitentiary — Copley being the cashier who got off with a lighter sentence because the judge and jury held him to be no more than a blind accomplice in the wrecking of the Thirteenth National — Mr. Trimm read closely every line that the papers carried about Copley's departure. But none of them had seen fit to give the young cashier more than a short and colorless paragraph. For Copley was only a small figure in the big intrigue that had startled the country; Copley didn't have the money to hire big lawyers to carry his appeal to the higher courts for him; Copley's wife was keeping boarders; and as for Copley himself, he had been wearing stripes several months now.

With Mr. Trimm it had been vastly different. From the very beginning he had held the public eye. His bearing in court when the jury came in with their judgment; his cold defiance when the judge, in pronouncing sentence, mercilessly arraigned him and the system of finance for which he stood; the manner of his life in the Tombs; his spectacular fight to beat the verdict, had all been worth columns of newspaper space. If Mr. Trimm had been a popular poisoner, or a society woman named as co-respondent in a sensational divorce suit, the papers could not have been more generous in their space allotments. And Mr. Trimm in his cell had read all of it with smiling contempt, even to the semi-hysterical outpourings of the lady special writers who called him The Iron Man of Wall Street and undertook to analyze his emotions — and missed the mark by a thousand miles or two.

Things had been smoothed as much as possible for him in the Tombs, for money and the power of it will go far toward ironing out even the corrugated routine of that big jail. He had a large cell to himself in the airiest, brightest corridor. His meals were served by a caterer from outside. Although he ate them without knife or fork, he soon learned that a spoon and the fingers can accomplish a good deal when backed by a good appetite, and Mr. Trimm's appetite was uniformly good. The warden and his underlings had been models of official kindliness; the newspapers had sent their brightest young men to interview him whenever he felt like talking, which wasn't often; and surely his lawyers had done all in his behalf that money — a great deal of money — could do. Perhaps it was because of these things that Mr. Trimm had never been able to bring himself to realize that he was the Hobart W. Trimm who had been sentenced to the Federal prison; it seemed to him, somehow, that he, personally, was merely a spectator standing to one side watching the fight of another man to dodge the penitentiary.

However, he didn't fail to give the other man the advantage of every chance that money would buy. This sense of aloofness to the whole thing had persisted even when his personal lawyer came to him one night in the early fall and told him that the court of last possible resort had denied the last possible motion. Mr. Trimm cut the lawyer short with a shake of his head as the other began saying something about the chances of a pardon from the

President. Mr. Trimm wasn't in the habit of letting men deceive him with idle words. No President would pardon him, and he knew it.

"Never mind that, Walling," he said steadily, when the lawyer offered to come to see him again before he started for prison the next day. "If you'll see that a drawing-room on the train is reserved for me — for us, I mean — and all that sort of thing, I'll not detain you any further. I have a good many things to do tonight. Good night."

"Such a man, such a man," said Walling to himself as he climbed into his car; "all chilled steel and brains. And they are going to lock that brain up for twelve years. It's a crime," said Walling, and shook his head. Walling always said it was a crime when they sent a client of his to prison. To his credit be it said, though, they sent very few of them there. Walling made as high as fifty thousand a year at criminal law. Some of it was very criminal law indeed. His specialty was picking holes in the statutes faster than the legislature could make them and provide them and putty them up with amendments. This was the first case he had lost in a good long time.

When Jerry, the turnkey, came for him in the morning Mr. Trimm had made as careful a toilet as the limited means at his command permitted, and he had eaten a hearty breakfast and was ready to go, all but putting on his hat. Looking the picture of well-groomed, close-buttoned, iron-grey middle age, Mr. Trimm followed the turnkey through the long corridor and down the winding iron stairs to the warden's office. He gave no heed to the curious eyes that followed him through the barred doors of many cells; his feet rang briskly on the flags.

The warden, Hallam, was there in the private office with another man, a tall, raw-boned man with a drooping, straw-colored moustache and the unmistakable look about him of the police officer. Mr. Trimm knew without being told that this was the man who would take him to prison. The stranger was standing at a desk, signing some papers.

"Sit down, please, Mr. Trimm," said the warden with a nervous cordiality. "Be through here in just one minute. This is Deputy Marshal Meyers," he added.

24

Mr. Trimm started to tell this Mr. Meyers he was glad to meet him, but caught himself and merely nodded. The man stared at him with neither interest nor curiosity in his dull blue eyes. The warden moved over toward the door.

"Mr. Trimm," he said, clearing his throat, "I took the liberty of calling a cab to take you gents up to the Grand Central. It's out front now. But there's a big crowd of reporters and photographers and a lot of other people waiting, and if I was you I'd slip out the back way — one of my men will open the yard gate for you — and jump aboard the subway down at Worth Street. Then you'll miss those fellows."

"Thank you, Warden — very kind of you," said Mr. Trimm in that crisp, businesslike way of his. He had been crisp and businesslike all his life. He heard a door opening softly behind him, and when he turned to look he saw the warden slipping out, furtively, in almost an embarrassed fashion.

"Well," said Meyers, "all ready?"

"Yes," said Mr. Trimm, and he made as if to rise.

"Wait one minute," said Meyers.

He half turned his back on Mr. Trimm and fumbled at the side pocket of his ill-hanging coat. Something inside of Mr. Trimm gave the least little jump, and the question that had ticked away so busily all those months began to buzz, buzz in his ears; but it was only a handkerchief the man was getting out. Doubtless he was going to mop his face.

He didn't mop his face, though. He unrolled the handkerchief slowly, as if it contained something immensely fragile and valuable, and then, thrusting it back in his pocket, he faced Mr. Trimm. He was carrying in his hands a pair of handcuffs that hung open-jawed. The jaws had little notches in them, like teeth that could bite. The question that had ticked in Mr. Trimm's head was answered at last — in the sight of these steel things with their notched jaws.

Mr. Trimm stood up and, with a movement as near to hesitation as he had ever been guilty of in his life, held out his hands, backs upward.

"I guess you're new at this kind of thing," said Meyers, grinning. "This here way — one at a time."

He took hold of Mr. Trimm's right hand, turned it sideways and settled one of the steel cuffs over the top of the wrist,

25

flipping the notched jaw up from beneath and pressing it in so that it locked automatically with a brisk little click. Slipping the locked cuff back and forth on Mr. Trimm's lower arm like a man adjusting a part of machinery, and then bringing the left hand up to meet the right, he treated it the same way. Then he stepped back.

Mr. Trimm hadn't meant to protest. The word came unbidden.

"This — this isn't necessary, is it?" he asked in a voice that was husky and didn't seem to belong to him.

"Yep," said Meyers. "Standin' orders is play no favorites and take no chances. But you won't find them things uncomfortable. Lightest pair there was in the office, and I fixed 'em plenty loose."

For half a minute Mr. Trimm stood like a rooster hypnotized by a chalkmark, his arms extended, his eyes set on his bonds. His hands had fallen perhaps four inches apart, and in the space between his wrists a little chain was stretched taut. In the mounting tumult that filled his brain there sprang before Mr. Trimm's consciousness a phrase he had heard or read somewhere, the title of a story or, perhaps, it was a headline — The Grips of the Law. The Grips of the Law were upon Mr. Trimm — he felt them now for the first time in these shiny wristlets and this bit of chain that bound his wrists and filled his whole body with a strange, sinking feeling that made him physically sick. A sudden sweat beaded out on Mr. Trimm's face, turning it slick and wet.

He had a handkerchief, a fine linen handkerchief with a hemstitched border and a monogram on it, in the upper breast pocket of his buttoned coat. He tried to reach it. His hands went up, twisting awkwardly like crab claws. The fingers of both plucked out the handkerchief. Holding it so, Mr. Trimm mopped the sweat away. The links of the handcuffs fell in upon one another and lengthened out again at each movement, filling the room with a smart little sound.

He got the handkerchief stowed away with the same clumsiness. He raised the manacled hands to his hat brim, gave it a downward pull that brought it over his face and then, letting his short arms slide down upon his plump stomach, he faced the man who had put the fetters upon him, squaring his shoulders

26

back. But it was hard, somehow, for him to square his shoulders — perhaps because of his hands being drawn so closely together. And his eyes would waver and fall upon his wrists. Mr. Trimm had a feeling that the skin must be stretched very tight on his jawbones and his forehead.

"Isn't there some way to hide these — these things?"

He began by blurting and ended by faltering it. His hands shuffled together, one over, then under the other.

"Here's a way," said Meyers. "This'll help."

He bestirred himself, folding one of the chained hands upon the other, tugging at the white linen cuffs and drawing the coat sleeves of his prisoner down over the bonds as far as the chain would let them come.

"There's the notion," he said. "Just do that-a-way and them bracelets won't hardly show at all. Ready? Let's be movin', then."

But handcuffs were never meant to be hidden. Merely a pair of steel rings clamped to one's wrists and coupled together with a scrap of chain, but they'll twist your arms and hamper the movements of your body in a way to constantly catch the eye of the passer-by. When a man is coming toward you, you can tell that he is handcuffed before you see the cuffs.

Mr. Trimm was never able to recall afterward exactly how he got out of the Tombs. He had a confused memory of a gate that was swung open by someone whom Mr. Trimm saw only from the feet to the waist; then he and his companion were out on Lafayette Street, speeding south toward the subway entrance at Worth Street, two blocks below, with the marshal's hand cupped under Mr. Trimm's right elbow and Mr. Trimm's plump legs almost trotting in their haste. For a moment it looked as if the warden's well-meant artifice would serve them.

But New York reporters are up to the tricks of people who want to evade them. At the sight of them a sentry reporter on the corner shouted a warning which was instantly caught up and passed on by another picket stationed half-way down the block; and around the wall of the Tombs came pelting a flying mob of newspaper photographers and reporters, with a choice rabble behind them. Foot passengers took up the chase, not knowing what it was about, but sensing a free show. Truckmen halted their teams, jumped down from their wagon seats and joined in. A man-chase is one of the pleasantest outdoor sports that a big city like New York can offer its people.

Fairly running now, the manacled banker and the deputy marshal shot down the winding steps into the subway a good ten yards ahead of the foremost pursuers. But there was one delay, while Meyers skirmished with his free hand in his trousers' pocket for a dime for the tickets, and another before a northbound local rolled into the station. Shouted at, jeered at, shoved this way and that, panting in gulping breaths, for he was stout by nature and staled by lack of exercise, Mr. Trimm, with Meyers clutching him by the arm, was fairly shot aboard one of the cars, at the apex of a human wedge. The astonished guard sensed the situation as the scrooging, shoving, noisy wave rolled across the platform toward the doors which he had opened and, thrusting the officer and his prisoner into the narrow platform space behind him, he tried to form with his body a barrier against those who came jamming in.

It didn't do any good. He was brushed away, protesting and blustering. The excitement spread through the train, and men, and even women, left their seats, overflowing the aisles.

There is no crueler thing than a city crowd, all eyes and morbid curiosity. But Mr. Trimm didn't see the staring eyes on that ride to the Grand Central. What he saw was many shifting feet and a hedge of legs shutting him in closely — those and the things on his wrists. What the eyes of the crowd saw was a small, stout man who, for all his bulk, seemed to have dried up inside his clothes so that they bagged on him some places and bulged others, with his head tucked on his chest, his hat over his face and his fingers straining to hold his coat sleeves down over a pair of steel bracelets.

Mr. Trimm gave mental thanks to a Deity whose existence he thought he had forgotten when the gate of the train-shed clanged behind him, shutting out the mob that had come with them all the way. Cameras had been shoved in his face like gun muzzles, reporters had scuttled alongside him, dodging under Meyers' fending arm to shout questions in his ears. He had neither spoken nor looked at them. The sweat still ran down his face, so that when finally he raised his head in the comparative quiet of the train-shed his skin was a curious grey under the jail paleness like the colour of wet wood ashes.

"My lawyer promised to arrange for a compartment — for

some private place on the train," he said to Meyers. "The conductor ought to know."

They were the first words he had uttered since he left the Tombs. Meyers spoke to a jaunty Pullman conductor who stood alongside the car where they had halted.

"No such reservation," said the conductor, running through his sheaf of slips, with his eyes shifting from Mr. Trimm's face to Mr. Trimm's hands and back again, as though he couldn't decide which was the more interesting part of him; "must be some mistake. Or else it was for some other train. Too late to change now — we pull out in three minutes."

"I reckon we better git on the smoker," said Meyers, "if there's room there."

Mr. Trimm was steered back again the length of the train through a double row of pop-eyed porters and staring trainmen. At the steps where they stopped the instinct to stretch out one hand and swing himself up by the rail operated automatically and his wrists got a nasty twist. Meyers and a brakeman practically lifted him up the steps and Meyers headed him into a car that was hazy with blue tobacco smoke. He was confused in his gait, almost as if his lower limbs had been fettered, too.

The car was full of shirt-sleeved men who stood up, craning their necks and stumbling over each other in their desire to see him. These men came out into the aisle, so that Meyers had to shove through them.

"This here'll do as well as any, I guess," said Meyers. He drew Mr. Trimm past him into the seat nearer the window and sat down alongside him on the side next the aisle, settling himself on the stuffy plush seat and breathing deeply, like a man who had got through the hardest part of a not easy job.

"Smoke?" he asked.

Mr. Trimm shook his head without raising it.

"Them cuffs feel plenty easy?" was the deputy's next question. He lifted Mr. Trimm's hands as casually as if they had been his hands and not Mr. Trimm's, and looked at them.

"Seem to be all right," he said as he let them fall back. "Don't pinch none, I reckon?" There was no answer.

The deputy tugged a minute at his moustache, searching his arid mind. An idea came to him. He drew a newspaper from his pocket, opened it out flat and spread it over Mr. Trimm's lap so that it covered the chained wrists. Almost instantly the train was in motion, moving through the yards.

"Be there in two hours more," volunteered Meyers. It was late afternoon. They were sliding through woodlands with occasional openings which showed meadows melting into wide, flat lands.

"Want a drink?" said the deputy, next. "No? Well, I guess I'll have a drop myself. Travelin' fills a feller's throat full of dust." He got up, lurching to the motion of the flying train, and started forward to the water cooler behind the car door. He had gone perhaps two-thirds of the way when Mr. Trimm felt a queer, grinding sensation beneath his feet; it was exactly as though the train were trying to go forward and back at the same time. Almost slowly, it seemed to him, the forward end of the car slued out of its straight course, at the same time tilting up. There was a grinding, roaring, grating sound, and before Mr. Trimm's eyes Meyers vanished, tumbling forward out of sight as the car floor buckled under his feet. Then, as everything — the train, the earth, the sky — all fused together in a great spatter of white and black, Mr. Trimm, plucked from his seat as though a giant hand had him by the collar, shot forward through the air over the seatbacks, his chained hands aloft, clutching wildly. He rolled out of a ragged opening where the smoker had broken in two, flopped gently on the sloping side of the right-of-way and slid easily to the bottom, where he lay quiet and still on his back in a bed of weeds and wild grass, staring straight up.

How many minutes he lay there Mr. Trimm didn't know. It may have been the shrieks of the victims or the glare from the fire that brought him out of the daze. He wriggled his body to a sitting posture, got on his feet, holding his head between his coupled hands, and gazed full-face into the crowning railroad horror of the year.

There were numbers of the passengers who had escaped serious hurt, but for the most part these persons seemed to have gone daft from terror and shock. Some were running aimlessly up and down and some, a few, were pecking feebly with improvised tools at the wreck, an indescribable jumble of ruin, from which there issued cries of mortal agony, and from which, at a point where two locomotives were lying on their sides, jammed together like fighting bucks that had died with locked

30

horns, a tall flame already rippled and spread, sending up a pillar of black smoke that rose straight, poisoning the clear blue of the sky. Nobody paid any attention to Mr. Trimm as he stood swaying upon his feet. There wasn't a scratch on him. His clothes were hardly rumpled, his hat was still on his head. He stood a minute and then, moved by a sudden impulse, he turned round and went running straight away from the railroad at the best speed his pudgy legs could accomplish, with his arms pumping up and down in front of him and his fingers interlaced. It was a grotesque gait, almost like a rabbit hopping on its hind legs.

Instantly, almost, the friendly woods growing down to the edge of the fill swallowed him up. He dodged and doubled back and forth among the tree trunks, his small, patent-leathered feet skipping nimbly over the irregular turf, until he stopped for lack of wind in his lungs to carry him another rod. When he had got his breath back Mr. Trimm leaned against a tree and bent his head this way and that, listening. No sound came to his ears except the sleepy calls of birds. As well as Mr. Trimm might judge he had come far into the depths of a considerable woodland. Already the shadows under the low limbs were growing thick and confused as the hurried twilight of early September came on.

Mr. Trimm sat down on a natural cushion of thick green moss between two roots of an oak. The place was clean and soft and sweet-scented. For some little time he sat there motionless, in a sort of mental haze. Then his round body slowly slid down flat upon the moss, his head lolled to one side and, the reaction having come, Mr. Trimm's limbs all relaxed and he went to sleep straightway.

After a while, when the woods were black and still, the half-grown moon came up and, sifting through a chink in the canopy of leaves above, shone down full on Mr. Trimm as he lay snoring gently with his mouth open, and his hands rising and falling on his breast. The moonlight struck upon the Little Giant handcuffs, making them look like quicksilver.

Toward daylight it turned off sharp and cool. The dogwoods which had been a solid color at nightfall now showed pink in one light and green in another, like changeable silk, as the first level rays of the sun came up over the rim of the earth and made long, golden lanes between the tree trunks. Mr. Trimm opened his eyes slowly, hardly sensing for the first moment or two how he came to be lying under a canopy of leaves, and gaped, seeking to stretch his arms. At that he remembered everything; he hunched his shoulders against the tree roots and wriggled himself up to a sitting position where he stayed for a while, letting his mind run over the sequence of events that had brought him where he was and taking inventory of the situation.

Of escape he had no thought. The hue and cry must be out for him before now; doubtless men were already searching for him. It would be better for him to walk in and surrender than to be taken in the woods like an animal escaped from a traveling menagerie. But the mere thought of enduring again what he had already gone through — the thought of being tagged by crowds and stared at, with his fetters on — filled him with a nausea. Nothing that the Federal penitentiary might hold in store for him could equal the black, blind shamefulness of yesterday; he knew that. The thought of the new ignominy that faced him made Mr. Trimm desperate. He had a desire to burrow into the thicket yonder and hide his face and his chained hands.

But perhaps he could get the handcuffs off and so go to meet his captors in some manner of dignity. Strange that the idea hadn't occurred to him before! It seemed to Mr. Trimm that he desired to get his two hands apart more than he had ever desired anything in his whole life before.

The hands had begun naturally to adjust themselves to their enforced companionship, and it wasn't such a very hard matter, though it cost him some painful wrenches and much twisting of the fingers, for Mr. Trimm to get his coat unbuttoned and his eyeglasses in their small leather case out of his upper waistcoat pocket. With the glasses on his nose he subjected his bonds to a critical examination. Each rounded steel band ran unbroken except for the smooth, almost jointless hinge and the small lock which sat perched on the back of the wrist in a little rounded excrescence like a steel wart. In the flat centre of each lock was a small keyhole and alongside of it a notched nub, the nub being sunk in a minute depression. On the inner side, underneath, the cuffs slid into themselves — two notches on each showing where the jaws might be tightened to fit a smaller hand than his — and right over the large blue veins in the middle of the wrists were swivel links, shackle-bolted to the cuffs and connected by a flat, slightly larger middle link, giving the hands a palm-to-palm play of not more than four or five inches. The cuffs did not hurt even after so many hours there was no actual discomfort from them and the flesh beneath them was hardly reddened.

But it didn't take Mr. Trimm long to find out that they were not to be got off. He tugged and pulled, trying with his fingers for a purchase. All he did was to chafe his skin and make his wrists throb with pain. The cuffs would go forward just so far, then the little humps of bone above the hands would catch and hold them.

Mr. Trimm was not a man to waste time in the pursuit of the obviously hopeless. Presently he stood up, shook himself and started off at a fair gait through the woods. The sun was up now and the turf was all dappled with lights and shadows, and about him much small, furtive wild life was stirring. He stepped along briskly, a strange figure for that green solitude, with his correct city garb and the glint of the steel at his sleeve ends.

Presently he heard the long-drawn, quavering, banshee wail of a locomotive. The sound came from almost behind him, in an opposite direction from where he supposed the track to be. So he turned around and went back the other way. He crossed a half-dried-up runlet and climbed a small hill, neither of which he remembered having met in his night from the wreck, and in a little while he came out upon the railroad. To the north a little distance the rails ran round a curve. To the south, where the diminishing rails running through the unbroken woodland met in a long, shiny V, he could see a big smoke smudge against the horizon. This smoke Mr. Trimm knew must come from the wreck — which was still burning, evidently. As nearly as he could judge he had come out of cover at least two miles above it. After a moment's consideration he decided to go south toward the wreck. Soon he could distinguish small dots like ants moving in and out about the black spot, and he knew these dots must be men.

A whining, whirring sound came along the rails to him from behind. He faced about just as a handcar shot out around the curve from the north, moving with amazing rapidity under the strokes of four men at the pumps. Other men, laborers to judge by their blue overalls, were sitting on the edges of the car with their feet dangling. For the second time within twelve hours impulse ruled Mr. Trimm, who wasn't given to impulses normally. He made a jump off the right-of-way, and as the handcar flashed by he watched its flight from the covert of a weed tangle.

But even as the handcar was passing him Mr. Trimm regretted his hastiness. He must surrender himself sooner or later; why not to these overalled laborers, since it was a thing that had to be done? He slid out of hiding and came trotting back to the tracks. Already the handcar was a hundred yards away, flitting into distance like some big, wonderfully fast bug, the figures of the men at the pumps rising and falling with a walking-beam regularity. As he stood watching them fade away and minded to try hailing them, yet still hesitating against his judgment, Mr. Trimm saw something white drop from the hands of one of the blue-clad figures on the handcar, unfold into a newspaper and come fluttering back along the tracks toward him. Just as he, starting doggedly ahead, met it, the little ground breeze that had carried it along died out and the paper dropped and flattened right in front of him. The front page was uppermost and he knew it must be of that morning's issue, for across the column tops ran the flaring headline: "Twenty Dead in Frightful Collision."

Squatting on the cindered track, Mr. Trimm patted the crumpled sheet flat with his hands. His eyes dropped from the first of the glaring captions to the second, to the next — and then his heart gave a great bound inside of him and, clutching up the newspaper to his breast, he bounded off the tracks back into another thicket and huddled there with the paper spread on the earth in front of him, reading by gulps while the chain that linked wrist to wrist tinkled to the tremors running through him. What he had seen first, in staring black-face type, was his own name leading the list of known dead, and what he saw now, broken up into choppy paragraphs and done in the nervous English of a trained reporter throwing a great news story together to catch an edition, but telling a clear enough story nevertheless, was a narrative in which his name recurred again and again. The body of the United States deputy marshal, Meyers, frightfully crushed, had been taken from the wreckage of the smoker — so the double-leaded story ran — and near to Meyers another body, with features burned beyond recognition,

34

yet still retaining certain distinguishing marks of measurement and contour, had been found and identified as that of Hobart W. Trimm, the convicted banker. The bodies of these two, with eighteen other mangled dead, had been removed to a town called Westfield, from which town of Westfield the account of the disaster had been telegraphed to the New York paper. In another column farther along was more about Banker Trimm; facts about his soiled, selfish, greedy, successful life, his great fortune, his trial, and a statement that, lacking any close kin to claim his body, his lawyers had been notified.

Mr. Trimm read the account through to the end, and as he read the sense of dominant, masterful self-control came back to him in waves. He got up, taking the paper with him, and went back into the deeper woods, moving warily and watchfully. As he went his mind, trained to take hold of problems and wring the essence out of them, was busy. Of the charred, grisly thing in the improvised morgue at Westfield, wherever that might be, Mr. Trimm took no heed nor wasted any pity. All his life he had used live men to work his will, with no thought of what might come to them afterward. The living had served him, why not the dead?

He had other things to think of than this dead proxy of his. He was as good as free! There would be no hunt for him now; no alarm out, no posses combing every scrap of cover for a famous criminal turned fugitive. He had only to lie quiet a few days, somewhere, then get in secret touch with Walling. Walling would do anything for money. And he had the money — four millions and more, cannily saved from the crash that had ruined so many others.

He would alter his personal appearance, change his name — he thought of Duvall, which was his mother's name — and with Walling's aid he would get out of the country and into some other country where a man might live like a prince on four millions or the fractional part of it. He thought of South America, of South Africa, of a private yacht swinging through the little frequented islands of the South Seas. All that the law had tried to take from him would be given back. Walling would work out the details of the escape — and make it safe and sure — trust Walling for those things. On one side was the prison, with its promise of twelve grinding years sliced out of the very heart of his life; on the other, freedom, ease, security, even power.

Through Mr. Trimm's mind tumbled thoughts of concessions, enterprises, privileges — the back corners of the globe were full of possibilities for the right man. And between this prospect and Mr. Trimm there stood nothing in the way, nothing but —

Mr. Trimm's eyes fell upon his bound hands. Snug-fitting, shiny steel bands irked his wrists. The Grips of the Law were still upon him.

But only in a way of speaking. It was preposterous, unbelievable, altogether out of the question that a man with four millions salted down and stored away, a man who all his life had been used to grappling with the big things and wrestling them down into submission, a man whose luck had come to be a byword — and had not it held good even in this last emergency? — would be balked by puny scraps of forged steel and a trumpery lock or two. Why, these cuffs were no thicker than the gold bands that Mr. Trimm had seen on the arms of overdressed women at the opera. The chain that joined them was no larger and, probably, no stronger than the chains which Mr. Trimm's chauffeur wrapped around the tires of the touring car in winter to keep the wheels from skidding on the slush. There would be a way, surely, for Mr. Trimm to free himself from these things. There must be — that was all there was to it.

Mr. Trimm looked himself over. His clothes were not badly rumpled; his patent-leather boots were scarcely scratched. Without the handcuffs he could pass unnoticed anywhere. By night then he must be free of them and on his way to some small inland city, to stay quiet there until the guarded telegram that he would send in cipher had reached Walling. There in the woods by himself Mr. Trimm no longer felt the ignominy of his bonds; he felt only the temporary embarrassment of them and the need of added precaution until he should have mastered them.

He was once more the unemotional man of affairs who had stood Wall Street on its esteemed head and caught the golden streams that trickled from its pockets. First making sure that he was in a well-screened covert of the woods he set about exploring all his pockets. The coat pockets were comparatively easy, now that he had got used to using two hands where one had always served, but it cost him a lot of twisting of his body and some pain to his mistreated wrist bones to bring forth the contents of his trousers' pockets. The chain kinked time and again as he groped with the undermost hand for the openings; his dumpy, pudgy form writhed grotesquely. But finally he finished. The search produced four cigars somewhat crumpled and frayed; some matches in a gun-metal case, a silver cigar cutter, two five-dollar bills, a handful of silver chicken feed, the leather case of the eyeglasses, a couple of quill toothpicks, a gold watch with a dangling fob, a notebook and some papers. Mr. Trimm ranged these things in a neat row upon a log, like a watchmaker setting out his kit, and took swift inventory of them. Some he eliminated from his design, stowing them back in the pockets easiest to reach. He kept for present employment the match safe, the cigar cutter and the watch.

This place where he had halted would suit his present purpose well, he decided. It was where an uprooted tree, fallen across an incurving bank, made a snug little recess that was closed in on three sides. Spreading the newspaper on the turf to save his knees from soiling, he knelt and set to his task. For the time he felt neither hunger nor thirst. He had found out during his earlier experiments that the nails of his little fingers, which were trimmed to a point, could invade the keyholes in the little steel warts on the backs of his wrists and touch the locks. The mechanism had even twitched a little bit under the tickle of the nail ends. So, having already smashed the gun-metal match safe under his heel, Mr. Trimm selected a slender-pointed bit from among its fragments and got to work, the left hand drawn up under the right, the fingers of the right busy with the lock of the left, the chain tightening and slackening with subdued clinking sounds at each movement.

Mr. Trimm didn't know much about picking a lock. He had got his money by a higher form of burglary that did not require a knowledge of lock picking. Nor as a boy had he been one to play at mechanics. He had let other boys make the toy fluttermills and the wooden traps and the like, and then he had traded for them. He was sorry now that he hadn't given more heed to the mechanical side of things when he was growing up.

He worked with a deliberate slowness, steadily. Nevertheless, it was hot work. The sun rose over the bank and shone on him through the limbs of the uprooted tree. His hat was on the ground alongside of him. The sweat ran down his face, streaking it and wilting his collar flat. The scrap of gun metal kept slipping

37

out of his wet fingers. Down would go the chained hands to scrabble in the grass for it, and then the picking would go on again. This happened a good many times. Birds, nervous with the spirit that presages the fall migration, flew back and forth along the creek, almost grazing Mr. Trimm sometimes. A rain crow wove a brown thread in the green warp of the bushes above his head. A chattering red squirrel sat up on a tree limb to scold him. At intervals, distantly, came the cough of laboring trains, showing that the track must have been cleared. There were times when Mr. Trimm thought he felt the lock giving. These times he would work harder.

Late in the afternoon Mr. Trimm lay back against the bank, panting. His face was splotched with red, and the little hollows at the sides of his forehead pulsed rapidly up and down like the bellies of scared tree frogs. The bent outer case of the watch littered a bare patch on the log; its mainspring had gone the way of the fragments of the gun-metal match safe which were lying all about, each a worn-down, twisted wisp of metal. The spring of the eyeglasses had been confiscated long ago and the broken crystals powdered the earth where Mr. Trimm's toes had scraped a smooth patch. The nails of the two little fingers were worn to the quick and splintered down into the raw flesh. There were countless tiny scratches and mars on the locks of the handcuffs, and the steel wristbands were dulled with blood smears and pale-red tarnishes of new rust; but otherwise they were as stanch and strong a pair of Bean's Latest Model Little Giant handcuffs as you'd find in any hardware store anywhere.

The devilish, stupid malignity of the damned things! With an acid oath Mr. Trimm raised his hands and brought them down on the log violently. There was a double click and the bonds tightened painfully, pressing the chafed red skin white. Mr. Trimm snatched up his hands close to his near-sighted eyes and looked. One of the little notches on the under side of each cuff had disappeared. It was as if they were living things that had turned and bitten him for the blow he gave them.

From the time the sun went down there was a tingle of frost in

38

the air. Mr. Trimm didn't sleep much. Under the squeeze of the tightened fetters his wrists throbbed steadily and racking cramps ran through his arms. His stomach felt as though it were tied into knots. The water that he drank from the branch only made his hunger sickness worse. His undergarments, that had been wet with perspiration, clung to him clammily. His middle-aged, tenderly-cared-for body called through every pore for clean linen and soap and water and rest, as his empty insides called for food.

After a while he became so chilled that the demand for warmth conquered his instinct for caution. He felt about him in the darkness, gathering scraps of dead wood, and, after breaking several of the matches that had been in the gun-metal match safe, he managed to strike one and with its tiny flame started a fire. He huddled almost over the fire, coughing when the smoke blew into his face and twisting and pulling at his arms in an effort to get relief from the everlasting cramps. It seemed to him that if he could only get an inch or two more of play for his hands he would be ever so much more comfortable. But he couldn't, of course.

He dozed, finally, sitting cross-legged with his head sunk between his hunched shoulders. A pain in a new place woke him. The fire had burned almost through the thin sole of his right shoe, and as he scrambled to his feet and stamped, the clap of the hot leather flat against his blistered foot almost made him cry out.

Soon after sunrise a boy came riding a horse down a faintly traced footpath along the creek, driving a cow with a bell on her neck ahead of him. Mr. Trimm's ears caught the sound of the clanking bell before either the cow or her herder was in sight, and he limped away, running, skulking through the thick cover. A pendent loop of a wild grapevine, swinging low, caught his hat and flipped it off his head; but Mr. Trimm, imagining pursuit, did not stop to pick it up and went on bareheaded until he had to stop from exhaustion. He saw some dark-red berries on a shrub upon which he had trod, and, stooping, he plucked some of them with his two hands and put three or four in his mouth experimentally. Warned instantly by the acrid, burning taste, he spat the crushed berries out and went on doggedly, following, according to his best judgment, a course parallel to the railroad. It was characteristic of him, a city-raised man, that he took no heed of distances nor of the distinguishing marks of the timber.

Behind a log at the edge of a small clearing in the woods he halted some little time, watching and listening. The clearing had grown up in sumacs and weeds and small saplings and it seemed deserted; certainly it was still. Near the center of it rose the sagging roof of what had been a shack or a shed of some sort. Stooping cautiously, to keep his bare head below the tops of the sumacs, Mr. Trimm made for the ruined shanty and gained it safely. In the midst of the rotted, punky logs that had once formed the walls he began scraping with his feet. Presently he uncovered something. It was a broken-off harrow tooth, scaled like a long, red fish with the crusted rust of years.

Mr. Trimm rested the lower rims of his handcuffs on the edge of an old, broken watering trough, worked the pointed end of the rust-crusted harrow tooth into the flat middle link of the chain as far as it would go, and then with one hand on top of the other he pressed downward with all his might. The pain in his wrists made him stop this at once. The link had not sprung or given in the least, but the twisting pressure had almost broken his wrist bones. He let the harrow tooth fall, knowing that it would never serve as a lever to free him — which, indeed, he had known all along — and sat on the side of the trough, rubbing his wrists and thinking.

He had another idea. It came into his mind as a vague suggestion that fire had certain effects upon certain metals. He kindled a fire of bits of the rotted wood, and when the flames ran together and rose slender and straight in a single red thread he thrust the chain into it, holding his hands as far apart as possible in the attitude of a player about to catch a bounced ball. But immediately the pain of that grew unendurable too, and he leaped back, jerking his hands away. He had succeeded only in blackening the steel and putting a big water blister on one of his wrists right where the shackle bolt would press upon it.

Where he huddled down in the shelter of one of the fallen walls he noticed, presently, a strand of rusted fence wire still held to half-tottering posts by a pair of blackened staples; it was part of a pen that had been used once for chickens or swine. Mr. Trimm tried the wire with his fingers. It was firm and springy.

40

Rocking and groaning with the pain of it, he nevertheless began sliding the chain back and forth, back and forth along the strand of wire.

Eventually the wire, weakened by age, snapped in two. A tiny shined spot, hardly deep enough to be called a nick, in its tarnished, smudged surface was all the mark that the chain showed.

Staggering a little and putting his feet down unsteadily, Mr. Trimm left the clearing, heading as well as he could tell eastward, away from the railroad. After a mile or two he came to a dusty wood road winding downhill.

To the north of the clearing where Mr. Trimm had halted were a farm and a group of farm buildings. To the southward a mile or so was a cluster of dwellings set in the midst of more farmlands, with a shop or two and a small white church with a green spire in the center. Along a road that ran northward from the hamlet to the solitary farm a ten-year-old boy came, carrying a covered tin pail. A young grey squirrel flirted across the wagon ruts ahead of him and darted up a chestnut sapling. The boy put the pail down at the side of the road and began looking for a stone to throw at the squirrel.

Mr. Trimm slid out from behind a tree. A hemstitched handkerchief, grimed and stained, was loosely twisted around his wrists, partly hiding the handcuffs. He moved along with a queer, sliding gait, keeping as much of his body as he could turned from the youngster. The ears of the little chap caught the faint scuffle of feet and he spun around on his bare heel.

"My boy, would you —" Mr. Trimm began.

The boy's round eyes widened at the apparition that was sidling toward him in so strange a fashion, and then, taking fright, he dodged past Mr. Trimm and ran back the way he had come, as fast as his slim brown legs could take him. In half a minute he was out of sight round a bend.

Had the boy looked back he would have seen a still more curious spectacle than the one that had frightened him. He would have seen a man worth four million dollars down on his knees in the yellow dust, pawing with chained hands at the tight-fitting lid of the tin pail, and then, when he had got the lid off, drinking the fresh, warm milk which the pail held with great, choking gulps, uttering little mewing, animal sounds as he drank, while the white, creamy milk ran over his chin and splashed down his breast in little, spurting streams.

But the boy didn't look back. He ran all the way home and told his mother he had seen a wild man on the road to the village; and later, when his father came in from the fields, he was soundly thrashed for letting the sight of a tramp make him lose a good tin bucket and half a gallon of milk worth six cents a quart.

The rich, fresh milk put life into Mr. Trimm. He rested the better for it during the early part of that night in a haw thicket. Only the sharp, darting pains in his wrists kept rousing him to temporary wakefulness. In one of those intervals of waking the plan that had been sketchily forming in his mind from the time he had quit the clearing in the woods took on a definite, fixed shape. But how was he with safety to get the sort of aid he needed, and where?

Canvassing tentative plans in his head, he dozed off again.

On a smooth patch of turf behind the blacksmith shop three yokels were languidly pitching horseshoes — "quaits" they called them — at a stake driven in the earth. Just beyond, the woods shredded out into a long, yellow and green peninsula which stretched up almost to the back door of the smithy, so that late of afternoons the slanting shadows of the near-most trees fell on its roof of warped shingles. At the extreme end of this point of woods Mr. Trimm was squatted behind a big boulder, squinting warily through a thick-fringed curtain of ripened goldenrod tops and sumacs, heavy-headed with their dark-red tapers. He had been there more than an hour, cautiously waiting his chance to hail the blacksmith, whose figure he could make out in the smoky interior of his shop, passing back and forth in front of a smudgy forge fire and rattling metal against metal in intermittent fits of professional activity.

From where Mr. Trimm watched to where the horseshoe-pitching game went on was not more than sixty feet. He could hear what the players said and even see the little puffs of dust rise when one of them clapped his hands together after a pitch. He judged by the signs of slackening interest that they would be stopping soon and, he hoped, going clear away.

But the smith loafed out of his shop and, after an exchange of bucolic banter with the three of them, he took a hand in their game himself. He wore no coat or waistcoat and, as he poised a horseshoe for his first cast at the stake, Mr. Trimm saw, pinned flat against the broad strap of his suspenders, a shiny, silvery-looking disk. Having pitched the shoe, the smith moved over into the shade, so that he almost touched the clump of undergrowth that half buried Mr. Trimm's protecting boulder. The near-sighted eyes of the fugitive banker could make out then what the flat, silvery disk was, and Mr. Trimm cowered low in his covert behind the rock, holding his hands down between his knees, fearful that a gleam from his burnished wristlets might strike through the screen of weed growth and catch the inquiring eye of the smith. So he stayed, not daring to move, until a dinner horn sounded somewhere in the cluster of cottages beyond, and the smith, closing the doors of his shop, went away with the three yokels.

Then Mr. Trimm, stooping low, stole back into the deep woods again. In his extremity he was ready to risk making a bid for the hire of a blacksmith's aid to rid himself of his bonds, but not a blacksmith who wore a deputy sheriff's badge pinned to his suspenders.

He caught himself scraping his wrists up and down again against the rough, scrofulous trunk of a shellbark hickory. The irritation was comforting to the swollen skin. The cuffs, which kept catching on the bark and snagging small fragments of it loose, seemed to Mr. Trimm to have been a part and parcel of him for a long time — almost as long a time as he could remember. But the hands which they clasped so close seemed like the hands of somebody else. There was a numbness about them that made them feel as though they were a stranger's hands which never had belonged to him. As he looked at them with a sort of vague curiosity they seemed to swell and grow, these two strange, fettered hands, until they measured yards across, while the steel bands shrunk to the thinness of piano wire, cutting deeper and deeper into the flesh. Then the hands in turn began to shrink down and the cuffs to grow up into great, thick things as cumbersome as the couplings of a freight car. A voice that Mr.

Trimm dimly recognized as his own was saying something about four million dollars over and over again.

Mr. Trimm roused up and shook his head angrily to clear it. He rubbed his eyes free of the clouding delusion. It wouldn't do for him to be getting light-headed.

On a flat, shelving bluff, forty feet above a cut through which the railroad ran at a point about five miles north of where the collision had occurred, a tramp was busy, just before sundown, cooking something in an old washboiler that perched precariously on a fire of wood coals. This tramp was tall and spindle-legged, with reddish hair and a pale, beardless, freckled face with no chin to it and not much forehead, so that it ran out to a peak like the profile of some featherless, unpleasant sort of fowl. The skirts of an old, ragged overcoat dangled grotesquely about his spare shanks.

Desperate as his plight had become, Mr. Trimm felt the old sick shame at the prospect of exposing himself to this knavish-looking vagabond whose help he meant to buy with a bribe. It was the sight of a dainty wisp of smoke from the wood fire curling upward through the cloudy, damp air that had brought him limping cautiously across the right-of-way, to climb the rocky shelf along the cut; but now he hesitated, shielded in the shadows twenty yards away. It was a whiff of something savory in the washboiler, borne to him on the still air and almost making him cry out with eagerness, that drew him forth finally. At the sound of the halting footsteps the tramp stopped stirring the mess in the washboiler and glanced up apprehensively. As he took in the figure of the newcomer his eyes narrowed and his pasty, nasty face spread in a grin of comprehension.

"Well, well, well," he said, leering offensively, "welcome to our city, little stranger."

Mr. Trimm came nearer, dragging his feet, for they were almost out of the wrecks of his patent-leather shoes. His gaze shifted from the tramp's face to the stuff on the fire, his nostrils wrinkling. Then slowly: "I'm in trouble," he said, and held out his hands.

"Wot I'd call a mild way o' puttin' it," said the tramp coolly. "That purticular kind o' joolry ain't gen'lly wore for pleasure."

44

His eyes took on a nervous squint and roved past Mr. Trimm's stooped figure down the slope of the hillock.

"Say, pal, how fur ahead are you of yore keeper?" he demanded, his manner changing.

"There is no one after me — no one that I know of," explained Mr. Trimm. "I am quite alone — I am certain of it."

"Sure there ain't nobody lookin' fur you?" the other persisted suspiciously.

"I tell you I am all alone," protested Mr. Trimm. "I want your help in getting these — these things off and sending a message to a friend. You'll be well paid, very well paid. I can pay you more money than you ever had in your life, probably, for your help. I can promise —"

He broke off, for the tramp, as if reassured by his words, had stooped again to his cooking and was stirring the bubbling contents of the washboiler with a peeled stick. The smell of the stew, rising strongly, filled Mr. Trimm with such a sharp and an aching hunger that he could not speak for a moment. He mastered himself, but the effort left him shaking and gulping.

"Go on, then, an' tell us somethin' about yourself," said the freckled man. "Wot brings you roamin' round this here railroad cut with them bracelets on?"

"I was in the wreck," obeyed Mr. Trimm. "The man with me — the officer — was killed. I wasn't hurt and I got away into these woods. But they think I'm dead too — my name was among the list of dead."

The other's peaky face lengthened in astonishment.

"Why, say," he began, "I read all about that there wreck — seen the list myself — say, you can't be Trimm, the New York banker? Yes, you are! Wot a streak of luck! Lemme look at you! Trimm, the swell financeer, sportin' 'round with the darbies on him all nice an' snug an' reg'lar! Mister Trimm — well, if this ain't rich!"

"My name is Trimm," said the starving banker miserably. "I've been wandering about here a great many hours — several days, I think it must be — and I need rest and food very much indeed. I don't — don't feel very well," he added, his voice trailing off.

At this his self-control gave way again and he began to quake violently as if with an ague. The smell of the cooking overcame him.

"You don't look so well an' that's a fact, Trimm," sneered the tramp, resuming his malicious, mocking air. "But set down an' make yourself at home, an' after a while, when this is done, we'll have a bite together — you an' me. It'll be a reg'lar tea party fur jest us two."

He broke off to chuckle. His mirth made him appear even more repulsive than before.

"But looky here, you wus sayin' somethin' about money," he said suddenly. "Le's take a look at all this here money."

He came over to him and went through Mr. Trimm's pockets. Mr. Trimm said nothing and stood quietly, making no resistance. The tramp finished a workmanlike search of the banker's pockets. He looked at the result as it lay in his grimy palm — a moist little wad of bills and some chicken-feed change — and spat disgustedly with a nasty oath.

"Well, Trimm," he said, "fur a Wall Street guy seems to me you travel purty light. About how much did you think you'd get done fur all this pile of wealth?"

"You will be well paid," said Mr. Trimm, arguing hard; "my friend will see to that. What I want you to do is to take the money you have there in your hand and buy a cold chisel or a file — any tools that will cut these things off me. And then you will send a telegram to a certain gentleman in New York. And let me stay with you until we get an answer — until he comes here. He will pay you well; I promise it."

He halted, his eyes and his mind again on the bubbling stuff in the rusted washboiler. The freckled vagrant studied him through his red-lidded eyes, kicking some loose embers back into the fire with his toe.

"I've heard a lot about you one way an' another, Trimm," he said. "'Tain't as if you wuz some pore down-an'-out devil tryin' to beat the cops out of doin' his bit in stir. You're the way-up, high-an'-mighty kind of crook. An' from wot I've read an' heard about you, you never toted fair with nobody yet. There wuz that young feller, wot's his name? — the cashier — him that wuz tried with you. He went along with you in yore games an' done yore work fur you an' you let him go over the road to the same place you're tryin' to dodge now. Besides," he added cunningly, "you come here talkin' mighty big about money, yet I notice you ain't carryin' much of it in yore clothes. All I've had to go by is yore word. An' yore word ain't worth much, by all accounts."

"I tell you, man, that you'll profit richly," burst out Mr. Trimm, the words falling over each other in his new panic. "You must help me; I've endured too much — I've gone through too much to give up now." He pleaded fast, his hands shaking in a quiver of fear and eagerness as he stretched them out in entreaty and his linked chain shaking with them. Promises, pledges, commands, orders, arguments poured from him. His tormentor checked him with a gesture.

"You're wot I'd call a bird in the hand," he chuckled, hugging his slack frame, "an' it ain't fur you to be givin' orders — it's fur me. An', anyway, I guess we ain't a-goin' to be able to make a trade — leastwise not on yore terms. But we'll do business all right, all right — anyhow, I will."

"What do you mean?" panted Mr. Trimm, full of terror. "You'll help me?"

"I mean this," said the tramp slowly. He put his hands under his loose-hanging overcoat and began to fumble at a leather strap about his waist. "If I turn you over to the Government I know wot you'll be worth, purty near, by guessin' at the reward; an' besides, it'll maybe help to square me up fur one or two little matters. If I turn you loose I ain't got nothin' only your word — an' I've got an idea how much faith I kin put in that."

Mr. Trimm glanced about him wildly. There was no escape. He was fast in a trap which he himself had sprung. The thought of being led to jail, all foul of body and fettered as he was, by this filthy, smirking wretch made him crazy. He stumbled backward with some insane idea of running away.

"No hurry, no hurry at all," gloated the tramp, enjoying the torture of this helpless captive who had walked into his hands. "I ain't goin' to hurt you none — only make sure that you don't wander off an' hurt yourself while I'm gone. Won't do to let you be damagin' yoreself; you're valuable property. Trimm, now, I'll tell you wot we'll do! We'll just back you up agin one of these trees an' then we'll jest slip this here belt through yore elbows an' buckle it around behind at the back; an' I kinder guess you'll stay right there till I go down yonder to that station that I passed comin' up here an' see wot kind of a bargain I kin strike up with the marshal. Come on, now," he threatened with a show of

47

bluster, reading the resolution that was mounting in Mr. Trimm's face. "Come on peaceable, if you don't want to git hurt."

Of a sudden Mr. Trimm became the primitive man. He was filled with those elemental emotions that make a man see in spatters of crimson. Gathering strength from passion out of an exhausted frame, he sprang forward at the tramp. He struck at him with his head, his shoulders, his knees, his manacled wrists, all at once. Not really hurt by the puny assault, but caught by surprise, the freckled man staggered back, clawing at the air, tripped on the washboiler in the fire, and with a yell vanished below the smooth edge of the cut.

Mr. Trimm stole forward and looked over the bluff. Half-way down the cliff on an outcropping shelf of rock the man lay, face downward, motionless. He seemed to have grown smaller and to have shrunk into his clothes. One long, thin leg was bent up under the skirts of the overcoat in a queer, twisted way, and the cloth of the trouser leg looked flattened and empty. As Mr. Trimm peered down at him he saw a red stain spreading on the rock under the still, silent figure's head.

Mr. Trimm turned to the washboiler. It lay on its side, empty, the last of its recent contents sputtering out into the half-drowned fire. He stared at this ruin a minute. Then without another look over the cliff edge he stumbled slowly down the hill, muttering to himself as he went. Just as he struck the level it began to rain, gently at first, then hard, and despite the shelter of the full-leaved forest trees, he was soon wet through to his skin and dripped water as he lurched along without sense of direction or, indeed, without any active realization of what he was doing.

Late that night it was still raining — a cold, steady, autumnal downpour. A huddled figure slowly climbed upon a low fence running about the house-yard of the little farm where the boy lived who got thrashed for losing a milk pail. On the wet top rail, precariously perching, the figure slipped and sprawled forward in the miry yard. It got up, painfully swaying on its feet. It was Mr. Trimm, looking for food. He moved slowly toward the house, tottering with weakness and because of the slick mud underfoot; peering near-sightedly this way and that through the murk; starting at every sound and stopping often to listen.

48

The outlines of a lean-to kitchen at the back of the house were looming dead ahead of him when from the corner of the cottage sprang a small terrier. It made for Mr. Trimm, barking shrilly. He retreated backward, kicking at the little dog and, to hold his balance, striking out with short, dabby jerks of his fettered hands — they were such motions as the terrier itself might make trying to walk on its hind legs. Still backing away, expecting every instant to feel the terrier's teeth in his flesh, Mr. Trimm put one foot into a hotbed with a great clatter of the breaking glass. He felt the sharp ends of shattered glass tearing and cutting his shin as he jerked free. Recovering himself, he dealt the terrier a lucky kick under the throat that sent it back, yowling, to where it had come from, and then, as a door jerked open and a half-dressed man jumped out into the darkness, Mr. Trimm half hobbled, half fell out of sight behind the woodpile.

Back and forth along the lower edge of his yard the farmer hunted, with the whimpering, cowed terrier to guide him, poking in dark corners with the muzzle of his shotgun for the unseen intruder whose coming had aroused the household. In a brushpile just over the fence to the east Mr. Trimm lay on his face upon the wet earth, with the rain beating down on him, sobbing with choking gulps that wrenched him cruelly, biting at the bonds on his wrists until the sound of breaking teeth gritted in the air. Finally, in the hopeless, helpless frenzy of his agony he beat his arms up and down until the bracelets struck squarely on a flat stone and the force of the blow sent the cuffs home to the last notch so that they pressed harder and faster than ever upon the tortured wrist bones.

When he had wasted ten or fifteen minutes in a vain search the farmer went shivering back indoors to dry out his wet shirt. But the groveling figure in the brushpile lay for a long time where it was, only stirring a little while the rain dripped steadily down on everything.

The wreck was on a Tuesday evening. Early on the Saturday morning following the chief of police, who was likewise the whole of the day police force in the town of Westfield, nine miles from the place where the collision occurred, heard a peculiar, strangely weak knocking at the front door of his cottage, where he also had his office. The door was a Dutch door, sawed through the middle, so that the top half might be opened independently, leaving the lower panel fast. He swung this top half back.

A face was framed in the opening — an indescribably dirty, unutterably weary face, with matted white hair and a rime of whitish beard stubble on the jaws. It was fallen in and sunken and it drooped on the chest of its owner. The mouth, swollen and pulpy, as if from repeated hard blows, hung agape, and between the purplish parted lips showed the stumps of broken teeth. The eyes blinked weakly at the chief from under lids as colorless as the eyelids of a corpse. The bare white head was filthy with plastered mud and twigs, and dripping wet.

"Hello, there!" said the chief, startled at this apparition. "What do you want?"

With a movement that told of straining effort the lolled head came up off the chest. The thin, corded neck stiffened back, rising from a dirty, collarless neckband. The Adam's apple bulged out prominently, as big as a pigeon's egg.

"I have come," said the specter in a wheezing rasp of a voice which the chief could hardly hear — "I have come to surrender myself. I am Hobart W. Trimm."

"I guess you got another thing comin'," said the chief, who was by way of being a neighborhood wag. "When last seen Hobart W. Trimm was only fifty-two years old. Besides which, he's dead and buried. I guess maybe you'd better think agin, grandpap, and see if you ain't Methus'lah or the Wanderin' Jew."

"I am Hobart W. Trimm, the banker," whispered the stranger with a sort of wan stubbornness.

"Go on and prove it," suggested the chief, more than willing to prolong the enjoyment of the sensation. It wasn't often in Westfield that wandering lunatics came a-calling.

"Got any way to prove it?" he repeated as the visitor stared at him.

"Yes," came the creaking, rusted hinge of a voice, "I have."

Slowly, with struggling attempts, he raised his hands into the chief's sight. They were horribly swollen hands, red with the dried blood where they were not black with the dried dirt; the fingers puffed up out of shape; the nails broken; they were like the skinned paws of a bear. And at the wrists, almost buried in the bloated folds of flesh, blackened, rusted, battered, yet still strong and whole, was a tightly-locked pair of Bean's Latest Model Little Giant handcuffs.

"Great God!" cried the chief, transfixed at the sight. He drew the bolt and jerked open the lower half of the door.

"Come in," he said, "and lemme get them irons off of you — they must hurt something terrible."

"They can wait," said Mr. Trimm very feebly, very slowly and very humbly. "I have worn them a long, long while — I am used to them. Wouldn't you please get me some food first?"

THE GALLOWSMITH

This man that I have it in mind to write about was, at the time of which I write, an elderly man, getting well along toward sixty-five. He was tall and slightly stooped, with long arms, and big, gnarled, competent-looking hands, which smelled of yellow laundry soap, and had huge, tarnished nails on the fingers. He had mild, pale eyes, a light blue as to color, with heavy sacs under them, and whitish whiskers, spindly and thin, like some sort of second-growth, which were so cut as to enclose his lower face in a nappy fringe, extending from ear to ear under his chin. He suffered from a chronic heart affection, and this gave to his skin a pronounced and unhealthy pallor. He was neat and prim in his personal habits, kind to dumb animals, and tolerant of small children. He was inclined to be miserly; certainly in money matters he was most prudent and saving. He had the air about him of being lonely. His name was Tobias Dramm. In the town where he lived he was commonly known as Uncle Tobe Dramm. By profession he was a public hangman. You might call him a gallowsmith. He hanged men for hire.

So far as the available records show, this Tobias Dramm was the only man of his calling on this continent. In himself he constituted a specialty and a monopoly. The fact that he had no competition did not make him careless in the pursuit of his calling. On the contrary, it made him precise and painstaking. As one occupying a unique position, he realized that he had a reputation to sustain, and capably he sustained it. In the Western Hemisphere he was, in the trade he followed, the nearest modern approach to the paid executioners of olden times in France who went, each of them, by the name of the city or province wherein he was stationed, to do torturing and maiming and killing in the gracious name of the king.

A generous government, committed to a belief in the efficacy of capital punishment, paid Tobias Dramm at the rate of seventy-five dollars a head for hanging offenders convicted of the hanging crime, which was murder. He averaged about four hangings every three months or, say, about nine hundred dollars

52

a year — all clear money.

The manner of Mr. Dramm's having entered upon the practise of this somewhat grisly trade makes in itself a little tale. He was a lifelong citizen of the town of Chickaloosa, down in the Southwest, where there stood a State penitentiary, and where, during the period of which I am speaking, the Federal authorities sent for confinement and punishment the criminal sweepings of half a score of States and Territories. This was before the government put up prisons of its own, and while still it parceled out its human liabilities among State-owned institutions, paying so much apiece for their keep. When the government first began shipping a share of its felons to Chickaloosa, there came along, in one clanking caravan of shackled malefactors, a half-breed, part Mexican and the rest of him Indian, who had robbed a territorial post-office and incidentally murdered the postmaster thereof. Wherefore this half-breed was under sentence to expiate his greater misdeed on a given date, between the hours of sunrise and sunset, and after a duly prescribed manner, namely: by being hanged by the neck until he was dead.

At once a difficulty and a complication arose. The warden of the penitentiary at Chickaloosa was perfectly agreeable to the idea of keeping and caring for those felonious wards of the government who were put in his custody to serve terms of imprisonment, holding that such disciplinary measures fell within the scope of his sworn duty. But when it came to the issue of hanging any one of them, he drew the line most firmly. As he pointed out, he was not a government agent. He derived his authority and drew his salary not from Washington, D. C., but from a State capital several hundreds of miles removed from Washington. Moreover, he was a zealous believer in the principle of State sovereignty. As a soldier of the late Southern Confederacy, he had fought four years to establish that doctrine. Conceded, that the cause for which he fought had been defeated; nevertheless his views upon the subject remained fixed and permanent. He had plenty of disagreeable jobs to do without stringing up bad men for Uncle Sam; such was the attitude the warden took. The sheriff of the county of which Chickaloosa was the county-seat, likewise refused to have a hand in the impending affair, holding it — and perhaps very properly — to be no direct concern of his, either officially or personally.

53

Now the government very much wanted the hybrid hanged. The government had been put to considerable trouble and no small expense to catch him and try him and convict him and transport him to the place where he was at present confined. Day and date for the execution of the law's judgment having been fixed, a scandal and possibly a legal tangle would ensue were there delay in the premises. It was reported that a full pardon had been offered to a long-term convict on condition that he carry out the court's mandate upon the body of the condemned mongrel, and that he had refused, even though the price were freedom for himself.

In this serious emergency, a volunteer in the person of Tobias Dramm came forward. Until then he had been an inconspicuous unit in the life of the community. He was a live-stock dealer on a small scale, making his headquarters at one of the town livery stables. He was a person of steady habits, with a reputation for sobriety and frugality among his neighbors. The government, so to speak, jumped at the chance. Without delay, his offer was accepted. There was no prolonged haggling over terms, either. He himself fixed the cost of the job at seventy-five dollars; this figure to include supervision of the erection of the gallows, testing of the apparatus, and the actual operation itself.

So, on the appointed day, at a certain hour, to wit, a quarter past six o'clock in the morning, just outside the prison walls, and in the presence of the proper and ordained number of witnesses, Uncle Tobe, with a grave, untroubled face, and hands which neither fumbled nor trembled, tied up the doomed felon and hooded his head in a black-cloth bag, and fitted a noose about his neck. The drop fell at eighteen minutes past the hour. Fourteen minutes later, following brief tests of heart and pulse, the two attending physicians agreed that the half-breed was quite satisfactorily defunct. They likewise coincided in the opinion that the hanging had been conducted with neatness, and with swiftness, and with the least possible amount of physical suffering for the deceased. One of the doctors went so far as to congratulate Mr. Dramm upon the tidiness of his handicraft. He told him that in all his experience he had never seen a hanging pass off more smoothly, and that for an amateur, Dramm had done splendidly. To this compliment Uncle Tobe replied, in his quiet and drawling mode of speech, that he had studied the whole thing out in advance.

"Ef I should keep on with this way of makin' a livin' I don't 'low ever to let no slip-ups occur," he added with simple directness. There was no suggestion of the morbid in his voice or manner as he said this, but instead merely a deep personal satisfaction.

Others present, having been made sick and faint by the shock of seeing a human being summarily jerked into the hereafter, went away hurriedly without saying anything at all. But afterward thinking it over when they were more composed, they decided among themselves that Uncle Tobe had carried it off with an assurance and a skill which qualified him most aptly for future undertakings along the same line; that he was a born hangman, if ever there was one.

This was the common verdict. So, thereafter, by a tacit understanding, the ex-cattle-buyer became the regular government hangman. He had no official title nor any warrant in writing for the place he filled. He worked by the piece, as one might say, and not by the week or month. Some years he hanged more men than in other years, but the average per annum was about twelve. He had been hanging them now for going on ten years.

It was as though he had been designed and created for the work. He hanged villainous men singly, sometimes by pairs, and rarely in groups of threes, always without a fumble or a hitch. Once, on a single morning, he hanged an even half-dozen, these being the chief fruitage of a busy term of the Federal court down in the Indian country where the combination of a crowded docket, an energetic young district attorney with political ambitions, and a businesslike presiding judge had produced what all unprejudiced and fair-minded persons agreed were marvelous results, highly beneficial to the moral atmosphere of the territory and calculated to make potential evil-doers stop and think. Four of the six had been members of an especially desperate gang of train and bank robbers. The remaining two had forfeited their right to keep on living by slaying deputy marshals. Each, with malice aforethought and with his own hands, had actually killed some one or had aided and abetted in killing some one.

This sextuple hanging made a lot of talk, naturally. The size of it alone commanded the popular interest. Besides, the personnel of the group of villains was such as to lend an aspect of picturesqueness to the final proceedings. The sextet included a full-blooded Cherokee; a consumptive ex-dentist out of Kansas, who from killing nerves in teeth had progressed to killing men in cold premeditation; a lank West Virginia mountaineer whose family name was the name of a clan prominent in one of the long-drawn-out hill-feuds of his native State; a plain bad man, whose chief claim to distinction was that he hailed originally from the Bowery in New York City; and one, the worst of them all, who was said to be the son of a pastor in a New England town. One by one, unerringly and swiftly, Uncle Tobe launched them through his scaffold floor to get whatever desserts await those who violate the laws of God and man by the violent shedding of innocent blood. When the sixth and last gunman came out of the prison proper into the prison enclosure — it was the former dentist, and being set, as the phrase runs, upon dying game, he wore a twisted grin upon his bleached face — there were six black boxes under the platform, five of them occupied, with their lids all in place, and one of them yet empty and open. In the act of mounting the steps the condemned craned his head sidewise, and at the sight of those coffins stretching along six in a row on the graveled courtyard, he made a cheap and sorry gibe. But when he stood beneath the cross-arm to be pinioned, his legs played him traitor. Those craven knees of his gave way under him, so that trusties had to hold the weakening ruffian upright while the executioner snugged the halter about his throat.

On this occasion Uncle Tobe elucidated the creed and the code of his profession for a reporter who had come all the way down from St. Louis to report the big hanging for his paper. Having covered the hanging at length, the reporter stayed over one more day at the Palace Hotel in Chickaloosa to do a special article, which would be in part a character sketch and in part a straight interview, on the subject of the hangman. The article made a full page spread in the Sunday edition of the young man's paper, and thereby a reputation, which until this time had been more or less local, was given what approximated a national notoriety. Through a somewhat general reprinting of what the young man had written, and what his paper had published, the country at large eventually became acquainted with an ethical

56

view-point which was already fairly familiar to nearly every resident in and about Chickaloosa. Reading the narrative, one living at a distance got an accurate picture of a personality elevated above the commonplace solely by the role which its owner filled; a picture of an old man thoroughly sincere and thoroughly conscientious; a man dull, earnest, and capable to his limits; a man who was neither morbid nor imaginative, but filled with rather a stupid gravity; a man canny about the pennies and affectionately inclined toward the dollars; a man honestly imbued with the idea that he was a public servant performing a necessary public service; a man without nerves, but in all other essentials a small-town man with a small-town mind; in short, saw Uncle Tobe as he really was. The reporter did something else which marked him as a craftsman. Without stating the fact in words, he nevertheless contrived to create in the lines which he wrote an atmosphere of self-defense enveloping the old man — or perhaps the better phrase would be self-extenuation. The reader was made to perceive that Dramm, being cognizant and mildly resentful of the attitude in which his own little world held him, by reason of the fatal work of his hands, sought after a semi apologetic fashion to offer a plea in abatement of public judgment, to set up a weight of moral evidence in his own behalf, and behind this in turn, and showing through it, might be sensed the shy pride of a shy man for labor undertaken with good motives and creditably performed. With no more than a pardonable broadening and exaggeration of the other's mode of speech, the reporter succeeded likewise in reproducing not only the language, but the wistful intent of what Uncle Tobe said to him. From this interview I propose now to quote to the extent of a few paragraphs. This is Uncle Tobe addressing the visiting correspondent:

"It stands to reason — don't it? — that these here sinful men have got to be hung, an' that somebody has got to hang 'em. The Good Book says an eye fur an eye an' a tooth fur a tooth an' a life fur a life. That's perzactly whut it says, an' I'm one whut believes the Bible frum kiver to kiver. These here boys that they bring in here have broke the law of Gawd an' the law of the land, an' they jest natchelly got to pay fur their devilment. That's so, ain't it? Well, then, that bein' so, I step forward an' do the job. Ef they was free men, walkin' around like you an' me, I wouldn't lay the weight of my little finger on 'em to harm a single hair in their haids. Ef they hadn't done nothin' ag'in' the law, I'd be the last one to do 'em a hurt. I wisht you could make that p'int plain in the piece you aim to write, so's folks would understand jest how I feel — so's they'd understand that I don't bear no gredge ag'inst any livin' creature.

"Ef the job was left to some greenhawn he'd mebbe botch it up an' make them boys suffer more'n there's any call fur. Sech things have happened, a plenty times before now ez you yourself doubtless know full well. But I don't botch it up. I ain't braggin' none whilst I'm sayin' this to you; I'm jest tellin' you. I kin take an oath that I ain't never botched up one of these jobs yit, not frum the very fust. The warden or Dr. Slattery, the prison physician, or anybody round this town that knows the full circumstances kin tell you the same, ef you ast 'em. You see, son, I ain't never nervoused up like some men would be in my place. I'm always jest ez ca'm like ez whut you are this minute. The way I look at it, I'm jest a chosen instrument of the law. I regard it ez a trust that I'm called on to perform, on account of me havin' a natchel knack in that 'special direction. Some men have gifts fur one thing an' some men have gifts fur another thing. It would seem this is the perticular thing — hangin' men — that I've got a gift fur. So, sech bein' the case, I don't worry none about it beforehand, nor I don't worry none after it's all over with, neither. With me handlin' the details the whole thing is over an' done with accordin' to the law an' the statutes an' the jedgment of the high court in less time than some people would take fussin' round, gittin' ready. The way I look at it, it's a mercy an' a blessin' to all concerned to have somebody in charge that knows how to hang a man.

"Why, it's come to sech a pass that when there's a hangin' comin' off anywhere in this part of the country they send fur me to be present ez a kind of an expert. I've been to hangin's all over this State, an' down into Louisiana, an' wunst over into Texas in order to give the sheriffs the benefit of my experience an' my advice. I make it a rule not never to take no money fur doin' sech ez that — only my travelin' expenses an' my tavern bills; that's all I ever charge 'em. But here in Chickaloosa the conditions is different, an' the gover'mint pays me seventy-five dollars a hangin'. I figger that it's wuth it, too. The Bible says the laborer is worthy of his hire. I try to be worthy of the hire I git. I certainly

58

aim to earn it — an' I reckin I do earn it, takin' everything into consideratiuii — the responsibility an' all. Ef there's any folks that think I earn my money easy — seventy-five dollars fur whut looks like jest a few minutes' work — I'd like fur 'em to stop an' think ef they'd consider themselves qualified to hang ez many men ez I have without never botchin' up a single job."

That was his chief boast, if boasting it might be called — that he never botched the job. It is the common history of common hangmen, so I've been told, that they come after a while to be possessed of the devils of cruelty, and to take pleasure in the exercise of their most grim calling. If this be true, then surely Uncle Tobe was to all outward appearances an exception to the rule. Never by word or look or act was he caught gloating over his victims; always he exhibited a merciful swiftness in the dread preliminaries and in the act of execution itself. At the outset he had shown deftness. With frequent practice he grew defter still. He contrived various devices for expediting the proceeding. For instance, after prolonged experiments, conducted in privacy, he evolved a harness-like arrangement of leather belts and straps, made all in one piece, and fitted with buckles and snaffles. With this, in a marvelously brief space, he could bind his man at elbows and wrists, at knees and ankles, so that in less time almost than it would take to describe the process, the latter stood upon the trap, as a shape deprived of motion, fully caparisoned for the end. He fitted the inner side of the crosspiece of the gallows with pegs upon which the rope rested, entirely out of sight of him upon whom it was presently to be used, until the moment when Uncle Tobe, stretching a long arm upward, brought it down, all reeved and ready. He hit upon the expedient of slickening the noose parts with yellow bar soap so that it would run smoothly in the loop and tighten smartly, without undue tugging. He might have used grease or lard, but soap was tidier, and Uncle Tobe, as has been set forth, was a tidy man.

After the first few hangings his system began to follow a regular routine. From somewhere to the west or southwest of Chickaloosa the deputy marshals would bring in a man consigned to die. The prison people, taking their charge over from them, would house him in a cell of a row of cells made doubly tight and doubly strong for such as he; in due season the warden would notify Uncle Tobe of the date fixed for the inflicting of the penalty. Four or five days preceding the day, Uncle Tobe would pay a visit to the prison, timing his arrival so that he reached there just before the exercise hour for the inmates of a certain cell-tier. Being admitted, he would climb sundry flights of narrow iron stairs and pause just outside a crisscrossed door of iron slats while a turnkey, entering that door and locking it behind him, would open a smaller door set flat in the wall of damp-looking grey stones and invite the man caged up inside to come forth for his daily walk. Then, while the captive paced the length and breadth of the narrow corridor back and across, to and fro, up and down, with the futile restlessness of a cat animal in a zoo, his feet clumping on the flagged flooring, and the watchful turnkey standing by, Uncle Tobe, having flattened his lean form in a niche behind the outer lattice, with an appraising eye would consider the shifting figure through a convenient cranny of the wattled metal strips. He took care to keep himself well back out of view, but since he stood in shadow while the one he marked so keenly moved in a flood of daylight filtering down through a skylight in the ceiling of the cell block, the chances were the prisoner could not have made out the indistinct form of the stranger anyhow. Five or ten minutes of such scrutiny of his man was all Uncle Tobe ever desired. In his earlier days before he took up this present employment, he had been an adept at guessing the hoof-weight of the beeves and swine in which he dealt. That early experience stood him in good stead now; he took no credit to himself for his accuracy in estimating the bulk of a living human being.

Downstairs, on the way out of the place, if by chance he encountered the warden in his office, the warden, in all likelihood, would say: "Well, how about it this time, Uncle Tobe?"

And Uncle Tobe would make some such answer as this:

"Well, suh, accordin' to my reckonin' this here one will heft about a hund'ed an' sixty-five pound, ez he stands now. How's he takin' it, warden?"

"Oh, so-so."

"He looks to me like he was broodin' a right smart," the expert might say. "I jedge he ain't relishin' his vittles much, neither. Likely he'll worry three or four pound more off'n his bones 'twixt now an' Friday mornin'. He oughter run about one hund'ed an' sixty or mebbe one-sixty-one by then."

"How much drop do you allow to give him?"

"Don't worry about that, suh," would be the answer given with a contemplative squint of the placid, pale eye. "I reckin my calculations won't be very fur out of the way, ef any."

They never were, either.

On the day before the day, he would be a busy man, what with superintending the fitting together and setting up of the painted lumber pieces upon which tomorrow's capital tragedy would be played; and, when this was done to his liking, trying the drop to see that the boards had not warped, and trying the rope for possible flaws in its fabric or weave, and proving to his own satisfaction that the mechanism of the wooden lever which operated to spring the trap worked with an instantaneous smoothness. To every detail he gave a painstaking supervision, guarding against all possible contingencies. Regarding the trustworthiness of the rope he was especially careful. When this particular hanging was concluded, the scaffold would be taken apart and stored away for subsequent use, but for each hanging the government furnished a brand new rope, especially made at a factory in New Orleans at a cost of eight dollars. The spectators generally cut the rope up into short lengths after it had fulfilled its ordained purpose, and carried the pieces away for souvenirs. So always there was a new rope provided, and its dependability must be ascertained by prolonged and exhaustive tests before Uncle Tobe would approve of it. Seeing him at his task, with his coat and waistcoat off, his sleeves rolled back, and his intent mien, one realized why, as a hangman, he had been a success. He left absolutely nothing to chance. When he was through with his experimenting, the possibility of an exhibition of the proneness of inanimate objects to misbehave in emergencies had been reduced to a minimum.

Before daylight next morning Uncle Tobe, dressed in sober black, like a country undertaker, and with his mid-Victorian whiskers all cleansed and combed, would present himself at his post of duty. He would linger in the background, an unobtrusive bystander, until the condemned sinner had gone through the mockery of eating his last breakfast; and, still making himself inconspicuous during the march to the gallows, would trail at the very tail of the line, while the short, straggling procession was winding out through gas-lit murky hallways into the pale dawn-light slanting over the walls of the gravel-paved, high-fenced compound built against the outer side of the prison close. He would wait on, always holding himself discreetly aloof from the middle breadth of the picture, until the officiating clergyman had done with his sacred offices; would wait until the white-faced wretch on whose account the government was making all this pother and taking all this trouble, had mumbled his farewell words this side of eternity; would continue to wait, very patiently, indeed, until the warden nodded to him. Then, with his trussing harness tucked under his arm, and the black cap neatly folded and bestowed in a handy side-pocket of his coat, Uncle Tobe would advance forward, and laying a kindly, almost a paternal hand upon the shoulder of the man who must die, would steer him to a certain spot in the centre of the platform, just beneath a heavy cross-beam. There would follow a quick shifting of the big, gnarled hands over the unresisting body of the doomed man, and almost instantly, so it seemed to those who watched, all was in order: the arms of the murderer drawn rearward and pressed in close against his ribs by a broad girth encircling his trunk at the elbows, his wrists caught together in buckled leather cuffs behind his back; his knees and his ankles fast in leathern loops which joined to the rest of the apparatus by means of a transverse strap drawn tautly down the length of his legs, at the back; the black-cloth head-bag with its peaked crown in place; the noose fitted; the hobbled and hooded shape perhaps swaying a trifle this way and that; and Uncle Tobe on his tiptoes stepping swiftly over to a tilted wooden lever which projected out and upward through the planked floor, like the handle of a steering oar.

It was at this point that the timorous-hearted among the witnesses turned their heads away. Those who were more resolute — or as the case might be, more morbid — and who continued to look, were made aware of a freak of physics which in accord, I suppose, with the laws of horizontals and parallels decrees that a man cut off short from life by quick and violent means and fallen prone upon the earth, seems to shrink up within himself and to grow shorter in body and in sprawling limb, whereas one hanged with a rope by the neck has the semblance of stretching out to unseemly and unhuman lengths all the while that he dangles.

Having repossessed himself of his leather cinches, Uncle Tobe would presently depart for his home, stopping *en route* at the Chickaloosa National Bank to deposit the greater part of the seventy-five dollars which the warden, as representative of a satisfied Federal government, had paid him, cash down on the spot. To his credit in the bank the old man had a considerable sum, all earned after this mode, and all drawing interest at the legal rate. On his arrival at his home, Mr. Dramm would first of all have his breakfast. This over, he would open the second drawer of an old black-walnut bureau, and from under a carefully folded pile of spare undergarments would withdraw a small, cheap book, bound in imitation red leather, and bearing the word "Accounts" in faded script upon the cover. On a clean, blue-lined page of the book, in a cramped handwriting, he would write in ink, the name, age, height, and weight of the man he had just despatched out of life; also the hour and minute when the drop fell, the time elapsing before the surgeons pronounced the man dead; the disposition which had been made of the body, and any other data which seemed to him pertinent to the record. Invariably he concluded the entry thus: "Neck was broke by the fall. Everything passed off smooth." From his first time of service he had never failed to make such notations following a hanging, he being in this, as in all things, methodical and exact.

The rest of the day, in all probabilities, would be given to small devices of his own. If the season suited he might work in his little truck garden at the back of the house, or if it were the fall of the year he might go rabbit hunting; then again he might go for a walk. When the evening paper came — Chickaloosa had two papers, a morning paper and an evening paper — he would read through the account given of the event at the prison, and would pencil any material errors which had crept into the reporter's story, and then he would clip out the article and file it away with a sheaf of similar clippings in the same bureau drawer where he kept his account-book and his underclothing. This done he would eat his supper, afterward washing and wiping the supper dishes and, presently bedtime for him having arrived, he would go to bed and sleep very soundly and very peacefully all night. Sometimes his heart trouble brought on smothering spells which woke him up. He rarely had dreams, and never any dreams unpleasantly associated with his avocation. Probably never was there a man blessed with less of an imagination than this same Tobias Dramm. It seemed almost providential, considering the calling he followed, that he altogether lacked the faculty of introspection, so that neither his memory nor his conscience ever troubled him.

Thus far I have made no mention of his household, and for the very good reason that he had none. In his youth he had not married. The forked tongue of town slander had it that he was too stingy to support a wife, and on top of that expense, to run the risk of having children to rear. He had no close kindred excepting a distant cousin or two in Chickaloosa. He kept no servant, and for this there was a double cause. First, his parsimonious instincts; second, the fact that for love or money no negro would minister to him, and in this community negroes were the only household servants to be had. Among the darkies there was current a belief that at dead of night he dug up the bodies of those he had hanged and peddled the cadavers to the "student doctors." They said he was in active partnership with the devil; they said the devil took over the souls of his victims, paying therefor in red-hot dollars, after the hangman was done with their bodies. The belief of the negroes that this unholy traffic existed amounted with them to a profound conviction. They held Mr. Dramm in an awesome and horrified veneration, bowing to him most respectfully when they met him, and then sidling off hurriedly. It would have taken strong horses to drag any black-skinned resident of Chickaloosa to the portals of the little three-roomed frame cottage in the outskirts of the town which Uncle Tobe tenanted. Therefore he lived by himself, doing his own skimpy marketing and his own simple housekeeping. Loneliness was a part of the penalty he paid for following the calling of a gallowsmith.

Among members of his own race he had no close friends. For the most part the white people did not exactly shun him, but, as the saying goes in the Southwest, they let him be. They were well content to enshrine him as a local celebrity, and ready enough to point him out to visitors, but by an unwritten communal law the line was drawn there. He was as one set apart for certain necessary undertakings, and yet denied the intimacy of his kind because he performed them acceptably. If his aloof and solitary state ever distressed him, at least he gave no outward sign of it, but went his uncomplaining way, bearing himself with a homely, silent dignity, and enveloped in those invisible garments of superstition which local prejudice and local ignorance had conjured up.

Ready as he was when occasion suited, to justify his avocation in the terms of that same explanation which he had given to the young reporter from St. Louis that time, and greatly though he may have craved to gain the good-will of his fellow citizens, he was never known openly to rebel against his lot. The nearest he ever came to doing this was once when he met upon the street a woman of his acquaintance who had suffered a recent bereavement in the death of her only daughter. He approached her, offering awkward condolences, and at once was moved to a further expression of his sympathy for her in her great loss by trying to shake her hand. At the touch of his fingers to hers the woman, already in a mood of grief bordering on hysteria, shrank back screaming out that his hand smelled of the soap with which he coated his gallows-nooses. She ran away from him, crying out as she ran that he was accursed; that he was marked with that awful smell and could not rid himself of it. To those who had witnessed this scene the hangman, with rather an injured and bewildered air, made explanation. The poor woman, he said, was wrong; although in a way of speaking she was right, too. He did, indeed, use the same yellow bar soap for washing his hands that he used for anointing his ropes. It was a good soap, and cheap; he had used the same brand regularly for years in cleansing his hands. Since it answered the first purpose so well, what possible harm could there be in slicking the noose of the rope with it when he was called upon to conduct one of his jobs over up at the prison? Apparently he was at a loss to fathom the looks they cast at him when he had finished with this statement and had asked this question. He began a protest, but broke off quickly and went away shaking his head as though puzzled that ordinarily sane folks should be so squeamish and so unreasonable. But he kept on using the soap as before.

Until now this narrative has been largely preamble. The real story follows. It concerns itself with the birth of an imagination.

In his day Uncle Tobe hanged all sorts and conditions of men — men who kept on vainly hoping against hope for an eleventh-hour reprieve long after the last chance of reprieve had vanished, and who on the gallows begged piteously for five minutes, for two minutes, for one minute more of precious grace; negroes gone drunk on religious exhortation who died in a frenzy, sure of salvation, and shouting out halleluiahs; Indians upborne and stayed by a racial stoicism; Chinamen casting stolid, slant-eyed glances over the rim of the void before them and filled with the calmness of the fatalist who believes that whatever is to be, is to be; white men upon whom at the last, when all prospect of intervention was gone, a mental numbness mercifully descended with the result that they came to the rope's embrace like men in a walking coma, with glazed, unseeing eyes, and dragging feet; other white men who summoned up a mockery of bravado and uttered poor jests from between lips drawn back in defiant sneering as they gave themselves over to the hangman, so that only Uncle Tobe, feeling their flesh crawling under their grave-clothes as he tied them up, knew a hideous terror berode their bodies. At length, in the tenth year of his career as a paid executioner he was called upon to visit his professional attentions upon a man different from any of those who had gone down the same dread chute.

The man in question was a train-bandit popularly known as the Lone-Hand Kid, because always he conducted his nefarious operations without confederates. He was a squat, dark ruffian, as malignant as a moccasin snake, and as dangerous as one. He was filthy in speech and vile in habit, being in his person most unpicturesque and most unwholesome, and altogether seemed a creature more viper than he was man. The sheriffs of two border States and the officials of a contiguous reservation sought for him many times, long and diligently, before a posse overcame him in the hills by over-powering odds and took him alive at the cost of two of its members killed outright and a third badly crippled. So soon as surgeons plugged up the holes in his hide which members of the vengeful posse shot into him after they had him surrounded and before his ammunition gave out, he was brought to bar to answer for the unprovoked murder of a postal clerk on a transcontinental limited. No time was wasted in hurrying his trial through to its conclusion; it was felt that there was crying

66

need to make an example of this red-handed desperado. Having been convicted with commendable celerity, the Lone-Hand Kid was transferred to Chickaloosa and strongly confined there against the day of Uncle Tobe's ministrations upon him.

From the very hour that the prosecution was started, the Lone-Hand Kid, whose real name was the prosaic name of Smith, objected strongly to this procedure which in certain circles is known as "railroading." He insisted that he was being legally expedited out of life on his record and not on the evidence. There were plenty of killings for any one of which he might have been tried and very probably found guilty, but he reckoned it a profound injustice that he should be indicted, tried, and condemned for a killing he had not committed. By his code he would not have rebelled strongly against being punished for the evil things he himself had done; he did dislike, though, being hanged for something some rival hold-up man had done. Such was his contention, and he reiterated it with a persistence which went far toward convincing some people that after all there might be something in what he said, although among honest men there was no doubt whatsoever that the world would be a sweeter and a healthier place to live in with the Lone-Hand Kid entirely translated out of it.

Having been dealt with, as he viewed the matter, most unfairly, the condemned killer sullenly refused to make submission to his appointed destiny. On the car journey up to Chickaloosa, although still weak from his wounds and securely ironed besides, he made two separate efforts to assault his guards. In his cell, a few days later, he attacked a turnkey in pure wantonness seemingly, since even with the turnkey eliminated, there still was no earthly prospect for him to escape from the steel strong-box which enclosed him. That was what it truly was, too, a strong-box, for the storing of many living pledges held as surety for the peace and good order of the land. Of all these human collaterals who were penned up there with him, he, for the time being, was most precious in the eyes of the law. Therefore the law took no chance of losing him, and this he must have known when he maimed his keeper.

After this outbreak he was treated as a vicious wild beast, which, undoubtedly, was exactly what he was. He was chained by his ankles to his bed, and his food was shoved in to him through the bars by a man who kept himself at all times well out of reach of the tethered prisoner. Having been rendered helpless, he swore then that when finally they unbarred his cell door and sought to fetch him forth to garb him for his journey to the gallows, he would fight them with his teeth and his bare hands for so long as he had left an ounce of strength with which to fight. Bodily force would then be the only argument remaining to him by means of which he might express his protest, and he told all who cared to listen that most certainly he meant to invoke it.

There was a code of decorum which governed the hangings at Chickaloosa, and the resident authorities dreaded mightily the prospect of having it profaned by spiteful and unmannerly behavior on the part of the Lone-Hand Kid. There was said to be in all the world just one living creature for whom the rebellious captive entertained love and respect, and this person was his half-sister. With the good name of his prison at heart, the warden put up the money that paid her fare from her home down in the Indian Territory. Two days before the execution she arrived, a slab-sided, shabby drudge of a woman. Having first been primed and prompted for her part, she was sent to him, and in his cell she wept over the fettered prisoner, and with him she pleaded until he promised her, reluctantly, he would make no physical struggle on being led out to die.

He kept his word, too; but it was to develop that the pledge of non-resistance, making his body passive to the will of his jailers, did not, according to the Lone-Hand Kid's sense of honor, include the muscles of his tongue. His hour came at sunup of a clear, crisp, October morning, when a rime of frost made a silver carpet upon the boarded floor of the scaffold, and in the east the heavens glowed an irate red, like the reflections of a distant bale-fire. From his cell door before the head warder summoned him forth, he drove away with terrible oaths the clergyman who had come to offer him religious consolation. At daylight, when the first beams of young sunlight were stealing in at the slitted windows to streak the whitewashed wall behind him with a barred pattern of red, like brush strokes of fresh paint, he ate his last breakfast with foul words between bites, and outside, a little later, in the shadow of the crosstree from which shortly he would dangle in the article of death, a stark offence before the sight of mortal eyes, he halted and stood reviling all who had a hand in furthering and compassing his condemnation. Profaning the name of his Maker with every breath, he cursed the President of the United States who had declined to reprieve him, the justices of the high court who had denied his appeal from the verdict of the lower, the judge who had tried him, the district attorney who had prosecuted him, the grand jurors who had indicted him, the petit jurors who had voted to convict him, the witnesses who had testified against him, the posse men who had trapped him, consigning them all and singly to everlasting damnation. Before this pouring flood of blasphemy the minister, who had followed him up the gallows steps in the vain hope that when the end came some faint sign of contrition might be vouchsafed by this poor lost soul, hid his face in his hands as though fearing an offended Deity would send a bolt from on high to blast all who had been witnesses to such impiety and such impenitence.

The indignant warden moved to cut short this lamentable spectacle. He signed with his hand for Uncle Tobe to make haste, and Uncle Tobe, obeying, stepped forward from where he had been waiting in the rear rank of the shocked spectators. Upon him the defiant ruffian turned the forces of his sulphurous hate, full-gush. First over one shoulder and then over the other as the executioner worked with swift fingers to bind him into a rigid parcel of a man, he uttered what was both a dreadful threat and a yet more dreadful promise.

"I ain't blamin' these other folks here," he proclaimed. "Some of 'em are here because it's their duty to be here, an' ef these others kin git pleasure out of seein' a man croaked that ain't afeared of bein' croaked, they're welcome to enjoy the free show, so fur ez I'm concerned. But you — you stingy, white-whiskered old snake! — you're doin' this fur the little piece of dirty money that's in it fur you.

"Listen to me, you dog: I know I'm headin' straight fur hell, an' I ain't skeered to go, neither. But I ain't goin' to stay there. I'm comin' back fur you! I'm comin' back this very night to git you an' take your old, withered, black soul back down to hell with me. No need fur you to try to hide. Wharever you hide I'll seek you out. You can't git away frum me. You kin lock your door an' you kin lock your winder, an' you kin hide your head under the bedclothes, but I'll find you wherever you are, remember that! An' you're goin' back down there with me!

"Now go ahead an' hang me — I'm all set fur it ef you are!"

Through this harangue Uncle Tobe worked on, outwardly composed. Whatever his innermost emotions may have been, his expression gave no hint that the mouthings of the Lone-Hand Kid had sunk in. He drew the peaked black sack down across the swollen face, hiding the glaring eyes and the lips that snarled. He brought the rope forward over the cloaked head and drew the noose in tautly, with the knot adjusted to fit snugly just under the left ear, so that the hood took on the semblance of a well-filled, inverted bag with its puckered end fluting out in the effect of a dark ruff upon the hunched shoulders of its wearer. Stepping back, he gripped the handle of the lever-bar, and with all his strength jerked it toward him. A square in the floor opened as the trap was flapped back upon its hinges, and through the opening the haltered form shot straight downward to bring up with a great jerk, and after that to dangle like a plumb-bob on a string. Under the quick strain the gallows-arm creaked and whined; in the silence which followed the hangman was heard to exhale his breath in a vast puff of relief. His hand went up to his forehead to wipe beads of sweat which, for all that the morning was cool almost to coldness, had suddenly popped out through his skin. He for one was mighty glad the thing was done, and, as he in this moment figured, well done.

But for once and once only as those saw who had the hardihood to look, Uncle Tobe had botched up a job. Perhaps it was because of his great haste to make an end of a scandalous scene; perhaps because the tirade of the bound malefactor had discomfited him and made his fingers fumble this one time at their familiar task. Whatever the cause, it was plainly enough to be seen that the heavy knot had not cracked the Lone-Hand Kid's spine. The noose, as was ascertained later, had caught on the edge of the broad jawbone, and the man, instead of dying instantly, was strangling to death by degrees and with much struggling.

In the next half minute a thing even more grievous befell. The broad strap which girthed the murderer's trunk just above the bend of the elbows, held fast, but the rest of the harness, having been improperly snaffled on, loosened and fell away from the twitching limbs so that as the elongated body twisted to and fro in half circles, the lower arms winnowed the air in foreshortened and contorted flappings, and the freed legs drew up and down convulsively.

Very naturally, Uncle Tobe was chagrined; perhaps he had hidden within him emotions deeper than those bred of a personal mortification. At any rate, after a quick, distressed glance through the trap at the writhing shape of agony below, he turned his eyes from it and looked steadfastly at the high wall facing him. It chanced to be the western wall, which was bathed in a ruddy glare where the shafts of the upcoming sun, lifting over the panels at the opposite side of the fenced enclosure, began to fall diagonally upon the whitewashed surface just across. And now, against that glowing plane of background opposite him, there appeared as he looked the slanted shadow of a swaying rope framed in at right and at left by two broader, deeper lines which were the shadows marking the timber uprights that supported the scaffold at its nearer corners; and also there appeared, midway between the framing shadows, down at the lower end of the slender line of the cord, an exaggerated, wriggling manifestation like the reflection of a huge and misshapen jumping-jack, which first would lengthen itself grotesquely, and then abruptly would shorten up, as the tremors running through the dying man's frame altered the silhouette cast by the oblique sunbeams; and along with this stenciled vision, as a part of it, occurred shifting shadow movements of two legs dancing busily on nothing, and of two foreshortened arms, flapping up and down. It was no pretty picture to look upon, yet Uncle Tobe, plucking with a tremulous hand at the ends of his beard, continued to stare at the apparition, daunted and fascinated. To him it must have seemed as though the Lone-Hand Kid, with a malignant pertinacity which lingered on in him after by rights the last breath should have been squeezed out of his wretched carcass, was painting upon those tall planks the picture and the presentiment of his farewell threat.

Nearly half an hour passed before the surgeons consented that the body should be taken down and boxed. His harness which had failed him having been returned to its owner, he made it up into a compact bundle and collected his regular fee and went away very quietly. Ordinarily, following his habitual routine, he

71

would have gone across town to his little house; would have washed his hands with a bar of the yellow laundry soap; would have cooked and eaten his breakfast, and then, after tidying up the kitchen, would have made the customary entry in his red-backed account-book. But this morning he seemed to have no appetite, and besides, he felt an unaccountable distaste for his home, with its silence and its emptiness. Somehow he much preferred the open air, with the skies over him and wide reaches of space about him; which was doubly strange, seeing that he was no lover of nature, but always theretofore had accepted sky and grass and trees as matters of course — things as inevitable and commonplace as the weathers and the winds.

Throughout the day and until well on toward night he was beset by a curious, uncommon restlessness which made it hard for him to linger long in any one spot. He idled about the streets of the town; twice he wandered aimlessly miles out along roads beyond the town. All the while, without cessation, there was a tugging and nagging at his nerve-ends, a constant inward irritation which laid a hold on his thoughts, twitching them off into unpleasant channels. It kept him from centering his interest upon the casual things about him; inevitably it turned his mind back to inner contemplations. The sensation was mental largely, but it seemed so nearly akin to the physical that to himself Uncle Tobe diagnosed it as the after-result of a wrench for his weak heart. You see, never before having experienced the reactions of a suddenly quickened imagination, he, naturally, was at a loss to account for it on any other ground.

Also he was weighted down by an intense depression that his clean record of ten years should have been marred by a mishap; this regret, constantly recurring in his thoughts, served to make him unduly sensitive. He had a feeling that people stared hard at him as they passed and, after he had gone by, that they turned to stare at him some more. Under this scrutiny he gave no sign of displeasure, but inwardly he resented it. Of course these folks had heard of what had happened up at the prison, and no doubt among themselves would be commenting upon the tragedy and gossiping about it. Well, any man was liable to make a slip once; nobody was perfect. It would never happen again; he was sure of that much.

All day he mooned about, a brooding, uneasy figure,

speaking to scarcely any one at all, but followed wherever he went by curious eyes. It was late in the afternoon before it occurred to him that he had eaten nothing all day, and that he had failed to deposit the money he had earned that morning. It would be too late now to get into the bank; the bank, which opened early, closed at three o'clock. To-morrow would do as well. Although he had no zest for food despite his fast, he figured maybe it was the long abstinence which was filling his head with such flighty notions, so he entered a small, smelly lunch-room near the railroad station, and made a pretence of eating an order of ham and eggs. He tried not to notice that the black waiter who served him shrank away from his proximity, shying off like a breechy colt, from the table where Uncle Tobe sat, whenever his business brought him into that part of the place. What difference did a fool darky's fears make, anyway?

Dusk impended when he found himself approaching his three-room house, looming up as a black oblong, where it stood aloof from its neighbors, with vacant lands about it. The house faced north and south. On the nearer edge of the unfenced common, which extended up to it on the eastern side, he noted as he drew close that somebody — perhaps a boy, or more probably a group of boys — had made a bonfire of fallen autumn leaves and brushwood. Going away as evening came, they had left their bonfire to burn itself out. The smoldering pile was almost under his bedroom window. He regretted rather that the boys had gone; an urgent longing for human companionship of some sort, however remote — a yearning he had never before felt with such acuteness — was upon him. Tormented, as he still was, by strange vagaries, he had almost to force himself to unlock the front door and cross the threshold into the gloomy interior of his cottage. But before entering, and while he yet wrestled with a vague desire to retrace his steps and go back down the street, he stooped and picked up his copy of the afternoon paper which the carrier, with true carrier-like accuracy, had flung upon the narrow front porch.

Inside the house, the floor gave off sharp little sounds, the warped floor squeaking and wheezing under the weight of his tread. Subconsciously, this irritated him; a lot of causes were combining to harass him, it seemed; there was a general conspiracy on the part of objects animate and inanimate to make

73

him — well, suspicious. And Uncle Tobe was not given to nervousness, which made it worse. He was ashamed of himself that he should be in such state. Glancing about him in a furtive, almost in an apprehensive way, he crossed the front room to the middle room, which was his bed chamber, the kitchen being the room at the rear. In the middle room he lit a coal-oil lamp which stood upon a small centre table. Alongside the table he opened out the paper and glanced at a caption running half-way across the top of the front page; then, fretfully he crumpled up the printed sheet in his hand and let it fall upon the floor. He had no desire to read the account of his one failure. Why should the editor dwell at such length and with so prodigal a display of black head-line type upon this one bungled job when every other job of all the jobs that had gone before, had been successful in every detail? Let's see, now, how many men had he hanged with precision and with speed and with never an accident to mar the proceedings? A long, martialed array of names came trooping into his brain, and along with the names the memories of the faces of all those dead men to whom the names had belonged. The faces began to pass before him in a mental procession. This wouldn't do. Since there were no such things as ghosts or haunts; since, as all sensible men agreed, the dead never came back from the grave, it was a foolish thing for him to be creating those unpleasant images in his mind. He shook his head to clear it of recollections which were the better forgotten. He shook it again and again.

He would get to bed; a good night's rest would make him feel better and more natural. It was an excellent idea — this idea of sleep. So he raised the bottommost half of the curtain-less side window for air, drew down the shade by the string suspended from its lower cross breadth, until the lower edge of the shade came even with the window sash, and undressed himself to his undergarments. He was about to blow out the light when he remembered he had left the money that was the price of his morning's work in his trousers which hung, neatly folded, across the back of a chair by the centre table. He was in the act of withdrawing the bills from the bottom of one of the trouser-pockets when right at his feet there was a quick, queer sound of rustling. As he glared down, startled, out from under the crumpled newspaper came timorously creeping a half-grown, sickly looking rat, minus its tail, having lost its tail in a trap, perhaps, or possibly in a battle with other rats.

At best a rat is no pleasant bedroom companion, and besides, Uncle Tobe had been seriously annoyed. He kicked out with one of his bare feet, taking the rat squarely in its side as it scurried for its hole in the wainscoting. He hurt it badly. It landed with a thump ten feet away and sprawled out on the floor kicking and squealing feebly. Holding the wad of bills in his left hand, with his right Uncle Tobe deftly plucked up the crushed vermin by the loose fold of skin at the nape of its neck, and with a quick flirt of his arm tossed it sidewise from him to cast it out of the half-opened window. He returned to the table and bent over and blew down the lamp chimney, and in the darkness felt his way across the room to his bed. He stretched himself full length upon it, drew the cotton comforter up to cover him, and shoved the money under the pillow.

His fingers were relaxing their grip on the bills when he saw something — something which instantly turned him stiff and rigid and deathly cold all over, leaving him without will-power or strength to move his head or shift his gaze. Over the white, plastered wall alongside his bed an unearthly red glow sprang up, turning a deeper, angrier red as it spread and widened. Against this background next stood out two perpendicular masses like the broad shadows of uprights — like the supporting uprights of a gallows, say — and in the squared space of brightness thus marked off, depending midway from the shadow crossing it at right angles at the top, appeared a filmy, fine line, which undoubtedly was the shadow of a cord, and at the end of the cord dangled a veritable jumping-jack of a silhouette, turning and writhing and jerking, with a shape which in one breath grotesquely lengthened and in the next shrank up to half its former dimensions, which kicked out with indistinct movements of its lower extremities, which flapped with foreshortened strokes of the shadowy upper limbs, which altogether so contorted itself as to form the likeness of a thing all out of perspective, all out of proportion, and all most horribly reminiscent.

A heart with valves already weakened by a chronic affection can stand just so many shocks in a given time and no more.

A short time later in this same night, at about eight-forty-five o'clock, to be exact, a man who lived on the opposite side of the unfenced common gave the alarm of fire over the telephone. The Chickaloosa fire engine and hose reels came at once, and with the machines numerous citizens.

In a way of speaking, it turned out to be a false alarm. A bonfire of leaves and brush, abandoned at dusk by the boys who kindled it, had, after smoldering a while, sprung up briskly and, flaming high, was now scorching the clap-boarded side of the Dramm house.

There was no need for the firemen to uncouple a line of hose from the reel. While two of them made shift to get retorts of a patent extinguisher from the truck, two more, wondering why Uncle Tobe, even if in bed and asleep at so early an hour, had not been aroused by the noise of the crowd's coming, knocked at his front door. There being no response from within at once, they suspected something must be amiss. With heaves of their shoulders they forced the door off its hinges, and entering in company, they groped their passage through the empty front room into the bedroom behind it, which was lighted after a fashion by the reflection from the mounting flames without.

The tenant was in bed; he lay on his side with his face turned to the wall; he made no answer to their hails. When they bent over him they knew why. No need to touch him, then, with that look on his face and that stare out of his popped eyes. He was dead, all right enough; but plainly had not been dead long; not more than a few minutes, apparently. One of his hands was shoved up under his pillow with the fingers touching a small roll containing seven ten-dollar bills and one five-dollar bill; the other hand still gripped a fold of the coverlet as though the fatal stroke had come upon the old man as he lifted the bedclothing to draw it up over his face. These incidental facts were noted down later after the coroner had been called to take charge; they were the subject of considerable comment next day when the inquest took place. The coroner was of the opinion that the old man had been killed by a heart seizure, and that he had died on the instant the attack came.

However, this speculation had no part in the thoughts of the two startled firemen at the moment of the finding of the body. What most interested them, next only to the discovery of the presence of the dead man there in the same room with them, was a queer combination of shadows which played up and down against the wall beyond the bed, it being plainly visible in the glare of the small conflagration just outside.

With one accord they turned about, and then they saw the cause of the phenomenon, and realized that it was not very much of a phenomenon after all, although unusual enough to constitute a rather curious circumstance. A crippled, tailless rat had somehow entangled its neck in a loop at the end of the dangling cord of the half-drawn shade at the side window on the opposite side of the room and, being too weak to wriggle free, was still hanging there, jerking and kicking, midway of the window opening. The glow of the pile of burning leaves and brush behind and beyond it, brought out its black outlines with remarkable clearness.

The patterned shadow upon the wall, though, disappeared in the same instant that the men outside began spraying their chemical compound from the two extinguishers upon the ambitious bonfire to douse it out, and one of the firemen slapped the rat down to the floor and killed it with a stamp of his foot.

MR. LOBEL'S APOPLEXY

The real purpose of this is to tell about Mr. Lobel's attack of apoplexy. What comes before must necessarily be in its nature preliminary and preparatory, leading up to the climactic stroke which leaves the distinguished victim stretched upon the bed of affliction.

First let us introduce our principal. Reader, meet Mr. Max Lobel, president of Lobel Masterfilms, Inc., also its founder, its chief stockholder and its general manager. He is a short, broad, thick, globular man and a bald one, wearing gold-rimmed spectacles, carrying a gold-headed cane and using a private gold-mounted toothpick after meals. His collars are of that old-fashioned open-faced kind such as our fathers and Mr. John D. Rockefeller, Sr., used to wear; collars rearing at the back but shorn widely away in front to show two things — namely, the Adam's apple and that Mr. Lobel is conservative. But for his neckwear he patronizes those shops where ties are exclusively referred to as *scarves* and cost from five dollars apiece up, which proves also he is progressive and keeps abreast of the times. When he walks he favors his feet. Mostly, though, he rides in as good a car as domestic currency can buy in foreign marts.

Aside from his consuming desire to turn out those surpassing achievements of the cellular-cinema art known as Lobel's Masterfilms, he has in life two great passions, one personal in its character, the other national in its scope — the first a craving for fancy waistcoats, the second a yearning to see the name of Max Lobel in print as often as possible and in as large letters as likewise is possible; and for either of these is a plausible explanation. Mr. Lobel has a figure excellently shaped for presenting the patternings of a fanciful stomacher to the world and up until a few years ago there were few occasions when he might hope to see the name Lobel in print. For, know you, Mr. Lobel has not always been in the moving-picture business. Nobody in the moving-picture business has always been in the moving-picture business — excepting some of the child wonders under ten years of age. And ten years ago our hero was the M.

Lobel Company, cloak and suit jobbers in rather an inconspicuous Eastern town.

What was true of him as regards his comparatively recent advent into the producing and distributing fields was true of his major associates. Back in 1911 the vice president and second in command, Mr. F. X. Quinlan, moved upward into a struggling infantile industry via the stepping-stone of what in the vernacular of his former calling is known as a mitt joint — summers at Coney, winters in store pitches — where he guided the professional destinies of Madame Zaharat, the Egyptian seeress, in private, then as now, Mrs. F. X. Quinlan née Clardy.

The treasurer and secretary, Mr. Simeon Geltfin, had once upon a time been proprietor of the Ne Plus Ultra Misfit Clothing Parlors at Utica, New York, a place where second-hand habiliments, scoured and ironed, dangled luringly in show windows bearing such enticing labels as "Tailor's Sample—Nobby—$9.80," "Bargain—Take Me Home For $5.60," and "These Trousers Were Uncalled For—$2.75."

The premier director, Mr. Bertram Colfax, numbered not one but two chrysalis changes in his career. In the grub stage, as it were, he had begun life as Lemuel Sims, a very grubby grub indeed, becoming Colfax at the same time he became property man for a repertoire troupe playing county-fair weeks in the Middle West.

As for the scenario editor and continuity writer, he in a prior condition of life had solicited advertisements for a trade journal. So it went right down the line.

At the time of the beginning of this narrative Lobel Masterfilms, Inc., had attained an eminence of what might be called fair-to-medium prominence in the moving-picture field. In other words, it now was able to pay its stars salaries running up into the multiples of tens of thousands of dollars a year and the bank which carried its paper had not yet felt justified in installing a chartered accountant in the home offices to check the finances and collect the interest on the loans outstanding. Before reaching this position the concern had passed through nearly all the customary intervening stages. Nearly a decade rearward, back in the dark ages of the filmic cosmos, the Jurassic Period of pictures, so to speak, this little group of pathfinders tracking under the chieftainship of Mr. Lobel into almost uncharted wilds of artistic endeavor had dabbled in slap-stick one reelers featuring the plastic pie and the treacherous seltzer siphon, also the trick staircase, the educated moustache and the performing doormat.

Next — following along the line of least resistance — the adventurers went in more or less extensively for wild-western dramas replete with stagecoach robberies and abounding in hair pants. If the head bad man — not the secondary bad man who stayed bad all through, or the tertiary bad man who was fatally extinguished with gun-fire in Reel Two, but the chief, or primary, bad man who reformed and married Little Nell, the unspoiled child of Death Valley — wore the smartest frontier get-up of current year's vintage that the Chicago mail-order houses could turn out; if Little Nell's father, appearing contemporaneously, dressed according to the mode laid down for Forty-niners by such indubitable authorities as Bret Harte; if the sheriff stalked in and out of lens range attired as a Mississippi River gambler was popularly supposed to have been attired in the period 1860 to 1875; and if finally the cavalry troopers from the near-by army post sported the wide hats and khaki shirts which came into governmental vogue about the time of the Spanish War, all very well and good. The action was everything; the sartorial accessories were as they might be and were and frequently still are.

Along here there intruded a season when the Lobel shop tentatively experimented with costume dramas — the Prisoner of Chillon wearing the conventional black and white in alternating stripes of a Georgia chain gang and doing the old Sing Sing lock step and retiring for the night to his donjon cell with a set of shiny and rather modern-looking leg irons on his ankles; Mary Queen of Scots and Catharine de' Medici in costumes strikingly similar; Oliver Goldsmith in Sir Walter Raleigh's neck ruff and Captain Kidd's jack boots.

But this season endured not for long. Costume stuff was nix. It was not what the public wanted. It was over their heads. Mr. Lobel himself said so. Wake him up in the middle of the night and he could tell you exactly what the public did and did not want. Divining the popular will amounted with him to a gift; it approximated an exact art; really it formed the corner stone of his success. Likewise he knew — but this knowledge perhaps had come to him partly by experience rather than altogether by intuition — that historical ten reelers dealing with epochal events in the life of our own people were entirely unsuited for general consumption.

When this particular topic untactfully was broached in his presence Mr. Lobel, recalling the fate of the elaborate feature entitled *Let Freedom Ring*, had been known to sputter violently and vehemently. Upon this production — now abiding as a memory only, yet a memory bitter as aloes — he had spared neither expense nor pains, even going so far as personally to direct the filming of all the principal scenes. And to what ends? Captious critics, including those who wrote for the daily press and those who merely sent in offensive letters — college professors and such like cheap high-brows — had raised yawping voices to point out that Paul Revere galloping along the pre-Revolutionary turnpike to spread the alarm passed en route two garages and one electric power house; that Washington crossing the Delaware stood in the bow of his skiff half shrouded in an American flag bearing forty-eight stars upon its field of blue; that Andrew Jackson's riflemen filing out from New Orleans to take station behind their cotton-bale breastworks marched for some distance beneath a network of trolley wires; that Abraham Lincoln signing the Emancipation Proclamation did so while seated at a desk in a room which contained in addition to Lincoln and the desk and the Proclamation a typewriter and a Persian rug; that at Manila Bay Admiral Dewey wore spats and a wrist watch.

But these primitive adventurings, these earlier pioneering quests into the realm of the speculative were all in limbo behind them, all wiped off the slate, in part forgiven, in a measure forgotten. Since that primitive beginning and those formulative middle periods Lobel Masterfilms had found their field, and having found it, now ploughed and tilled it. To those familiar with the rise and the ever-forward movement of this, now the fourth largest industry in the civilized globe — or is it the third? — it sufficiently will fix the stage of evolutionary development attained by this component unit of that industry when I state that Lobel Masterfilms now dealt preponderantly with vampires. To be sure, it continued to handle such sidelines as taffy-haired ingénues from the country, set adrift among the wiles and pitfalls of a cruel city; such incidentals as soft-pie comickers and chin-whiskered by-Hectors; such necessary by-products as rarely beautiful he-juveniles with plush eyelashes and the hair combed slickly back off the forehead in the approved Hudson seal effect — splendid, manly youths these, who might have dodged a draft or two but never yet had flinched from before the camera's aiming muzzle. But even though it had to be conceded that Goldilockses and Prince Charmings endure and that while drolls and jesters may come and go, pies are permanent and stale not, neither do they wither; still, and with all that, such like as these were, in the Lobel scheme of things, merely so many side lines and incidentals and by-products devised and designed to fatten out a program.

Where Mr. Lobel excelled was in the vamp stuff. Even his competitors admitted it the while they vainly strove to rival him. In this, his own chosen realm of exploration and conquest he stood supremely alone; a monarch anointed with the holy oils of superiority, coroneted with success's glittering diadem. Look at his *Woman of a Million Sins!* Look at his *Satan's Stepchild*, or *How Human Souls are Dragged Down to Hell*, in six reels! Look at *A Daughter of Darkness!* Look at *The Wrecker of Lives!* Look at *The Spider Lady*, or *The Net Where Men Were the Flies!* Look at *Fair of Face Yet Black of Heart!* All of them his, all box-office best bets and all still going strong!

Moreover by now Lobel Masterfilms had progressed to that milestone on the path of progress and enterprise where genuine live authors — guys that wrote regular books — frequently furnished vehicles for stardom's regal usages. By purchase, upon the basis of so much cash or — as the case might be — so little cash down on the signing of the contract and the promise of so much more — often very very much more — to be paid in royalties out of accrued net profits, the rights to a published work would be acquired. Its name, say, was *A Commonplace Person*, which promptly would be changed in executive conclave to *The Cataract of Destiny*, or perhaps *Fate's Plaything*, or in any event some good catchy title which would look well in electrics and on three sheets.

This important point having been decided on, Mr. Ab Connors, the scenario editor, would take the script in hand to labor and bring forth the screen adaptation. If the principal character in the work, as originally evolved by her creator, was the daughter of a storekeeper in a small town in Indiana who ran away from home and went to Chicago to learn the millinery business, he, wielding a ruthless but gifted blue pencil, would speedily transform her into the ebon-hearted heiress of a Klondike millionaire, an angel without but a harpy within, and after opening up Reel One with scenes in a Yukon dance hall speedily would move all the important characters to New York, where the plot thickened so fast that only a succession of fade-outs and fade-ins, close-ups and cut-backs saved it from clabbering right on Mr. Connors' hands.

The rest would be largely a matter of continuity and after that there was nothing to worry about except picking out the cast and the locations and building the sets and starting to shoot and mayhap detailing a head office boy to stall off the author in case that poor boob came butting in kicking about changes in his story or squawking about overdue royalty statements or something. Anyhow, what did he know — what could he be expected to know — about continuity or what the public wanted or what the limitations and the possibilities of the screen were? He merely was the poor fish who'd wrote the book and he should ought to be grateful that a fellow with a real noodle had took his stuff and cut all that dull descriptive junk out of it and stuck some pep and action and punch and zip into the thing and wrote some live snappy subtitles, instead of coming round every little while, like he was, horning in and beefing all over the place.

And besides, wasn't he going to have his name printed in all the advertising matter and flashed on the screen, too, in letters nearly a fifth as tall as the letters of Mr. Lobel's name and nearly one-third as tall as the name of the star and nearly one-half as tall as the name of the director and nearly — if not quite — as tall as the name of the camera man, and so get a lot of absolutely free advertising that would be worth thousands of dollars to him and start people all over the country to hearing about him? Certainly he was! And yet, with all that, was there any satisfying some of these cheap ginks? The answer was that there was not.

There was never any trouble, though, about casting the principal rôle. That was easy — a matter of natural selection. If it could be played vampishly from the ground up, and it usually could — trust Mr. Connors for that — it went without question to Vida Monte, greatest of all the luminaries in the Lobel constellation and by universal acknowledgment the best vampire in the business. In vampiring Vida Monte it was who led; others imitatively followed. Compared with her these envying lady copy cats were as pale paprikas are to the real tabasco. Five pictures she had done for Lobel Masterfilms since placing herself under Lobel's management and a Lobel contract, all of them overpowering knock-outs, sensations, sure-fire hits. On the sixth she now was at work and her proud employer in conversation and in announcements to the trade stood sponsor for the pledge that in its filming Monte literally would out-Monte Monte.

Making his word good, he took over volunteer supervision of the main scenes. His high-domed forehead glistening with sweat, his spectacles aflame like twin burning glasses, his coat off, his collar off, his waistcoat off, he snorted and churned, a ninety-horse dynamo of a little fat man, through the hot glary studio, demanding this improvement, detecting that defect, calling for this, that or the other perfect thing in a voice which would have detained the admiring ear of an experienced bull whacker. Before him Josephson, the little camera man, quailed. From his path extra people departed, fleeing headlong; and in his presence property men were as though they were not and never had been. Out of the hands of Bertram Colfax, born Sims, he wrenched a megaphone and through it he bellowed:

"Put more punch in it, Monte — that's what I'm asking you for — the punch! Choke her, Harcourt! Choke him right back, Monte! Now-w-w then, clinch! Clinch and hang on! Good! And now the kiss! You know, Monte, the long kiss — the genuwine Monte kiss! Oh, if you love me, Monte, give me footage on that kiss! That's it — hold it! Hold it! Keep on holding it!"

"But, Mr. Lobel, now," protested Colfax, born a Sims but living it down and feeling that never more than at this minute, when rudely the steersman's helm had been snatched from his grasp, was there greater need that he should be a Colfax through and through — "but, Mr. Lobel, it was my idea that up to this point anyway the action should be played with restraint to sort of prepare the way for —"

"What do you mean restraint?"

"Well, I thought to emphasize what comes later — for a sort of comparative value — that if we were just a little subtle at the beginning —"

"Sufficient, Colfax! Listen! Don't come talking to me about no subtles! When you're working the supporting members of the cast you maybe could stick in some subtles once in a while to salve them censors, but so far as Monte is concerned you leave 'em out!"

"But — but —"

"Don't but me any buts! Listen! Ain't I taken my paralyzed oath that this here picture should make all the other vamp pictures which ever were taken look like pikers? I have! Listen! For Monte, the way I feel, I shouldn't care if she don't do a single subtle in the whole damn picture."

He had taken his paralyzed oath and he kept it. It was a wonderful story. The queen of the apaches, ruling the Parisian underworld by her fire, her beauty, her courage, accepts German gold to betray her country, and attempts by siren wiles to seduce from the path of duty Capt. Stuyvesant Schuyler of the U. S. A. general staff; almost succeeds too because of his blind passion for this glorious, sinful creature. At the crucial moment, when about to surrender to his Delilah secrets which would destroy the entire Allied cause and open the gates of Paris to the conquering foe, he is saved by a vision of his sainted, fade-in-and-fade-out mother's face. Overcome with remorse, he resigns his commission, and fleeing from temptation returns to America, a broken-hearted man; proves heart is broken by constantly pressing clenched hand to left breast as though to prevent pieces from slipping down into the abdominal cavity. Distress of the apache queen on finding her intended victim gone. Suddenly a real love, not the love of the wanton, but a purer, deeper emotion wakens in her breast. Close-up showing muscular reflexes produced upon the human face by wakening processes in the heart.

Quitting the gay life, she follows him to the Land of Free. Finds him about to marry his sweetheart of childhood, a New York society girl worth uncounted millions but just middling looking. Prompt bust-up of childhood sweetheart's romance. Abandonment of social position, wealth, everything by Schuyler, who declares he will make the stranger his bride — accompanying subtitle, "What should we care what the world may say? For after all, love is all!" Discovery on day before marriage of papers proving that Lolita — that's the lady apache's

85

name — is really Schuyler's half sister, due to carryings-on of Schuyler's late father as a young art student in Paris with Lolita's mother, a famous gypsy model. Renunciation by Lolita of Schuyler. Her suicide by imbibing poison from secret receptacle in ring. Schuyler, after registering copious grief, re-enters American Army under assumed name as a private in the ranks. Returns to battlefield in time to take part in decisive action of the war. All the officers in his brigade above the rank of corporal having apparently been killed by one devastating blast of high explosive, he assumes command and leads dauntless charge of the heavy artillery through the Hindenburg Line. Is made a colonel on the spot. Rides up Fifth Avenue alongside of Pershing in grand triumphant parade of home-coming First Division, carrying a large flag and occasionally chatting pleasantly with Pershing. On eve of marriage to childhood's sweetheart, who remains faithful, he goes to lonely spot where Lolita lies buried and places upon the silent mound her favorite flower, a single long-stemmed tiger lily. Fade out — finish!

Artistically, picturesquely, from the standpoint of timeliness, from the standpoint of vampirishness, from any standpoint at all, it satisfied fully every demand. It was one succession of thrilling, gripping, heart-lifting scenes set amid vividly contrasting surroundings — the lowest dive in all Paris; the citadel at Verdun; grand ballroom of the Schuyler mansion at Newport; the Place Vendôme on a day when it was entirely unoccupied except by moving-picture actors; Fifth Avenue on its most gala occasion — these were but a few samples. The subtitles fairly hissed to the sibilant swishing of such words as traitress, temptress, tigress and sorceress. And the name of it — you'd never guess — the name of it was *The She-Demon's Doom!* When Mr. Lobel spoke those words inspired he literally took them up in his arms and fondled them and kissed them on the temples. And why not? They were his own brain children.

He had kept his paralyzed word and he could prove it. For because this Vida Monte was one of those mimetic pieces of flesh which, without any special mental coöperation, may alter the body, the face, the muscles, the expression, the very look out of the eyes, to suit the demands of prompters and teachers; because of the plan of direction so powerfully engineered by the master mind of Lobel and, under Lobel, the lesser mind of Colfax, born

Sims; because of the very nature of the rôle of Lolita the abandoned, this picture was more daring, more sensual, more filled up with voluptuous suggestion, with coiling, clinging, writhing snakiness, with rampant, naked sexuality — in short and in fine was more vampirishly vampiratious than this, the greatest of all modern mediums for the education, the moral uplift and the entertainment of the masses, had ever known.

And then one week to the day after Mr. Lobel shot the last scene she up and died on him.

That is to say, a woman named Glassman, a Hungarian by birth, in age thirty-two years, widowed and without children or known next of kin, died in a small bungalow in a small town up in the coast range north of Los Angeles. When the picture was done and Vida Monte took off the barbaric trappings and the heavy paste jewels and the clinging reptilian half gowns of the rôle she played, with them she took off and laid aside the animal emotionalism, the theatricalistic fever and fervor, the passion and the lure that professionally made up Vida Monte, movie star. She took off even the very aspect of herself as the show shop and as patrons of the cinemas knew her; and she put on a simple traveling gown and she tucked her black hair up in coils beneath a severely plain hat and she became what really she was and always had been — a quiet, self-contained, frugal and — except for her splendid eyes, her fine figure and her full mobile mouth — a not particularly striking-looking woman, by name Sarah Glassman, which was, in fact, her name; and quite alone she got on a train and she went up into the foothills to a tiny bungalow which she had rented there for a month or so to live alone, to do her own simple housekeeping, to sew and to read and to rest.

It was the day after the taking of the last segment of the picture that she went away. It was four days later that she sickened of the Spanish influenza, so called. It was not Spanish and not influenza, though by any other name it would have been as deadly in its devastating sweep across this country. And it was within forty-eight hours after that, on a November afternoon, that word came to the Lobel plant that she was dead. Down there they had not known even that she was sick.

"The doctor in that there little jay town up there by the name Hamletsburg is the one which just gets me on the long-distance telephone and tells me that she died maybe half an hour ago."

87

Mr. Lobel in his private office was telling it to Vice President Quinlan and Secretary-Treasurer Geltfin, the only two among his associates that his messenger had been able to find about the executive department at the moment. He continued:

"Coming like a complete shock, you could 'a' knocked me down with a feather, I assure you. For a minute I couldn't believe it. This doctor he has to say it to me twice before I get it into my head. Shocking — huh? Sudden — huh? Awful — what? You bet you! That poor girl, for her my heart is bleeding. Dead and gone like that, with absolutely practically no warning! It don't seem possible! Taken down day before yesterday, the doctor says, and commenced getting from bad to worse right away. And this morning she goes out of her head and at two-forty-five this afternoon all of a sudden her heart gives out on her and she is dead before anybody knows it. Awful, awful!"

Mr. Lobel wagged a mournful poll.

"More than awful — actually it is horrifying!" quoth Mr. Geltfin. Visibly at least his distress seemed greater than the distress of either of the others. "All off alone up there by herself in some little rube town it must come to her! Maybe if she had been down here with specialists and surgeons and nurses and all she would 'a' been saved. Too bad, too bad! People got no business going away from a big town! Me, I get nervous even on a motor trip in the country and —"

"Everything possible which could be done was done," resumed Mr. Lobel. "So you don't need you should worry there, Geltfin. The doctor tells me he can't get no regular trained nurse on account there is so much sickness from this flu and no regular nurses there anyway, but he tells me he brings in his wife which she understands nursing and he says the wife sticks right there day and night and gives every attention. There ain't nothing we should reproach ourselves about, and besides we didn't know even she was sick — nobody knew.

"Dead and gone, poor girl, and not one week ago — six days, if I got to be exact — she is sitting right there in that same seat where you're sitting now, Geltfin, looking just as natural and healthy as what you look, Geltfin; looking just as if nothing is ever going to happen to her."

Mr. Geltfin had hastily risen and moved nearer the outer door.

"An awful thing — that flu!" he declared. "Lobel, do you think maybe she could 'a' had the germs of it on her then?"

"Don't be a coward, Geltfin!" rebuked his senior severely. "Look at me how I am not frightened, and yet it was me she seen last, not you! Besides, only to-day I am reading where that big doctor in Cincinnati, Ohio — Silverwater — says it is not a disease which you could catch from somebody else until after they have actually got down sick with it. Yes, sir, she sits right there telling me good-by. 'Mr. Lobel,' she says to me — I had just handed her her check — 'Mr. Lobel,' she says, 'always to you,' she says, 'I should be grateful. Always to you,' she says, 'I should give thanks that two years ago when I am practically comparatively unknown you should 'a' given me my big chance.' In them very words she says it, and me setting here at this desk listening at her while she said so!

"Well, I ain't lost no time, boys. Before even I sent to find you I already got busy. I've got Appel starting for up there in half an hour in my car to take charge of everything and with orders to spare no expense. The funeral what I am going to give that girl! Well, she deserves it. Always a hard worker, always on the job, always she minds her own business, always she saves her money, always a perfect lady, never throwing any of these here temperamentals, never going off in any of these here highsterics, never making a kick if something goes wrong because it happens I ain't on the lot to run things, never —"

It threatened to become a soliloquy. This time it was Quinlan who interrupted:

"You said it all, Lobel, and it's no need that you should go on saying it any more. The main points, I take it, are that we're all sorry and that we've lost one swell big asset by her dying — only it's lucky for us she didn't take ill before we got through shooting *The She-Demon*."

"Lucky? Huh! Actually, lucky ain't the right word for it!" said the president. "When I think of the fix we should 'a' been in if she hadn't finished up the picture first, I assure you, boys, it gives me the shivers. Right here and now in the middle of being sorry it gives me the shivers!"

"It does, does it?" There was something so ominous in Mr. Geltfin's sadly ironic remark — something in tone and accent so lugubriously foreboding that his hearers swung about to stare at him. "It does, does it? Well, all what I've got to say is, Lobel, you've got some shivers coming to you! We've all got some shivers coming to us! Having this girl die on us is bad business!"

"Sure it is," agreed the head, "but it might be worse. There's one awful big salary cut off the pay roll and if we can't have her with us no longer there's nobody else can have her. And the profits from that last picture should ought to be something positively enormous — stupendous — sensational. Listen! I bet you that from the hour we release —"

"You ain't going to release!" broke in Geltfin, his wizen features sharpening into a peaky mask of grief.

"Don't talk foolishness!" snapped Mr. Lobel. "For why shouldn't we be going to release?"

"That's it — why?" Mr. Quinlan seconded the demand.

"Because you wouldn't dare do it!" In his desire to make clear his point Mr. Geltfin fairly shoveled the words out of himself, bringing them forth overlapping one another like shingles on a roof. "Because the public wouldn't stand for it! Always you brag, Lobel, that you know what the public want! Well then, would the public stand for a picture where a good, decent, straight girl that's dead and will soon be in her grave is for six reels doing all them suggestive vampire stunts like what you yourself, Lobel, made her do? Would the public stand for calling a dead woman names like she-demon? They would not — not in a thousand years — and you should both know it without I should have to tell you! With some pretty rough things we could get by, but with that thing we could never get by! The public, I tell you, would not stand for it. No, sir; when that girl died the picture died with her. You just think it over once!"

Out of popped eyes he glared at them. They glared at him, then they looked at each other. Slowly Mr. Lobel's head drooped forward as though an unseen hand pressed against the back of his neck. Quinlan casting his eyes downward traced with one toe the pattern of the rug under his feet.

On top of one sudden blow, heavy and hard to bear, another now had followed. Since Lobel had become one of the topnotchers with a reputation to maintain, expenses had been climbing by high jumps, but receipts had not kept pace with expenses. There were the vast salaries which even the lesser drawing cards among the stars now demanded — and got. There were war taxes, excess profit taxes, amusement taxes. There was to be included in the reckoning the untimely fate of *Let Freedom Ring*, a vastly costly thing and quickly laughed to death, yet a smarting memory still. Its failure had put a crimp in the edge of the exchequer. This stroke would run a wide fluting of deficit right through the middle of it.

The pall of silence lasted no longer than it has here taken to describe how it fell and enveloped them. Mr. Geltfin broke the silence without lifting the prevalent gloom. Indeed his words but depressingly served to darken it to a very hue of midnight.

"Besides," he added, "there is anyhow another reason. We know what a nice clean girl she was in private life. We know that all them wild romance stories about her was cooked up in the press department to make the suckers believe that both on and off the screen she was the same. But she wasn't, and so I for one should be afraid that if we put that fillum out she'd come back from the dead to stop it!"

He sank his voice, glancing apprehensively over his shoulder.

"Lobel, you wouldn't dare do it!"

"Lobel," said Quinlan, "he's right! We wouldn't dare do it!"

"Quinlan," admitted Lobel, "it's right — I wouldn't dare do it."

In that same instant of his confession, though, Mr. Lobel bounded out of his chair, magically changing from a dumpy static figure of woe into the dynamo of energy and resourcefulness the glassed-in studios and the out-of-door locations knew.

"I got it!" he whooped. "I got it!" He threw himself at an inner door of the executive suite and jerked it open. "Appel," he shouted, "don't start yet! I got more instructions still for you. And say, Appel, you ain't seen nobody but only Quinlan and Geltfin — eh? You ain't told nobody only just them? Good! Well, don't! Don't telephone nobody! Don't speak a word to nobody! Don't move from where you are!"

He closed the door and stood against it as though to hold his private secretary a close prisoner within, and faced his amazed partners.

"It's a cinch!" he proclaimed to them. "I just this minute thought it up myself. If I must say it myself, always in a big emergency I can think fast. Listen! Nobody ain't going to know Monte is dead; not for a year, not maybe for two years; not until this last big picture is old and worn out; not until we get good and ready they should know. Vida Monte, she goes right on living till we say the word."

"But — but —"

"Wait, wait, can't you? If I must do all the quick thinking for this shop shouldn't I sometimes get a word in sideways? What I'm telling you, if you'll please let me, is this: The girl is dead all right! But nobody knows it only me and you, Quinlan, and you, Geltfin, and Appel in this next room here. Even the doctor up there at Hamletsburg he don't know it and his wife she don't know it and nobody in all that town knows it. And why don't they know? Because they think only it is a woman named Sarah Glassman that is dead. Actually that sickness no doubt changed her so that even if them rubes ever go to see high-class feature fillums there didn't nobody recognize her. If they didn't suspect nothing when she was alive, for why should they suspect something now she is dead? They shouldn't and they won't and they can't!

"What give me the idea was, I just remembered that when the doctor called me up he spoke only the name Glassman, not the name Monte. He tells me he calls up here because he finds in her room where she died a card with the name Lobel Masterfilms on it. And likewise also I just remembered that in the excitement of getting such a sad news over the telephone I don't tell him who really she is neither."

"Holy St. Patrick!" blurted Quinlan, up now on his feet. "You mean, Lobel —"

"Wait, wait, I ain't done — I ain't hardly started!" With flapperlike motions of his hands Mr. Lobel waved him down. "It's easy — a pipe. Listen! To date her salary is paid. The day she went away I gave her a check in full, and if she done what always before she does, it's in the bank drawing interest. Let it go on staying in the bank drawing interest. So far as we know, she ain't got no people in this country at all. In the old country, in Hungary? Maybe, yes. But Hungary is yet all torn up by this war — no regular government there, no regular mails, no American consuls there, no nothing. Time for them foreigners that they should get their hands on her property one year from now or

92

two years or three. They couldn't come to claim it even if we should notify them, which we can't. They don't lose nothing by waiting. Instead they gain — the interest it piles up.

"Should people ask questions, why then through the papers we give it out that Miss Vida Monte is gone far off away somewhere for a long rest; that maybe she don't take no more pictures for a long time. That should make *The She-Demon* go all the better. And to-morrow up there in that little rube town very quietly we bury Sarah Glassman, deceased, with the burial certificate made out in her own name." He paused a moment to enjoy his triumph. "Boys, when I myself think out something, am I right or am I wrong?"

He answered his own question.

"I'm right!"

By the look on Quinlan's face he read conviction, consent, full and hearty approval. But Geltfin wavered. Inside Geltfin superstition wrestled with opposing thoughts. Upon him then Lobel, the master mind, advanced, dominating the scene and the situation and determined also to dominate the lesser personality.

"But — but say — but look here now, Lobel," stammered Geltfin, hesitating on the verge of a decision, "she might come back."

"Geltfin," commanded Lobel, "you should please shut up. Do you want that we should make a lot of money or do you want that we should lose a lot of money? I ask you. Listen! The dead they don't come back. When just now you made your spiel, that part of it which you said about the dead coming back didn't worry me. It was the part which you said about the public not standing for it that got me, because for once, anyhow, in your life you were right and I give you right. But what the public don't know don't hurt 'em. And the public won't know. You leave it to me!"

It was as though this argument had been a mighty arm outstretched to shove him over the edge. Geltfin ceased to teeter on the brim — he fell in. He nodded in surrender and Lobel quit patting him on the back to wave the vice president into activity.

"Quinlan," he ordered as he might order an office boy, "get busy! Tell 'em to rush *The She-Demon!* Tell 'em to rush the subtitles and all! Tell 'em to rush out an announcement that the big fillum is going to be released two months before expected —

on account the demand of the public is so strong to see sooner the greatest vampire feature ever fillumed."

Quinlan was no office boy, but he obeyed as smartly as might any newly hired office boy.

If it was Mr. Lobel's genius which guided the course of action, energizing and speeding it, neither could it be denied that circumstance and yet again circumstance and on top of that more circumstance matched in with hue and shade to give protective coloration to his plan. Continued success for it as time should pass seemed assured and guaranteed, seeing that Vida Monte, beyond the studios and off the locations, had all her life walked a way so secluded, so inconspicuous and so utterly commonplace that no human being, whether an attaché of the company or an outsider, would be likely to miss her, or missing her, to pry deeply into the causes for her absence. So much for the contingencies of the future as those in the secret foresaw it. As for the present, that was simplicity.

As quietly as she had moved in those earlier professional days of hers, when she played small roles in provincial stock companies; as quietly as she had gone on living after film fame and film money came her way; as quietly as she had laid her down and died, so — very quietly — was her body put away in the little cemetery at Hamletsburg. To the physician who had ministered to her, to his good-hearted wife, to the official who issued the burial certificate, to the imported clergyman who held the service, to the few villagers who gathered for the funeral, drawn by the morbid lure which in isolated communities brings folk to any funeral — to all of these the dead woman merely was a stranger with a strange name who, temporarily abiding here, had fallen victim to the plague which filled the land.

Of those who had a hand in the last mortal rôle she would ever play only Lobel's private secretary, young Appel, who came to pay the bills and take over the private effects of this Sarah Glassman and after some fashion to play the roles of next friend and chief mourner, kenned the truth. The clergyman having done his duty by a deceased coreligionist, to him unknown, went back to the city where he belonged. The physician hurried away from the cemetery to minister to more patients than he properly could care for. The townspeople scattered, intent upon their own affairs. Appel returned to headquarters, reporting all well.

At headquarters all likewise went well — so briskly well in fact that under the urge for haste things essential were accomplished in less time by fewer craftsmen than had been the case since those primitive beginnings when Lobel's, then a struggling short-handed concern, frequently had doubled up its studio staffs for operative service in the makeshift laboratory. Reporting progress to the president, Mr. Quinlan expanded with self-satisfaction.

"I'm fixing to show you something in the way of a speed record," he proudly proclaimed. "The way I looked at it, the fewer people I had rushing this thing through the factory the less chance there was for loose talk round the plant and the less loose talk there was going on round the plant the less chance there was for maybe more loose talk outside. Yes, I know we'd figured we'd got everything caulked up air-tight, but I says to myself, 'What's the use in taking a chance on a leak if you don't have to?'

"So I practically turned the big part of the job — developing and all the rest of it — over to Josephson, same as we used to do back yonder when we was starting out in this game and didn't have a regular film cutter and the cameraman had to jump in and develop and cut and assemble and print and everything. Josephson shot all the scenes for *The She-Demon* — he knows the run of it better even than the director does. Besides, Josephson is naturally close-mouthed. He minds his own business and never butts in anywhere. To look at him you can't never tell what he's thinking about. But even if he suspected anything — and, of course, he don't — he's the kind that'd know enough to keep his trap shut. So I've had him working like a nailer and he's pretty near done.

"Soon as he had the negative ready, which was late yesterday afternoon after you'd went home, I had it run off with nobody there but me and Josephson, and I took a flash at it — and, Lobel, it's a bear! No need for you to worry about the negative — it was a heap too long, of course, in the shape it was yesterday, but it had everything in it we hoped would be in it — and more besides.

"So then without losing a minute I stuck Josephson on the printing machine himself. I'd already gave the girl on the machine a couple of days off to get her out of the way. Josephson stayed on the job alone pretty near all last night, I guess. He had things to himself without anybody to bother him and I tell you he shoved it along.

"Connors ain't lost no time neither. He's got the subtitles pretty near done, and believe it or not, as you're a mind to, but, Lobel, I'm telling you that this time to-morrow morning and not a minute later I'll have the first sample print all cut and assembled and ready for you to give it a look! Then it'll just be a job of matching up the negative and sticking in the subtitles and starting to turn out the positives faster than the shipping-room gang can handle 'em. I guess that ain't moving, heh?"

"Quinlan," said Mr. Lobel, "I give you right."

By making his word good to the minute the gratified Mr. Quinlan derived additional gratification. At the time appointed they sat in darkness in the body of the projection room — Lobel, Quinlan, Geltfin and Appel, these four and none other — behind a door locked and barred. Promptly on Quinlan's order the operator in the box behind them started his machine and the accomplished rough draft of the great masterpiece leaped into being and actuality upon the lit square toward which they faced.

The beginning was merely a beginning — graphic enough and offering abundant proof that in this epochal undertaking the Lobel shop had spared no expense to make the production sumptuous, but after all only preliminary stuff to sauce the palate of the patron for a greater feast to come and suitably to lead up to the introduction of the star. Soon the star was projected upon the screen, a purring, graceful panther of a woman, to change at once into a sinuous python of a woman and then to merge the feline and the ophidian into a sinister, splendid, menacing composite bespeaking the dramatic conception and the dramatic presentment of all feminine evil, typifying in every move of the lithe, half-clad body, in every shift of the big eyes, wickedness unleashed and unashamed.

Mr. Lobel sitting unseen in the velvet blackness uttered grunts of approbation. The greatest of all film vampires certainly had delivered the goods in this her valedictory. Never before had she so well delivered them. The grunting became a happy

96

rumble.

But all this, too, was in a measure dedicatory — a foretaste of more vivid episodes to follow, when the glorious siren, displaying to the full her powers of fascination over the souls and the bodies of men, would rise to heights yet greater and the primitive passion she so well simulated would shine forth like a malignant jewel in a setting that was semibarbaric and semicivilized, too, and altogether prodigal and lavish. The first of these bigger scenes started — the scene where the queen of the apaches set herself to win the price of her hire from the Germans by seducing the young army officer into a betrayal of the Allied cause; the same scene wherein at the time of filming it Mr. Lobel himself had taken over direction from Colfax's hands.

The scene was launched, acquired headway, then was halted as a bellow from Mr. Lobel warned the operator behind him to cut off the power.

"What the hell!" sputtered the master. "There's a blur on the picture here, a sort of a kind of smokiness. Did you see it, Geltfin? Right almost directly in front of Monte it all of a sudden comes! Did you, Quinlan?"

"Sure I seen it," agreed Geltfin. "Like a spot — sort of."

"It wasn't on the negative when I seen it day before yesterday," stated Quinlan. "I can swear to that. A little defect from faulty printing, I guess."

"All right then," said Mr. Lobel. "Only where you got efficiency like I got it in this plant such things should have no business occurring.

"Go on, operator — let's see how goes it from now on."

Out again two shadow figures — the vampire and the vampire's prey — flashed in motion. Yes, the cloudy spot was there, a bit of murky shadow drifting between the pair of figures and the audience. It thickened and broadened — and then from the suddenly constricted throats of the four watchers, almost as though all in the same moment an invisible hand had laid gripping hold on each of their several windpipes, came a chorused gasp.

For they saw how out of the drifting patch of spumy wrack there emerged a shape vague and indistinct and ghostly, but taking on instantly the sharpened outlines of one they recognized. It was the shape, not of Vida Monte, the fabled wrecker of lives, but the shape of her other self, Sarah Glassman, and the face it wore was not the face of the stage vampire, aflame with the counterfeited evil which the actor woman had so well known how to simulate but the real face of the real woman, who lay dead and buried under a mound of fresh-cut sods seventy miles away — her own face, melancholy and sadly placid, as God had fashioned it for her.

Out from the filmy umbra it advanced to the center, thus hiding its half-naked double writhing in the embrace of the deluded lover, and clearly revealed itself in long sweeping garments of pure white — fit grave clothes for one lately entombed — with great masses of loosened black hair falling like a pall about the passionless brooding face; and now lifting reproachful eyes, it looked out across the intervening void of blackness into their staring eyes, and from the folds of the cerement robes raised a bare arm high as though to forbid a lying sacrilege. And stood there then as a wraith newly freed from the burying mold, filling and dominating the picture so that one looking saw nothing else save the shrouded figure and the head and the face and those eyes and that upheld white arm.

Cowering low in his seat with a sleeve across his eyes to shut out the accusing apparition, Mr. Geltfin whispered between chattering teeth: "I told him! I told him the dead could maybe come back!"

Mr. Quinlan, a bolder nature but even so terribly shaken, was muttering to himself: "But it wasn't in the negative! I swear to God it wasn't in the negative!"

It is probable that Mr. Lobel heard neither of them, or if he heard he gave no heed. He had a feeling that the darkness was smothering him.

"Shut off the machine!" he roared as he wrenched his body free of the snug opera chair in which he sat. "And turn on the lights in this room — quick! And let me out of here — quick!"

Lunging into the darkness he stumbled over Appel's legs and tumbled headlong out into the narrow aisle. On all fours as the lights flashed on, he gave in a choking bellow his commands.

"Burn that print — you hear me, burn it now! And then burn the negative too! Quick you burn it, like I am telling you!"

"But, Lobel, I'll swear to the negative!" protested Quinlan, jealous even in his fright for his own vindication. "If you'll look at

98

the neg—"

"I wouldn't touch it for a million dollars!" roared Lobel. "Burn it up, I tell you! And bury the ashes!"

Still choking, still bellowing, he scrambled to his feet, an ungainly embodiment of mortal agitation, and ran for the door. But Mr. Geltfin beat him to it and through it, Quinlan and Appel following in the order named.

Outside their chief fell up against a wall, panting and wheezing for breath, his face swollen and all congested with purple spots. They thought he was about to have a stroke or a seizure of some sort. But they were wrong. This merely was Nature's warning to a man with a size seventeen neckband and a forty-six-inch girth measurement. The stroke he was to have on the following day.

Probably Quinlan and Geltfin as experienced businessmen should have known better than to come bursting together into the office of a stout middle-aged man who so lately had suffered a considerable nervous shock and still was unstrung; and having after such unseemly fashion burst in, then to blurt out their tidings in concert without first by soft and soothing words preparing their hearer's system to receive the tidings they bore. But themselves, they were upset by what they just had learned and so perhaps may be pardoned for a seeming unthoughtfulness. Both speaking at once, both made red of face and vehement by mingled emotions of rage and chagrin, each nourishing a perfectly natural and human desire to place the blame for a catastrophe on shoulders other than their own two pairs, they sought to impart the tale they brought. Ensued for an exciting moment a baffling confusion of tongues.

"It was that Josephson done it — the mousy little sneak!"

These words became intelligible as Quinlan, exerting his superior vocal powers, dinned out the sputtering inarticulate accents of Geltfin.

"He fixed it so that you'd spill the beans, Lobel! He fixed *The She-Demon* — Josephson. And me trusting him!

"How should I be knowing that all this time him and that girl was secretly engaged to be married? How should I be knowing that he would find out for himself the day after the funeral that she was dead and yet never say a word about it? How should I be knowing that he would have all tucked away somewhere a roll of film showing her dressed up like a Madonna or a saint or a martyr or a ghost or something which he took privately one time when they was out together on location — slipping away with her and taking 'em without nobody knowing about it? How should I be knowing that without tipping his hand he would cook up the idea to work a slick fake on you, Lobel, and scare you into killing off the whole thing? How should I be knowing that while he was on the printing machine all by himself the other night that he would work the old double exposure stunt and throw such a scare into you in the projecting room yesterday?"

By reason of his valvular resources Mr. Quinlan might shout louder than Geltfin. But he could not shout louder than Mr. Lobel. Nobody in that section of Southern California could. Mr. Lobel outblared him:

"How should you be knowing? You come now and ask me that when all along it was you that had the swell idee to stick him into the laboratory all by himself where he could play some funny business? You!"

"But it was you, Lobel, that wouldn't listen to me when I begged you to wait and not burn up the negative. I tried to tell you that the negative was O. K. when I'd seen it run off."

"You told me? It's a lie!"

"Sure I told you! Geltfin remembers my telling you, don't you, Geltfin? You're an old bird, Lobel — you ought to know by now about retouching and doctoring and all. You know how easy it is to slip over a double exposure. But it was only the sample print that was doctored. The negative was all right, but you wouldn't listen."

"That's right too, Lobel!" shrilled Geltfin. "I heard him when he yelled out to you that you should wait!"

Quinlan amplified the indictment.

"Sure he heard me — and so did you! But no, you had to lose your nerve and lose your head just because you'd had a scare throwed into you."

"I never lose my head! I never lose my nerve!" denied Mr. Lobel. He turned the counter tide of recriminations on Geltfin.

"Anyhow, — it was you started it, Geltfin — you in the first place, right here in this room, with your craziness about the dead coming back. Only for your fool talk I would never have had the idee of a ghost at all. And now — now when the cow is all spilt milk you two come and —"

"Oh, but Lobel," countered Geltfin, "remember you was the one that made 'em burn up the negative without giving it a look at all!"

"He said it, Lobel!" reinforced Quinlan. "You was the one that just would have the negative burned up whether or no. And now it's burned up!"

Mr. Lobel was not used to being bullied in his own office or elsewhere. If there was bullying to be done by anyone, he was his own candidate always. Surcharged with distracting regrets as he was, he had an inspiration. He would turn the flood of accusation away from himself.

"Where is that Josephson?" he whooped. "He is the one actually to blame, not us. Let me get my hands on that Josephson once!"

"You can't!" jeered Quinlan. "He's quit — he's gone — he's beat it! He wrote me a note, though, and mailed it back to me when he was beating it out of town, telling me to tell you how slick he'd worked it on you." He felt in his pockets. "I got that note here somewhere — here it is. I'll read it to you, Lobel — he calls you an old scoundrel in one place and an old sucker in another."

"Look out — catch him, Quinlan!" cried Mr. Geltfin. "Look at his face — he's fixing to faint or something."

The prime intent of this recital, as set forth at the beginning, was to tell why Mr. Max Lobel had an attack of apoplexy. That original purpose having been now carried out, there remains nothing more to be added and the chapter ends.

THE UNBROKEN CHAIN

In the year 1819 a string of twenty-one black slaves was passing along an African game trail bound for Mombassa. In this connection the word *string* advisedly is used. These twenty-one blacks were hitched in a tether, one after another, like a mess of fish on a stringer. Only, in the case of the fish the cord would have been threaded through the gills; this lot were yoked together.

They were chained, neck by neck. Each one of them wore an iron collar, clamped on. A four-foot length of iron chain, springing from this collar in front, teamed him with the fellow going before him; a similar chain joined him fast to the slave following next in order. This left his legs free for the march and his hands for carrying a burden – if one were given him to carry – or for scratching himself or for beating himself on the breast in lamentation for his captivity; yet in all respects held him well secured.

If there were any places of favour they belonged to the pair who traveled at the far ends of the leash. The file leader had no chain dragging him under his chin but only a chain at his back. The one at the extreme rear likewise had to support just half the burden of metal which each of the nineteen intermediaries bore.

The gang lived and ate and slept in their chain. At nighttime they lay down in a ring, their feet pointing to a common focus where a fire burned to keep off the leopards and the lions. By day they moved along to the accompaniment of a constant grating and clanking, each using his free hand, if he had one, to ease the pressure of the neck ring upon the base of his throat or where its rivets irked the top jointings of his chine behind. They were all adult males and therefore, in the eyes of their present proprietors, rather more to be prized than the run of a mixed assortment would have been. They were members of a tribe living well back in the country, in the foothills of the mountains; their tribal mark was the filing of their upper front teeth to sharp points. They had been taken in a night raid of the valorous Masai. Formerly they would have been massacred on the spot by the light of the blazing huts or reserved for sacrificial torture on the return of the victors to their own village. But lately the Masai had found a more profitable if less congenial way for disposing of all able-bodied prisoners.

Now they bound them and brought them out to a place called Kilwa and lodged them in a barracoon. To this place the Arabs came up from the sea – and once in a while the Portuguese – and these exporters bargained with the Masai for their human spoils and carried them away. On this side of Africa the trade had not attained the proportions which made the trade on the Guinea Coast so enormously profitable. Indeed, on the Indian Ocean the traffic never amounted to a fifth of what it did where the Congo ran down to the Atlantic; but at this time it was growing fast – thanks to a steadily rising market and a steady demand for prime and prize offerings in certain parts of the world, notably Persia and Turkey in the East, and Cuba, Brazil and the more southerly states of the new North American republic on the other side of the world.

This especial group of slaves was in herd to six Arabs who bore weapons for defense and heavy hippo-pelt whips for disciplining their purchases. If the subchief who strode on ahead to set the pace wished to halt the procession, he cut backward at the nearest pair of bare legs; if his squad sought to stimulate the train to brisker speed they made general play with their lashes on the limbs and bodies most convenient to them. Thus it was that without words the commands and the desires of the owners were made manifest – and obeyed – by the newly bought. In any tongue, or lacking any, a rawhide speaks a parable which the dullest wit may comprehend.

Of a morning when the Arabs and their yoked commodities still were ten days from salt water, an adventure and a disaster befell the little caravan. On this day they were moving east by south across a high plateau. We who have never been there are accustomed to think of interior Africa as one great jungle, dark, miasmic, knotted with poisonous tropic growths. But here stretched a vast upland plain lying some thousands of feet above sea level. It was clothed in a rich pasturage through which game trails crossed and crisscrossed like the wrinkles in the palm of a washwoman's hand. It was parked with fine trees in an effect of studied and ordained landscaping. It was fairly well watered, and it literally rippled with game both great and small – birds and beasts and some reptiles; grass-eaters and flesh-eaters and bug-eaters. Wild animals – and not so very wild, either, some of them – abounded in a plenitude which those of us who know only the temperate zones are accustomed to associate with our ideas of insect life in midsummer, but not with four-legged or with two-legged creatures. Where the antelope and zebra fed they filled the scope of the eye, multiplying themselves by thousands and uncountable thousands. When, taking panic from real or fancied dangers they fled to other grazing grounds, they streaked away interminably in a suggestion of driven rain slanting across the earth; and the noise of their hoofs made suitable thunder for the living storm-burst that they were.

At a point where the herbage grew rank and high a bull rhino charged the travelers. There were no elephants in this part; here the rhino was the largest of all the brutes as, indeed, next only to the elephant, he is the largest quadruped to be found anywhere in the world and, for his bulk and his swiftness and his malignant disposition, almost the most dreaded and the most dreadful. He may stand six feet and more at the shoulder, may, in the instance of a full-grown male specimen, weigh up to six thousand pounds – the strength of a three-ton struck, the sheathing of an armored tank, the power and speed of a runaway switch engine; and with all this, the snout of a unicorn, the eyes of a mole, the brain of a very stupid boar pig, but a scent and a hearing as keen as any and keener than most, and as quick on his feet, to check and to pivot, as a toe dancer.

In the British Protectorate and farther south, toward the tip of the continent, they kill them today up to this size and heft. A hundred years ago, away back yonder in 1819, they certainly ran, by average, no smaller than they run today, and their tempers probably were just as uncertain. A century, more or less, works no material change in a rhino's mood. His mood, like his shape, has come down unimpaired and substantially unaltered since the day when he emerged, all plated and scaly and dripping, from the primordial mists.

The rhino which assailed the passing troop was as big as they grew and as mean natured. Probably the sound made by the convoy as it drew near him – the *pat-pat* of naked feet padding upon the hard trodden path, the clangor of all that jouncing metal ware, perhaps the crack of a well-aimed whiplash and the agonized screech of its mark as his flesh flinched and wealed under the stroke – was an irritation to him. From Cummings and Speke on down to this present time the game hunters have told us that about the sulky bull rhino you never can be sure. He may take it into his horned and leathery head to run away from a single stalker, or in a sudden fit of purblind rage may elect to attack a whole *safari*. But whatsoever he takes it into his head to do, that he does, bulging straight ahead at a gait which is incredibly fast for a thing so lumbersome and, while at rest, apparently so awkward. Forward on he rushes, an irresistible, crushing, ripping, rending projectile; vicious, fearless, devilish; seeming more a machine than a mammal, more the spectacle of a monstrous wound-up mechanism than an affair of blood and bones.

It was so with this particular rhino which on this particular bygone time charged down upon the slave squad. He heaved himself up into sight from a trampled wallow some two hundred yards distant, at the left-hand side of the trail, just as these invaders on the privacy of his bedchamber were abreast of him. He squealed once or twice, sniffed at the taint in the air, and then, lowering his front until the slobbery lower lip almost touched the earth, he came at right angles thundering down upon the travelers, uttering sharp, furious snorts, that were like the blasts of a steam whistle, as he came.

For the Arabs the tooted danger signal was ample. They scattered, leaping spraddle legged into the high grass and making for some trees which rose nearby. From personal experience and from hearsay they knew that, once they cleared out of the direct way of the brute, he probably would not swerve from his course to pursue a single fugitive unless possibly the wind, blowing from one of them to him, informed his nose of what his poor eyes could not tell him. Even so, they veered off frantically toward the trees with intent to climb them.

Brief as the time was, the slaves likewise had full warning of what was upon them. All in a frenzied half-minute or so they did many futile, purposeless things. They gibbered and shrieked, they fought at their fetters, they dragged the line out to its full length, trying, all of them, to flee from the point of greatest peril; they huddled in together next, tangling themselves in the chain, then once more swung away from the common centre, so that for an instant there was presented this tragic grotesquerie – it was like a figment from a nightmare – of ten joined black shapes straining to move in one direction and ten more striving to move in the opposite direction; but each batch, by its own crazed efforts, defeating the intent of the other; and in between, as the connecting link for this foolish and antic tug-of-war, a dancing and dangling puppet figure of a black man, his head half twisted off his shoulders, his distorted body writhing and capering, his toes lifted bodily off the earth, his eyes bulging from his skull as he glared full-face upon the misshapen deadly mass which bore him down.

The rhino struck this fairest of all possible targets a perfect bull's-eye, impaling it on the longer of his two horns. For an instant the Arabs, looking back from among the tree trunks, beheld an even more fantastical japery than the one of a moment before. In the middle space of their vision they saw the armed prow of the beast, with the spitted wretch held high up on the great head which now was upraised; and from this clumped apex there stretched out to right and left a slanted, rigid, V-formation – a prong forty feet long from tip to tip, formed on either plane of naked forms, ten this side and ten that, regularly spaced apart, the necks lengthened inordinately, the heads aiming all the same way, the poised taut bodies pulled straight out behind, the arms set and trailing aft, the legs drawn back horizontally and kept so by the might which had lifted and now carried them forward – for all the world like a wedge of black geese in ordered geometric flight along the flanks of a swift craft that had shoved her bow into their alignment.

For the briefest of timable spaces this triangled phenomenon endured. Then the hurtling phalanx lost shape, flapped down, folded in on itself and collapsed in the grass when the rhino, freeing his head of that which cumbered it, whirled about to slash and trample the confused litter underfoot and then was gone from sight, puffing out the last of his vented spleen as he vanished.

Cautiously the dispersed Arabs tracked back to the trail. The damage to them in property values was greater than they feared it would be. Indeed, the loss well-nigh was a total loss. The middle slave practically was in bits; his breast was little more than a great hole, and where the gross brute, turning back, had side swiped at him, the flesh was sheared away from his ribs like fillets from a dressed cod; some such casualty as this they had expected, naturally. But from this chief victim's chain-mates they found the life gone, also. No hangman's noose ever had cracked a single spine more expeditiously than those iron necklets under that terrific jolt had cracked the spines of the hapless bondsmen. Broken-necked, they lay in the coil of their own heaped bodies.

At first look it seemed the entire twenty-one were dead. But as it turned out there was an item for possible reclamation. A slave whose station had been at the extreme rear of the string was found to be breathing. His chest was battered and his chin torn and his shoulders were all roweled by the tough grass blades through which he had been ploughed and dragged; but his neck lay straight in its collar band, not twisted about as were the necks of the twenty; and soon he groaned and moved and threshed with his body.

His escape from the common fate might reasonably be accounted for. By virtue of his having been at the tail end of the tether, the colliding jerk which killed the rest had come to him from one way only – from in front; also, in the instant following the impact, there had been no pendent weight of dragged forms behind him to help snap his vertebrae for him. Moreover, just before the rhino struck, he either had the wit to seize the chain in his two hands and hold it fast, with a few precious inches of slack between him and his grip, or else involuntarily he had done this. At any rate, it had been his salvation; his fingers still were cramped in the links. Under prodding he presently sat up.

He hardly seemed worth saving, though. He was idiotic from fright. He continued to tug at his coupling, trying to drag himself farther from the dead pile which anchored him. In his blubbering, bubbly speech repeatedly he shrieked out words which the Arabs took to be his name for a bull rhinoceros. Nevertheless, they elected to take him along with them; better a scrap of salvage from the calamity than none at all.

By a species of butchers' work which need not here be described, but it was done with knives and spear blades, they redeemed their hampered ironmongery and they lashed the jarred imbecile to his feet and resumed the interrupted trek, going now seven all told where before there had been twenty-seven. Since they traveled light they also traveled fast. That night they overtook at its camping place a larger convoy under the command of their sheik and accompanied by a Portuguese factor. Having told their story they incorporated their remaining chattel with the main stock and drove him on down to Mombassa. There a dhow took him and his new companions aboard and carried them to an appointed rendezvous offshore. Being young and able-bodied and in good case, save for his abiding fright, he was bartered at current rates to a lanky Yankee skipper who, at home in the state of Maine, was a church deacon and a citizen walking in most mindful ways.

Chained now at wrist and ankle instead of neckwise, the solitary survivor of the rhino's pettishness was stowed, with sundry hundreds of his kind in the 'tween decks of a smart, fast, American-built clipper ship. This being done, Captain Hosea Plummer and his crew of good men and true had up the mudhook and headed away for a far distant place of entry on the soil of their own, their native land of freedom.

The Middle Voyage, as they called it then, was without mishap and with no more than the average percentage of mortality among the live freightage. Having successfully eluded the British and the American men-of-war which popularly were supposed to keep watch for such as he, the master in due time dropped anchor in a certain estuary well sheltered behind a certain island lying between Charleston and Savannah. Here he smuggled to shore his cargo – or what part of it had lived out the trip – and then, having dealt for cash with his consignees and with a fine jag of money in his pockets, went up the coast to the godly Down-East town of Portland for a period of vacation and sober thanksgiving.

For, mind you, Captain Hosea Plummer not only was a pious soul but was a grateful one.

In the year 1920 a Mr. G. Claybourne Brissot was living the life of a gentleman in retirement near Smithtown, Long Island. He was known to be by birth Southerner, but he spoke with scarcely a trace of Southern accent. Judging by his speaking voice, you would have said he came of some cultured New England stock; only when he spoke rapidly or under stress did there slur into his tone a suggestion – a trace, as a chemist might say – of the softening of the consonant *r* and the slovenly treatment of the final *g*. This, though, might easily be accounted for. It would appear that in his early youth he had been sent North to be educated. Up here he had been tutored; later he went through Harvard and thereafter remained in the North, living first, for a while in New York City and now on this estate which he owned north of Smithtown village, on a site half a mile back from the Sound.

He seemed to have no ties in the section where he had been born. He never visited the South although his wealth, which was considerable, had been created there; and he rarely spoke of it. Nor did he make mention, ever of any kinspeople, living or dead, that he might have down there. He did not belong to the Southern Society in New York or to any of the state societies. It was almost inevitable that as a child he must have had black playfellows or, at least, a black nurse, but in his household staff there were no negroes whatsoever; a rather unusual thing when you remember that most transplanted Southerners like to have colored domestics about them. His valet was a Frenchman; his cook an Armenian – Mr. Brissot liked his foods highly spiced and well oiled – his chauffeur a second generation Italian; his head gardener a Scot, and his maidservants usually were Irish girls or Swedish.

He lived very much to himself; really, you might call him a recluse. When he traveled he traveled alone excepting that he took along his valet and occasionally his chauffeur. I meant to say he had no traveling companion of his own sort. He knew Europe thoroughly and especially southern Europe, where he had motored extensively, but of his own country all he now saw was a narrow strip along the Eastern seaboard. As a young man he had married, but it would appear that within a year or two after his marriage he and his wife, who since was dead, had separated and thereafter had lived apart. There had been one child and, according to a more or less vague hearsay, the child still lived, although the father was not known ever to have spoken of it. By one report, the child had been born with a deformity on it or a blemish of some sort and had been put away elsewhere by the father. This was only gossip; proofs to back it were lacking.

Mr. Brissot was not a member of any club. Apparently he had no intimate, no confidant whatsoever, unless his lawyer in New York, Mr. Cyrus H. Tyree, might be termed such. The acquaintance he has with his neighbors on Long Island, many of them persons of refinement and property, was little more than a bowing acquaintance. Not one, speaking with truth, could say he was a friend to this reserved and secluded gentleman. For such associates as he had he mainly preferred foreigners, and notably Frenchmen. Once in a while he had some visiting foreigner for his guest. Otherwise he did no entertaining; accepting very few invitations and extending practically none at all. Perhaps the typical educated Frenchman's tolerance, his racial freedom from so many of the prejudices which bind so many of us – perhaps these appealed to him. Or perhaps his preference might be explained on the ground – since he had a French name and presumably was, on one side at least, of Latin descent – that some handed-down sentiment in his nature inclined him to seek the company of men of a Latin strain.

He loved music, being himself a fair pianist and better than a fair singer. In his singing and his playing invariably he favored French and German and Italian music. For our native folk-songs and for our more ambitious work he seemed not to care at all. As for the rest, he was a plump man of middle age and medium height, with straight, dark hair, rather sensitive features, brooding brown eyes and an aloof, almost a shrinking manner. It was as though, having a distinct personality of his own, he nevertheless strove to subdue it, to hide it away from people as he hid himself away. Always he wore plain, dark, well-cut garb, but always, too, he wore a bright colored necktie and on his fingers heavy jeweled rings; and these stipplings of florid color, taken with his otherwise somber garments and his air, seemed oddly out of place.

Naturally, Mr. Brissot was an object of interest to his neighbors. People discussed him in the terms of a mild and restrained curiosity; they wondered about him; some probably built up mythical and more or less fantastic theories of their own to account for him and his ways. So there was a distinct stir of polite surprise one afternoon when he came to an amateur race meet on a private half-mile tract at the Blackburn estate, which adjoined his own.

Staying at the Blackburn place at this time was Judge Martin Sylvester, who before his elevation to the federal bench had been a member of the lower house of Congress and before that lieutenant-governor of one of the South Atlantic states. That same night, meaning by that the night following the racing, Mr. George Blackburn sat with his distinguished visitor on the terrace of the house overlooking the Sound. It was after midnight; the other members of the household had gone off to bed. The two men, both of them elderly, were having the last of a last smoke before they turned in. There befell between them one of those small silences which come sometimes when a pair of men in excellent accord with each other and reasonably well content smoke good cigars together. It was the guest who broke the spell of it.

"Blackburn," he said, "what's the greatest tragedy, almost, that our American civilization has to offer?" Without pausing he went on, answering his own question: "I'm going to tell you what I think it is. I think that about the cruelest tragedy we've got in this country today is the man with a tincture of negro blood in his veins – the infinitesimal trace which according to our laws of consanguinity nevertheless brands him a negro – and who still has education, good taste, refinement, even may have in him an artist or a creator. But in our national scheme of things, North or South, there's no place for him at all.

"Life must be hell for such a man – it's bound to be. Think of it – he goes through his days despising his enforced contact with the run of his own race – the race to which we arbitrarily and, as I hold, properly assign him – and yet denied association on equal terms with white people of his own cultural rating. Oh, yes, yes, I know you Northerners sometimes make a pretence of according him companionship of a sort, but it's only a pretence – a shadow and not the substance of the social equality for which he must crave, world without end. Mind you, I'm not arguing in favor of any other convention for treating him. I have the orthodox convictions of an orthodox Southerner – prejudices you'd call 'em, some of 'em – but even so I can't help from seeing the pitiable side of it.

"And the most pitiable part of it is that there's nothing he can do or you or I can do, or would do, to better things for him. We've got to keep our own stock clean and undefiled if we can –

111

got to sacrifice the exceptional individual for the sake of ourselves and our race. One drop of black ink in a pint of clear water discolors the whole cupful – the stain goes all the way through from top to bottom. That's true in chemistry; it's true in biology; true of all creation and all procreation. And you can't get away from it. You can't buck against the everlasting laws. You're only a fool and a criminal if you try. But that don't keep you from being sorry sometimes, does it?

"I can think of just one other tragedy to equal it – and a kindred tragedy, this is, and maybe it's a greater one. And that's the case of a man who, let us say, has in him only a sixteenth or a thirty-second or even a sixty-fourth degree of the negroid admixture, a man who passes for a pure Caucasian, who goes unsuspected and yet must go always with a curse hanging over him – the curse of the fear that some day, somehow, somewhere, some word from him, some involuntary spasmodic act of his, some throw-back manifestation of motive or thought that's been hiding in his breed for generation after generation, will betray his secret and utterly undo him. Call it by what scientific jargon or popular term you please – hereditary instinct, reversion to type, transmitted impulse, dormant primitivism, elemental recurrence – still the haunting dread of it must be walking with him in every waking minute. It must be there always, poisoning his private thoughts and warping his nature. *Ugh!*"

"Say, Judge," asked Blackburn, "conceded that all you say is true – and I guess it is, every word – what on earth set you off at that unhappy tangent upon such a night as this?"

"Oh, I don't know," said the Southerner. He laughed a cryptic little laugh. "The moonlight, I reckon. It's the sort of moon which Private John Allen of Mississippi liked to say we used to have down South before the War. It's set me to thinking of things I've seen and heard down in my country – distressing things mainly. Now, I remember once –" He broke off, considering his shriveled peak of cigar ash as though this were a thing immensely important.

Presently he spoke again, making his tone casual: "Blackburn, this next door neighbor of yours – this Mr. Brissot who was over here this afternoon for a little while – he interested me."

"He must have – judging by the questions you've been

112

asking about him ever since he left. Well, there's not much I can tell you that I haven't already told you, and that's precious little: Brissot is by way of being our one small neighborhood mystery. He's a puzzle to you, I take it. Well, I'm not surprised at that – he's been a puzzle to us these last four or five years since he moved in."

"Yes," said the Judge, "he is a puzzle. Or, at any rate, I'd say he was a rarity. I only saw him for a few minutes – only talked with him a few minutes, I mean – but I've had him on my mind ever since. There were certain things about the man –" Again he left a sentence unfinished before it was well begun. For his next words he lowered his voice and before uttering them glanced behind him as though to make sure no servant was within hearing.

"Blackburn, I might as well get it off my chest. But remember what I'm going to say is said in the strictest confidence – on the square." He stressed the last word with a special intonation.

"I get you," said his host, putting the same ritualistic emphasis into his answer. "We're in Lodge; the door's locked and the Tyler on guard. But why all this secrecy?"

"Because, lacking proof, I commit an indiscretion when I even hint at what's been working inside my brain. It's the sort of thing that a man down my way doesn't even whisper unless he's prepared, in case of a show-down, to back up his insinuation with sworn evidence or a gun or both. Even then compassion might make him hesitate. But that's enough for a preamble. I reckon we understand each other.

"Now, this Mr. Brissot – while we were being introduced I felt sort of drawn to him. Someway, in all that big crowd of fine, clever, kindly people, he seemed so terribly alone. And when you happened to mention that he was also from the South, I decided right off that at least we'd have one congenial topic to talk over together – one thing in common. But, as it turned out, we didn't. Because when I spoke of families and said I had a sister-in-law whose mother had been a Claybourne – you remember you called him by his full name in introducing us – he shied away from the subject like a galled colt that's been flicked on a raw place. And he didn't have any state pride about him, either – not a particle – and that's a blamed peculiar thing, too, in a Southerner born.

113

"To have been born in certain states of this union is an incident. But to have been born in certain others is, to the man who was born there, a profession. Take a man, let's say, from Ohio. Unless he happens to be a Republican candidate for President he makes no capital out of the circumstance that his parents chose to set up housekeeping in Ohio instead of Illinois or Iowa or Michigan. Ask him where he was born and he says 'Ohio,' like that, and lets it go at that. But it's apt to be different with a man who hailed originally from Indiana or with one from California – being a Native Son is a thing for him to advertise – and to a degree the same thing applies up here in the North, to a Massachusetts man, if he came from Boston, or to a Philadelphian or to one of your old Knickerbocker line in New York.

"As for the South – well, go anywhere below Mason and Dixon's Line and see what happens. Especially if you take a Virginian or a Marylander or a Kentuckian or a Louisiana man or a Carolinian – above all a South Carolinian. He may be modest enough in most regards but just mention his home state and he'll start bragging as though a special virtue resided in it and a special virtue in him for having had the forethought and the good taste to have been born there. He never forgets it and he's not likely to let you forget it, either. Ninety-nine times out of a hundred, family means a lot to him. Probably he had a Confederate daddy or a Revolutionary great-granddaddy that he's proud of. Or maybe an ambassador for a cousin or somebody for a great-uncle who was in Buchanan's cabinet.

"I know how it is because I'm a victim of the habit myself. I come from a stock that boasts the loudest. One of my grandfathers came from Richmond and my mother was a Charleston woman – born in one of those old houses down on the Battery, a house that has been in her family for more than a hundred years. See there – I'm beginning to take credit to myself for my forbears even while I'm describing how the other fellow behaves. It's in us – we just naturally can't get away from it.

"But your hermit friend over here next door – why, he actually flinched when I tried to talk family with him. And yet, if his name counts for anything, he's of that old Huguenot stock down there in the tidewater country who're vainer even, as a rule, than the rest of us are. Funny – very funny! It's as though he

114

had something to conceal, as if – well, what would you say about it yourself?"

"But surely just because of that you wouldn't suspect the – the other thing?" said Blackburn. "The man is sallow, I admit – dark-skinned, in fact, but –"

"That has nothing to do with it," said Judge Sylvester. "In my time I've known a hundred men of the so-called Nordic strain – clean-bred Anglo-Saxon or straight Celtic – who were darker by ten shades than he is. I'm right smart of a brunette myself, if it comes to that, or anyhow I used to be before my hair turned white. And his fingernails would pass muster – I looked closely at them, and the little half-moons at their bases were as clear as yours are or mine – no suggestion there of the tell-tale dark blush that's like a bruise. Nor any chalk, as we say, in his eyeballs, either; they had the right bluish-white cast. But as he turned away from me – I was studying him closely – I don't know why, but I was – there suddenly came into his face as I saw it in profile a sort of – well, I won't say a cast; I don't know how to put it in words – but a something or other as if another face under the skin were fitting itself into the contour of his face, a face that – oh, thunder, I can't express it and yet I sensed it, felt it, recognized it intuitively! I don't want to be morbid but just to satisfy my own curiosity I'd certainly like to have a look at the man stripped."

"Why stripped, of all things in the world?"

"I'll tell you why – it's the final test for the negroid smudge. Or at least that's what the people down in my country all firmly believe. I don't know what ethnologists would say about it, but we believe that if a human being has in him the smallest possible tincture of African blood it will reveal itself in a sort of stain or streak or smear right down the middle of his back. The eyes, the nails, the arches of the insteps – they may all be as Caucasian as George Washington's were, or Lord Byron's – but along the line of the spine, thicker and darker at the base of the column and growing fainter and lighter as the vertebrae grows smaller at the top, where the nape is, will run that faint unmistakable smear that's like the stroke of a tar brush. Like a stroke of the Tar Brush – to put it brutally!

"I repeat – I don't want to be morbid, Blackburn, but I surely would like to have a look at your neighbor's spine. Mind you,

115

though, no living soul is ever to know what I've just said. Maybe I'm wrong – the Lord knows I hope I am."

But of course Judge Sylvester never had his curious wish. Two days later he finished out his visit and went back to his home near Augusta, and two weeks later, to the day, Mr. Brissot was dead at a grade-crossing of the Long Island railroad after an electric locomotive ran into his automobile.

He instantly was killed and so was his chauffeur. The third occupant of the car was the famous explorer and big game hunter, Colonel Bate-Farnaro, who had licked the desert and bested the jungle only, by this ironic trick of destiny, to be smashed up while riding on a paved avenue through a modern real estate development in a suburban addition to one of Greater New York's outlying suburbs.

This noted man, who was English by birth and of mixed English and Italian ancestry, had been staying a couple of days with his friend, Mr. Brissot. The two men had known each other abroad, and when the Colonel came over here to lecture, Mr. Brissot invited him down to his place for a quiet week-end in the country before the beginning of the tour. On a Monday morning they started back for town in Brissot's closed car, bringing with them the visitor's luggage. Being mainly British, the Colonel might travel across Tibet with a tooth brush for equipment – if he had to – but by the same token could not bring himself to go Friday-to-Mondaying without taking along at least one very large, very English looking kit bag and a suitcase or so.

Where the collision occurred, one of the electrified branches of the railway bisected the highroad at acute angles. The junction for the moment and for some reason or other was untended; there were no guard gates and the watchman was away from his post. It was a bad time, as it proved, for him to be absent from his duties. For a high-powered locomotive was moving west at high speed, carrying a single flat with an emergency crew aboard and bound for the scene of a small freight derailment a few miles farther down the line. Word of the tie-up had been flashed to division headquarters a few minutes earlier; the engineer of the wrecker had orders to make time, for traffic temporarily was tied up, and he was making it – giving his motor all the juice she would take.

Two hundred yards distant the locomotive tore out of a

shallow cut into view of the crossing just as the Brissot car came up a slight elevation approaching the right-of-way. The engineer did what he could which was mighty little, seeing he could not materially check his gait in so short a distance. He sounded his whistle in warning and he shut off his power and braked down hard.

The chauffeur did his best, too; but it would seem the trouble with him – a fatal trouble, as it turned out – was that in the imminent and impending face of the whizzing menace which so suddenly had come upon him, he altogether lost his head. Subsequent inquiry tended to develop the fact – or rather the theory – that first he tried to get over the track before the onrushing locomotive reached there and then that he changed his mind and tried to halt his car on the nearer side and that the upshot was he killed his motor. Be that as it may, the outstanding circumstance was this: The automobile, at a dead stop, stood squarely straddling the rails for an appreciable period of time before the squatty locomotive, bleating in sharp staccato blasts, struck it broadside and flung it sixty feet in a scrapheap of crumpled metal and broken parts.

Mr. Brissot and Luigi, his chauffeur, were both of them dead when they were picked up. The latter terribly was mutilated; he was scrodded like a fish where he had been hurled through his wind-shield. By some freak of physics or of fate, Colonel Bate-Farnaro had been spared his life. He had a broken leg though, and several of his ribs were caved in. He was carried, unconscious, to Jamaica and thence to a hospital in the city. At first it was feared his skull might be fractured. As it proved, he was suffering from a considerable concussion of the brain; that, mainly, was what kept him unconscious so long. It was two days later when he came to his senses and a day after that before the surgeons allowed him to see visitors.

The first to see him then was the late Mr. Brissot's lawyer. Mr. Cyrus Tyree had come hurrying from town immediately on hearing of the lamentable thing that had happened; he had returned that night and had been waiting, ever since, for this opportunity to get from the injured Englishman his version of the affair. Mr. Tyree anticipated, since Colonel Bate-Farnaro was an adventure-seeker of acknowledged repute and therefore probably accustomed to tragedy and quick danger, that the latter had kept his head and should be able to give a reasonably coherent account of what passed in those few dreadful seconds between the appearance of the wrecker and its collision with the stalled automobile. Nor was the lawyer disappointed in this hope. But almost the first extended remark by the bandaged-up Englishman, after Mr. Tyree had been presented to him and the nurse had left the room, seemed profoundly to disturb the caller.

"Ever since I got my wits back I've been lying here puzzling over a most extraordinary circumstance connected with this distressing occurrence," said the invalid. "In the midst of my regret for the shocking death of my host and my reflections on my own close squeak, I've not been able to put it out of my mind. Poor dead Brissot, God rest him, always struck me as being a remarkably close-mouthed person – not in the least given to idle talk about this and that, I mean to say. But why he should have been so secretive regarding his African experiences – I mean to say, why to me, of all persons, he should have been so secretive – well –"

"Pardon me," interrupted Mr. Tyree, in a suddenly concerned way; "did you say his African experiences?"

"Yes, yes," – the Britisher moved his swathed head impatiently. "He had knowledge, naturally, of the years I'd spent in interior Africa. If only he'd chosen to tell me that he'd been there too we'd have had something in common, something that would have been most confoundedly interesting for both of us to talk about."

"But Mr. Brissot was never in Africa," said Mr. Tyree, still in that strained tone; "I can positively assure you of that."

"My dear sir, I can't possibly be mistaken." The Colonel spoke emphatically.

"I can only repeat that you must be mistaken," stated Mr. Tyree gravely. "My late client had traveled extensively, as you probably know. But he never visited Africa. There were reasons why, of all the places in the world, he would never have gone –" He broke off and started afresh: "I give you my word of honor, Colonel, that Claybourne Brissot never in his life set foot on African soil."

"Your pardon again, my dear fellow, but surely you are the one who is wrong. We practically are strangers; even so, I assume that as Brissot's solicitor and presumably as his friend, you enjoyed his confidence?"

"I did, to a greater extent than any living being did."

"Well then, in that case, there was a chapter in his life he could not have told you of. I may be a bit knocked about and I confess to a nasty headache, but, in view of past experiences I myself have had, there are certain matters regarding which I could not possibly be deceived. Why, from my recollection of that horrid disaster on Monday there stands out above all the rest of the details a certain phase of it which absolutely convinced me of this: Brissot, at some time or another, must have had intimate acquaintance with African wildlife – with the language of a certain very remote tribe – with matters that one could learn only at first hand, out there, on the spot."

Mr. Tyree bent forward where he sat alongside the bed. There was a curious intent look, almost a startled look, on his face, and his eyelids lowered until his eyes were mere slits.

"Colonel," he said, "would you please tell me in detail exactly what happened – with particular reference to these – these disclosures which, you say, aroused your – hum – suspicion?"

"There isn't so much to tell. There we were and yonder was that cursed engine coming down upon us. Here I sat, penned up in that confounded coop of a car, and here just alongside me was Brissot, and there, just directly in front of us, was the chauffeur, who all at once seemed to have gone quite mad from fright and was screaming out most horribly. You see, we all three of us had sufficient time for apprehending what was about to happen. In a time like that things may pass in a flash – but you see them all, and if you live through it you remember them afterwards.

"We even had opportunity for making a move to get out of the car. I don't say we could have succeeded, any of us, but at least there was an appreciable time for trying.

"No use, though! The chauffeur seemed to be entangled in his steering wheel – quite a stoutish chap he was, with a snug fit for his seat, I should say. And the car door on my side of the car was caught. We'd noticed that morning before we left Brissot's place that the running board upon the other side – my luggage had been piled upon the other side – the side from which the locomotive was coming – my luggage had been piled up and tied on after we got in. So there we were, you see, all three of us practically prisoners and quite helpless.

"Poor Brissot did his best. He seized the door handle on his side and he turned it and tried to shove his way out. But his head was all he succeeded in getting entirely out. I figure my larger kit bag – it was quite heavy, really – must have slumped down or slipped forward in some way just at that instant – possibly his sudden push at the door shifted it – for the door was forced directly back again, pinching Brissot by the throat so that he stuck fast, as though his neck were locked in a vise; and there he stayed, poor chap, like one set in a pillory, unable to move either way and directly facing his doom until the blow came.

"I recall the entire thing very clearly, even though it all happened in much less time than I require now to tell you of it. It was as though I had one eye for Brissot's hideous plight and one for the chauffeur's state and an extra one for watching that engine approach and for calculating, by its speed, how long it would be before we were struck. Somehow my interest in myself was semi-detached, as you might say – I'd made up my mind already that I, for one, had no earthly chance to escape. I've noticed the same thing before in emergencies that might be called comparable to this one – once with a Cape buffalo when my gun-bearer deserted me after I'd fired and missed, and once again in a bit of a mess with a wounded tiger out in India.

"And it was just then, at that precise moment, while poor Brissot's head was held so tightly, that he cried out the words which made me know he had been where, in my time, I have been – away up the interior, well on toward the Uganda district. As he uttered them I too, in spite of all else, was struck by the same paralleling fact which, through some abnormal spasmodic trick of memory, must have driven itself then and there right into his brain. It was a curious freak; probably one of these psychological sharps could explain it. I can't. I only know that I also was impressed, even in the one brief instant and under those circumstances, by the graphic resemblance which the locomotive rushing straight at us, snorting and grinding and tooting, bore to a bull rhino charging, as the brute always does, with its head down and its belly hugging the earth."

"Do you actually mean to say he called out the word rhinoceros?"

"Yes and no; the thing was more remarkable even than if he

had used the English word. What he exclaimed – shrieked, rather – was a phrase of two native words. The very looks of that approaching monster must vividly have brought those words back to him now, years and years perhaps after he first heard them used, no doubt under somewhat similar circumstances.

"He cried out – not once but three times – '*Niama tumba! Niama tumba! Niama tumba!*' just so. And that is from the language of the Mbama, a tribe now almost extinct, who lived beyond the country of the Masai on the inner side of our British Protectorate in what was formerly Portuguese East Africa. There are only a few of them left – the slave trade first and the white man's diseases afterwards, long ago decimated them. The words, literally translated, mean 'great animal' – and that's the Mbamas' only name for the bull rhino. Extraordinary coincidence, I call it – if one may speak in such a sense of such a thing being coincidence?"

Mr. Tyree made no answer. For a bit he sat like a man stunned by an incredible tale of an incredible manifestation.

THE SECOND COMING OF A FIRST HUSBAND

If only Mrs. Thomas Bain had been content to compare Mr. Thomas Bain with men about him he, for his counter-arguments, would not have been put to a serious disadvantage. Out of her ammunition locker he might have borrowed shells to be fired in his own defense. Did she, for instance, cite the polished beauty of Mr. So-and-So's drawing-room behavior, speaking with that subtle inflection which as good as said that his own society manners left much to be desired, Mr. Bain's rebuttal would have been prompt and ready: He would have spoken right up to point out the fact that So-and-So notoriously neglected his family or that he drank entirely too much for his own good or that he habitually failed to pay his just debts. Mr. Bain was no scandal-monger, understand, still a man must fight back with such weapons as he may command.

But Mrs. Bain's method of attack was entirely too subtle for him; it left him practically weaponless. Out in the world he amply was competent to fend for himself. Beneath the domestic roof-tree, when his wife sat in judgment on him, and his ways, on his small short-comings or his larger faults, he completely was at a loss for proper rebuttal. It gave him such a helpless feeling! It would have given any normal man a helpless feeling. And Mr. Bain was in all essential regards a normal man – a good citizen, a good provider and, as husbands go, an average fair husband.

I would do Mrs. Bain no injustice. She was a normal woman, too. But it is only natural when destiny has fashioned an advantage to fit one's hands that one employs it. Her advantage was a very great one. Her criticisms of Mr. Bain took the form of measuring him off against the mental picture of her first husband.

And her first husband was dead. Now, in common decency, an honorable man – and Mr. Bain was an honorable man – may not speak ill of the dead. What is more, had he, under stress of provocation, been minded to retort that after all Mrs. Bain's first husband was not exactly perfection either, he could have produced no proof in support of the assertion. For he had never seen his predecessor. He knew nobody who had known the deceased. The present Mrs. Bain had been for three years a widow when first he set eyes on her. She had lately returned from Honolulu; it was in Honolulu that she had been bereft, as the saying is, by the hand of death. And Honolulu is a long distance from Brockway, Mass., where Tom Bain's people, a stay-at-home stock, had lived these five generations past.

So, on those frequently recurring occasions when Mrs. Bain, with a saddened, almost a wistful, air was moved to remind herself of her first husband's marvelous qualities – his temperament, his flawless disposition, his tact, his amiability or what not – there was for her second husband nothing to do except to suffer on in impotent silence. It is not well that anyone on this earth – and more especially a husband – should be required to suffer discomforts in silence. Suffering calls for vocal expression.

Otherwise, as human beings go, Mr. and Mrs. Bain were well suited, one for the other. It was that dead first husband of hers, who, invoked by her, kept rising up to mar the reasonable happiness which might have been theirs. The thing was getting on his nerves. Indeed, at the time this account begins, it already had got upon his nerves. He had come to the point where frequently he wished there had never been such a thing as a first husband.

There were times when he almost permitted himself the wish that there never had been such things as second husbands, either.

With the acute vividness of a war-scarred veteran remembering the time he was shot, he could recall the occasion when Mrs. Bain's first husband first came into his life. They had been married only a few weeks; the honeymoon was over; he who always had traveled singly was adjusting himself to the feel of double harness. This was an easier job for the lady than for her mate; she had been through the process once before. But while Tom Bain might be a green hand at this business of being married, still subconsciously he already was beginning to adjust himself in his ordained and proper place in the matrimonial scheme as it related to him and this very charming lady. In other words, he had reached the period where he was slipping out of the bridegroom pose into the less studied and more matter-of-fact status of a husband. He was ready to quit acting a part and be his own self again always, though with regard for the limitations and restrictions imposed by the new estate upon which he had entered.

The campaign against him – we may as well call it a campaign – opened on the evening following their return from the trip to White Sulphur. That first day at his desk had been a hard one; so much which seemed to require his personal attention had accumulated while he was away. He left the office pretty well fagged out. On his way home he built up a pleasant vision of a nice quiet little dinner and then a peaceful hour or so in the living-room in slippers and an old smoking jacket.

Mrs. Bain met him at the door with a greeting that put him in thorough good humor. This, he decided, was the best of all possible worlds to live in and his, undoubtedly, was the best of all possible ways of living.

"You're late, dearest," she said. "You've just time to run upstairs and slip on your evening clothes. I've laid them out for you."

"Why, there's nobody coming in for dinner, is there?" he asked.

She drew away from him slightly.

"No, there's no one coming," she said. "What difference does that make?"

"Well," he said, "I'm rather tired and so I sort of thought that, seeing there'd be only the two of us, I'd come to the table just as I am."

"Very well, dear," she said, "suit yourself."

But, as a newly married man, how could he suit himself? He clad himself in the starchy shirt, the high tight collar that nipped his throat, the pinchy patent leathers and all the rest of the funereal regalia in which civilized man encases himself on any supposedly festal occasion. She gave him an approving look when ten minutes later he presented himself before her.

"Tom," she said as they sat down, "I think you always should dress for dinner. Arthur always said that a gentleman should dress for dinner."

He stared at her, puzzled for a moment.

"Arthur?" he echoed.

124

"My first husband," she explained. "Arthur looked so well in his evening clothes."

"Oh," he said, like that. That was all he said for a minute or so. He was thinking.

She was thinking, too. Practically all women are popularly supposed to have intuition, and certainly this particular woman had her share of it. Probably it was in that very moment of reflection that the lady decided on a future plan of action.

At any rate, this was the beginning. Eventually, Mr. Bain awoke to a realization that he was the victim of a gentle tyranny – that he had fallen captive to an enemy force made up of an affectionate but somewhat masterful lady and the memory of a dead and gone personality. Mrs. Bain's first husband was persistently dogging Mrs. Bain's second husband. Daily, after one fashion or another, he was reminded of Arthur. Arthur, it seemed, had never lost his temper. What made the comparison hurt the more was the indubitable fact that Mr. Bain occasionally did lose his. Arthur had never raised his voice above a well low-pitched key of innate refinement – no matter how irritated he might be. Arthur had been so tidy; Arthur never left his clothes lying about where he dropped them. Arthur had never given her a cross word in all the seven years of their life together. Arthur invariably had been so considerate of her feelings. It was Arthur this and it was Arthur that; she realized her power and she used it. Mrs. Bain's first husband was ever, so to speak, at the elbow of Mrs. Bain's second husband, by proxy chiding him, admonishing him, correcting him, scolding him, even. And for all that he was a naturally sunny-natured and most companionable person, Mrs. Bain's second husband, at the end of the first year of his married life, was in a fair way to become a most unhappy person. Their matrimonial craft was sliding down the rapids toward a thundering Niagara and she didn't realize it and he, thoroughly under the dominion of forces with which he found himself somehow powerless to cope, only dimly and dully appreciated the peril. He wanted above all things to have and to hold his wife until death did them part. But always there was Arthur tagging along, making a crowd of three out of what might have been a congenial company of two.

But, as someone most aptly said, it's always darkest just before the dawn. In this instance, though, deliverance came to

125

the oppressed, not with the graduations of the spreading dawn but rather with the solid emphasis of a bolt from the blue. There was an evening of bridge with the Tuckers and Bain, who played well, had for a partner Mrs. Tucker who didn't. It is barely possible that he had betrayed a passing emotion of testiness once or twice. At midnight as they were entering their house Mrs. Bain renewed her remarks on an issue to which reference already had been made on the way home in the cab.

"My dear," she was saying, "I really must repeat again that, to my way of thinking, no amount of exasperation could have justified you in showing your feelings as you did show them at least twice at that cardtable. Now, Arthur would never –"

At this instant Mr. Bain's finger found the push-button just inside the jamb of the living-room door and the lights flashed on. What next ensued – the vocal part of it, I mean – might have suggested to an eavesdropper, had there been one, that the vowel sounds were being repeated by two persons laboring under a strong excitement.

"Ay?" That was his startled ejaculation.

"E-e-e-e!" A shrill outcry, part scream, part squeal, from her.

"I-I-" Mr. Bain again.

"Oh!" Mrs. Bain's turn.

"You!" Her startled gasp of recognition.

"Yes, Evelyn, that's who it is." This, in matter-of-fact tones, was a third party speaking.

After this for a moment the spell of a terrific stupefaction held both Mr. and Mrs. Bain silent.

Standing in the middle of the floor facing them, was a shadow. I use the language advisedly. With equal propriety I might write down "apparition" or "wraith" or "shape" or "spirit" to describe that which confronted them. I prefer the word "shadow."

It had the outline, somewhat wavery and uncertain, of a man. It had the voice of a man – a voice calm, assured, almost casual. It had the garb of a man or at least it had the nebulous faint suggestion of garbing. But it had no substance to it, none whatsoever. It had no definable color, either. It had rather the aspect of a figure of a man done in lines of very thin smoke. You could look right through it and distinguish, as through a patch of haze, the pattern of the wall-paper behind it. And now, as it spoke again, you could in some indefinable sort of way see its voice starting from down in its chest and traveling on up and up and so out at its lips. It was no more than a patch of fog, modeled by some unearthly magic into the semblance of a human form. It was inconceivable, impossible, an incredible figment of the imagination, and yet there it was.

Its second speech was addressed to Mr. Bain, who had frozen where he was, his finger still touching the push-button, his eyes enlarged to twice their size and his lower jaw sagged.

"You are astonished? Permit me to introduce myself. I am Arthur – Mrs. Bain's first husband. I am glad to meet you."

Mr. Bain came to himself all of a sudden. The shackles of twelve months of bottled-in restraint fell from him.

"Are you?" he answered. "Well, I'm damned if I'm glad to meet you."

"I understand." The voice was gentle, almost compassionate. "But you will be glad later on, I think – very glad. Shall we sit down, all of us?"

The Thing took a chair. And the back of the chair cloudily revealed itself as a sub-motif for the half-materialized torso of its occupant. Mechanically, moving jerkily, Mr. Bain followed suit; he also took a chair. Mrs. Bain, uttering whimpering sounds down in her throat, already had fallen upon a couch and was huddled there. It was just as well the couch had been handily near by, for her legs would no longer support her.

Her first husband – we may as well call him that – turned to her.

"Control yourself, Evelyn," he bade her. "There is no occasion for any excitement. Besides, those curious sounds which you are now emitting annoy me. I haven't long to stay and I have much to say."

He cleared his throat – the process might be followed by the eye as well as with the ear – and proceeded:

"I have been endeavoring for months past to bring about this meeting. In fact, ever since shortly after your second marriage to this gentleman, I have sought to return to earth for the one purpose which brings me tonight. But it was difficult – very difficult." He sighed a visible sigh. "It is not permitted that I should explain the nature of the obstacles. I merely say that they were very great. As you will notice, I am not able to even yet

127

attain the seeming solidity – the weight and specific density which I craved to take on. So I just came along in the somewhat sketchy and incomplete guise on which you now see me.

"My reason for coming is simple. I desire to see justice done. Where I was, I could not rest in peace knowing that you, Evelyn, were lying so outrageously and, what was worse, making me an unwitting accomplice, as it were, to your lying.

"Evelyn, you have been a wicked woman. You have done this gentleman here –" including Mr. Bain with a wave of a spectral arm –"a cruel wrong. But what, from my point of view, is even worse, you have done me a grave wrong as well. I may be only a memory – I may say that that precisely is what I am – but even a memory has its feelings, its sense of responsibility, its obligations to itself.

"Very well, having made that point clear, I shall proceed: Sir, for nearly a year past you have been intimidated by the constantly presented image of a paragon. Am I not right? Your peace of mind has been seriously affected. And I resent the slander on my name. It has been an insult which no self-respecting memory should be compelled to stand. Sir, I wish you to know the truth: I was not a paragon, and I thank God for it. I was not the perfect husband this woman would have you believe. I was fussy, faulty, crotchety – and I am proud of it!"

"Oh, Arthur!" Mrs. Bain, under attack, was reviving, rallying to her own defense as powers of coherent speech returned to her.

"Don't 'Oh, Arthur' me – but listen. And you, too, sir, if you will be so good? We quarreled frequently in those years of our married life. She complained of my brusque ways, of my fits of irritability, of my refusal to like many of the people that she persisted in liking, of my tastes and my habits and inclinations. She didn't care for some of my friends; I didn't care for many of hers. I objected to any number of things about her – and rarely refrained from saying so. She has told you that between us there was never a cross word. *Bah!* – there were tens of thousands of cross words. When we got on each other's nerves, which was often, neither of us hesitated to let it be known. When we disagreed over something – or anything – we argued it out – quarreled it out, frequently. We loved each other, it is true, but merely loving did not make either of us angelic. We fell out and made up and fell out again. There were times when we were like

128

a pair of cooing doves and again there were times when the proverbial monkey and parrot had little, if anything, on us. In short, and in fine, sir, we behaved just as the average reasonably well-mated married couple do behave. And for my own sake, and incidentally for yours, sir, I would not have you believe differently.

"That, I believe, is practically all I had to say to you. Having said it, I wish to add a final word to our wife, here. Evelyn, speaking with such authority as is befitting a first husband, I wish to state that, so far as my observations from another sphere have gone, your present husband is a first-rate fellow. I like to think of him as my successor. And I intend to see that he has a fair deal from you. I trust this visit from me has been a lesson to you. Hereafter, in your dealings with him you will please be so good as to stand on your own merits. You will kindly refrain from dragging me into your arguments as an advocate on your side. My stock of patience is no greater than it was before I became a memory – remember that. I sincerely trust it will not be necessary for me to admonish you personally a second time. Because I warn you here and now that next time I shall return under circumstances that may be most embarrassing to you. Next time there will be no privacy about my appearance; I shall appear to you in public. You'll be a talked-about woman, Evelyn. There'll be pieces about you in the paper and spiritualists and trance mediums and delvers into the occult – a meddlesome nosey lot, too, I may add – will make your life a burden for you. So have a care, Evelyn!

"Sir, to you I extend my best wishes. I'm sorry we didn't meet before. Well, some of these days we'll make up for lost time – when you join me on the plane where I am at present residing. Well, I guess that will be about all... Oh, if you don't mind, I'll just dissipate into air and float up the chimney – it's more convenient." Out of a nothingness near the fireplace came a voice growing thinner and fainter: "Good-bye, Bain, old chap; good-bye, Evelyn – and don't forget."

It was at this juncture that Mrs. Bain went off into a swoon. It also should be noted down that even as he sprang to her side to revive her Mr. Bain wore on his face a look of husbandly solicitude and concern, but his feet twittered in a dance measure.

Personally, I do not believe in ghosts. I assume, reader, that

129

you do not believe in ghosts, either. But Mrs. Bain does, and as for Mr. Bain he does, too, firmly – and, as a happily married man is each day renewing and strengthening his belief in them

MASTERPIECE

Looking back on it all, Staggner could see no flaws and no blow-holes in the murder he committed. The best proof of that was that the police never once singled him out from the others who were in the house at the time, for direct suspicion or even for special scrutiny.

In fact, the police never really suspected anybody in particular. They might talk big about "theories" and "investigations along new lines," and they did talk big about those things. They might dig up so-called "clues" and go through the motions of following so-called "leads," but they only traveled in circles, like a horse with the blind staggers, and came back where they started from.

So Staggner could look over his shoulder without real apprehension and certainly without remorse. Regret that his original object had failed? Yes, naturally he had that. But remorse? – no, none whatsoever. His chief feeling was rather one of satisfaction for his own smartness.

This feeling prevailed with him during those first few weeks when public interest was febrile and brisk, and before the case began to be listed among the "unsolved mysteries" of the year. Along there his main sensation might have been likened to that of a player who, single-handed and for high stakes, plays a difficult and unfamiliar and exciting game against a whole troupe of skilled adversaries and at each turn of the cards wins, and wins, and keeps on winning.

All through his life Staggner had been hearing of the fool-proof murder, the perfect crime, in which the criminal leaves behind no loose ends for detectives to pick up, no trails for bloodhounds to smell out. Often enough he had heard it said or had read that this perfect crime likewise is the impossible crime because, being a thing of human contriving, the equation of human error inevitably must enter into it. Murder Will Out! That was an old saying.

Now, lo and behold, the perfect crime had been committed and he, of all men alive, was the man who had committed it.

Why, he was one in a million. Indeed, if the United States census figures didn't lie about it, he was one in about a hundred and twenty millions.

He wasn't a professional killer, either. Far from it. This Olivia Thames was the only person he had ever killed. He never expected to have to kill any one else. He wasn't the sort to go around killing people, although he was beginning to understand how such a career might have a kind of fascination for an individual who succeeded at it.

To make it all the stranger, he was without prior experience along the lines of criminal endeavor. Finally, there was this to be said: it is not an act which in advance had been planned or contemplated even. It had grown out of an unforeseen contingency, so that all the covering-up of tracks, all the destroying of dangerous evidence, had to be done after the event, and done within a space of minutes, and some part of it done before the eyes of witnesses.

Nevertheless, he, Wally Staggner, and he a rank amateur, had killed this fat beldame of a woman deftly, quietly, quickly, and as you might almost say, cleanly, and had come out of the subsequent emergency and general messiness as smooth as a whistle and as free as a bird. He told himself he couldn't blame himself for being a bit toploftical over the outcome. With him, his confidence fed on his conceit and his conceit fed on his confidence, and both grew fatter rather than lean.

Nobody had known how desperately he had wanted a lot of money. That had helped. The fact that nobody was aware he wanted money stood him in good stead during all those prolonged inquiries when the police were prying about and casting about, lifting the lid on this one's life and that one's life, trying to find a possible motive, a plausible reason, any peg upon which to hang an accusation.

He wanted this money so he might marry that alleged Polish countess he had met in Italy during the summer. She wouldn't marry any man who hadn't plenty of money. She told him so, practically in so many words. But nobody over here knew of his infatuation for this woman with her chinchilla-colored eyes and her honey-colored hair, and nobody at all, with the possible exception of the lady adventurer herself, knew how, with so desperate a craving, he craved for money.

132

He had come home panting after her as the hart is said to pant after the water-brooks and with a brain whirling to a desire for money and plenty of it. Oh, she'd spend it for him once he got it and she got him. He appreciated that all right enough, but for what might follow in their future together he took no thought nor gave any heed. Possession of her – that was what his whole being demanded, and since a heap of good hard Yankee dollars was the price he must pay for his season in a lover's paradise, why, so be it.

The big notion which led to everything else came to him the Friday night in October when he drove up to Winchester for the week-end party that was being given by Solly Lennix, the moving-picture man, and Solly Lennix's newest wife. Two factors entered into the sudden forming of his purpose. The first of these was the presence of this Mrs. Olivia Thames. Besides being a woman who still kept, embedded in unwholesome bloat, some few traces of a beauty which once had made her notorious, this Thames woman was at least four other things: namely, a former actress, a frequent divorcee, a habitual souse and a reputed hophead.

Staggner, having been shown to his room on arrival and having dressed, came down to the overdone library, to find her there with the Lennixes and most of their guests. She blazed with jewels and already was incandescent with brandy or whatever it was she drank between times in private when not engaged in drinking cocktails or high-balls or wine or what-have-you in company.

Giving her a nod and a quick glance of appraisal, Staggner merely remarked inwardly that already she was pretty thoroughly illuminated, even for her. That, for the moment, was all the thought he gave her.

A minute later, when the butler came to him offering a laden tray, Staggner, with a little interior throb, recognized the man. Less than three months before, getting local color for an underworld scenario on which he was working, he had gone down to Police Headquarters one morning for the crooks' line-up, and there, unless he was mistaken now – and he wasn't mistaken now; of that he was sure – this selfsame smug-faced, light-stepping individual who now offered him cocktails had been paraded out as one of the catch of the preceding twenty-

133

four hours before an audience of masked plain-clothes men; and the master of ceremonies, a Central Office lieutenant, had gabbled off the routine about this here party being Somebody, alias Somebody Else, sneak, inside worker, general thief, number so-and-so in the Gallery, such-and-such previous convictions, picked up on suspicion, and so on and so forth.

The incident of the fellow's arraignment stood out in Staggner's mind. Something about this particular person's manner or appearance had impressed itself upon him at the time and the memory had stuck.

Staggner's first impulse was to draw Solly aside and warn him that he had a rogue, probably with forged credentials, in his household staff but just then, snap! – like that – an idea clicked in his brain, an idea in which, thus quickly and thus soon, he was coupling the pussy-footed butler with Olivia Thames. Over his tilted glass, he studied her by piecemeal and, with suddenly covetous eyes, summed up what two minutes before he casually had been cognizant of. On fingers and arms and breast she was burdened with jewels – diamonds, emeralds, rubies and, looped about her great throat and dangling below her problematical waistline, a certain famous rope of matched pearls, reputed formerly to have been the possession of a refugee Russian princess, and bestowed on the present possessor by the most recent of her string of affluent husbands. It would be like her to go about, a perambulating hock-shop, with all the precious junk she owned on display. She was the type.

And a good thing, too, that she was the type, because all in one swift instant he was saying to himself that assuming, just for instance, some of her jewels or, for that matter, all of them, should disappear and on top of that, assume further, it developed that a notorious thief, a rascal with a long police record, was masquerading as a servant under the same roof with her at the moment of their disappearance, why, then, in such case what more natural, yes, what more inevitable a conclusion could any one conceive of than that official suspicion would center upon the exposed scoundrel for long enough to enable the real culprit to make a clean get-away with the swag? He didn't take into account that purloined gems of great value and of reputation among the gem-dealers might be hard things to dispose of.

Swiftly, over and over again, he was telling himself that the pearls alone were said to be worth, by expert valuation, two hundred thousand dollars and to be insured for some such sum. All that concerned him – and this should help to show what a novice at larcenous games was Staggner – was the certainty that with the worth of half what that overfleshed caricature yonder wore draped on her frame, he could buy the favor of his Polish countess.

Give him a chance, give him but an opening to make a chance and he'd have a brisk try for it. All in this flash of time his resolution took on a shape and substance.

It was a typical Solly Lennix dinner – persons who were smartly polished and persons who merely shone with the thin shellac of a sudden affluence; boisterous ones and sinister-looking ones and simple-looking ones sitting down together, twenty-odd strong, at an overburdened table: and plenty to eat and drink there, and plenty to laugh at and be noisy over. As an established but not a notable free-lancing scenario writer, Staggner, in a way, fitted the setting and, in another way, did not.

From where he sat among the lesser fry down toward the foot of the table, sandwiched in between the flashy wife of a flashy Wall Street man named Glosscup and a somewhat stringy and faded woman playwright named Baylor, he could watch Olivia Thames whose place was almost opposite him. He did watch her and, with a secret glow of satisfaction, marked how steadily she punished Solly's sweet champagne.

Solly, up yonder at the head, was in his best form or his worst; it depended on how you took Solly. Whatever else you might say about Solly you had to give him credit for being game. About him there was nothing to indicate that he was in deep waters financially and about to be in still deeper; in fact, clear over his head.

Within three months' time Solly would be out of the moving-picture game and out of this house, and the house and its contents and the contents of his big city apartment would be for sale to pay off some of the judgments against him. The wolves would be on him then, picking his bones clean. But to-night he was the life of the party.

The guzzling Thames woman proved her capacity. Not until the dinner ended did the liquid ballast begin to shift on her so that she lurched and listed heavily as she rose to her feet. Her waddle had changed to a stagger. She reached the doorway, though, before she went down on her knees, her gross face becoming suddenly blank of all expression.

There was a guffaw from some of the men, a giggle from some of the women, and two men who hadn't laughed heaved her up on her feet. They had to prop her upright. She was dead to the world. Her legs flopped and waggled under her.

"Help her up-stairs, will you, boys?" said little Mrs. Solly. "Get her into her room – it's the Blue Room on the second floor, first door on the right at the top of the steps. She didn't bring her maid with her; her maid's sick or something. I'll trail along and get her undressed. No need for anybody to watch her – she'll be like that till morning."

She laughed over her shoulder as she started up the stairs behind the helpers with their sagging burden between them.

"Smart gal, Olivia," she said gaily. "She always knows when she's got enough. She knows it about half an hour after she's got it."

Coffee and brandy had been served by the time she reappeared in the doorway. Glosscup was just getting under way, telling one of his off-color stories. Mrs. Solly's prompt return interrupted him.

"All done," she announced. "Mama's off to Shut-eye Town. Trust little Fannie Fix-it, the Camp-fire Girl. Say, how long are you boys going to loll around here, being dirty? Don't you hear those dames sharpening their teeth on the other side of this hall? There'll be three tables of bridge and a free-for-all poker table, dealer's choice and heaven's dome for the limit; everybody's set to go as soon as you big Camemberts get through pawing into the city dump. So make it snappy."

"Beat it," said Solly with affectionate violence. "Let them female sharks wait; these poor fish will be along soon enough. This gag Glossy's pullin' is too good to miss."

Glosscup's story posthumously begot another like it from the same abundant source, and then a third. Solly looked at his watch.

"By gosh, it's later than I thought!" he exclaimed. "Quarter to twelve already, if this kettle's right."

"Twelve minutes of, to be exact," said the man next him. "I

set mine in town to-day by Western Union."

"Let's go," ordered Solly. "Gamblers to the center! Serious drinkers can stick right here or else go to the bar in the library. A library makes a swell bar – once you've throwed out enough of them fool books."

By intent, Staggner was at the tail of the procession which at once was straggling across the broad entrance hall of this big Georgian barn of a house and on into one or the other of the twin drawing-rooms. Here at once there was a clamor of preferences being shrilly stated, of partners being drawn, of chips being counted and, on the part of a few, of refusals to play anything at all.

Nobody, whether servants or fellow-guests, was paying any attention to Staggner. That suited his book admirably. He was sure then – and later had confirmation for it – that his leisurely dawdling withdrawal was unobserved. Once out of sight of the rest, his retreat up the stairs was swift but not so swiftly timed as to breed suspicion, did some person come unexpectedly into view either from above or from below.

The broad upper corridor was dimly lighted. He slipped into a still darker side hall, took a handkerchief from his pocket and, drawing it across the bridge of his nose, tied it behind his ears. It covered the lower part of his face; made a good-enough improvised mask. He meant to run no risk of recognition should the sleeper awake.

Emerging from the crossway, he crept to the first door on the right. A light shone through the keyhole but through the keyhole came no sound that he could detect. So softly and very gently he turned the knob and pushed. As he had expected, the door was unlocked. He pushed it farther, slipped through and closed and bolted it behind him.

Now, being inside, he heard the woman's heavy breathing. Partly undressed, she lay on the bed, face upward, puffing through her painted lips. There was a comforter over the lower part of her body. The bed light alongside her was on. It made plenty of illumination. One pudgy arm, on top of the coverlet, still carried its load of broad bracelets. But her throat had been stripped of its rich burden:

Had the pearls been locked away? No, there they were in a coil on the dresser between the two windows, making a lustrous little heap. Silently he crossed the room to where they were. There were other things with them – a huge diamond sunburst, emerald earrings, a diamond hair ornament, various costly gauds.

The job, thus far, had been so ridiculously easy that almost it was funny. He had only to scoop up the spoils and tiptoe out.

In the act of scooping them up a problem unforeseen until the present moment beset him. When discovery of the robbery came, as inevitably and within a few hours it must, there would be a house-wide search. In justice to the servants, in justice to one another, all hands would surely submit to an examination of their persons and their belongings and their rooms. Where, then, would be the safest place to hide this loot until that phase passed?

With the treasure clinking in his grasp, he gave consideration to this puzzle. In the midst of it he was aware, all of a sudden, that the thick breathing behind him had stopped short. Startled, he swung about.

Her eyes wide open, her jaw agape, the Thames woman was sitting up in bed – indeed, was moving to get out of bed. She did not offer to scream, but as plainly as a drawing taking shape against a canvas, a conscious understanding was replacing the blank stupor on those swollen features. Shock was sobering her; was sobering her with a miraculous swiftness.

Squinting hard at him, she flung the covers aside, thrust her legs out of bed, got on her feet and stood barring his path to the door. There was no fear in the scowl on that dissipated face, no panic betrayed in the glare from those bleared eyes, but only a great hostility.

Then he came to himself and took a step toward her and as he did this he felt his badly tied disguisement slipping off his nose. He threw up his free hand to hold it and his fumble at it completed the damage. The handkerchief fell down about his throat and in the virago's staring look, along with the rage, there was now recognition. She knew him, so that settled her hash for her.

"You dirty dog!" she said in a sort of slow fierce undertone. "I've got you! You'll pay –"

In that same flash he struck her down. She took the first blow on an upturned forearm but the second, delivered with all his might and main, landed squarely on her unprotected head and he could feel the sink of the weapon's iron butt right into the bone structure.

She was down now, face forward, on the thick bearskin before the hearth, which had muffled the soft thud of her dropping. And he was standing over her, ready to strike again, holding poised the heavy ornamental poker which he had caught up from the side of the fireplace.

Afterward he could not remember dropping the jewels and snatching for the poker. He must have acted instinctively. But he remembered everything else – how very clearly he did remember it all, reconstructing each detail in his mind!

She was dead, all right – no cause for worry there. The very sprawl of her body told him she was dead. Besides, the top of her skull was bashed in.

He was perfectly calm. Even in that hurried phase of it, he subconsciously marveled that he should be so entirely calm and marveled also that he should marvel. Of course, taking the jewels was now out of the question. Who would dare to risk being caught with a murdered woman's jewels in his possession? Who would dare try to market them?

There they were – scattered on the floor. So he gathered them up, making sure no article was missing, and put them on the dresser where he had found them. But before he did this, he slid the poker under the bed on the side nearer the body, leaving the brass handle exposed. There was method in this partial concealment of the poker.

He undid the handkerchief from his throat and wadded it into his pocket. Next he came and stood over the dead woman and thought very hard. What else, if anything, was to be done? A crowning inspiration flashed across his brain.

IIis victim's pulpy left arm was outstretched. It had a crumpled, curiously foreshortened aspect to it. He bent and looked closer, and that was when he got his inspiration. Where his first blow had fallen, her wrist was shattered. The stroke had smashed the gemmed band which held her wrist-watch in place. The watch, though, was not injured; only the band was.

He slid the wrecked bracelet out from beneath the broken wrist and put the watch to his ear. It ticked steadily. So he turned the hands back from twelve-seven until they registered eleven-

139

forty-six, and then tapped the face of the watch against his heel until the crystal smashed and the mechanism failed.

Again applying the mistreated bauble to his ear, he made sure it had quit running. He shook it, listened once more. Its tick was silenced. With his handkerchief he wiped it well and, keeping it nested in the handkerchief to avoid touching it again, he deposited the watch on the rung a finger's length from its late owner's relaxed left hand.

He drew the bolt, passed out of the door, closing it softly behind him and, meeting no one in his descent, was immediately back down-stairs, making a leisurely reappearance in the front drawing-room. No person there so much as lifted a head or cocked an inquiring eyebrow at his sauntering, indifferent entrance. Well, all told, he'd only been away a matter of some seven or eight minutes.

Casually, he stationed himself behind two others – dumb kibitzers – who were standing back of one of the players at one of the bridge tables. The player was a woman.

A deal was played out; the woman and her partner had gone down.

"My luck is terrible," she declared. "Not a decent hand since we started."

"That's right," said Staggner sympathetically, "I've been looking over your shoulder and you haven't had a really good hand since you began playing."

She glanced up at him, grimacing and nodding. Staggner meant that the alibi he had built should have no chinks in it. Big things counted in its construction, but trifles might help too. He was sure this woman would be willing, in perfect good faith, to testify that he had been in her vicinity all the while.

He idled off to another table and lingered, observing the play for perhaps a quarter of an hour more. He wasn't the least bit nervous.

He was still there near this second quartet of player when from up-stairs came a shrill frightened outcrop – Solly Lennix's wife's voice.

"Come quick, somebody!" she was screaming. "Something's happened to Olivia. Come quick!"

There was a scuffle, a stir of bodies suddenly galvanized into movement. A table went over with a small crash, a glass smashed, chips were clattering in a cataract and Mrs. Lennix was repeating her call.

In the excited jostling rush up the stairs, Staggner was one of the first; not the first – he saw to that – but one of the first.

Very pale, Mrs. Lennix met them at the head of the steps.

"I slipped up to see how Olivia was," she was screechily proclaiming, "and she's flat on the floor! And she's all over blood! I took one look and ran. Something's happened – oh, something terrible's happened!"

Staggner shoved forward. He was over the threshold hard on Lennix's heels, bumping into Solly as that pudgy person balked at the dread sight before him.

"*Gott!*" cried Solly, relapsing into the accents of his early youth. "Keep the women out from here," he barked over his shoulder. "Keep out from here – you women. Come on, some of you men."

He still hesitated himself. With others, Staggner shoved past Solly. At once there was a ringed huddle of men's bodies about the shape on the rug. A futile clamor of interlaced, overlapping voices arose.

"Get a doctor quick," somebody was saying but himself making no move to do so. "Phone for a doctor."

"She's dead," somebody else was saying, "she certainly looks dead, boys."

"Maybe – maybe she fell out of bed and hurt herself," a third somebody was saying but in a strangely flattened tone.

"And maybe she didn't," snapped Staggner, his voice dominating the small tumult so that it ended and a quick tense hush ensued. "Look at her head! And look at her arm! Never mind getting any doctor. What we need here is the police!"

"*Mein Gott*, then it's moider!" yelled Solly hysterically.

"And look at this!" added Staggner. He stooped and from beneath the bed drew the heavy brass-handled poker. "Here's what it was done with, I'd guess."

He passed the poker into the hands of a neighbor. The neighbor happened to be Glosscup. And immediately another man, seized with a morbid inquisitiveness, took it away from Glosscup.

"See if that poker doesn't fit that dent in her head," Staggner bade him. "I'm no good at that sort of thing – makes me sick!"

Glosscup – and for it Staggner was secretly grateful to him – said now what Staggner had meant to say in a moment or two. He took the words right out of Staggner's mouth and Staggner was glad of it.

"We've played hell!" declared Glosscup. "Handling that poker was all wrong. There might have been finger-prints on it. And now we've messed 'em all up with our finger-prints."

"That's so," agreed Staggner contritely. "Lay it down and don't anybody touch it again."

Glosscup, it would seem, was by way of being an amateur detective; probably was a reader of crime fiction. For he dropped down on his knees and closely eyed the ruined wrist-watch; next was stooping closer and applying his ear close to it.

"Be still," he commanded. "I want to see if this watch is still going." He straightened up. "It's stopped," he stated. "It stopped when that lick hit it – no wonder. Her wrist's all smashed up. It stopped at exactly forty-six past eleven – that's when this killing was done! We've got that much to go on."

"*Gott!*" cried Solly. "Chust almost the very minute when I was saying to you fellows down-stairs that we'd better be joinin' the wimmin. You remember?"

Haply, he appealed to Staggner.

"I remember," said Staggner.

"So do I," put in Walters, the effeminate little costume designer. "You asked me, Solly, and I told you it was exactly twelve minutes of twelve. The whole crowd of us gabbling down there and this going on up here. Let me out of here, men – I'm getting sick, too."

Glosscup, all palpitant with his self-appointed role, was delivering an order now. "Lock the outside doors!" he proclaimed with tremendous authority. "Nobody leaves this house until the police get here – nobody! This looks like an inside job to me. By the way, where's all her jewelry – those pearls and everything?"

"Right here on this dressing-table," stated an eager voice. "A whole pile of 'em."

"Oh!" grunted Glosscup as though baffled or at least disappointed. "So that's how it stands, eh?"

So it stood and so, until the end of the chapter, it continued to stand. The crime must have been committed by some person on the premises. The city detectives who came up from town to aid the Westchester County constabulary in its gruesome guessing contest agreed with the local cops on that point.

Likewise they all agreed that the woman must have been stricken down at eleven-forty-six – her wrist-watch proved that much, so they all decided. But at eleven-forty-six practically all the guests and practically all the servants could account, at least approximately, for their whereabouts.

And why had it been done at all? What reason other than an outburst of homicidal insanity – and that a frenzied thing without any reason to it – was there for it? What cause? Nobody in all the wide world, so far as was known, hated this chronic grass widow of an Olivia Thames, or had a grudge against her even. Some might have contempt for her; some undoubtedly had pity. The poor vain weak creature had been her own worst enemy, with no other identifiable enemy anywhere.

After the first few hours – after the false butler had been recognized and locked up, after each individual on the place had been pumped and badgered and cross-questioned – the case just stood still. The butler spent a month or two in jail, where he learned things about the third degree he never knew before. The rest underwent a week or two of being interviewed for the press and being photographed for the press and being resummoned for more futile, footless examinations by harassed police chiefs and perplexed police underlings and by a pestered district attorney.

Then some newer nine-day sensation bobbed up and the "House-party Mystery," as the head-lines had dubbed it, was put upon the shelf. Only the gaudy Broadway prominence of a few of the names concerned in it had kept it alive for as long as it did live.

Staggner, feeling altogether comfortable and assured, waited until January before he drew out of the bank what cash he had there and went abroad. He was going over to see if his Polish countess wouldn't take him just as he was, financially speaking. He crossed on an Italian liner and landed at Genoa, and the day he landed read in the Paris edition of the *Chicago Tribune* that his countess had been married to an Argentine nabob.

So he went on one spectacular lone-handed drunk and then he turned around and started back home again. He wasn't by any means as broken-hearted as he had figured he was going to be when he first heard the news.

Still, he was unhappy and most depressed. His conceit had taken an awful wallop. He drank hard on the steamer. He turned in groggy every night of the return voyage and would be at it again, headachy and shaky, as soon as he waked up next morning. He kept mostly to himself.

On the afternoon before they landed at New York he was sitting alone, mopy and morose, in a chair in the smoking-room when, with a sudden jolt, it came to him, cutting through the alcoholic haze which enveloped his brain, that he was beginning to think more about the dead woman, the worthless one he had killed, than about the live woman, the delectable one he had lost; that in his mind he was repetitiously calling up the repugnant image of that spraddled corpse on that bear-skin robe. Why should he be doing that?

He shook his head, to clear it of the fumes and the memory. Probably he'd been brooding so much over his latest disappointment that by some vague mental phenomenon, some twisted relationship of ideas, the unpleasant vision of what had happened last October kept recurring. That must be it.

Anyway, he'd been hitting the hard liquor pretty constantly. That was enough, by itself, to unsettle a fellow temperamentally.

Whatever the explanation was, the thing persisted all through that night. He drank in his berth, sending his steward to the bar for high-balls until the bar closed, but somehow couldn't drug himself into sleep. He lay awake, foggily miserable, until nearly daylight and that wasn't like him. And when he did sleep he had dreams – that same lurid dream invariably repeating itself and the dream had to do with Olivia Thames, with her skull caved in, spraddled at his feet.

So when he got up he decided that if his head was going to play him these funny tricks, it was time to soft-peddle on the drinking. Conscience didn't enter into the situation at all. Neither then nor thereafter did conscience enter into it. It was imagination, that's all – just a freak of the imagination. Why, it naturally had to be.

Things went along in this fashion for two months or so. There

144

was a harassed-looking, morose-acting literary man, a young man steadily losing in flesh and in spirits, a man by turns abstracted or garrulous with an almost feverish intensity, a man seeking company to-day and to-morrow avoiding it; by spells working hard at his trade, and by spells engaged in restless idling; a man who tried cutting down on his consumption of liquor and once, for a week, cutting it out altogether – only that seemed to make the situation worse – and finally a man who reached the stage where he kept constantly in a sodden state; and this man all the while seeking desperately to rid himself of a certain retrospective mind-picture which refused to fade out but instead grew stronger and more vivid and, waking or sleeping, bided with him through the days and nights.

Along in the early spring, another and an infinitely more disconcerting phase developed itself. One bright windy afternoon toward the end of March this man was walking up Madison Avenue on his way to keep an appointment with an independent producer who wanted him to redraft the dialogue of a "talkie" script. He was waiting at Fifty-Seventh Street for the cop to stop the cross-traffic when right in front of him appeared the scene of the murder, reproduced, with setting and physical accessories and all, against a shifting perspective of cars and pedestrians and buildings.

He felt himself going stiff and chilly, felt the little hairs on the back of his neck pricking and rising stiffly. For this was altogether different from what had gone before. Before always he had seen the apparition within his brain only. But now he was seeing it, life-size and complete, in broad harsh daylight, seeing it with his eyes. It seemed inconceivable that none of these persons about him likewise saw it with their eyes. None of them did, though. They streamed past, oblivious and unconcerned.

To the frozen Staggner it was as though he stood facing a three-sided stage, as in a theater. Barring that the two ends and the top and bottom of the stage blurred off into the background, instead of making a sharp framing, he might have been the lone spectator of the thrillsome silent episode in a melodrama, a preliminary, say, to a strong second-act climax.

For here, directly ahead of him, was the sprawled body on the bearskin rug, and, alongside it to the left, the fireplace and beyond it the door to the hall, and behind these the rumpled bed and the burning bed light on the stand, and farther on and slightly to the right, the dresser between the two draped windows, and, for a finishing touch, the far corners of Mrs. Solly Lennix's Blue Room shading off into gloominess – a perfect replica of every detail of the original occurrence, save only that his own figure was missing from down-stage, so that the dead woman's shape dominated the whole scene, her broken arm stiffly outthrust, her cropped yellow-dyed hair gleaming except where the matted red stain at the poll of the head showed, her bare bleached feet revealed below the hem of a twisted undergarment.

Staggner's first impulse, where he stood enveloped in a rigor of cold clamminess, was to turn and run away. By an almost visible effort, he rid himself of that desire. Exerting his will power to the uttermost he forced himself to advance across the sidewalk toward the curb and toward the embodied hallucination, or whatever it was. On that the mirage – if you could call it that? – became dim and dimmer, hazy and hazier, and then vanished.

Staggner didn't keep his engagement with the independent producer up on Fifty-Ninth Street. Instead, he hailed a taxi cruising south and rode down-town to his bachelor apartment on Washington Square, having a hard chill on the way.

Reaching his quarters he locked himself in and sought comfort in a full quart of Scotch. Before he found comfort, or any thin semblance of it, the bottle was empty and Staggner was very full.

And next morning while he, still dazed and befuddled, was crossing through Times Square to the Paramount Building – of all unlikely places for daytime nightmares – the thing recurred. And that afternoon when, in an effort to get away from himself he was riding up Riverside Drive on top of a bus, it duplicated itself for the second time within the space of six hours, springing up ten feet high on the horizon of the river shore and fading out as the bus lumbered closer to it. But to the murderer it seemed that perceptibly it endured for a breath of time longer than either of its predecessors had, as though it were reluctant to shred off into the air.

Promptly, then, Staggner went to an eye specialist and the specialist subjected him to various tests and told him that for a person of his age and sedentary pursuits he had excellent vision. So then – but he felt this was merely another utterly vain gesture on his part – he visited a stomach specialist, saying to the latter that he was troubled with a sort of shifting spottiness before his gaze when he stared intently at outdoor objects, and especially when he stared at the sky-line. As he put it, he thought perhaps indigestion might be responsible for this optic derangement. The physician agreed with him that he might be right and prescribed a simple diet, regular habits, outdoor exercise – the customary ritual.

Staggner nodded as though converted and paid the fee but had no intention of following the advice. He had knowledge which no one else would ever have unless – unless – and from this point a certain dire foreboding came to add to his burden of hidden distress. It was this: Suppose others should begin to see what he was seeing almost daily, and, on some days, several times in a day? No one yet had beheld the manifestation, for all that now it was lingering longer so that advancing on it, he almost could enter the scene before it dissipated.

To himself he began saying: "If ever it turns solid, if ever it stays there until I can touch it and feel it with my own fingers, I'm gone. I'm gone then; I'll have to quit fighting then. I'm licked."

Although the thing presented itself oftener in the open, in public or semi-public places, than when he was alone, he now sought spots where there were masses of people and plenty of stir and movement. Conceded that from nursing his delusion his mind was sick with a subtle disease, Staggner nevertheless had a purpose behind this preference for multitudes, this deliberately seeking out surroundings where strangers numerously were.

It was a sort of testing of his security. For so long as no one else saw what he was seeing he would be safe. So he punished himself with long walks on busy thoroughfares, attended theater openings, a solitary, liquor-saturated figure; frequented prize-fights, ball games, even the cheaper amusement resorts.

One hot June evening when New York was frying in its own grease, the dipsomaniac that Staggner had become rose on a sightseeing car, with a flock of gaping out-of-towners for his fellow-passengers, down to Coney Island. Coney was packed and jammed – it was the first big night of the opening season there – and was brilliant with lights and blatant with a thousand discordant noises. It was Coney at its gayest and best and, by that same token, its most delirious worst.

Staggner, more alone in the midst of these two hundred thousand bedraggled pleasure seekers than he would have been as a castaway on a desert island, went shambling along a board walk in a whisky fog. He traveled the board walk for hours, bumping into people and getting cursed for his clumsiness, being bumped into and paying no heed.

All day he had been drinking hard – harder even than usual. He had a flask on his hip. At intervals he entered into some darker corner – a pocket behind a refreshment stand, a byway leading into a labyrinth of rear entrances, any convenient recess – and took a swig.

It got to be very late. The crowds thinned out; the shows and the concession booths were closing. A good many of them already had closed, and Staggner, with no remembrance of how and when he had quitted the board walk or how he came to be where he was now, found himself at the farther end of a sort of blind alley opening back from Surf Avenue.

Gusts of freshened air were blowing in off the sea and there was comparative quiet about him. A misty, indefinite distaste for the bumpy trip back to Manhattan, through the steaming side streets of Brooklyn, took possession of him. Besides, he felt so fearfully tired.

He'd sleep a while right here at Coney, lying on the sand where it was cool, as tenement dwellers often did on a hot night, and go home in the morning. As a matter of fact he was in a semi-coma already, and very near the end of his endurance.

He fumbled at his flank for his flask. A good long drink of the biting raw spirits was still in it. He emptied the bottle, tossed it aside and sat down in a doorway. He lurched back into an easier posture and behind him a poorly secured latch clicked and the door, under the pressure of his shoulders, slid slowly open, revealing near at hand a clutter of mechanical odds and ends, and on beyond an inviting, still darkness. Why wouldn't it be better to rest a while in this secluded harborage rather than down yonder on the gritty beach? It would be better.

The new inclination hoist him to his feet. He pulled his heavy, uncertain feet over the low shelf of the entryway and blindly invaded the building. He was sketchily conscious of passing down a sort of narrow, dimly lighted corridor, then of turning a corner, where he stumbled into projecting solid obstacles that felt like boxes or trunks, and then of moving along a wider passage, flanked on either side by open-faced cubicles or booths.

The beginnings of the flimsy partitions between these spaces he could make out but their interiors were inky-black. Midway of this crossway weariness overcame him – weariness, plus bootlegger's Scotch – and he lay down on his back on the bare planking, with a bent arm for a pillow, and was immediately asleep.

He slept there until nearly three o'clock in the morning. A bright glare, flashing on suddenly and shining down from above into his upturned face, was what roused him. He blinked his gummed eyelids apart and sat up, staring about him in bewilderment. He was in some perfectly strange place and for the drowsy moment had no recollection of how he got there.

The truth was that a slovenly night watchman was just then operating a switchboard at the front of the building, turning on one set of overhead electrics after another, the better to see his way about as he started his belated first round of the place since closing time. The watchman, who had an uneasy nagging feeling that he had forgotten to lock the alley exit, as was his bounden duty, didn't see Staggner then or thereafter, and didn't hear his departure.

The watchman was still in a cuddy just behind the barred main entrance, out of sight and earshot of the intruder. Nor did Staggner see the watchman at all, while the two of them were together under that high-corniced roof.

What Staggner did see – and it drew him up on his feet as though strong invisible wires pulled at him – was what he had seen so many times before since springtime, but never like this, never in just this hideous fashion. Solly Lennix's Blue Room was there right in front of him, not ten feet away and, as always, complete to the final familiar touch. It was the same thing as before and still not the same. It was the Real Thing.

Here it was at last, all solid, substantial, indubitable. One faltering foot dragging behind the other, Staggner forced himself forward, step by step, until he crossed the dividing line between the boards from which he had risen and the verge of that three-sided Blue Room. He sensed the yielding texture of the carpet through his soles, got next the softer nap of the bearskin robe before the fireplace.

He was sure, but he must make very sure. He reached across to the mantel and touched an ornament – some sort of vase. It joggled to his touch – it had the genuine feel to it. He half straddled the dead woman's body and bent over and gripped the handle of the poker, where it lay half under and half from under the tousled bed. It was heavy and solid in his grasp and made a small muffled sound when he let it slide out of his fingers.

And the woman was real too – the waxy-looking naked white feet, the stiff distorted figure, the distorted arm, the matted red stain on the yellow bobbed head. He didn't touch her. He didn't need to. When a man was licked, he was licked, and that was all there was to it.

He backed away until he stood beyond The Thing. Being all at once sobered, he recalled in a cloudy way how he had come to this place. Besides, the path of his retreat was well illuminated now. Quietly but briskly, looking neither to the right nor to the left, he issued forth by the alley door and hurried out of the alley and passed into Surf Avenue, looking for a policeman.

He came upon a policeman, a bored-looking young policeman, after he had traveled perhaps a quarter of a mile. Staggner went up to him.

"Officer," he said. "I would like to give myself up."

"Oh, you would, would you?" said the policeman. "And what have you been doin'" – he caught a whiff of Staggner's breath – "besides drinkin' a lot of bum hooch?"

"Yes," admitted Staggner, "I've been drinking. And I was drunk, I guess. I'm not drunk now. I know what I'm doing and I know what I'm saying. I killed somebody."

"You killed somebody?" The policeman's tone was sharper but still edged with cynicism. Coney abounds in freaks, and not all of them are in side-shows either.

"Yes; a woman."

"When?"

"Last year – in October. So I want to give up – I've got to, that's all. I don't believe they'll do much to me. Either I'm going crazy, or else the whole world's gone crazy around me. They can't send a crazy man to the chair."

"They send a lot of 'em to the bug-house but others have luck. Last October you say it was?"

"Yes."

"Well, what's delayed you so long about comin' clean? Why pick on me now?" He was still skeptical.

"Because she's here now – her body, I mean."

"Where?"

"I can show you; it's not far. It won't be gone when we get there, I know that."

"Oh, it won't?" He'd humor this poor fish along. "Well, did you kill her here and keep her hid all this time, or did you just fetch her here so as to give me a treat?"

"No, the place where I killed her is fifty miles from here – maybe sixty. And I didn't bring her here. But she's here. Devils from hell must have brought her. I'll show you, and then you'll have to believe me."

"You'll show me a pair of heels, getting' away from here to where you belong at, that's what you'll show me. You be off out of this now, and you go and sleep off that load that you're carryin' around with you and in the mornin' you'll feel different about all this here murder stuff."

"I think you'll be sorry," said Staggner. "Well, there's only one other thing left for me to do." He turned his face toward where the surf just yonder was slapping against the beach.

"Here, just a minute. What's your name?"

Staggner turned to him.

"Spell it out?"

Staggner spelled it out. The name seemed to strum some thin fiddlestring of recollection in the policeman's brain. Where had he heard that name before?

"Come along, then," agreed the cop. "You get your wish. I'll leave you recite your piece to the desk man over at the station. Whatever kind of nut you are, my guess is you need to be took in out of the wet."

Behold, how on such small hinges do the big gates of circumstance sometimes swing. Had that blasé young policeman obeyed his first inclination, Siggy Gottschalk's concession at

Coney might have finished out the season as it had begun it – deep in the red ink. A wiser and a shock-proof generation must have grown up since the Chamber of Horrors at the old Eden Musée made money and the Gallery of Famous Criminals at Huber's on Fourteenth Street was turning 'em away. Siggy had figured that his Grotto of Great Murder Mysteries, with a good ballyhoo outside and a swell flash for the front entrance, ought to suck the suckers in, but from the start-off he had been a heavy loser.

Not any more though. Not with the newspapers giving him a billion dollars' worth of free advertising on their front pages; not with the dimes rattling down at the door and the boobs stampeding in and rushing on past the Elwood Case layout and the Dot King layout and the Arnold Rothstein layout to jam, with goggling eyes and round mouths and greedy ears for the spiel of the official orator – and he getting fresh dope every day out of the head-lines – in front of the section devoted to the Olivia Thames Case.

All along that Olivia Thames layout had been Siggy's pride and his masterpiece. The rest of the stuff, however true to the original models, was synthetic stuff. But this was absolutely, positively authentic. Hadn't Siggy bid in, at the sheriff's sale, the furnishings and the hangings and the other contents of Solly Lennix's Blue Room and set it up just as it was, except, of course, that the figure on the rug in the foreground was a waxworks figure, although most lifelike, so Siggy claimed? He had done that very little thing back in May, had smart Mr. Siggy. He didn't know then how smart he was. But in July he knew and everybody else knew. Siggy's masterpiece was Siggy's meal ticket now, and from now on.

JANUARY THAW

From where he sat, day after day, with his broken leg propped on a padding of pillows, the young Englishman could look out of his bedroom window upon what the citizens of the village proudly called Sugar Loaf Park.

The worthy burghers had reason for being proud of their Sugar Loaf Park. If their boasts were to be credited, there was no other town in the northern chain which had a winter playground to match this town's winter playground. Search the district through and where else but here, they asked, could you find so perfect a combination of climate and altitude, of natural setting and provided facility for enjoying cold-weather sports? Pointing out that for the past three seasons both of the hotels and all of the boarding places had been crowded as never before and that this season the crowd was the biggest yet, the claimants answered their own eager inquiries.

The young Englishman was newly come to the States, as he, being English, called them, and this was his first visit in this part of this state, but, speaking for himself, he conceded he could not imagine a finer picture of Arctic beauty than the one which his window-casings framed for him. He had, as you might say, a front seat for the show. The small house where he was lodged stood on a ledge of a steep declivity, with Finger Peak rearing up behind it, and far down below at the foot of the slope, Twisted Pond lying in the mouth of a narrowly enclosed clove which wound off and away through its skewed cleft between two neighbor-mountains toward Saranac and the larger lakes.

Because of this situation the invalid had a perfect view of the hillside. The slide for the coasters began at a point directly in front of him, and by turning his head he could follow it, with its slick paving of smoothly joined ice blocks and its steep walk-back to flank it, as it ran abruptly down like a ribbony strip cut from the selvage of a glacier.

Opposite him also, but somewhat farther distant, was the take-off for the ski-jumpers, a tousled nubbin of a knoll jutting out over the slanted drop of the land. Down yonder, where

153

perspective brought the walls of the ravine together with a sharp V, the cleared rink for the curlers' game showed like a gleaming target in the notch of a gun-sight.

All about, up and down the slope, back in among the ranked evergreens and out on the glary open, in fact, nearly everywhere one looked, were the figures of men and women and animals and like creations, all done in snow. Some of them were mere crude white clumps and some, being more ambitiously modeled, purported to represent whole family groups or famous characters in history or horses or dogs or deer or what-not.

This Annual Exhibition of Snow Statuary, to quote the grand language of the publicity printed in the city papers and in the home weekly, was a distinctive feature of the village activities, a fancy which each fall was widely advertised. There were contests for the best sculpturing, with many contestants and with judges who took their work most seriously, and with substantial prizes in each specified class. After the competition ended, volunteers added their less elaborate contributions to the display.

Whenever and for so long a time as the snow stayed soft enough and moist enough to be molded, it was quite the thing for a tobogganing party or a bobsledding party, or indeed almost anybody, to build an image before leaving the heights. In a vague way, local pride entered into the thing. It was more than a fad; it was a custom.

By now, the massy white forms stood about so numerously that when a newer design was set up, nobody except possibly its maker had any special eye for it. Besides, each succeeding storm superimposed layers of powdery fine particles on each shape of the array, blurring its contours and fattening out its bulk so that presently the effect was as though all the soldiers of a small skirmishing army had gone dropsical together.

They told the young Englishman the vista into the valley was at its loveliest during the brief Indian summer of this high country, when the hardwoods blazed out with color from their backgrounds of spruces and pines and hemlocks, but it suited him as it was now. On fine, bright, windless days he could watch the coasters and the skaters and the curlers and all, where their sweaters and Mackinaws made gay, moving splashes against the white of the drifts and the frigid blue-white of the ice.

Down to fifteen or eighteen or twenty below zero the

temperature might fall, or even lower than twenty, but so marvelously dry was the air, and so still, that none of them seemed to mind what the thermometer said about it. On the whole, though, the onlooker liked it better when the weather turned blizzardly and a great invisible force came roaring down over Finger Peak to swirl up the loose snow in a dense smother and bite the long, frozen stalactites off the eaves of the cottage and drive all living things to cover. And at night, after the wind had died down, as generally it did die down with the sunset, he, lying warmly in his bed, could hear the distant cracking of riven ice on the pond, and the nearer sharp reports as the winter split stout tree limbs asunder and when silence fell again, he could hear through it a gritty, gentle sound where the cold was etching its patterned scrolls on his window-panes; and he liked that best of all.

Smiling to himself and hugging himself, he would be comforted by one heartening thought, which thought, though he did not go so far as to put it in words, was constantly with him. And the core of this thought was that with all their splendidly friendly agencies – with their congealing frosts by night and their whipping gales by day and the white banks which grew higher and stiffened harder, both by day and by night, the polar gods unceasingly were at work to lock in his Secret all the tighter and all the faster, and make it the safest, surest secret that ever was.

He took good care to let no human creature see him smiling. Coming in on him, the middle-aged woman who was his hostess and his housekeeper, and who since his accident had been also his nurse, would find him in his armchair at his window, with the encased leg resting on the bolstered-up footstool, and he staring out with a concerned and serious look upon the snowscape beyond; and she, doing small offices for his comfort, would make commiserating little clucks with her tongue, and going out, would say to her husband:

"That nice poor good-looking young feller! It gives me a fair ache in the heart to see him settin' in there a-broodin' over his friend and a-worryin' and wonderin' over what could have happened to him and what could have become of him."

"He ain't the only one," her husband would say. "All the time I been livin' in these Adirondack regions, and that's all my life, I ain't never heard of no such a curious case as this here one, let alone us bein' drug into it ourselves, as you might say."

"But him bein' a foreigner and so lonesome and gettin' lamed-up besides – that's what makes it so bad on him," she would say.

"Yes, that would make it worse on a chap – natchelly."

The young Englishman professed to be grateful for their sympathy. Daily he discussed the mystery with one or with both of them. And he discussed it with the doctor on the occasion of the latter's professional calls. It never got any of them anywhere – all their talking; always they came back to the starting point. But they talked it over and over, and so did the village at large.

Among the villagers the crippled man went by the name of Champney – Hubert Champney. That was the name on his passport, which was a passport procured through forgery. Nobody hereabouts knew that, though. Indeed, since the disappearance of his companion nobody at all on this side of the Atlantic and nobody on the other side either, except certain individuals who for motives of self-protection might be depended upon not to betray him, knew he was using a false name and carrying fraudulent credentials.

The other man, the one now so strangely missing, had traveled hither under the name of Mortimer. By means of these aliases and by various devices, the two of them had succeeded not only in hiding their true identities but in breaking any connection between the individuals they were across the Atlantic and the fugitives – imposters, rather – they had been since reaching American soil.

They both were well-bred, plausible, shrewd young Britishers gone badly wrong, but without recorded criminal histories at home. They were smugglers of narcotics; in the jargon of the venders of those illicit goods, "dope-shovers." Mortimer, as self-styled, was himself a confirmed addict of the opium habit. Champney had never used the stuff except this once, as a merchandise.

Posing as tourists, they had landed less than two months before from a French ship, bringing with them, concealed in false trunk bottoms, large quantities of drugs which by pooling their funds they had obtained cheaply – and of course unlawfully – at a certain Continental port. It was Champney's first venture in this – if one carried it off safely – highly lucrative business.

156

Mortimer had made one such voyage before. As a habitué and as one having prior experience, he knew avenues for the quick distribution of their wares once they safely were through the gateway. They were lucky there. Their stratagem was undetected; they themselves were not suspected.

Having got by the customs people at New York, they did speedily dispose of the stuff at current prices in the underworld market. Each took his share of the proceeds in currency, in large bills; and each thereafter carried his share on his person, Champney in a money-belt worn at all times about his middle, Mortimer in a flat pouch on a slender, stout chain necklace beneath his shirt.

They had it in mind to hide for a short while and very quietly somewhere in this country – the strain on their nerves had been severe and both felt the need of a rest – and then, leaving by way of Canada, to sail from Vancouver for the Orient, there to gather a fresh supply of the forbidden products. This time they meant to deal direct with native traffickers and, by cutting out European middlemen and Yankee agents and the like, get all the profit of the import for themselves, rather than a part of it. That was Mortimer's idea and, at the beginning, it was Champney's idea, as well.

It also was by Mortimer's suggestion that they chose for their vacation this pleasant village in the north woods. He vetoed the notion of staying on in New York. The city having been the scene of their recent lucrative operations, there was, in the event of raids or arrests or confessions, danger of exposure by one of their resident accomplices, and likewise there was a remoter danger of being recognized by some one who had known them overseas.

Florida was held to be out of the question. Mortimer, being well acquainted with America, pointed out that the more southerly resorts were filled at this season with sophisticated travelers – especially Florida resorts. But he knew of a proper retreat up in the northern part of New York state.

For their present purposes it was, geographically speaking, most admirably situated. Should an unforeseen emergency arise, should one desire expeditiously to get off of Yankee territory and move beyond the jurisdiction of Yankee authorities, why, there, adjacent by just a few miles – a motor trip or a train journey of less than two hours – was the international boundary.

Moreover, this asylum offered another and a greater advantage, a prime benefit: It was a smallish community and comparatively isolated, but unlike most small interior communities, here was one wherein strangers were not conspicuous targets for local scrutiny. The reason for this lay in the facts that, to begin with, it was an all-the-year-round refuge for tubercular patients, which meant sanitariums and hotels and a shifting transient class; and in the second place, its popularity as a winter play-place brought to it at this particular time large numbers of outsiders whose comings and goings and doings were not likely to create gossip or undue curiosity.

Accordingly, in the rôles of sightseers who had heard of the magnificent climate and the scenic attractions of these parts and desired to enjoy both at their leisure, they arrived by rail on a morning in the latter end of November, following the first heavy snowfall and the first hard freeze. Their explanation was entirely acceptable to the populace – especially the parts about the climate and the scenery. Had they been Californians, these good people hardly could have been more grateful for their natural boons than they were, or more vocal when extolling the same.

For private motives, the newcomers sought a measure of privacy. They found it, and along with it, comfort, as occupants of a two-room extension of the cottage of Mr. and Mrs. Simeon Tupper, facing the farther reaches of Sugar Loaf Park. Thus established, they might watch the sports and yet not stir abroad; and they had seclusion without remoteness from the center of local things.

The Tupper house was the uppermost of a string of houses which straggled along a road, by courtesy called a street, that climbed one flank of the ravine. The main body of the village – the shops, the hotels, the sanitariums, the larger boarding places – were out of sight behind an outjutted shoulder of mountain but within convenient walking distance down the precipitous grade to the gore of the valley.

Mrs. Tupper was a hospitable body and a heaven-sent cook. She took paying guests as much for the pleasure of feeding them and mothering them as for the money they paid her. Mr. Tupper likewise favored the arrangement. It gave him company – and an audience, he being a conversationalist of renown. He was a retired guide.

Champney's project for doubling his working capital by doing away with his ally was, when first it came to him, not so much a plot as a thought, a craving. You might call it an ambition, vague as yet and formless, but persistent and alluring. To destroy that slovenly addict of a Mortimer should be an easy-enough job, he reckoned.

In his mind, before the pair of them left New York, he had canvassed various ways for accomplishing that grim result. But when a man killed a man, his work was just begun. There remained the victim's body – the *corpus delicti*, as the lawyers called it – to be disposed of. And that was the hard job, the difficult spot where so many deft assassins before him so utterly had failed and, for their failures, had gone to prison or to the rope or the chair. To eliminate this day-dreaming morphine-eater from life was one thing; but to hide the dead from mortal eyes until the killer safely was away, with his bridges burned behind him and the trail confused and broken against pursuit – that now was another and a different thing altogether.

The solution of the major problem came to Champney all of a sudden. It came to him within the second week after the two aliens were domiciled with the Tuppers. It was in the afternoon and they had just returned from a stroll – he and Mortimer – and the shivering Mortimer had gone on indoors to thaw out by the kitchen fire, and he, out on the small front porch, was kicking the balled slush off his heavy boots, when he chanced to look back over his shoulder and saw the now familiar scene on the near-by terrain – laden bobsleds whizzing down the incline and each sled loaded with whooping, thrilled passengers; a group of small boys throwing snowballs at one another over yonder in "Statuary Row" at the far edge of the slide; a party of hikers on snowshoes laboring amateurishly across the crust which coated the footway below the bouldered outcrop of the ski-jump – and in one darting flash the puzzle which had fretted him was a puzzle no longer.

It was so marvelous and yet so simple that even in that inspired and exultant moment he caught himself wondering why he had not read the riddle before, when all the while the answer to it had been spread there, plain as blue-prints, right under his nose, right in front of his eyes. In that instant the final plan began shaping itself in his brain.

Before he had clunked the length of the elbowed hallway leading to the "L" where he was housed, the design was full-developed and finished; that was how quickly it had grown up. The execution of it waited only on an opportunity, which meant waiting for certain conditions, and within the span of half a week the favorable conditions were vouchsafed and with them the opportunity.

Up to the point where Champney slipped on a glittery ice patch and fell and snapped the larger bone of his right leg just above the ankle, no hitch, no mishap occurred. And that happened fully two hours after the murder was an accomplished fact, and after the cunning strategy subsequent to the murder, in the silence and in the darkness, had been carried out.

These matters came to pass shortly before the beginning of Christmas week, on a night when there was a brisk snow-flurry on. Spilled out of some warmer cloud-current above, the snow came down thickly for a time, putting a newer and smoother coverlid on the already deeply blanketed earth. Within a little while after its fall the fierce cold would make it crisp and firm and creaky under foot-pressure. But as they fell the big flakes were moist and pliant.

The Tuppers were in their kitchen. Winters they made a sitting-room of their kitchen. Ten o'clock having struck, Mr. Tupper shut off the radio as a preliminary step to banking the coals in the range and going to bed.

"Hark, Tupper," commanded Mrs. Tupper, whose ears were keener than her husband's. "Seems like I hear something threshin' round outside."

She was right. To them from the direction of the front stoop came muffled thumping sounds as though some one with gloved fists drummed on a wooden panel, and with these, a distressed voice heard dimly.

They hurried through their cold hall, she carrying a lamp, and he opened the thick door.

"Land of Goshen!" exclaimed Mrs. Tupper.

A man was sprawled face downward across the little porch, and all smeared with white where he had dragged himself along on his hands and knees. He lifted his face to them, straining his neck, and by the lamplight they saw who he was and saw that his face was twisted with pain and fatigue.

160

"Why, it's our Mr. Champney!" cried Mrs. Tupper. "Land of Goshen, Mr. Champney, what's happened? Land of Goshen, whatever are you doin' out here?"

"I'm hurt," he told them, panting on his words. "I fell – fell just out there and hurt myself... Mind!" He gasped the warning sharply as Mr. Tupper stooped and laid hold on him and sought to heave him upright. "Careful, please. One of my legs is quite helpless; sprained, I'm afraid – or broken."

Between them the couple managed to get him back to the hot kitchen and stretched on a sofa that was there, a clammy perspiration breaking out on his skin as they eased him down.

"You do what you can for him, Mother," Mr. Tupper bade her from a closet, where he pawed for his boots and his ulster. "I'll run over next door to Mitchell's phone and git a doctor up here quicker'n scat!"

"Wait!" commanded the injured man, speaking from between his clenched teeth. "While you're about it, get through to your local constabulary and have them send some of their men up at once."

"Our local which?" asked Mr. Tupper blankly.

"Your police agency. And scurry about the neighborhood, too, for men. We shall need aid to find Mortimer." (Thereafter the plotter was to congratulate himself that even in that time of agony he had bethought him to ask for searchers; it strengthened his story; gave it plausibility, made it appear that his prime concern had been not for himself but for his friend.)

"Mortimer?"

"Surely – Mortimer. He's out there somewhere. I went out seeking for him – that's how I was hurt. After wandering about calling for him everywhere, I started back to notify you. It was then that I fell on a slickness of ice. An hour ago – perhaps longer – I missed him from his room. His greatcoat was there – he'd left it behind. He must have gone out quietly by the door of the side passage behind out rooms. Otherwise you in here would have seen him or heard him."

"Whyn't you call me to help you hunt?" demanded Mr. Tupper. "I got a flash-light. I know the lay of the land better'n you gentlemen do."

"There was a reason – a reason why I preferred to go alone."

"But land of Goshen, Mr. Champney, what could 'a' took him

out a night like this without his overcoat on and it cold as Greenland and snowin' besides?"

"That I must tell you. I meant to keep it from every one – for his sake. But of course now it must come out. I'm sorry. Mortimer – poor chap – is a drug fiend; has been one for years, I think. You may have noticed his tendency at times – and especially toward evening – to behave peculiarly; to turn dull and drowsy?"

"Land of Goshen, but ain't I noticed it, though? Gettin' so logy right after his supper! And us never guessin' why!"

"Quite so, Mrs. Tupper. To-night I thought him even more under the influence than usual. I got him to his room early, you remember, and heard no more from him; then, presently, went in to see whether he was asleep." (How cunningly now, he told himself as he paused a space as though from exhaustion, was he combining fact with falsehood to make a suspicion-proof fabric. Who hereafter would have cause to guess out the truth – a half-stupefied wretch lured on specious pretext to venture out-of-doors, to be led stumblingly along, dumb and unwitting, to his quick, bloodless end? And then the sequel, the wonderful crafty sequel to this violent chapter!)

"So, as I tell you, I went to see how he fared – and he was gone, and his bed not disturbed. And unless he returned by the same way, while I was casting about the vicinity, I sorely fear for him."

"Lemme look!" called Mr. Tipper, and on that was lumbering through the rear hall; then as speedily lumbering back again with his news. "Not there and no signs of him neither," he proclaimed, his own alarm – in his case a genuine alarm – rising within him.

"It's as I feared. I'm afraid in his dazed condition he wandered into some awkward quarter. So please, Mr. Tupper, before you summon a physician for me – I'm easier now – please notify your chief constable's office and take steps to rouse some of your neighbors."

"Land, yes, Tupper, and be spry as you can. Why, likely it's ten below out there right this minute."

"I'm gone," promised Mr. Tupper, and on the instant was.

Afterward the young Britisher was glad, really glad, that he had smashed his leg; it was good fortune disguised as ill fortune, he figured. Elsewise the impulse to get away might have been too strong for him. Had he yielded to that perilous temptation – and looking back on it, he almost was sure he must have yielded – his departure, if too quick a departure, might have been interpreted as flight. Besides, as things stood, he must bide on and could watch, without trepidation, but instead with a growing satisfaction, the course of the search for the vanished man; a quest conducted first with intensity, then diminishing, and finally altogether abandoned as a thing still unsolved but utterly hopeless.

Lying helpless, with weights hitched to his leg and dangling by a harness of straps over the footboard of his bed, he had at the first some hidden perturbations – as naturally he would. But at once, with a mounting inner confidence, he saw how all natural forces conspired together to be his dependable allies.

To begin with there were no tracks to lead those nocturnal searchers in any given direction. The snow, coming down so thick and fine and soft, had covered up any footprints within a space of minutes after they were recorded. The furrowed marks of his own crawling and floundering route, from the place where he fell in the Park to the Tuppers' door-yard, were obliterated by the time the hastily recruited posse of volunteers turned their lanterns on the smooth white carpeting there.

The snowfall ceased about midnight so that when daylight came the body of a frozen man should have been easily discernible by the eyes of those who diligently explored in every cleft and cranny of the mountainside, and crossed and recrossed every thicketed edging of the ridge. A dead body would have been partly covered, true, but it would not wholly have been buried from sight. There was no body and no sign of one. And the ice on Twisted Pond was steel-hard and a foot thick and showed no proof of having lately been broken.

From the outset, all possibility that the missing man could have quitted the town by his own volition was eliminated. No person answering to his description had boarded the one train which during the night halted at the local station; no such person had sought to hire a privately owned vehicle. It wasn't humanly possible that over the ice-coated, drift-walled highways leading out of the village any thinly clad man afoot could have traveled far before he dropped; or that his stiffened shape could by any

163

natural agency completely have been hidden from view after he did drop.

Altogether, it was quite incredible that a grown man so entirely and without trace could vanish exactly as though he had been caught up bodily into the skies; and yet, incredible as it was, it was the fact. The languishing search narrowed into nothing at all, and at nothing, through what was left of December and through nearly all of January, it remained.

Outwardly all grieved solicitude, Champney repeated his narrative over and over for the benefit of sundry official investigators – the village police chief, the persistent county prosecutor, the sheriff of the county, a representative of the nearest British consulate, who came to inquire and remained to marvel, and went away as baffled as the rest. It was evident to Champney that on its face and for the full of its face value, they accepted his story.

He told them what he professed to know of Mortimer's antecedents, giving to the other a purely fictional and sketchy background which, however, was accepted without question since, to his hearers, there seemed to be no reason why any one of them should question it. Moreover, its main points found seeming confirmation in Mortimer's effects – his few papers, his passport and all. No one gave a sign of doubting Champney's statement that he had met Mortimer on shipboard and, finding him congenial and pitying him for his habit, had chummed with him.

On his own suggestion, Champney sent off letters to a mythical address in London, he being privately very well assured that long before those letters came back as unclaimed – if indeed they came back at all – he would be on his way into Western Canada under another name than Champney and moving by a devious and purposely misleading itinerary. But if by any chance they did come back before he left the country, what would it matter except to strengthen the already well-buttressed assumption that Mortimer, by reason of his secret vice, had broken contact with his people. Becoming an itinerant, a foot-loose and more or less irresponsible peregrine?

By fault of a distemper in his blood or his marrows, Champney's fracture, under its cast and its bindings, was somewhat slow in knitting, so that after he ceased to be bedfast, he still was house-bound. At length, though, he was provided with crutches and now, a month after his injury, was learning to use them. By their aid he could get about his room, could swing himself along to his meals. In another week, at most within ten days, he would be ready to move on.

What he liked best to do was to sit at his window, the splinted limb outstretched and resting on a mound of Mrs. Tupper's sofa cushions, his crutches against his chair, a book or a newspaper on his lap, the money, all of the money, in the belt about his middle where through his clothing he could touch and fondle the bulges it made, and he peering out to see how, on the rough days, the wind came sweeping down over the scuffed and rumpled slope and snapped the thick but brittle icicles off the clashing tree limbs and off the audibly wheezing roof ledges, and piled the loose snow in windrows, only to flatten these as soon as they were fashioned; and on fair days to see the young fellows in their gay lumbermen's shirts skylarking on skis or skates or with sleds, and the pretty girls – for they all looked pretty, what with their hair flying and their cheeks reddened by the chill – the pretty girls shrieking gleefully as they sped down the toboggan lane on past the close-ranked gallery of swollen snow-figures, gathering speed miraculously and all in a breath becoming small flying dots in the clear distance half a mile away.

And just to think, now, that through every hour and every minute of every hour the dependable tireless elements wrought at their crafts to keep the secret of his guilt safe from any human eye but his eye! There could be no treachery, no turn of fickleness in helpers so steadfast and so constant. He could hug himself at the very thought of it. When no one was by, he sometimes did hug himself – literally.

There was a night when he slept badly. The customary night noises – those clamorous outbursts when the ice was crackled or the trees were split apart, those lesser grating, scratchy sounds of frost-pictures forming on the windows and the groanings of the solid timbers of the house and the minor craunching protests which the snow gave off sometimes if the northern lights were playing across the horizon – had come to be a part of his subconsciousness, soothing him to sleep.

But this night there was a new and rifty note which disturbed the customary harmonies. It disturbed him into wakefulness a full hour before his regular hour for awaking. It was a prevalent *drip-drip-drip* note. He couldn't make it out. It depressed him. It somehow was disturbing to him, almost ominous, akin to an outright foreboding.

Before the tardy daylight had strengthened, Mr. Tupper came in with a lamp to stoke up the live embers in the drum stove and replenish the fire with cordwood chunks and open the dampers; and the now acutely uneasy Champney said to him:

"Good morning. Surely it can't be raining?"

"Nope," said Mr. Tupper, tinkering with the drafts; "not yit."

"Not yet?"

"Not yit, but soon. That what you've been hearin' is melted stuff pourin' off the roof. But it will be rainin' a plenty soon, the way the clouds is bankin' up to the south-erd and the way the air feels. She's comin' – fact, you might go so fur as to say she's already arrove. Wind's swung 'round and blowin' spang right out of the south. And you ought to see the way the mercury outside my window is started humpin' up the tube. Climbin' same as if it has a flame under it. Yes, sir, she's practically already here!"

"She? What do you mean by she?"

"Why the January thaw, tubby sure," explained Mr. Tupper, and he much pleased to be the bearer of news. "She's a mite late this year, but she's busy declarin' her intents and purposes even this early in the day. Sometimes, but that ain't usual, she don't come at all and sometimes she don't come till February and onc't or twic't, in a specially mild winter, I seen her come back and repeat herself two-three times. But generally speakin' she's due in January. So that's why we call her the January thaw."

"But I thought you told me often that your springs were invariably much belated – that sometimes the ice did not clear from your streams until April or even early in May." Champney was striving to keep the quickening anxiety out of his voice.

"Oh, it's jest a temporary thing; it ain't got a mite to do with real spring. Everything'll stiffen up again good and hard; don't let nobody worry about that. And the ice won't go out of the brooks, not for six weeks yit at the least. It'll mush up some and git rotten on the top down in the pond, so as to spile the skatin' and the other games fur the time bein', but it won't break plum' up – nope!"

"Oh!" There was a world of relief in the word. "Then by your January thaw you mean a slight softening only?"

"Slight softenin' be dern! If she stays this way – and my guess is she's likely to stay this way for the better part of a week, anyhow – you'll see somethin'. By this time to-morrow, if not sooner, you're liable to see that fancy slick-mer-slide out yonder turnin' into a regular waterfall. And the drifts meltin' away like butter on a spittin'-hot spider. And a smoky-lookin' mist risin' everywhere. And seepy bare mud – great wide shoals of it – showin' through where now everythin's two feet deep in solid white." Garrulous Mr. Tupper, bringing his light, came nearer to the bed to expand his tale at close range, and Champney, knowing full well that naked fear must be looking out of his eyes, turned his face away.

"I remember one time – right after New Year's it was – she hung on and hung on till, exceptin' maybe for a few sheltered corners like down in deep hollows, every last par-tickle of snow was absolutely gone. Joke certainly was on them big spraddle-footed snowshoe-rabbits then. Fellow with a gun couldn't hardly miss one if he tried. Way the weather's actin' now, you're likely to see that same sight repeatin' itself – them poor old bewildered hares bobbin' round on the wet brown ground, lookin' big as woolly elephants.

"Nope, Mr. Champney, till you've seen one of our genuwine January thaws you ain't seen nothin'. But mark my words, you'll be seein' one in full swing before sunset this evenin'... Well, Mother'll be fetchin' you your breakfast soon as you git up and git yourself dressed."

Champney got up and got dressed. But he ate no breakfast. He couldn't eat. His panic, a tangible thing, having solidity to it and weight, made a lump in his throat; made heavy dead feelings at the pit of his stomach. Nor could he touch the midday meal.

He hurt Mrs. Tupper's feelings by refusing to go to the dinner table; by declining to have her bring him his victuals on a tray. He didn't feel just right, he said; his appetite was poorly, telling her this with his head averted so that she might not read the pulsing-hot terror that was on him.

Through that long day of desperation, he huddled behind his window watching the incredibly swift disintegration of a vast white-and-blue pageantry. Before his sickened eyes he saw how the splendid ironwork of winter, forged on winter's clanging anvils into tight hoops to band the imprisoned world in, was coming unwelded.

He saw how the very structures of his defense were crumbling and disintegrating. For he saw the rain coming down in sheets upon the deserted hill; saw the snow lose its sharp crystalline aspect and go sodden and honeycombed; saw runlets of water grow to impetuous small cataracts; saw first one bloaty snow effigy and, later on, a second give a drunken lurch and topple over; saw the icicles shrinking, as little streams ran from their yielding tips; saw in every trickling drop and every loosening formation a hideous, unrelenting threat for him; saw the moment of his exposure advancing on him, inevitably, inexorably.

If only the wind would veer north before it was too late! If only he could get away! But whither could a man flee who hobbled on two sticks, who was as plainly fixed in his true person as though he carried a banner to advertise his identity? But he must do something to save himself. He has to do something to fend off, to delay destruction. His frantic need honed his wits without sharpening his wits – an agony rasping at his brain but only making it the more futile.

He had to do something! After a while, through his travail, he knew what that something would be. But he must wait – if for so long he could hold himself back – for darkness to cloak him or at least for twilight, before he set about doing it; a mad thing, but the only thing left for him to do.

He couldn't hold himself back, though. His control snapped – snapped before the dusk was thick enough to hide his movements. It wouldn't have mattered, though, not in the long run, because his doom already had him tagged and labeled.

Between four and five o'clock Mr. Tupper, with the collar of his leather jacket turned up against the driving rain, and with his rubber boots making squashy noises, came out of the kitchen door and took the left turn behind the house, bound for the wood-pile. With a small start of astonishment he noted that the door at the end of the wing was open. So he went nearer and there were fresh tracks – footprints – and spaced beyond them, like punctuation marks, round deep holes plainly signifying the use of crutches; and this trail led down the steps and around the lower corner of the extension. By stooping and squinting, Mr. Tupper could make them out.

Now, why should that young fellow choose such an hour and such a day for his first excursion outdoors? This thing was mighty funny; a thing calling for an investigation. Mr. Tupper got his flash-light out of the pocket of his windbreaker, where he carried it for emergencies, and flipped the light on and followed the tracks where they led him through the murk out of the yard and diagonally across the slope beyond. He mended his gait, splashing into the sloppy, semiliquid underfooting and sending his narrow dart of light spying this way and that on ahead.

Out of the gloom the long pencil of light at once picked up a black figure down in a huddle on the soft snow clear over yonder in "Statuary Row," as it was called. From where he was, it looked to Mr. Tupper as though Mr. Champney, having gone that far, had fallen and was wriggling about in an effort to get up again. That was the impression he got.

So he broke into a lumbering canter, at the same time calling out. There was no answer to his hail. Mr. Champney seemed not to hear him, seemed not to be aware of his presence or of the illumination he brought, even when he puffed up alongside and turned the bulb so that its focused radiance made a bright circle on things thereabouts. Oblivious to all else, Mr. Champney was down on all fours frantically employed on a crazy business of his own.

Mr. Tupper saw now what that business was, and he gave a shrill horrified hoot. He saw a man who had been strangled; whose body had been laid by then, with the legs spraddled and the arms outstretched until a ten-below-zero temperature had made it rigid in that posture – what a time of waiting that must have been! – which body then had been set upright and braced with props, while the slayer was encasing it inches deep in a plastic perfect covering against detection.

To be exact about it, Mr. Tupper did not in that one tremendous moment see all of this grisly spectacle. All of it was to be seen by him later, as a physical exhibit, and confirmed as to its details by a confession. The part revealed to Mr. Tupper was one frozen leg showing from the knee downward – a trousered stark leg upon which Mr. Champney was furiously plastering

169

scooped-up handfuls of soppy snow in a frenzied and foolish effort to remake his dead man into a good snow-man again.

CABBAGES AND KINGS

The wind came up with the sun, so for an hour or so at our point we have fairly good shooting, mainly on mallard and teal. But before eight o'clock the wind fell away and soon then died on us and the flight was over. Barring when an occasional single buzzed across the stool, we got no chance to warm our gun-barrels.

From down the twisted bayou where Long and Atkins were stationed, we could hear, about once in so often, a shot or a couple of shots and by that we knew they weren't doing much for their country either. The flocks would be drowsing outside beyond the bar, in rafts and flotillas, and there they would stay until evening unless the breeze picked up again, which didn't seem likely with the weather as it was. Our decoys sat as still as you please, each with a shadow under it which exactly mirrored the original, color and all, and that show was calculated to deceive none but a very near-sighted or very absent-minded duck. Out of our sight in the saw-grass we could hear a whole synod of grebes chattering and spattering, but the sky above us showed as a blue Delft bowl, not a cloud in it – nor a bird. With our gum-booted feet in the mud we relaxed, and the old thermos was brought forth to yield a swig of coffee apiece, and Thorne lighted his pipe and I lighted a cigar and we let the world wag on as we talked of this and that. Our guide wouldn't be bringing the push-boat for us until toward noon. Among many virtues a duck-hunter must have is patience.

All at once, from behind us there was a silken whistling of stout wings, and a big bull-mallard whizzed by, banking on an acute angle. It seemed he must have been making a late breakfast in the rice-stubble, otherwise there was no earthly excuse for him to be curving out of that quarter at this time of the day and in such a rush. Thorne grabbed up his automatic and made a swell snap-shot, and that large passer-by came slanting down, kerflop, in the edge of the marsh to the right, and made the first and only ripples on the water that we had seen for an hour or more. He righted himself and Thorne poised, ready to give him a finishing load in case he made for the tall rushes. But this fellow wasn't a cripple, he was a real casualty.

Swimming in small circles, he began nodding like a drunken man who automatically agrees with everything you're saying. He nodded faster and faster, then slower and slower, and then in a fine valedictory flutter turned bottomside up, with his broad, bright-yellow feet folding in like two pond-lilies at sundown, and immediately after that was no more. Thorne waded out, going carefully through the soft ooze, and fetched deceased in and dumped him with the rest of our bag at the back of the blind.

"We kind of stole that baby, didn't we?" he said as he sat down again alongside me.

"We? You flatter me."

"Anyhow, he's ours." He retamped his pipe. "Say, tell me," he said next, "did I ever tell you about the Doctor Trout murder case?"

"No," I said, "but you're going to, I can see that. Whatever put the Whatyoumaycallem murder into your mind?"

"Old Mr. Green-head here did – in a way of speaking."

"Was there a dead duck or a load of duck-shot or something else duckish mixed up in the thing, then?"

"No, it wasn't that way at all. Say, did you ever stop to think how one thing reminds you of another thing and that thing of something else and so on until in about a minute you're a million miles away from where you started? And you stop and wonder how the dickens that particular subject came to hop into your mind? But if you'll only work back, you'll see how it's all part of an unbroken chain – one link tied to another and each one suggesting something else that's more or less vaguely related to it. The Walrus in *Alice in Wonderland* wasn't so daffy when he said the time had come to talk about shoes and ships and sealing-wax, and cabbages and kings. I claim he wasn't. Why wouldn't cabbages bring up kings if there was a connection somewhere? Now, you take this fat drake that just got plastered: While he was passing out, out yonder, I said to myself he ought to make a lovely meal for somebody, but wasn't it a pity that guide's wife of ours didn't know how to cook a duck decently but must always fry him good and hard? And that made me think of the way a good French chef can fix up a duck so he'll just naturally get up off the platter and fly down your throat; and I said to

172

myself, wasn't it a pity our country people couldn't handle food the way those French peasants can? And that reminded me of some of the bad cooking I'd run into at company messes and even regimental messes when I was with the A.E.F. over there in France; and that brought up field-kitchens at the front; and that brought up what I saw a shell do once to one of our field-kitchens, and that brought up something that I took, that time, off a dead soldier – or what was left of him; and that brought up the Trout murder case; and there you are, all in about one-twentieth of the time I'm taking now to map out the sequence of it for you."

"All of which would seem to make you an exciting back-number of the *North American Review*," I said. "Well, go on with the tale, because that's where you're heading for. I'm one of those rarely gifted geniuses that can listen with one eye and watch the heavens for stray birds with the other."

"You're darned tooting that's where I'm head for," he agreed. The board under us creaked as he settled himself back to begin. I may say right here that this friend of mine, Dan Thorne, is of a rare species. He's almost the only one of his sort I've ever met. He's an educated man who deliberately chose to be a policeman; not that all policemen are uneducated men, because to claim that would be claiming what's untrue. I've known college graduates – yes, one ex-college professor – who wore brass buttons and pounded beats in thick-soled shoes. But here, understand, was a man who, having no need for the money he might earn at the calling, and belonging to a family whose male members were professional men if they weren't business men or planters, yet elected to join the Memphis police force when he came out of the University of Virginia, after having taken a law course there. He was ordinary patrolman at first, but he didn't stay ordinary patrolman for long. His chief discovered he had natural aptitude along certain trends and took the youngster out of uniform and put plain clothes on him and pretty soon he was making better than a local name for himself as a detective. Before we got into the war he took a leave of absence and entered an officers' training-camp, and when the break came he had his commission and went overseas as a captain in one of the first contingents to get over. His inclinations were for service in the line but with his schooling the Military Intelligence section was plainly indicated

173

for him and, for a wonder, a man especially fitted for a particular job was given that job by those little tin gods on wheels who spent so many congenial hours trying to fit the round peg into the square hole, and then wondered why the gears wouldn't mesh sometimes. After the mess was ended he came home, limping a trifle – a machine-gun bullet bored his knee three days before Armistice – and since then he had been rather at loose ends for regular occupation, with plenty of money to spend, an uncle having died and left him a really handsome estate. He didn't feel like settling down, he said. For the sport of the thing, the love of the game, he sometimes did help out the authorities in his part of the South, when there was a puzzling crime to be unraveled, working under cover, though, as a sort of unpaid volunteer aide. But in the open season on wild fowl he gunned pretty steadily; for to him no call was so strong as the call of the marshes. This was the second fall for the two of us, shooting together down in the Gulf country, and out of his store of experience I already had heard yarns which were worth listening to and, some of them, useful for fabrication into copy. So this morning, during the lull, when he showed signs of getting set to tell a tale, my inner ears twitched, even though I might pretend to being only mildly interested.

He made the board creak again and was off: "That Trout killing now;" he said, "that was one killing that I managed to untangle up all by my little self and then just kept my trap closed and let the party that had done the killing get away with it, so that the only credit I got out of it was out of my own conscience. I figure it might not have been exactly ethical for me to do that, that is it wouldn't if I'd still been a regular cop working for wages and bound by an oath. But as a free lance, which I was – well, anyhow, I'll let you say when I'm through whether I did the right thing.

"It happened about a year and a half after I got back from the other side. By then my leg was as good as it's ever going to be. I'd had a couple of operations and a lot of treatment but it was evident the joint would always be stiff. Fussing around with hospitals and specialists had given me occupation for a spell but now I was restless and inclined to drift with the current. The after-effects of war take lots of fellows that way, as you know. I thought for a while of going into the government secret service –

they offered me a berth – but I passed that up after going up to Washington and talking it over with the head of the bureau. Then I went on to New York for a while. On the way back home that trip I stopped over in Chattanooga for a day or so with an old classmate of mine who'd been shot and gassed both, during the St. Mihiel drive and was in bad shape. On my second morning there I was knocking about down-town and ran into a fellow I'd known ever since the old days – Fred Gaither was his name and he came from Baltimore originally. He had been a Burns operative once. Now, so he told me right off, he'd opened up shop as a private detective. He asked me what I was doing and I said I wasn't doing anything in particular and found it rather a tiresome job. As I said that, I saw a kind of light come into his eyes and he asked me if I had ten minutes to spare. I told him yes – ten minutes or ten days or ten months, so far as that went. 'Great,' he said. 'Come along with me then. My office is right up-stairs here.'

"So when we got up there he said, 'Dan, I've got something that's right down your street – a murder case with some mighty unusual features to it. I've been working on it myself; had a couple of my best men working on it, too, and we've got nowhere. Now,' he says, 'there's a nice juicy reward posted – five hundred offered by the state and a thousand more that the widow of the man who was killed added on. If you care to tackle it and can run down the guilty party, whoever he is, I'll make any sort of deal about the money end that's agreeable to you, except that I'd like to see this agency get the glory. It's the case of a certain Dr. Adrian Trout, who was assassinated up here in the mountains not far from the Kentucky line, at Uniondale. Maybe you read something about it?'

"I had – a dispatch in a Washington paper. 'But that was three or four weeks ago,' I said. 'The trail's cold by now.'

"'No colder than it was from the beginning,' he says. 'This trail was born cold and hasn't warmed up since. I'll be honest with you,' he says; 'this is a tough puzzle, this Trout killing. But I'll stand all expenses and if you come through with it you can have the whole fifteen hundred or, if you want to split on any sort of basis, you just name the terms and I'm agreeable to whatever you say.'

"'I don't require expenses and I don't need the money,' I said.

175

"'Well, I do,' he says. 'I've just started up on my own hook and expenses have been heavy and business is still slow although I've picked up one or two accounts – banks and business houses – that bring in something. But what this concern of mine needs more than anything else to make it a go is a reputation. And if somebody on my staff cleared up this killing after the local people and the imported investigators, including myself, have fallen down, why, the free advertising we'd get here would be worth a lot to me personally. Won't you join in with me, Dan,' he says, 'for old times' sake? Besides,' he says, 'you might get a big kick out of it.'

"'Well,' I said, 'if you put it that way –'

"'I do put it that way,' he says. And with that he began hauling records and reports and newspaper clippings and what-not out of a filing cabinet.

"Well, the upshot was that I got steamed up and spent the morning going over the stuff and discussing the different angles of it with Fred Gaither, and the next day I was on my way with him in his car into the mountains northwest of Chattanooga. Where the decent highway ended I left him and he turned back – it had been agreed that I should handle the thing by myself – and I hired a buckboard and rode the last eighteen miles into this little town of Uniondale over one of the worst apologies for a road on God's green earth. You couldn't get in there by rail or anywhere near it by rail. It's a county-seat but it's tucked away there in the knobs, miles from anywhere – a typical mountain town, one of the few that are left just as they were before the automobiles came – and it's populated by typical mountain people. You know the type, being from Kentucky yourself?"

I nodded and at the same time pointed. To our left, one lonesome ring-neck was flipping to and fro over the rushes in the hurried but aimless fashion of the ring-neck tribe. We made ready for him but all of a sudden he remembered that this wasn't the place where he'd left his umbrella and quit hunting for it and flickered past, forty yards distant, and vanished downstream like a wind-blown leaf.

Thorne laid his gun back down and went on: "I got there about dark, and put up at the leading hotel. It had to be the leading hotel because it was the only one. You've guessed it – about eight guest-rooms and you carry up your own ice-water and towels – it you can find any towels – and they have pink water-proof soap and they call it the Fifth Avenue or the Grand. They called this one the Grand. I didn't pretend to be a canvasser taking orders for crayon portraits or a timber-cruiser or a solicitor getting subscriptions for some farm magazine – that's old stuff and doesn't get you anywhere, either. I didn't pretend to be anything but what I was, and so the first thing I did after I'd taken a bath in a wash-basin and eaten supper with everything fried except the coffee – and it might have been improved if they'd fried it – was to go out and hunt up the sheriff and the coroner and the county attorney, and lay my cards on the table and tell them frankly who I represented. In a way, I spoke the same language they spoke, and in another way I didn't – we were all of us native Tennesseans but they were mountaineers and I was a lowlander. Anyhow, I told 'em what I was there for and, of course, inside of fifteen minutes the news must have been all over the place.

"Probably I'd better give you a sort of picture of the case, the way it stood when I got there. This murdered man, Dr. Adrian Trout, had been born and raised in the county on a creek with the interesting name of Stubtoe Creek. His people must have been more prosperous than the run of their neighbors because they'd been able to send him off to medical college, and after he'd graduated he came back and opened up for practise among his own folks. If you stirred up the undercurrents of popular opinion it didn't take you very long to find out he'd never been exactly popular, either as a young hillbilly growing up or as a citizen. For one thing, his general disposition was against him – he was inclined to be dictatorial and overbearing and stuck-up over the fact that he'd had an education – and besides, his reputation for running after women wasn't as good as it might be. Then, in '17 he'd served as medical examiner for the local draft-board and that wasn't calculated to make friends for him – up there in the knobs they didn't always look very kindly on the draft. France was an awful long distance off to those people. Even so, it didn't appear that he'd had any real outspoken enemies. His family never had been mixed up in any of the old feuds; fact was this particular county never had a feud in it. There was no record that he'd ever been in a serious fight or been threatened by anyone. He just wasn't trusted, that was all, and he never had been liked in the community. But, you'd say that not being liked was no reason why anybody should want to bump him off, and wait months or years for the chance to do it, too.

"Well, be that as it may, while the war was still on or about the time it ended, he up and married a well-to-do widow from near Nashville, a woman who was considerably older than he was. He must have been about thirty-five then. And he moved down to the town where she lived and never once came back again until four days before he was killed.

"He came back on account of some legal formalities in connection with the settling up of a little scrap of an estate in which he had an interest. It would seem he did quite a bit of strutting up and down the main street, which was almost the only street worth the name. He was showing off his city-made clothes and his affluence and his importance. Well, on the fourth day, shortly after dinner-time, which would make it about one-thirty o'clock in the afternoon, he went to the county clerk's office, which was in the fore part of the little court-house, to get a copy of a certain transcript. The clerk hadn't quite finished copying it – they kept most of their records in longhand up there – and Trout told him he'd go outside, it being cooler out there than it was inside, and wait until the job was done. He was aiming to leave that same day.

"Well, according to the clerk, it couldn't have been more than two minutes after that when he heard a thump and a sort of scuffling sound at the front entrance. He dropped what he was doing and ran out. Trout was lying sprawled in the doorway. He'd been shot in front, right through the heart. He was dead by the time the clerk got to him. There was nobody in sight – on a warm day in a little country-town people are not apt to stir about much for an hour or so after midday; you know that without me telling you. The clerk looked up and down and he said that for an appreciable space, before people who'd heard the report began to hop outdoors, the little square and the street in front of it were absolutely deserted. If there was any eyewitness to the killing, nobody ever found him or her.

"Immediately, though, it was easy enough to figure where the shot had been fired from. It had been fired from somewhere upon a rather steep little hill which rose on the far side of the street and faced the county square. There was a store and a

178

harness-shop directly across from the court-house but the shot couldn't have come from that level. The course of the wound proved that – the shot had slanted downward at rather a steep angle, proving that it must have been fired from well above the opposite house-line. Now, above the shops up on the hill were two buildings and only two – both of them dwellings, one stuck in the side of the hill a few yards above the other, and both reached by footpaths from the street. Otherwise the hill was bare – no trees on it, no thick bushes, no anyplace where a human being could hide. What's more, the clerk stuck to it that he glanced at that hill a moment after he reached Trout's side. In fact, he said he did more than just glance; he said he searched the whole side of it with his eye and saw nothing moving. Measurements showed that if Trout was sitting down on a bench that stood just outside the court-house doorway, the shot might very well have come from the general direction of the lower one of the two hillside houses opposite; from inside of it or from behind it or from under it – it stood on posts a foot and a half off the ground – or even from just over the ridgepole of its roof. On the other hand, if he was standing up, the shot might have come from the approximate direction of the uppermost of the two houses. But nobody could testify whether he was standing or sitting, and that complicated things. No weapon was found in or near either of these two houses, no footprints either, although, the grass being fairly thick in places and the footpaths hard and dry, it would have been difficult to find foot-tracks if they were there. And, so far as the residents of the two houses were concerned – I'll come to them individually in a minute – there wasn't any earthly reason for anybody to suspect that they or any one of them could have had a hand in the killing or any knowledge of it before or after. There wasn't any earthly reason to suspect anybody at all. The most commonly accepted theory was that the assassin must have been lying in ambush under or behind one or the other of the houses and either that he got away unobserved in the first hullabaloo of excitement, or that he stayed concealed right where he was until things had quieted down, and then escaped. But to offset that, the county clerk – and a reasonably alert, intelligent chap he was – said his first scrutiny of the face of the hill had been thorough even though it was a hasty one, and besides, inside of five minutes after Trout dropped searchers led by a deputy sheriff who happened to be in the back part of the court-house building, were swarming all over the slope. It was exactly as though death had come leaping at the man from the rounded slant of that hill – like a bolt of lightning, like a dart out of the earth, like anything uncanny and mysterious and unhuman that you want to imagine.

"But wait, that wasn't the freakiest feature of it, not by a long shot it wasn't. They had an autopsy on the body – sort of an autopsy, anyhow. The bullet, passing through the body at that downward slant it took, had stopped just under the skin in the small of the back, almost touching the spinal column. They dug it out and it wasn't a regular bullet at all. It wasn't even lead. It was a roughly circular slug or chunk of some dull hard metal. At first they thought it might be brass. Afterward it turned out to be a bronze composition. It might have been a mutilated button or a pounded-up scrap of a badge or a lodge emblem – something of that nature. There was no telling for sure."

Thorn stopped and tamped a fresh charge into his pipe and borrowed a match from me. There was hardly a breath of air stirring; the blue smoke of his tobacco rose straight up in a solid-looking little spindle. There in the shelter of our ambuscade it was like an August day for warmth and stillness. He went on:

"That's a rough sketch of how matters stood when I struck this little town of Uniondale. I slept on it that night and next morning I climbed the knoll and met the members of the two households that lived up there. I'll take the first house first. I'll boil the facts down: First house: three rooms, plank construction, unpainted, fairly new. Owned by one Anderson Padgett, carpenter by trade. He built it himself, odd times. He lives there with his wife and a new baby. Straightforward, hard-working young pair; stand well with their neighbors. Here's Padgett's story to me: He's sitting in the middle room, nursing the baby while his wife, back in the kitchen, is washing up the dinner dishes. He hears a shot, and knows it must have been fired from close by, but can't make up his mind exactly where it came from owing to being indoors and owing also to the echo against the hill. For the moment he isn't deeply concerned; in a country where shooting at a mark is still a favorite outdoor pursuit of the inhabitants, a shot generally doesn't mean much. After a minute or two, though, decides to see what's doing, if anything. Puts the

180

baby on the bed, goes to the front door, and across the way he sees the county clerk alongside a body and sees people coming at a run. His wife confirms his account. Her experience is practically the same as his except that she rather thinks the gun cracked at the back of their house toward the left, whereas he's inclined to say it might have been slightly below and, if anything, off to the right. Innocence written all over both of them; both formerly acquainted with Trout but no record that either of them ever had any dealings with him or bore him any grudge. That's that. Let's temporarily eliminate Padgett and move on; he's a short horse and soon curried.

"Now then, we're going to climb sixty feet up the slope to the second house. It's an old-time log cabin – what they call a double cabin. You know the style – two rooms, separate cabins, really, set side by side, with one roof to cover 'em both and an open space or 'gallery' – to give it the country name – in between. Two women live here – a sick young woman that's bedfast, and an old crippled woman that's looking after her. The young woman's name is Byers – Martha Byers, according to the data in my hands. She's married but she's shy a husband. His name is Tobe Byers, harmless enough but a pretty tolerable worthless party, by all accounts. They've been married less than two years. She'd always been in poor health but lately when she became a confirmed invalid he just up and ran off and left her and nobody knows his present whereabouts – the trifling, dirty scoundrel! After he abandons her, she gets word to the old crippled woman who's no kin to her but who, it seems, was a sort of foster-mother to her before her marriage, and the old woman leaves her own shack back up in the mountains somewhere and comes down to nurse her and look after her. Other than this old woman there isn't a soul to whom the young woman can turn. One look at her and you can write this poor little thing's ticket. She's got consumption and is almost through. The death-look is on her; her voice is almost gone. And her arm-bones are like pipe-stems. The old woman is a character. Everybody calls her 'Aunt Lizzie' except the dying girl and she calls her 'Mom'; on Gaither's notes she's down as 'Lizzie Johnson, unmarried, commonly known as Aunt Lizzie.' She's close to seventy, I'd say, but well-preserved for her age. Before she fell off a mule years before and broke her hip, she could do a man's work, so they say, and could handle

181

tools almost like a man. Now she hobbles about on a crutch – an awkward-looking thing, painted a bright red and heavily padded at the arm-crotch and the hand-grip with rags, evidently a home-made crutch. Offhand, my guess is that it's one she made herself. Considering her weight – she's a broad, heavy woman – she gets about on it pretty briskly, though.

"She can do a woman's work, too – that's plain to be seen. That little shanty is clean as a pin inside and everything in apple pie order. She's absolutely devoted to the sick woman; anybody can see that. She wears a pair of rusty old glasses with thread wrapped around the part that goes over the bridge of the nose, and she still has all her teeth, and she has a broad placid face and she chews tobacco, just like a man, and she talks like a house afire – I never met such a chronic old chatterbox in my life – and altogether impresses me as a competent, honest, ignorant, not very shrewd old female – loose-tongued but well-meaning. Now, you'd say that here wasn't very promising material to work on, either, when you were looking for a cold-blooded assassin – a dying girl and a garrulous, gossipy old countrywoman – and that's the way it struck me.

"Still, I made 'em both go over their stories. There isn't much to the deserted wife's evidence; she gives it to me in a whisper, with coughing spells in between. She was asleep in the bedroom; didn't hear the shot although she had a sort of drowsy feeling that something was happening outside. Then 'Mom' came and roused her and told her about the shooting, and right after that there were posse-men searching the house and searching all about it. I asked her as few questions as possible.

"I didn't have to ask the old crippled woman any – no need to prompt her; she was primed to go. Right away I found out that there was no hope of pumping her dry – hers was a bottomless reservoir of talk. And you couldn't steer her in any given direction. You just had to let nature take its course. And so, eventually, by scraps and fragments, and all mixed-in and mixed-up with a thousand topics that had no bearing on the main subject, I got her story out of her. I pieced it together afterward: She had just crossed the gallery from the sick-room to the twin cabin where the cooking was done, when she heard the shot close by somewhere. She was as vague as the Padgetts had been as to the direction – couldn't be sure, she said, whether it

182

sounded from this side or that, from above or from below. I remember her description: 'Mister,' she says, 'hit didn't crack, nice and sharpish; it seemed more to quote.' Now if you'll look it up in Marlowe – or maybe it's Spenser – you'll find that she was using 'quote' in the sense that our Elizabethan ancestors – and hers – used it: to denote a reverberating sound, a sound handed on. Up in the mountains they still speak Chaucerian English, as you know.

"Anyhow, she tells me that she turned around on her crutch and looked out of a little front window and saw what Padgett also claimed he saw, except that in her case no citizens had as yet begun to appear and there was no one in her sight for the moment except the dazed county clerk and the dead man spraddled out over there in the court-house door.

"She made no bones of not caring for the late unlamented Trout. An outspoken old party, this was, thumping about over her cabin floor while I listened, with her shiny red crutch under her arm and the big brass ferule on the bottom of it striking against the loose boards; and her lower jaw just working overtime. She said more than once that she'd known him from the time he was a child, and that he was from childhood an 'unlikely one' meaning that, I took it, of an unpleasant or a sinister personality. She didn't stress her feelings against him nor did she minimize them. She merely had the candid matter-of-fact air of expressing a common prejudice which she shared with numbers of others. And then immediately she'd be off down some side-alley, airing her own views on this and that or dragging in some perfectly irrelevant neighborhood reminiscence.

"I came down off that hill with my eardrums throbbing – and feeling licked. So far as these households were concerned, I told myself I'd have to count them out of the equation; would have to look elsewhere for clues, if any. I'd given the terrain surrounding the two places only the most cursory of examinations; I did that before I scrambled down. After nearly four weeks there'd be no use looking for physical evidences on the flank of that bleak little knob and it sticking up out of the center of the town like a sore thumb. So far, I was certainly up against it.

"Do you ever have hunches? Well, I do, and sometimes they've yielded dividends when I've been up against a hard

183

proposition. I wouldn't exactly call it intuition; I'll swear it's not deduction, because the reasoning process doesn't enter into it at all. I guess the right word is just hunch. Well, while I was eating dinner – they called it dinner – at the Grand, and giving the resident house-flies a hard battle between bites, all of a sudden a hunch came. And what the hunch told me to do was to go back up the hill. I followed the urge, too – didn't even wait for the green-apple pie – and in less than two hours from that time, that murder mystery was all wrapped up, signed, sealed and delivered, and I was packing my bag to leave Uniondale for good and all and ever.

"I stopped first by the Padgetts'; made them repeat their statements; tried to draw them out along new lines. There weren't any new lines to draw them out on. So I knew – somehow I knew it – that my hunch hadn't sent me here. Then it must be the log-house higher up. It just naturally had to be. The moment I got there and saw the lame woman sitting in an old rocking-chair in the gallery between the twin cabins sewing on something or other, I knew I was getting 'warm,' as we used to say when we were kids playing some hide-and-seek game. I knew that, too. Don't ask me how I did. But I did – that's enough.

"She didn't seem surprised to see me back so soon – neither surprised not concerned. She said the sick woman was asleep and invited me to sit down. So I sat on the edge of the gallery where I could lean back against a side-wall and watch her, and I told her that to make sure I had things straight I wanted her, if she didn't mind, to tell me all over again what she remembered about the shooting. She said, very calmly and very casually, that she didn't mind.

"It was a peaceful, drowsy afternoon – a Sunday. If it hadn't been for the preacher's voice coming booming up to us from a little church diagonally down below us where the Primitive Baptists were holding one of their all-day services, there wouldn't have been a sound, hardly, except birds calling and bees humming and locusts going it in the trees along the main street. I had the feeling that a hound must have when he hits on a blind scent that's still confused and pretty faint, but a trail, all the same, that's going to lead him somewhere sooner or later.

"I gave her her head and she went to it. Sandwiched in between all sorts of extraneous side-issues, the same entirely plausible tale I'd already heard from her came forth, by degrees. It was exactly the same – no contradictions, no changes, no stressing of this incidental point, no slurring-over of that important one. Something told me just having her repeat her story wouldn't help any. That subtle indefinable sign I was looking for would have to emerge from another source. Sitting there pretending to be taking in all her guinea-hen chatter, I studied her movements, the way she handled herself, the play of her expression and all. Now I observed little peculiarities of habit, little mannerisms about her which had more or less escaped me that morning during my preliminary scouting. For one thing, I noticed how full and firm her frame was. She might be overweight but she wasn't flabby. And when she gripped her crutch as she got up once to cross the floor and get something, her grip was strong and the tip of it came down hard and brisk on the planks. Sitting down, she kept the crutch balanced across her knees and she had a little trick of running her hand along it while she gassed along. For all her solidity, there was something mighty motherly about her.

"Still I wasn't getting anywhere; I realized that. At the end of an hour I felt baffled – maybe 'thwarted' is the better word – as though the big secret was eluding me and yet was hiding right around the corner every minute of the time. It was somewhere close by if only I had the sense to put my finger on it. Finally, more to be making motions than for any really valid reason, because I already knew her story off by heart, I pulled out a note-book, telling her I intended to jot down the headings of what I'd found out from her and from the other witnesses in her vicinity.

"'Let's see now,' I said, just stalling along, you understand, 'let's see – your name is Miss Elizabeth Johnson? Or is it Mrs. Johnson?'

"'I hain't never been wedded, ef that's whut you mean,' she says. 'And the fust name ain't 'Lizabeth nor nuthin' very much like it.'

"'But everybody around her calls you Aunt Lizzie,' I said, mildly astonished. 'It's set down so by my friend who was up here immediately after the killing.'

"'Then your friend wuz pyure wrong,' she says. 'It mout sound like Lizzie but it ain't – hit's Lissy, fur short. My full entitled name, only I ain't heard it fur so long a spell that I mouty nigh furgit it myself sometimes, is Melissa Remembrance Johnson.'

"I almost fell of that rickety little porch – it was so like a lick between my eyes. Not plain Elizabeth Johnson, about as common a name next to Mary Smith, as you could think of, but Melissa Remembrance Johnson, a name in a million. A name that fairly jumped at me out of the back part of my brain. And all in a flash I was reconstructing in my mind the picture of that field-kitchen of ours that a stray German shell, a nine-point-five, came along and scored a direct hit on, one August morning of 1918 up in front of Château Thierry. I saw myself helping to straighten out the mangled fragments of the four boys who'd been wiped out in that burst. I saw myself taking the 'dog tag' and what was left of the messed-up service papers off of one of those four bodies. I saw myself fumbling in the pockets of a coat, which had been blown half off of the poor kid, for further marks of identification, and finding the last page of a misspelt letter – part of the last page, rather, for the rest of that page and the rest of the letter were just so much charred, ripped-up scrap. But the part that was left bore words that because of what they said had branded themselves into my mind and it bore also a signature that I'd never forgotten and never would. I heard myself listening again while a young second lieutenant, the commander of the platoon to which the four boys belonged, said of this particular boy: 'Rotten luck for that poor kid. He was marked to be sent back for discharge. Why the dam' fool doctors at home and at the base ever qualified him for active duty I don't know. But they did. And now, when he's as good as mustered out of the service, this gift from the Heinies comes over and scatters him all over the shop.'

"And I, out of all the people in France and out of all the people in the world, must be the one to hear what the young lieutenant said, and the one to read that tail-end fragment of a letter and then, moved by an impulse I can't explain, to tuck it back into that burnt pocket to be buried with that dead boy. And now I had to be the one to sit on this back-country hillside, with my brain whirling like a merry-go-round to the shock of an incredible discovery, while I fitted together, or tried to fit together, the pieces of this amazing, tragic jig-saw puzzle. It was a tremendous coincidence, of course. What was it then – nemesis, fate, judgment? You can tell me when I'm done.

"I could see light ahead of me, I was certain of that, but I didn't let on. Putting the next question, I tried to make my tone indifferent and I think I must have succeeded for she apparently never saw where I was driving for until a little farther along. 'You had a sort of foster-son who died in the service, didn't you?' I said, holding the pencil poised for a bluff at taking down the answer.

"'No,' she says, 'he wuzn't no Foster, nor ary kin to 'em. The Foster connection, they live higher up the waters of Stubtoe than us. He wuz a Triplett – Johnny Tom Triplett was his name – and I taken him ez an orphant child after his own maw and paw died, and raised him like he wuz my own. He's the one died over thar in that fur-off land of France.'

"'Oh, an adopted son?' I said.

"'That's the word I've heared some of 'em use – "'dopted,"' she says, 'but wuz jest the same ez my flesh and blood to me.'

"'I'm sure of it,' I said.

"'He had a little baby sister, too,' she goes on. 'I taken her the same time I taken him.'

"'Then it's probable,' I said, 'that on his papers – his soldier's papers – he would put down his sister's name as his next of kin, wouldn't he?'

"'Yes, I reckin' so,' says she.

"'And his place of residence?' I said; 'would he put that down as Uniondale?'

"'No, suh,' she says, "'cause whar us-all-three lived at before he wuz tuck fur a soldier up at Farleyville six mile frum here up the creek; that wuz our post-office then. But in gin'ral us mounting folks don't call a settlement by no 'special name; we jest calls it "town." Ast one of us whar we lives at and we air prone to say on the waters of sich-and-sich a fork or sich-and-sich a creek.'

"'Farleyville, eh?' That filled in the next blank for me; I was out in the clear now, making game steadily. 'And the sister's name?' I said.

"'Likely it would be writ down on them papers ez Marthy Triplett,' she says.

"'And where is she now?' I asked.

"'Why, layin' right here in this house, Mister,' she says.

187

"'Twuz quite some months after he wuz tuck away that she married off with that thar sorry scound'el of a Tobe Byers that's lately done run off and left her to live or else perish, ez mout be.'

"If the old woman suspected anything yet she didn't show it, not by look or voice or anything. The only thing was that for the first time she was making direct replies instead of flying off at tangents. That might not mean anything, though; probably it didn't. So I made ready to fire straight and hard at her. I said:

"'You wrote to your adopted son after he went overseas, I presume?'

"'Yes,' she says; 'of'entimes I writ him.'

"But unless I was wrong, I had detected just a barely perceptible pause, an instantaneous spell of hesitation, between this question and her answer. 'You wrote him shortly before his death?'

"'Doubtless I done so,' she says, but says it slowly, warily, almost reluctantly, as though sensing a trap set for her feet.

"'Yes, you wrote him then,' I said, and as I said it I stood up and faced her. 'You wrote him a letter and you signed that letter with your full name.' I wasn't asking her now, I was telling her. 'And in that letter you used these words: "Son-boy, if you don't come back I'm going to kill the one that sent you there. He knowed you ain't fitten for a soldier but still he took and shoved you on in. And you and me both knows why he wanted for to get you out of the way. If you don't come back, it will be pure murder on his soul and I aim to kill him for it if it's the last thing I ever does. But say nothing; you and me will be the onliest two that ever does know about this."'

"'You wrote that,' I said, 'and the man you meant was the man you killed four weeks ago – Adrian Trout.'

"She stiffened until the muscles of the back of her hands where she gripped her crutch stood out like ropes. But her expression didn't change – I can swear to that.

"'Mister,' she says, 'air you a conjure? Have you got in you the witchin' power?'

"'Never mind that,' I says. 'You killed that man, didn't you?'

"'Even so,' she says, keeping her voice flat and keeping it down. 'Through me the will of the 'vengin' Lawd God Almighty wuz made manifest, and I kilt him.'

"'Did you shoot him from this gallery or from inside this

house?' I said.

"'From right back behind whar I'm a-settin' now,' she says. 'That's whar I done it frum, me sort of leanin' aginst them logs to stiddy myself and him a-standin' down thar whar the Lawd God, a-answerin' of my constant prayer, had done delivered him into my hands.'

"'You'd been practicing to shoot him, hadn't you?' I said.

"'No,' she says, 'that wuzn't needful. I never shot ary shoot before then; I ain't never shot nary one sense, Mister. I ain't rememberin' that I tried fur to draw a bead on him, even. I didn't have to, 'cause it done had come to me long before that when the time come, the bullet would be guided to find his wicked breast.'

"'About the bullet, now,' I said. I was guessing a little although the answer seemed pretty plain. 'You made that bullet out of a soldier's button, didn't you?'

"'Out of a button off'en Johnny Tom's coat,' she says. 'When I went down on them steamcars to that thar camp in Caroliny, where they had him herded up ag'inst the day they'd ship him away – the onliest time I ever set foot out of these native mountings – I asked him fur one button offen his coat. He 'lowed I craved it fur a keepsake and so he give it to me. Johnny Tom wuz ever a most biddable boy. I didn't tell him whut I purposed fur to do with it. I never told him nur ary livin' whut wuz my intent – only to him in that thar last letter. Mister, all whut I'm a-narratin' to you is the pyure truth.'

"But I knew that without her telling me – knew it wasn't in her to lie. I said: 'In that letter you intimated that there was some second reason other than his having pushed your son through the draft-board examination, why you hated this man you've confessed to killing. Hadn't you better tell me what that reason was?'

"'I'm a-comin' to that,' she says. 'He lusted after Marthy, same ez he had lusted after many another pore gal in these mountings. And Johnny Tom, puny ez he wuz, stood betwixt him and his carnal cravin's. So he aimed fur to git Johnny Tom out of his path, and this here draft give him his bounden chance. So with Johnny Tom snatched up and carried off fur a soldier there ain't nobody left a-standin' 'twixt him and Marthy excusin' it's me. So to save her pore weak body frum him and to save her pore soul frum everlastin' torments of Hell's fire, I aiged her on

189

into weddin' with this here Tobe Byers, a-knowin' him fur a low-down, no-worth fiest, but a-doin' it 'cause it seemed like there wuzn't no other way out. And so this here Tobe Byers, he starves her thin and wears her down and breaks her little heart, and when she's done plum' wore-out, he flees frum her and leaves her fur to die. Johnny Tom and Marthy – my onliest two – one gone and other one goin' – and one man to blame fur 'em both.'

"There's no passion in her voice while she's saying this. She's just saying it, just so, that's all. And I know that every word she's saying is the truth, as she sees it. Then she says, still without any dramatics: 'Well, Mister, now that you know all, whut do you aim fur to do with me? I ain't 'shamed fur whut I done and I wouldn't be 'feared fur whut's to come to me, only fur Marthy. With me in the jail-house, whut'll Marthy do? That's all I'm feared fur.'

"She wasn't pleading, understand. She merely was stating a case.

"'I'll tell you what I'm going to do with you,' I said; my decision was already made and confirmed. 'I'm going to leave you right here where you are. I'm not going to say a word about this to the sheriff or anybody, and unless you should talk yourself, nobody is going to be any the wiser about what the two of us know.'

"She didn't thank me in words; the look she gave me and the nod she gave me were enough. I held out my hand, not to shake hands with her but for something else, and she knew what I wanted and handed it over – her crutch. Oh, yes, I'd had my eye on that crutch for some little time past. It was a very heavy, very cumbersome thing, and I'd say it had about six separate coats of red paint on it, not to speak of the elaborate cloth padding. And why wouldn't it be heavy and cumbersome, and why wouldn't it be well painted and well-padded when the stock part of it was the octagonal barrel of an old-fashioned, muzzle-loading squirrel-rifle with the forearm shaved away; and with its stock cut down and fitted into the arm-crotch, and with that big brass ferule slipped over the muzzle; and with the lock part – the trigger and trigger-guard and the hammer – so nicely hidden away under the cloth where the hand-grip came. A beautifully done job, if you're asking me. I hefted it, fingered it all over, slipped off the ferule, slipped it back on again and hammered it fast, and then handed the thing back to her. 'Aunt Lissy,' I said to her, reaching for my hat, 'I've told you what I'm going to do with you – and that's nothing whatsoever. Now I'm telling you something I'm going to do for you: I'll be in Chattanooga by this time to-morrow. As soon as I get there I'm going to buy you a regular crutch out of a store and send it back up here by a messenger that can be trusted. As soon as you get that new crutch I want you to take this old one of yours and break it up and bury the pieces separately, deep down underground where nobody can ever find them.'

"'I will, Mister,' she says.

"We shook hands on it and I came on away. And so that's the story that old Mr. Green-head here reminded me of... Any more coffee left in that bottle, d'ye think?"

"Wow!" I said. "I'd like to write that yarn sometime and try to sell it."

"Go right ahead," Thorne said. "It couldn't do any harm. Marthy's dead and Aunt Lissy died two years ago – I sort of kept track of her. And if you don't use my right name and change some of the other names I can't see where writing it could do any harm, although it might jar up Fred Gaither a little. Oh, by the way, while we're on the subject, I want to ask you something: What would you say was the most unusual feature of the whole thing – my having been the one who read that scrap of writing over in front of Château Thierry that time? Or that old woman, using one of the most awkward weapons you can imagine – a stock that she couldn't get up to her shoulder because of its added length, and a barrel that she couldn't aim down – that old woman being able to fire right center to the target of a man's heart seventy-five yards away from her? Or what?"

I did some swift but intensive thinking. Then:

"I'd say the strangest part of it was her ability to keep the secrets of her deadly hate and her deadly plot to herself when, as you tell me, she was such an ever-lasting gabbler on every other possible subject."

"Proving," said Thorne, "that great minds run in the same channel. That's exactly what I claim... Well, yonder comes Jerome with the pirogue. It's just as well, there'll be no more gunning to-day."

WE CAN'T ALL BE THOROUGHBREEDS

Among his own people his name signified "The One Who Laughs." But his smile was imminent danger and his laughter it was death. There was sudden destruction in it and also there was shuddering, lingering torture. He laughed at burning homes, at mutilated corpses and – when he had the leisure for such diversions – at the agony of victims dying by slow torments at the stake or where they were spread-eagled and pegged down on ant-hills to be eaten piecemeal.

For years on end, through a drawn-out campaign which endures in our history as the cruelest and almost the bloodiest epic of our Indian-fighting age, this gay red murderer laughed at pursuit. Finally he was captured and lived out his time on an Oklahoma reservation as the caged ward of a forgiving and beneficent government, a tiger with its claws drawn, selling his autograph at a dollar a throw to tourists whose scalps he lovingly would have lifted and whose eyelids he would have been proud to shear from their living eyeballs. To call him by his white man's name which is a Spanish name, he was Geronimo, the spindly scourge of the old but not so very old Southwest.

Under his wily leadership, a stripped-down and painted-up war party closed in, one burning forenoon, on a settler's isolated cabin of 'dobe and wattles in what is now the state of Arizona and not many miles north by east of the National Boundary. The raiders came afoot as was their way, silently sliding like so many sidewinders through the scanty desert herbage and over the naked alkali smears.

This was a district where the mountains met the table-lands which the band had not invaded until now. This, then, was their first foray across this particular flat.

The head of that remote household was a shiftless young Irishman whose name doesn't matter and indeed long since has been forgotten; and he was away from his home-place that day. He was ill-fitted to play the dry-farmer's game on these lonesome high plateaus. But he was the life of the party at any frontier saloon. In the cabin were his wife and his baby: the wife a homely, grubby-looking little Saxon of twenty or there-abouts, an immigrant recently come from overseas, as her husband had; the baby a lusty man-child some six months old.

The woman had a short warning; not that it did her any good. A Mexican herder, fleeing for his life, checked and cried out to her as she, hearing the quick thump of hoofs, came to the door and, shading her eyes with her hand, looked out across the hot glare. Then he dusted on down the trail, riding hell-for-leather to the nearest settlement. He could not have taken her along with him, anyhow. His lathered pony already was carrying double, his own woman riding behind him and she gelatinous with terror.

The German girl didn't know what the Mexican said but she knew what he meant, all right. She ran back into the shanty and caught up the sleeping babe from his flour-barrel crib and, with him in her arms against her breasts, darted into the greasewood and the chaparral and the sage-brush at the rear of their claim.

Two hundred yards back, she faced west, being minded to head for the gap between the snaggled peaks yonder. If she made it, she would have a better prospect of hiding in the broken ground there than here on her own mesa, where a cactus plant was the tallest thing in view and a mesquite bush the densest.

She never made it. Probably she never could have made it. The slim swift figures moving in on the homestead from all four quarters were, as any old soldier out of our old army will tell you, the shrewdest trackers and the keenest-eyed tribesmen on this continent. Perhaps she knew that; her actions would seem to indicate as much.

Even so, none of the trotting enemies sighted her until she had sighted a brace of them. Squatting a moment for breath in the small shelter of a clump of mesquite she saw, three hundred yards away, bobbing up over a small dip like the obscene black-and-red blossoms of some poisonous poppy, two heads of long slick hair, each bound around with a gay turban of traders' cloth.

As I say, the flankers hadn't seen her yet. Did she bide on where she was, motionless and mute, there was, let's say, one chance in a thousand for her. Because from the time the fugitive quitted the 'dobe, either instinctively or by design, she had been traveling upon an upthrust of lava which almost was free of sand

and on which her feet left few or no prints.

Now then, this drab piece of steerage fruit did a thing of stark heroism. Deliberately she threw away her one faint hope of salvation for the sake of her baby. She thrust the little moist warm bundle that was he in among the roots and the stems of that mesquite. Then on her hands and knees she crawled a few rods farther along the narrowing gritty outcrop. Then, turning herself about at right angles, she boldly stood up and ran south at top speed.

Actually she covered more than a quarter of a mile before one of the slender pursuers overhauled her and sank the blade of his war hatchet deep into her skull. Without tarrying to scalp her, he hurried off to join the other bucks in the rapid looting of the shack and the lean-to horse shed behind it. Well for him that he did, the child slept on until the Apaches were gone, as very soon they were gone. Strike fast and get away fast – that would have been skinny old Geronimo's motto, if grinning old Geronimo ever had any mottoes.

A troop of sun-finished regulars, with a squad of friendlies to scout for them and a handful of civilians to reenforce them, reached the ravaged shack before dark that same evening. They were in a hurry, naturally. So the woman's body was buried where they found it, and one trooper who had repute for piety said the Lord's Prayer over the shallow hole before they hastily shoveled her under and, for her, that was that and that was all.

About the time the burial was finished, somebody heard something mewing in the undergrowth and searched about and found the famishing baby in his brushy cache. After a brief but highly alcoholic period of mourning, the child's father sloughed off his domestic obligations and went away drunk and went away for good. A well-meaning couple named Jacobs took his abandoned offspring and gave that hungry derelict a place among their own increasing progeny.

These Jacobses weren't so happy in that land of mirages and massacres. They moved on to southern California and bought a quarter-section for practically nothing and as one of their brood, and under the name of Renfrew Jacobs, the adopted orphan grew up out of infancy into boyhood. When oil was struck on their property, he, being then of an age suitable for the higher education, shared in the sudden prosperity which came to the family.

He was sent off to college and took a course in mining and was graduated with honors, since he was smart and a good student and ambitious, and began the career which, by the time he was fifty, had put him in the front rank of the conspicuously wealthy and conspicuously strong business magnates of North America. Long before that, though, he had proved to an admiring world and an envying profession that he was a great engineer.

Being translated from field-work to office-work, he next proved that likewise he was a great and most scientific executive. Along about then it seemed a proper season for him to take unto himself a wife and start rearing a dynasty. Both of which, in the order named, he straightway did.

At forty he had been president of Interhemispheric Copper. At fifty he was chairman of the board and even by the Mellons and the Morgans was indeed very highly thought of. And at fifty-one he died of a highly fatal combination, to wit, as follows: rich living, overwork and just one tiny blood clot on the motor area of the left lobe.

The widow who survived him and who mourned his loss for substantially nine lively months before she remarried herself to a refugee prince from Russia, a land where princes appear once to have abounded in the utmost profusion, was a daughter of an old Knickerbocker stock, a stock that had been rooted in the friendly Manhattan schist for several snooty generations, and so she had come to his bosom handsomely dowered with the semi-regal tradition and that air of a true and inborn culture which so often is counterfeited but so rarely with success. To match with this lady's almost royal lineage, Renfrew Jacobs had, right from the beginning of his financial and social prominence, fashioned out of somewhat shoddy materials a fine blue studbook for himself.

He knew the early facts about himself and about his immediate forebears. In confidence, when he was old enough to understand and, as they mistakenly trusted, to appreciate the measure and the beauty of his real mother's supreme sacrifice, his foster-parents had told him who and what he was. With a precocious wisdom, having first sworn them to secrecy, he chose for ever after to bask in the shade of a blossomy and fragrant although, as you will perceive, an almost purely synthetic family tree.

Another man might have been proud to the point of boasting over so gorgeous a maternal heritage. Curiously, Renfrew Jacobs was not built that way. Besides, he was busy at shaping himself according to a different and a more refined model. Before the flattering mirror of his inner soul and to some extent before the eyes of the admiring multitude, he became a sort of glamorous fiction character, a craftily constructed acting part; and in times to come, if posterity only does right by our captains of industry, will be one of an immortalized constellation of Aryan myths.

As a background for this grand future rôle, he created, or he suffered to be created, a common assumption that he was the result of the mating of scions of two old southern lines. Well, in a way of speaking, he was an all-southern product – South German on one side, South of Ireland on the other. But once the elder Jacobs had passed on, no living soul save Renfrew Jacobs knew that. You bet he wasn't passing the news around. The hidden truth burned inside of him like a little warm spot of shame.

Such gross vanities as he had – this especial one among the rest – might have made a lesser man ridiculous. But in this fair republic a man who piles ninety millions into one heap never can be made ridiculous by anything or anybody.

He was at the very height of his material leadership and of his seeming health, neither he nor any one else suspecting he was about to be snatched up to everlasting glory by what the attending physicians – eight in number at the final consultation – would diagnose as apoplexy, when a staff representative called by appointment at the Jacobs summer home in Lenox to question him on behalf of *Dynamic Individualities*, an inspirational monthly, and subsequently to write for the pages of that valued publication what would be in part a personality sketch, a study rather, and in part the consolidated tale of a massive succession of achievements.

The pair of them – the grateful interviewer and the graciously interviewed – sat on the latter's veranda looking out over an estate big enough for a barony, and presently the eager author put this one to the blandly majestic proprietor:

"Mr. Jacobs, what romantic incident – something like that makes a good starter for an article such as this is going to be –

what picturesque or thrilling episode was there that occurred in your early life or, better still, in your childhood?"

Mr. Jacobs gave an inner guilty start. "And why do you ask that – of me?" he demanded suspiciously.

"Oh, it was just a vague idea of Mr. Laidlaws, our editor, that's all." The caller's tone was most respectful, in fact almost humble. "He thought that inasmuch as you came from the Far West, and were born and brought up there at a period when the last wave of the crude but gallant pathfinding element was pushing its way out to the Coast, maybe it was possible that in your own youth there had been something exciting – something in the nature of an adventure or an experience which would make good copy, sir."

"Ah, I see," said Mr. Jacobs, now completely reassured, and he smiled a gentle smile betokening regret that the publishers and their subscribers must be disappointed. "I'm sorry to say, young man, that unless I should draw upon my fancy – which is not my habit – I can not gratify your readers in this regard. My people could hardly be called home-seekers, or even Argonauts, much less pioneers. True, they went from the South at what seems now a comparatively remote age in our country's development, but they went from refined and cultivated surroundings to an environment which, while possibly primitive in some respects, was yet immediately invested, as it were, with a translated refinement.

"I might add – if it is of any popular interest – that for at least a century before that my people had been part and parcel of the old South as it was in the antebellum days and on back into the Colonial days. In a community of gentlefolk, slave owners, plantation owners, luxury-loving people – that was where I was born. There is, I believe, some Huguenot blood in my veins, and some of the strain of the Cavaliers also.

"My mother, now –" Through a well-spaced and finely dramatic moment he paused, meanwhile looking out with softened eye upon his formal gardens and upon the only slightly less formal terraces, all ornated and groomed, which fell below, and then in a mildly sentimentalized tone of reminiscence continued: "My mother, now. She was the daughter of a rather famous soldier in the Confederacy – a brevet brigadier, a Kentuckian out of the Blue Grass regions but of Virginia descent.

"She passed away when I was a small boy. But I faintly remember her. Very small and fragile, I recall, and always wearing a bit of fine lace at her throat. Ah, me!" His small sigh was so cleverly done that it achieved genius – a thing so beautifully theatrical that it didn't sound theatrical at all.

Perhaps it was by coincidence that at this precise moment a cock pheasant crowed derisively from somewhere quite close by down the landscaped slope. It was, however, a common barnyard cock which gave similar proof to Apostle Peter that the prophecy touching on *his* words of betrayal had been fulfilled.

Mr. Jacobs, now pacing to and fro along his veranda, went on: "However, I hold that a display of pride in honorable and even – ahem – distinguished ancestry, however laudable it may be on some occasions and under some conditions, has no place really in a story such as I gather you propose to write. If you insist on mentioning it in passing, that is your own concern.

"To be born right is something; to be reared right is better still – granted. But the point I would make and emphasize – you may quote me here in full – is that the opportunities for rising to commercial supremacy in this splendid country of ours are open to those who spring from the most – how shall we phrase it? – well, the most prosaic, the most commonplace circumstances and often from the lowliest of parentage.

"Take, for example, the late lamented Andrew Carnegie, a man without benefit of early advantages, and yet look at his record. Take my dear friend, Charley Schwab. Take Mr. John D. Rockefeller, Senior. Take almost any one of my recent or present contemporaries in the realm of big business." He said almost sadly, as though grieving for sundry ones: "No, my worthy young friend, we can't all be thoroughbreds, can we?"

"Quite so, sir. Thank you, sir. And now, sir, not changing the subject, but for the inspiration of our youth of to-day, to what do you ascribe, primarily and basically, I mean, your own preeminence?"

"In a word," answered Mr. Jacobs, meaning by that a considerable number of words – "in a word, to hard work. To keeping the faith with all men and all women regardless of the consequences. To punching the time clock on the dot always. To never watching the hands of the clock. To telling the plain truth, no matter what the cost..."

And so on and so forth for ten elaborating minutes – right out of the old copy-book. But good stuff for the younger generation – splendid stuff.

In the printed column or even in the rough proofs, Mr. Jacobs would have been greatly pleased to scan – that would seem to be the proper word, or anyhow the stylish word – to scan that which this talented young man went back to the office and wrote. Unhappily such pleasure was to be denied him. Six weeks later, when the subject-matter was going into type for the magazine and the magazine people would be ready pretty soon now to close up that number, Mr. Jacobs had his untimely stroke and lay unconscious until the end.

It so befell that the issue of *Dynamic Individualities* containing the write-up came out only two days before his death and less than a week before the funeral. So the rewrite men on the newspapers drew upon it freely; and what had been meant for a condensed biography ironically served the posthumous purposes of obituary.

The published list of clubs to which Mr. Jacobs belonged was a compendium of the worth-while clubs of Manhattan Island. The published list of the pallbearers, active and honorary, read like several important pages out of the Directory of Directors. In a bronze and marble mausoleum which cost ninety thousand dollars, and which is a conspicuous feature of a marcelled vista in what the ribald-minded call "Millionaires' Row," he rests in trust, sleeping the sleep which knows no waking, at the most exclusive, the most conservative, the most fashionable of all up-town cemeteries – a cemetery having so exclusive a membership that unless the candidates' remains really belong, they'll blackball 'em out the very minute they come up before the admissions committee.

Irrigation has reclaimed much of the mesa lying just under a certain notch in the range, so that alfalfa ripples where the savage mesquite once sprouted and a lone 'dobe shack once squatted in the midst of a fearsome desolation. In a strip of still unwatered and therefore arid silt between two of the cultivated grass-fields, a gang of Mexican laborers were excavating foundation trenches for a proposed addition to the Pinto Buttes

Dude Ranch when about four feet down, the pick-point of a worker tinked against something solider than the light ash-like subsoil.

Under the direction of the foreman, a few minutes more of careful digging revealed a human body, a woman's body, which, lying for no telling how long in that moistureless altitude and shielded beneath layers of that dry volcanic loam, was mummified, the parchmented skin being here corrugated and there drawn as tight as drumheads over the fragile but still intact framework.

For fear of breaking some of those brittle bones, the foreman wouldn't let his Mexies lift the cadaver out of the hole. He got down in the hole himself and with his fingers scooped up the coarse dirt and flung it out so that the entire shape was exhibited, and with it some crumbling fragments of the heavy woolen cerements in which obviously the dead crudely had been shrouded.

He left the grim find thus and went to the main ranch house to give in the word. With the morbid little crowd of hands and guests who followed him back to the spot came Daddy Lem Doolittle, spraddling along on his bowed and unsteady old legs like a set of animated calipers.

Daddy Lem was an octogenarian relic of the early times, a surviving bit of local color retained by the management to be picturesque and quaintly philosophical all over the place, and most of all to regale paying pilgrims from the East with tales that were as high, wide and handsome as the views of this, his original habitat – in other words, the official hired liar of the establishment and, considering his age and the amount of liquor he had in his day consumed and his advanced stage of decrepitude, a very good liar, resourceful, ready, dependable.

This ancient's present mood, though, was not a mood for romancing. He squinted down into the opened grave, and then broke in on a babble of exclamations and theories and surmises coming from natives and visitors as well.

"You-all are all wrong," he stated decisively. "This here ain't no squaw. It couldn't be no squaw. Injuns never buried their female folks in no sich a fashion ez this. 'Sides, the hair wuzn't dead black, to begin with. It's bleached out a heap and faded, but you kin tell yit that it must 'a' been light brown or mebbe yaller.

200

"So this here must be a white woman's body you boys have done uncovered." His voice, already shrill with age, grew shriller: "And, by Tunket, now I know who that white woman wuz! It comes back to me: The sorry feller, that she wuz his wife or leastwise his woman – I furgit his name, though, ef ever I knowed it – he had a claim staked out right in this here identical spot. She wuz a Dutch gal, but he wuz Irish and no durned good neither, I've heared tell.

"And the day the 'Paches come through this deestrict, slaughterin' and stealin' and ravishin' – not the last time they come but the time before the last – he wuz off frum home somewheres that day. And she – this here very Dutch gal that I'm tellin' you about – she tuck out across the desert with her baby in her arms and she dropped her kid in the bushes and kept runnin' till one of them onmerciful little devils run her down and knocked her skull in with a tomahawk.

"Why, jist look, you-all, and you kin see where the wound wuz, there in the back of her –" The shock of a new and strange discovery made Daddy Lem break off. "Who's been messin' about with her?" he demanded. "Who's been disturbin' that poor thing's molderin' remainders?"

"Not nobody," answered back the foreman. "I'm the only one touched her and I didn't move her none, neither – jist cleared out the hole."

"Then whut's she doin' restin' that way?"

"Way I found her, I'm tellin' you. But it does look funny, don't it? I been wonderin'."

"It looks dam' funny!"

All the others were silent, harkening to these two. The foreman hazarded a guess: "Maybe – maybe it might have been that whoever it was stuck her away was in such confusion they accidentally tumbled her in upside down?"

"Not nary a chanct. You're talkin' now, son, to somebody that knows whut he's talking about. You're listenin' to Arizony history, boy. Fur while I wuzn't here myself, my older brother, the late Pierce Doolittle, deceased, he wuz here. He come in here with the posse that come in here with the soldiers that same evenin'. That wuz when they found the gal with her brains all spilt out on the ground and found the baby mouty hungry and terrible sunburnt but still livin'.

201

"Somebody or other taken the kid fur to raise. And ef I heared Pierce say it onct endurin' his lifetime, I heared him say it a hundred times, that whilst they wuz all set to light out and ketch up with them 'Paches before they could do some more fresh devilment, still they taken the time to lay the woman away decent and proper and Christian-like – foldin' her hands on her breast and wroppin' her up in a saddle blanket offen one of the cav'rymen's spare mounts – by Tunket, onless I'm mistaken, and I ain't, that's whut's left of the blanket still folded around her – and even coverin' up her face with a handkerchief off of somebody's neck to keep the dirt out of her face."

A fascinated and awe-stricken listener put in his oar: "Had you thought of this? Wouldn't it be possible that she was still breathing – that they buried her alive and in her struggles, poor thing, she wriggled and rolled over until she was face downward?"

"Huh!" The aged historian was very scornful about it. "You never knowed no 'Paches when they wuz in their prime. Ef a 'Pache ondertaken a job of killin' somebody, no matter how big a rush he wuz in, he finished that there killin' job before he quit – nary record of ary failure there! Nur you seemin'ly don't know whut layin' out in Arizony sunshine all day would do to you, let alone your skull bein' split plum' wide open behind."

"Well, then, what's your explanation?"

"Me, I ain't got none. I'm jist sayin' it's dam' funny – 'scuse me, I furgot about there bein' ladies present... Hold on, boys, I got me kind of a loose idée! It mout be foolish but sich ez 'tis, I've got it: Ain't you never heard 'em say it, jokin'-like, I'll admit, but still and all sayin' it, that ef a dead person has been laid away in the silent tomb and somebody, no matter how many years afterward, deliber'tly does that there dead person dirt – I mean to say, does their memory dirt – that then that there dead person will turn smack over in the grave?"

"Surely you don't believe that, Daddy Lem?" asked a tourist.

"I ain't sayin' ez how I believe it, neither I ain't sayin' ez how I disbelieve it," answered Daddy Lem. "Till this minute I ain't never given it nary thought nur study. The older I git the less inclined I am to be certain shore about ary thing in this world or the next. But jist the same," – and he pointed a long fleshless finger into the hole – "jist the same, look down there and tell me

202

ef this here thing ain't damnation funny!"

QUEER CREEK

Connors, if that was his name, rode easily. He rode in front, breaking trail. The city man, Bauer, was much the lighter man of the two but he slumped in the saddle, a dead weight, punishing the tired mare under him. The pack-pony, which was half hidden beneath its load of shabby dunnage, stumbled along behind him. That was all there was of the cavalcade.

They went down a steep draw and up a steep grade at its outlet and then were on a small table-land. Looking back, they could see a narrowed vista of the desert they had crossed. Looking ahead, they could see the foot-hills rising from the farther of this little plateau and, on beyond the foot-hills, could see also the first of the real mountains. Mainly they looked ahead; they were going in that direction, which was west. Anyhow, the desert was an old and a wearisome story. They had spent four days getting across it.

They clumped along over the flat, and pretty soon were nearing some jack-pines. The alkali dust was gone now. It had gone all of a sudden. The sage-brush and the junipers were thinning out. There was grass under the horses' worn feet. There were beginning to be clumps of dwarf manzanita and bush-willow.

Connors checked his fatigued mount. He spoke to himself rather than to his companion, giving no backward glance. He said:

"Unless that there nester I walked to yistiddy was wrong about it, we oughter to strikin' that creek along about now. Yonder's that scald-face peak he told me about and this here must natchelly be the mesa that he said was right here. Unless he was all wrong it can't be more'n a coupler miles more till we hit runnin' water."

It was less than that, it turned out.

He jerked his horse's bent head out of the herbage and the procession straggled on and entered the pines, winding in and out between their slender tight-ranked trunks but, largely by trained instinct on Connor's part, holding to a reasonably direct course. Within ten minutes they issued from the stunted fringe into an opening, a sort of tiny natural park, where ferns grew rank and the scattered timber was taller than in the close-set stuff through which they had just passed.

The creek they sought curved along two flanks of the meadow, making a sharp bend here. In the East it would have been called a river, for it was swift and it was good and wide – forty to sixty feet wide – and that dry-farmer of yesterday had told them it was over a hundred miles long. But out here in this western country it was a creek. The sight of it was grateful to them and the sound of it, too.

The three plugs had been sniffing and snorting for some little time. They had one advantage over their owners. They could smell sweet water at a distance. Now they quit their single-file formation and ran at a shambling gallop to bury their muzzles in the tumbling stream and flood their famished throats. Bauer was almost shaken off the mare. He cursed her viciously and struck at her and clung to the high pommel. He was no horseman.

"We'll camp here," said Connors when the beasts had drunk their fill. "We'll camp here to-night and stay here part of to-morrow restin' up these here cayuses, and then we'll make fur the pass and git on over to the fur side of the range. We gotta rest 'em up a little without we want 'em dying under us. They're plum' played out."

His tone, which had been authoritative, became contemptuous. He said to Bauer:

"See ef you got the gumption to git the duffel off that pinto and the saddles off them other two and throw 'em loose to graze. You can't pack nothin'; you done proved that. But maybe you *have* got sense enough to unpack. And after that see ef you know enough to rastle up a little dead wood and start a fire so's I kin cook somethin'. And then you kin git the bed-rolls spread down. I ain't keerin' where you spread yours, but you'd better see to it that mine are spread on a nice soft place with no rocks nor roots not nothin' stickin' up underneath."

"And while I'm doing all that, what'll you be doing?" demanded Bauer, but there was no force in his demand. This was one time when he was too spent even to quarrel.

"Me?" Connors laughed that high whinnying laugh of his that was so hateful a sound to hear. "Whut'll I be doin'? Why, bo,

205

I'll be stretched out under a tree easin' myself and figgerin' up how much more you'll be owin' me to-night on top of whut you already owe me."

Bauer gave him a venomous stare but said nothing. Being helpless, what could he say? As he set to work obeying his orders, every awkward fumbling movement betrayed in him the novice at this menial business. Connors looked on from where he lay on his back with his head pillowed on his hands, and from time to time nickered derisively. That almost drove Bauer crazy. As a matter of fact, it was driving him desperate.

The partnership between these two travel-grimed wayfarers was an enforced companionship. They shared a common danger and that literally was the only bond between them. Briefly, the connection was this:

Bauer, a Chicago product, was a common thief but a fairly versatile one. He had been a gangster, a hijacker, a racketeer, a yeggman of sorts. He had been where killings were done, but to date had killed no one. Bauer was his right name; he had an alias or two. He was going under the name of Bowman at present.

He had to get out of Chicago on account of the enmity of a more powerful gang than the gang with which he customarily affiliated. A dispute over beer-running privileges had led to an open break, and Bauer presently was listed with a number of young men who were scheduled to be wiped out. So he took time by the forelock and a fast train for the West. Once started in that direction, he kept on going until he reached Spokane. Feeling safe now, he stopped there a while.

His cash was running low when he fell in with Connors, an ex-ranch hand, gone the whole route wrong. Through Connors he met Mattingly, a petty gambler and a former railroad brakeman who aspired to be a crook. They would meet at a pool-room and colleague together.

For Connors, the sinister personality of the slim and dapper Bauer had a fascination. Connors was not slim, neither was he dapper. He liked to listen to Bauer's accounts of life in the city with its code of underworld ethics, which were so different from any he knew, and he strove diligently but without notable success to acquire the argot and the accent which Bauer used. This was at the beginning. Afterward there was to be a change of heart. In a lesser degree Mattingly seemed to share these sentiments.

It was Connors' idea that the three of them should team up. He knew of a plum ripe for the picking – a prosperous country bank in a small town not very far from the Nevada-Oregon line. He had the notion that it might be a good thing to go down there and hold up this bank.

They did go down there and they held up the bank and tied up the paying-teller and a clerk and got away with upward of eighteen thousand dollars in a tidy little leather sack. But coming out of the bank on the way to their automobile, they bumped into the chief of police of the town and it seemed expedient for Connors and Mattingly to shoot him. They did shoot him, not once but several times.

As he went down on one elbow he got his own gun into action and his first bullet bored Mattingly through the skull, and that person leaned up against the side of the bank building and died there with a look of almost comic astonishment on his face. But the chief's next two shots went wild and he passed out on the sidewalk before he could pull on his fourth cartridge.

In the car, Connors and Bauer made their getaway with the eighteen thousand. The sparsely settled country rose behind them; likewise it rose before them and all about them; the chief had been a well-liked man and prominent in county politics. They circled around communities and they outran one posse and by rare luck dodged two more. For forty-eight hours they drove day and night, spelling each other at the wheel. They crossed their own track and recrossed it, doubling back and forth to confuse the chase. They abandoned their car and stole another, and in this second car, traveling west by north, they got through a cordon too thinly patrolled and reached an area where settlements were few and far apart. They were on the border-line of exhaustion, Bauer more so than Connors, but they kept on. Mainly they were living on nerve and canned goods.

It was on Connors' suggestion that finally they tried a desperate but, as it developed, a successful expedient. Representing themselves to be Oregon deputies searching for the two surviving bank robbers, they rode boldly up to a remote homestead at the edge of the desert and bargained with the homesteader for mounts for themselves and for a pack-animal and for camping equipment.

207

Their story was that they believed the bandits were on ahead of them in the rough country nearer the coast. They meant to follow, being minded, they said, to earn for themselves the rewards which were offered for the capture of the criminals. To give color of plausibility to their tale, they asked if they might leave their car in the custody of the resident until they got back or could send for it.

Their real intention was to lose themselves from local pursuit in the broken waste-lands on beyond and work their way through the short range and then make for some sizable place on salt water – Seattle, for choice, or, failing that, Astoria, perhaps. That much accomplished, it would be time to think of separating.

The native suspected nothing. As Connors gleefully stated after they parted from him, he didn't seem to know about the war being over. And Bauer said what else could you expect from a poor fish who was content to live in such an empty, God-forsaken dump as this? But before that, he provisioned them and rather scantily outfitted them and sold them three head of indifferent stock.

So they set out on what proved to be a four-day trudge across a dismal and arid expanse. They missed one water-hole, couldn't find it at all. So that night they made what Connors called a dry camp. On the third day they got traveling instructions from a forlorn settler on a barren claim; and in the late afternoon of the fourth day they came to the cleft at the base of the hills and alongside the pleasantly roaring creek of which he had told them.

From the hour of taking to horseback, Connors openly assumed the leadership. As a matter of fact, his had been the directing mind all along but now he was in full command. He quit consulting with Bauer on this point or that. Immediately he assumed a hectoring attitude; very soon it was domineering, overbearing, was full of sneerings and fault findings. He began playing the tyrant.

In Chicago or some other great city, the relations between them might have been reversed, probably would have been reversed. There Bauer would have had the westerner at a disadvantage. But here the advantages, all of them, were on Connors' side. He could ride well; he could throw a hitch on a pack; he understood the care and handling of horses; he could cook; could make a camp; could wield an ax or a spade expertly; could take care of himself in a waste or a wilderness; could steer for their flight by the sun or the stars or, lacking these, by landmarks.

Bauer, the tenderfoot, could do none of these things; was dependent in nearly every regard; was obviously frightened by their isolation, by their remoteness from the facilities and comforts upon which all his life he had depended. This sort of game wasn't his sort of game at all. He complained of the heat and the bitter-tasting dust in the daytime, of the searching chill that descended after dusk.

Connors' scornfulness for Bauer grew by the hour. He cursed the city man for his ineptness, for his clumsiness, for his sulkiness; at frequent intervals reminded him that in the duel outside the bank he alone had fired no shot, and that thereafter he had been no help but merely a hindrance and a nuisance. And Bauer, circumstanced as he was, dare not physically rebel. He snarled back or sometimes turned sullen and silent for hours at a stretch, but further than that he dared not go.

On the evening of their first day in the desert, the oppressor had delivered an ultimatum from where he lay under his tarp with his feet to their camp-fire.

"I've been figgerin'," Connors said. "I figger that out of your split you're goin' to owe me quite a chunk of money before we're done with this here trip."

"Money for what?" asked Bauer, raising a surprised head from a huddle of blankets.

"Why, fur lookin' after you, fur takin' care of you, fur wet-nursin' you along. Where'd you be without me? In one devil of a fix, that's where you'd be. So I'm aimin' to charge you fur it." It was apparent that he meant what he said. He went blithely on:

"Before we git out of this here mess back into civilization, we'll square up the books. Let's see, now, my guidin' fee will be two hundred and fifty dollars a day. And fur saddling' up fur you and unsaddlin' and fur cookin' and fur wranglin' the plugs single-handed and fur general service and all these here other roustaboutin' jobs, big and little – well, I reckon about two hundred and fifty more a day would be about right fur that. Call it five hundred a day, without somethin' special extry should come up unexpected. I'll collect it, too, bo; don't worry none about that part of it."

There had been more of that mental arithmetic on the next night and the next, and this night there would be still more. Regarding the mounting indebtedness there had been other references from time to time. Not content merely with rubbing a thing in, Connors was the kind who liked to rub it all the way through and out on the other side. On Connor's part, this was a fatal defect. By overplaying his hand he lost the pot and along with it his life.

That following morning he was bending over the fire to hearten the flame under the coffee-pot, when Bauer came softly up behind him and bored him between the shoulders – *whang, whang, whang!* – three times, like that. He died very quickly with his face among the live ashes and his booted toes drumming grotesquely against the turf.

Since the second night before, Bauer had been planning this killing. He had meant, though, to hold in until they were out of the woods. For him, that would be the safer and therefore the more sensible course. But the sight of the bully with his back turned and he all unsuspicious – that, plus a particularly aggravating sneer uttered by Connors half a minute before – had been too much for him. Tempted beyond all restraint, he drew and crept close and cut down at short range.

But the moment the act was completed, with the victim quietly sprawled in the hot embers, Bauer began to feel that he had been overly impulsive. This was a swell revenge, all right, but it had been poor judgment; he had to admit as much in common with himself there in the daunting and subtly uncomfortable hush which had fallen upon the small empty glade. It would have been better had he withheld his hand while Connors piloted him through the range and down the continental slant until they were within easy striking distance of one or another of the seaports. That has been his original idea.

Still, it was done and he was the richer by a gratifying sum of money, and the nagging of Connors was ended. For the last time Connors had sounded that grating rackety horse-laugh, which thought for the moment was a pleasant thought to contemplate.

This, though, was not the place nor was it the hour, either, for regrets over the fit of impetuosity or for celebration of the accomplished result. The next thing to do and the important thing to do was to catch up the mare and the pony and load essential parts of the gear and get on away. Already this spot, with its eternally silenced occupant, was getting on Bauer's nerves.

He holstered his gun. He rummaged from the victim's bed-roll the small leather satchel containing the money, which was in currency and therefore compact and light. Heretofore Connors had constituted himself the custodian of the fund.

While doing this, Bauer was spying about for the plugs. They should be browsing somewhere close at hand. The mare wore hobbles on her forelegs at night to keep her from straying far, and the others stayed with her. Connors never seemed to have any trouble in rounding them up of a morning. Now Bauer was annoyed because he could see no sign of them. Yet he was positive he had seen them not five minutes before; had made a subconscious note of their presence at the farther side of the pasture-ground. Perhaps the shooting had scared them a little bit; they must be near by, though.

That, precisely, was what had happened – the shots had scared them, or rather had startled them. As the mare gave a jump, one of her leather hobbles snapped, leaving her free except for the short chain trailing from her left foreleg. It hampered her, this dangling fetter, but did not check her gait to any great extent, and at this moment she and her two corral-mates were shoving through the jack-pines, their bellies full of good water and good grass. Homesickness was on them. Jaded though they were, the instinct to return where they belonged was upon them.

Bauer, making search, heard them now threshing and stamping on beyond somewhere. He pushed into the labyrinth, calling soothing words to them. Possibly the truants might have heeded the sound of Connors' voice, which had become familiar to them. On preceding days it was Connors who had baited them from the small store of grain which sustained the animals on the trip across the barren strip. But Bauer's voice meant nothing to them except the prospect of interference with their liberty. They snorted, picked up speed, drew away from that strange voice bleating behind them.

Although he hurried along, following by ear, Bauer spent nearly half an hour in crossing the belt of jack-pines. When he emerged into the clear, the cayuses were three steadily moving dots – one white dot and two dun dots – at the farther end of the mesa.

As he watched them, straining his eyes to peer into the glare of the sunrise, they vanished altogether; and by that he knew they had entered the dip of land leading on out into the desert. From the elevation where he stood, the desert was spread below him, dim and gray in the distance except for certain patches of it which shimmered faintly, and it was very flat-looking, except for certain low ridges which seemed to heave gently under the white brilliance which already filled the eastern horizon.

Something told him he never could hope to overtake them; that the brutes were gone and gone for good. Yet a desperation growing out of his alarm led him on. He ran across the plateau. He was still running as he went down into the draw, was walking, though, and panting hard when he emerged from it. He stopped then, his hands against his heaving short ribs, his eyes blurred, his feet aching inside his low boots.

When his vision had cleared and his breathing was easier, he looked for hoof-marks and saw none at all. He had had prints to guide him almost to this point but now these had disappeared. He retraced his steps a few rods and picked them up, but immediately they petered out on a ledge of hard-baked earth.

He did not venture out on the desert proper, being moved by a faint hope of coming unawares upon the runaways just over the next swale, say, or the swale after that. In this way he traveled perhaps three miles farther. Then something daunting, something which never before had entered into his scheme of things, brought him up short.

Away up yonder above the sky-line, he saw green trees, many green trees, a whole double line of them, in fact; and he saw among the trees what appeared to be a row of buildings dotted along a road. But the whole lot – trees and road and buildings – were turned wrong way to, were floating upside down above the bleak and empty sage-brush of the desert; were suspended between the heat-waves below and the burnished heavens on high.

Never having beheld such a phenomenon before, never having heard that such optical illusions are not exactly uncommon in these parts, Bauer stared, amazed and confounded. As he stared, his imagination played him a trick. He

212

took it into his head that this capsized picture was the identical picture of the cottonwood-shaded side-street through which he and Connors had sped so fast after Mattingly and the police chief passed out.

Now, that town must be at least four hundred miles away; it was fully that far away, maybe more than that. And here it was dancing and shimmering on its head in the sweep of a zenith that had gone crazy and turned itself into a blazing mirror.

Bauer was in no fit frame of mind for calm consideration of any causes whatsoever. The superstitious side of him rose and took possession of him. This must be a sign, a supernatural warning foretelling disaster, a notice to him that he must go no farther along that return route.

No, he must get away from this spot and get quick – abandon the hunt for the horses and go back to the camp place and make new plans. He turned about and shambled away on his chafed feet, gasping a little because of the summer weather and the high altitude. Presently he looked back, cautiously. The reflected presentment was gone from the sky. Bauer figured his interpretation of the thing had been the right one.

He had no trouble in the confusing maze of the jack-pines. It was past noontime, so he judged by the gnawing in his stomach, before he broke through the last of them and came out in the glade.

While he was making a hurried meal of tinned beef and stale crackers, he kept his eyes and his thoughts steadfastly turned from the spot where Connors' shape lay, half in and half out of the dead camp-fire. Having fed, he canvassed the situation and reached the conclusion that, the transformed conditions being what they were, there remained for him but one logical line of action to follow.

Afoot, he must move on through the foot-hills, then must find the pass in the mountains and make his way down the slope to the ocean. He would carry a blanket and the hand-ax; would take along as heavy a load of provisions as he could pack on his back. If he ran out of supplies before he made the grade, he must subsist on the country. There ought to be berries and edible roots in the woods.

In an emergency there ought to be ways to trap the ground-squirrels which played about so fearlessly or, easier still, ways to catch some of these trout that darted to and fro in the shallows of the creek. And if the worst came to the worst, he could go hungry for a spell. Having food in him, he felt at the moment that he dreaded the solitude more than the possibility of starving for a day or two at the latter end of his adventure.

One thing was certain: He did not propose to let the sun go down on him and he still in this lonesome spot with only the stiff of the man he had killed for company. Besides, he needed the sun to steer by. For the remainder of this day, at least, he had only to head for where the sun would set. His path was westward, almost due westward, according to his understanding.

In half an hour he had waded across the creek and was on his way. He had wit enough to hold a swinging course which kept the sun slightly to his left. After it disappeared below the timbered rim, he traveled as straight as he could toward its afterglow. He kept on until the last reddish tinge faded, until walking became difficult in the growing darkness and then, well content with the progress he had made, Bauer started a campfire, ate something, took a swig from his canteen and slept under his blanket against the lee of a low bank in a dense place of aspens and willows.

Those next two days were prolonged repetitions of what the first afternoon's tramp had been – with this exception: Those two days he had no sun to guide him; there was an impenetrable haze over the sun. In this latitude it almost was time for the autumnal rainy spell to set in, so the clouds were thickening, were draped across the whole firmament in heavy dropsical masses.

Even so, Bauer figured he must be trudging in the right direction. He got into mazes of foot-hills, traveled through thick underbrush, crossed many small cold streams, or perhaps it was that he recrossed the same stream many times; regarding this he couldn't be definite. Still, he figured every dragging mile must carry him farther and farther away from the glade on the roaring creek.

At times doubts assailed him, as was to be expected, he being a novice at woodcraft, but in the main he kept telling himself that eventually he must reach the gap in the mountains and after that his travels ought to be simplified. He wasn't just wandering about, of that he was sure. He must be getting somewhere. What puzzled him was that the mountains seemed to be as far distant as they had been at the beginning.

There were times when, through breaks in the timber, or when he had scaled intervening ridges, he could see the tips of two tall peaks – sort of twin peaks, they were. They did not shift about; always when he caught peeps at them, they approximately were where, according to his calculations, they should be. And that was comforting, even though he appeared to be making such slow headway toward them.

But he remembered having been told that in this country objects far off often seemed closer than they really were, and vice versa; which reflection also had its comfort. He was bothered in his mind but he wasn't really bewildered. He kept saying to himself that he was not bewildered, was not growing flighty. Terribly tired, that was it, but not light-headed.

In the forenoon of the following day of his travels, which would make it the third day since the shooting, he strayed into an interminable and perplexing girdle of jack-pines. He spent hours limping in and out among the trunks, while spiny, springy boughs lashed his face, before he saw a thinning in the treetops that betokened an opening on ahead.

Moreover, the land here was almost flat, with a gentle downward slant toward the right. Now, to the right was the quarter where the woods thinned. Perhaps the beginning of the pass was there. He limped along faster.

He came out of the trees and stood on the edge of a natural clearing which somehow seemed vaguely familiar. He stared harder across the space, and then a terrifying conviction fixed itself in his brain. There could be no mistake about it. Yonder, not fifty yards away, was the rummaged heap of heavy duffel that he had abandoned. On beyond was the tumbling creek, with its waters sparkling where it poured over miniature rapids. He was back where he had started.

He stilled a desire to turn and run away from this haunted vista. That would be fatal. Torn by conflicting emotions, he forced himself, foot by foot, across the glade until he halted a stone's throw from the body in the ashes. Coyotes or other vermin had been at the body, but it was Connors' body, all right enough. He recognized the boots on the spraddled legs, the

215

holstered gun on the upturned flank.

Bauer sat down in the grass, his head in his hands and the head rocking to and fro. What dreadful agency, what hostile power or force was it that had thrown up an apparition in the sky to drive him off the desert, that had translated him back again to the very spot which he had been trying so hard and at such pains to get away from? Bauer did not believe in any God but he did believe in what his sort called hunches, meaning by that, nemesis or fate or luck.

Panic racked him as he squatted there. By a supreme effort of his will, he summoned a measure of calmness. He compelled his brain to reason about things, to canvass things, take stock of them.

Was it altogether bad luck that had returned him hither? That was the question. Assuredly there was a store of food here; the scavenger animals had pawed over the edibles but the tinned stuff was safe from their teeth and their claws. And he was practically out of food himself. Despite his careful husbanding, he had eaten nearly all of the supply he took away with him three days before.

He could reprovision himself; he rose up and proceeded to do so. He could make a fresh attempt to get across the range. But since the first effort had ended in this, how would he shape his second flight?

All at once an inspiration came to him, and in a cracked voice he shouted aloud for joy. He remembered something which Connors had said on the night before the shooting. Connors had said that, having passed over the Second Divide, they now were where all streams ran westward to empty into the Pacific Ocean or to empty into larger streams which did empty into the ocean.

No matter how tortuous a course any given stream might pursue, no matter how it might meander and wind and twist, eventually its waters found their way to tide-water – Connors had said that, and at the moment he, Bauer, had paid small heed, his mind being busy with other matters. Connors had added that only an idiot would try to follow a watercourse when he could go dry-shod. So, naturally, the statement had not registered deeply – then. But now – now things were different.

Here was this creek – tough traveling but, in the long run, a sure road to escape. Quickly he made a new pack, taking as much food as he could roll in his blanket and sling on his back. He made sure he had plenty of matches. He took his hand-ax in one hand and his precious satchel in the other and he stepped into the creek and was off down-stream.

Immediately, by experiment, he found that it was easier going if he waded than if he tried to force a path along the shores. There were rounded loose boulders on the bottom, there were swift little rapids, there were occasional unsuspected deep pools where the water rose thigh-deep on him, but with all that, he very soon realized that he could make better time in the stream than in the dense thickets bordering it.

That night he had no camp-fire. His matches, which he had been carrying in a breast pocket of his shirt, were wet as a result of a fall. Before embarking on this sort of trip, a woodsman would have corked his matches in a bottle, or at least would have made sure the receptacle which held them was water-tight; but Bauer, in his ignorance, had taken no such precautions. So, in his soaked garments he slept cold, and next morning was so stiff that for a while every wincing movement meant a stab of sheer agony through his joints.

He went on, though. For days he went on. He lost count of days, lost all notion of compass points. The thing turned into a continuous nightmare. His boots became so much slimy pulp. His feet, inside the boots, rubbed raw and swelled and got very sore.

The small rapids made him dizzy; the pools were pitfalls, full of scoured-out deep holes into which he tumbled, studded with treacherous small round stones over which he tripped, and with bigger stones against which he bruised his legs. At irregular intervals he scrambled ashore, chopped open a can of beans or a can of beef, made a meal – if you could call it that – repacked, reshouldered his sodden burden, reentered the winding creek, staggered on again, going with the current.

Presently he had put himself on short rations, for his stock was running low. In this, however, was a small compensation. The less that he had to carry, the lighter the weight upon his back. To a man growing steadily weaker, that meant something. After every stumble it was harder for him to regain his feet. Even in still water he tottered, leaning heavily upon a staff which he had cut for himself. His posture was that of a very old, very feeble man; his movements were stiffly mechanical, his thoughts disordered and mixed.

He kept on, though.

There was an afternoon when he reached one of the comparatively clear meadowlike patches past which, once in a while, the stream flowed. Bauer was only half aware of this break in the borderings of overhanging growth. He was entirely out of food, and had been since the night before.

That morning he had chewed at twigs, had gnawed at roots which he hoped might contain sustenance. There were no berries or, if there were, he hadn't been able to find any of them. He was on the verge of delirium; had been seeing things which weren't there; had had curious hallucinations as he crept along downstream.

He was cognizant of little bright-colored fishes racing over the shallows. Some of them almost brushed his legs. He stooped, and with his right hand tried to grab one of the swift fingerlings. There was a way to catch these baby trout but it was a way known only to deft experts. Greenhorn-like, Bauer snatched and clutched, and the small creatures easily eluded his fingers and fled away. It was no use.

The exertion made him faint. On all fours, he crawled to the bank and lay face downward in the sunshine. Its warmth was very grateful to him. His blanket was gone and his ax, too. He didn't remember when or where or how he lost either or both. All he knew was they were gone.

Also he had thrown away his pistol; but he dimly remembered about that. Dragging at his hip, it had felt as though it weighed a ton. He still had the leather satchel containing the eighteen thousand dollars. Through everything, he had clung fast to that.

When he was somewhat rested and recovered, he lifted his head and sniffed. A reek as of carrion had come to his nose. He sniffed again, and with a languid motion wiped the dripping plastered hair out of his eyes and raised his head higher, looking about him.

He did not have to look far. Not sixty feet from him was the body of Connors – what was left of it – and there, on beyond,

218

was the tumbled remnant of the camp equipment centered in the familiar setting of the little park. His eyes gaped wider and wider in a frozen stare, and his mouth fell open in a square shape and stayed so, but no sound issued from it.

After all his travail, after all his tortured sufferings, he was, for the third time back where he had started. The third time would be the last time for Bauer. This jinx was unbeatable. Dumbly, as though answering a question in the affirmative, he nodded, then slid backward down the low bank into the water and held his head under until he drowned.

With his last conscious thought he believed that it was his destiny which had licked him, whereas it merely was his lack of acquaintance with purely natural causes. To begin with, he didn't know about mirages being fairly common manifestations in these parts and explainable on scientific grounds. In the second place he didn't know that a man afoot and lost in a wild country almost invariably moves in a circle, by reason of the fact that one foot – usually it's the left foot – is longer by an almost infinitesimal degree than the other foot, thus causing the pedestrian to go in an orbit rather than on the straightaway.

And finally he did not know – how was he to know it? – that on the charts of the state forestry service, this particular creek was called by the name of Queer Creek because hereabouts it made a long freakish loop, circling back to within a scant hundred yards of itself before sliding off westward to make its way down the continental watershed toward the seaboard – or, in other words, you could save thirty-odd miles of creek travel by a three-minute stroll through the grass.

But then of course, ignorance, before now, has been the ruination of better men than Bauer was.

ACE, DEUCE, TEN SPOT, JOKER

THE TEN SPOT

More than almost anything else, one bothering thing kept its grip on The Suet while he was holed-up like a hibernating woodchuck in that combination of rooming-house and sweat-shop over on Lexington Avenue. It was a nagging, buzzing doubt as to whether he had been wise to stay on in town after his break with his old mob rather than to get out of town and stay out until the air cleared.

So far as the cops were concerned, everybody knew you couldn't pick a better hide-out than New York. In New York all was likely to be jake with you unless you had a harelip or a clubfoot or an arm missing – some obvious mark such as that – which made you stand out as different from the run of the shoal. Just so you sang soft and low, you probably would be, even to the inquiring eye, merely an undistinguished one of the seven or eight millions or whatever by the latest census figures the number of human atoms was. But just go for temporary retreat into some lesser community and no matter how small and inconspicuous you made yourself, nevertheless you were a stranger and any minute some hick bull might lamp you and get to thinking, which sometimes was just too bad because what he might get to thinking was where he had read your description or seen your mug smeared across one of these posters headed WANTED. No sir, for crossing up John Law's boys, you couldn't ask a better spot than the middle of little old Manhattan Island.

For the present moment The Suet wasn't dodging John Law. To be sure, any stray Central Office dick who recognized him might take the notion to give him the old runaround or ride him down to Headquarters on general principles. But what of it? You took it and you laughed it off.

Now, though, The Suet was in retirement because of an enemy infinitely more to be dreaded than any cop in or out of uniform – an enemy uncannily shrewd and, by nature, most unforgiving and of a fearsome resourcefulness, so that you never could dope it in advance when he'd be coming at you or whence or how – especially how.

In the Detective Bureau and in the newspapers this enemy still was being referred to by his familiar early name, to wit: Torpedo Mike Romano. They didn't know yet – the "tecs" and the reporters – that within various inner and interrelated circles this distinguished personage was wearing a newer title, one which carried with it a tribute to his latest and greatest series of achievements. Being credited with having devised and in some instances having personally directed the successful plans for extinction, one by one, but all within a six-months' period, of nine of the obnoxious Heiney Schlagel beer mob up in the Bronx, the campaign then suitably concluding with the spectacular rubbing-out of Heiney himself, Torpedo Mike privately had been re-christened so that to admiring intimates he had become The Ten Spotter, which by a quick erosion became The Ten Spot, which inevitably and almost immediately became Big Casino. By these same poetic interpretations, Sammy The Suet was called Sambo because he happened to be so dark of complexion as to suggest negroid blood and nearly always was given the alliterative suffix because he was fat with a greasy and a glistening fatness.

Seeing that before the recent misunderstanding came up he had been an esteemed member of Big Casino's outfit, nobody in all this wicked world would know better than he did that when a guy fell out with Big Casino, said guy sooner or later, but probably sooner, was likely to become an object of interest to one undertaker and a number of florists. The main issues here involved were, first, The Suet stood accused of having willfully failed to execute a lethal commission which had been entrusted to him, and, second, and what was worse, was under further suspicion of attempting to betray his chief's intents in this particular matter to the subject marked for elimination. Obedience, codal discipline, good faith, were all involved in these alleged acts of treachery, hence the affair took on an ethical aspect. Casino was most fussy touching on ethics. Considered in that light, one might call him high church – a ritualistic stylist, a stickler for all the little formalisms.

Thus we observe how essential it was to Sammy The Suet's well-being that he see to the secrecy and the safety of his present place of withdrawal. As to those important details, he should have been fairly satisfied. For his part, there was no visible reason to fear that he had been traced to this asylum, which was a staunchly built five-story brick building several miles south of his late Harlem habitat and situate in the approximate middle of a compact block. His room was a front room on the third floor, which meant that between him and the roof was a full floor and above that in turn a so-called loft, both of these being populated by sewing-machine operators during work hours and very securely locked up at all other hours.

On his own level and for the two below, there were rooms for boarders – not transients but established occupants known to the landlord and vouched for by him. And the landlord he could trust so far as any mortal of their cultural grouping might be trusted. At his back was a good thick wall and one very strong door opening upon a hallway. Facing him from the other side was a single window letting upon the smooth façade of the house and commanding a slantwise view of a brief strip of the avenue. From that direction – since the fire escapes cascaded down the rear elevation – his seclusion was guaranteed against any human intrusion whatsoever unless the intruder brought along scaling-ladders, which wasn't probable, or could fly, which wasn't plausible. Finally, the proprietor brought his meals to him along with such other supplies as he required, and in a corner of his room behind a board partition, was a private bath of sorts.

So, while he waited for the grudge of his late chief to abate itself or for the coming of a time deemed to be appropriate for making overtures looking to a truce, or happily, a permanent peace, he might bide on in these snug quarters, sleeping pleasantly in his bed and reading there or, provided he stayed well back behind the lowered shade, looking outward and down through the panes of the bolted window upon the life of the street. It was the middle of November, so keeping the window sash bolted didn't much matter.

In such undisturbed fashion then, the self-imprisoned fugitive spent a week and part of another week. He had a routine. He slept, woke up, breakfasted, read the news of the day and the magazines of the week – some of them, anyhow; the books of the month as well; smoked. Paced the floor for exercise, looked out of the window some more, smoked some more, dined, smoked, read, went to bed. It was not greatly diverting but it was ever so much better than being in a box with plated silver handles down the sides and a blanket of tuberoses and lilies-of-the-valley over the top. It was better than being surrounded by all these expensive flowers – his crowd went in for swell funerals for fallen brothers – and yet not smelling any of them.

There was just one main drawback to the solitary tenant's comfort and that drawback had a temperamental rather than a physical background. The trouble with him was he had an active imagination. To persons of his dangerous calling, an active imagination is an inconvenience always and sometimes 'tis a positive handicap. For such a person, brooding on the past is bad and projecting the thoughts into the future is worse. With very little of anything except leisure on his hands, Sammy was annoyed by recurring brainpan pictures. He saw Big Casino or one of Big Casino's lieutenants spying out his whereabouts. He saw the favorite rendezvous of the mob, a back parlor of a discreet speakeasy in East One Hundred and Sixteenth Street – saw it down to the very roaches skirmishing over the wainscotings – with the boss sitting there sipping a seltzer lemonade – the boss handled the hard stuff but drank only the soft – sitting there with a droll smile on his plump and placid face; just sitting there, artistically figuring out bright fresh plans of reprisal against him. For the boss, outside of his love of sundry tribal rites, was ever fertile-minded and never more so than when sheering away from the hallowed traditions of their craft to conjure up some shapely, sprightly form of murder which would be as a piquant sauce, adding spice of novelty to the red gravy of his vengeance. Sammy saw these things, and he felt things. For instance, he felt bullets striking his flesh with sharp stinging pains, or piercing his flesh with a terrible burning sensation. In the kind of novels he liked to read, a bullet either stung or burned – invariably did one or the other. And between times he kept worrying about whether or not he had made a mistake by denning-up in New York when he might just as well have gone somewhere else.

Oh, yes, indeed, to poets and to stock promoters and

advertisement writers, an imagination may be an asset but it's a liability for a killer turned hermit.

Sheltered behind the dingy window curtains, the recluse fought off boredom by studying the foreshortened panorama opposite and beneath him. Before the first week of his captivity was over, knew even the numbers on some of the surface cars that went up and down, down and up. By now, the habitués of the block were familiarized to him: the uniformed doorman of the cheap department store on the corner below and the deputy who understudied for that gaudy notable; the mounted cop at the crossing, and his relief; the patrolmen who in daytime alternated on the post of which his circumscribed vista was a part; the proprietor of the stationery shop yonder on the far side, who spent so many hours lounging in his doorway; the newly established apple vendor who risked disaster while he diagonaled back and forth seeking customers in the traffic; the old lady in garments which seemed outlandish because they were twenty years behind the mode – high-buttoned shoes, longish skirts, balloon sleeves and the rest of it – who at eleven o'clock every morning and again every afternoon at three, promenaded the far sidewalk, holding a decrepit pug dog on an unnecessary leash.

Whenever there was an addition to the small fleet of taxicabs which commonly cruised the roadway hereabouts or ranked themselves in the parking space slightly to the north, he knew it. And he was aware of any newcomers appearing among the standbys in that restless ebb and flow of the tides of pedestrian travel. For instance, there was a sandwich man, cased fore and aft with flat boards, who arrived on the fifth day. This one made the third of these human terrapins, these upended turtle shapes, now shambling along this particular beat. His twin shells proclaimed the merits of a cheap restaurant, whereas, of his already established brethren, one perambulated on behalf of a shoe-repairer and the other crawlingly advertised an auction sale which apparently never ended. The way each of these fellows had of dragging his feet and his way of suddenly sticking one hand out like a flapper from behind his carapace to offer printed cards to the passer-by, accentuated the resemblance to a tortoise reared upon its hind legs.

Likewise there was a ragged beggar-man with heavy black

glasses over his eyes, who presently joined the resident mendicants. He appeared on the sixth day. A boy brought him that morning and left him posted in an angle alongside an areaway on the opposite side of the avenue three doors south, where all day thereafter he teetered on his pins and patiently rattled a metal cup and at intervals rapped briskly with a cane upon a large placard which hung from a cord about his neck and which proclaimed him the victim of a powder explosion – with a large family.

This goggled figure, swaying like a channel buoy anchored in an eddy at the verge of some narrow sluiceway, at once became an accepted neighborhood fixture, also.

It got so with Sammy The Suet, and he watching there hour after hour, that he would have missed any one of the regulars who failed to show up. But he told himself that most of all he would have missed the old-fashioned old lady with her funny clothes and her pet specimen of a practically extinct species, that ancient pug dog. She fascinated him. Frequently, in his less perturbed moments, that imagination of his dealt speculatively with her.

The warning came without any warning. There was a smearing of significant drama – a kind of slick and sinister gloss – over the method employed for advising him that his number was up.

On the ninth day, late in the afternoon, he was lying on the bed, propped against the pillows, waiting for his host to bring him the afternoon papers and a fresh stock of cigarettes. The lights were on, the window shade, of course, being drawn.

He heard something – the faintest and tiniest of slithering sounds. He sat up straight and peered over the footboard in the direction of that sound and he saw something. He saw something white, something small and sharply angled, like one corner of an envelope, say, which was crawling, so to speak, through a crack under the bottom of the door and sliding across his threshold. More and more of it came in. It was an envelope. It came in until it was almost entirely in and then it stopped moving and lay there as though waiting for him to pick it up, a flat pale oblong, lying sealed-side up.

Like a chicken entranced by a chalk mark drawn under its beak, he stared at it and stared and stared, his neck stretching, his jaw lolling. For all his hypnotized pose, he didn't forget, though, to listen for noises, however small, from without – the rustle of a body against his bolted door, the stealthy tiptoe of a retreat along the hallway. But there were no such noises.

After a while – maybe five minutes, maybe ten, he very slowly, very cautiously, got up and went and stooped and picked up the envelope and turned it over. In typed letters it was addressed:

Mr. Salvatore Terrafino

Which was all, but which, for The Suet's understanding was enough. That would be Big Casino's deft ironic touch – to call him by his real name, the name which he almost had forgotten was his, so long had it been since he himself had used it or heard it used.

With fingers already turned cold and numbish at their tips, he opened the envelope. The message it contained also was ample and sufficient in its meaning. It was merely a new clean card from a deck of ordinary playing-cards. But it was the ten of diamonds, and, to The Suet, frozen in a stiffly wooden posture, every one of those ten bright little pips was like a separate petal of some scarlet graveyard flower ready to flutter loose and drift down on a coffin lid.

That's what The Suet got for having so much imagination. From that source he got plenty more of trouble through that night and through that next day.

He didn't dare try to make his break during the night; not in the darkness when any black corner in the building, any cranny or sidewalk recess for a block either way might be sheltering the torpedoes. Nor, temperamentally constituted as he was, could he stay on where he was until they came and dug him out of his hole. His only chance – if it was a chance – would be to try for it in broad daylight with people and cops about and all.

In the morning and on through the morning, from behind the slitted shade, he watched the street scene for dangerous-looking strangers. If they were down there – and they must be down there somewhere – he couldn't spot them. He saw all the regulars: the old lady with the pug dog, the apple pedler and the rest of them, but no suspicious newcomers could he see loafing along or idling about or pacing the abbreviated stretch lying within his reach of vision.

So about three o'clock, when the crowds were good and thick, he went down the stairs, one step at a time, with his stubby automatic in his right hand and all the while figuring himself to be no better than a hundred-to-one shot.

The odds were even longer than that.

For him to creep down the narrow stairwell from the second flight to the street level must have taken all of five minutes. Sucking his breath in with a big gulp, he stepped out of the doorway and stood upon the pavement, his back to the building and he trying to look every way at once.

Unless you had been there and seen it with your own eyes, you could never have believed a thing like that could happen so swiftly – yea, and so smoothly.

The apple pedler who, it would subsequently develop, had his station just one door down and on the same side, gave a signal by suddenly flinging a whole platter of apples high in the air, at the same time whistling shrilly. His share being performed, the apple pedler vanished.

The blind man – only it seemed he wasn't a blind man at all – cast off his black glasses and out with a gun and ran then across the roadway, firing briskly as he drew nearer.

The newest one among those three saurian-men closed in on the victim from another flank but his tactics were different. Reaching the curbing, he stopped and squatted so that his front sandwich board made a portable breastwork for him while he swapped shots with their trapped target. A grand breastwork it made, too, seeing it was a sheet of light tough steel painted over so two of The Suet's bullets that struck it zinged and glanced off, leaving gouges in the paint, which details subsequently interested the police department and public press no little. Likewise the abandoned placard of the first gunner had its share of attention. It also was of tempered metal, an excellent shield to the lungs and heart of its wearer.

In half a minute, maybe less, the sandwich-man was freed of his defensive plating and the "blind" man had discarded his armor and the pair of them were racing for a taxicab which just then opportunely cruised past. It slowed up for long enough to take both aboard and fled east by north, flashing a set of forged and therefore misleading license plates in the faces of a confused and, for the most part, a panic-stricken multitude.

As for the properly riddled Suet, he passed out where he had dropped on the pavement before the entryway, and his last conscious thoughts were elsewise directed than to the workmanlike manner of his undoing, there being in these farewell thoughts of his neither deep chagrin over the outcome nor reluctant admiration for the system employed. In these last conscious moments, what filled his mind was a vague wondering – a wondering with an element of shocked astonishment in it – that on penetrating one's person bullets neither stung nor burned, as the story-writers had claimed, but, on the contrary, hit with heavy and stunning impacts, thumps, really, like blows of a club or kicks of a mule's hoof.

THE ACE AND THE DEUCE

Coming out of the Tombs, Mr. M. J. (Slats) Horan obligingly halted to accommodate the waiting newspaper photographers, which the same, as it turned out, was an irreparable error on his part.

But how – we might ask you – was poor old spindle shanked Slats to figure that? The way he figured it, this probably was his last good chance to be photographed for publication. And Slats certainly did love the bright lights, spot-, foot-, or flash-, as the case might be. Also, and by the same token, it would be the last chance for the boys to get a posed likeness of him, inasmuch as this afternoon early he would be off to the United States penitentiary. This was the twenty-third of December, a nice clear day for traveling. And by this time to-morrow he would be Away Down South in Dixie – hooray, hooray! – reaching Atlanta in ample time to get settled and be all primed and ready to wish the warden a Merry Christmas.

Seeing that he very much preferred to be found by St. Nick on a bunk in the Big House rather than on a slab at the Morgue, this promised to be not such an un-Merry Christmas for Slats, either. Of two contingent evils he deliberately had chosen the one which by infinitely long odds was the lesser. As a ward of the government and a temporary guest of the County of New York, he had been safe enough these past few weeks here in the Tombs

228

while awaiting transportation to the bigger prison; and most assuredly he would be safe – safer than a bug in a rug and practically as snug as one – down yonder in Georgia, that hospitable land of cotton for which so many homesick darkies are by so many popular song writers supposed to yearn with an unappeasable yearning. Well, Slats had done some yearning in that general direction on his own account. His four-year bit for violating the income-tax laws didn't matter. Once he got at it, he could, as the saying went, do it standing on his head. What was more, in four years a good many things could happen and undoubtedly would. This might be forgiven and that might be forgotten; such-and-such a one might die or quit or even soften to the point of letting bygones be bygones.

Howsomever, until this bygoer was absolutely begone, the chief of the Homicide Bureau at Headquarters, knowing, that wise old head, what he did know and having, as he did have, the somewhat battered good name of the Department at heart, meant that no mishap which possibly was avoidable should befall during these final hours while Slats remained in the home bailiwick. The national arm might have taken over this lengthy young man for its very own, but until he passed beyond this venue there were the matters of local jurisdiction and local protection to be considered; and in these matters the Department felt a quite pressing responsibility.

Accordingly, for purposes of better insurance against accidents and such, an escort squad of four Central Office men were waiting outside the Tombs when Slats, handcuffed to a Federal deputy-marshal, came forth into the smacky winter sunshine. Furthermore, a special detail of six men in uniform assisted the brace of patrolmen on regular post duty there to maintain a ring around the police wagon that was drawn up at the curb and to form a sort of living aisle across the pavement of Lafayette Street from the door of the jail to the door of the wagon.

Inside the cordon were the newspaper photographers, five or six pushy, enterprising young men, all with their cameras unslung and loaded. Somebody said once that photographers had come to be to newspapers what cooties are to a war – bothersome but inevitable.

"Hey, Slats, old-timer," called out Haley, of the *Evening*

Review, who many a time and oft before had snapped this familiar subject. "How about a nice going-away picture, eh?"

"Sure," said Slats, and smiled.

"Stick right where you are then on that top step," commanded Schlosser, of the *Daily Pictorial*.

So the Central Office men drew off to this side and that, leaving the coupled pair standing between the stone jambs of the doorway. Just below these two the photographers jockeyed for angle and focus, squinting through their finders to make sure of good close-ups.

In chorus their shutters clicked. But no one there heard the clickings, because those sounds were swallowed up in a sharp and not far-distant crackle of gunfire from somewhere above and somewhere beyond the cameramen and the cops.

There was a quick scatteration this way and that, what with policemen whirling about to face eastward and reaching for their own guns, and photographers scurrying for refuge behind the patrol-wagon or behind one another or behind something else; and the United States deputy tried to scrouge in for shelter against the portico pillars but found he couldn't very readily make it by reason of being tethered to a corpse.

So soon as all that, Slats was dead and gone. There he was, down on the broad of his back, and just at the inner corner of his left eye a small-calibre bullet-hole.

It would seem that the *Review* man recovered his wits and his nerve quicker than any of his competitors. He shifted plates and got a grand picture of Slats and the deputy, with Slats all flattened out except for one long thin arm held tautly aloft where it was chained, wrist by wrist, to the shying deputy, and on the deputy's face about the most comical look of surprise and scare you could imagine. It made a swell full-page, front-page layout for the *Review's* Five Star edition that evening – the swellest layout, everybody in tabloid journalism agreed, that had been run in this man's town since another tab's staff star with a baby camera up his leg, got that lovely picture of Ruth Snyder in the Chair up at Sing Sing, that time.

It was a clean beat for the *Review*. Because, by the time the rival photographers got over their fright and returned to the spot subsequently marked X in the newspaper diagrams – at least two of them had run entirely around the corner of Chambers Street –

the handcuffs had been unlocked and the deputy was somewhat recomposed. Indeed, one of the photographers who fled never returned at all. When he dusted around the corner he kept right on with his dusting. At first, in the excitement and the hullabaloo and all, he wasn't missed. Anyhow, nobody was searching for him then. For the moment, the hunt was for whoever it was that had done that volley-firing over on the far side of the little plaza fronting the Tombs.

It was later – fully an hour later – before this entirely vanished individual became an object of official interest; and it was through the days and weeks which followed that thousands upon thousands of good people all over America memorized his printed description in the hope of meeting up with him, though none of them did, or at least if any of them ever did, didn't recognize him.

That, however, was understandable in view of the fact that the persons who collaborated in getting up the reward notice had so little to go on. They didn't know what his real name might be or his aliases, if any. They didn't have his likeness in the Gallery or his finger-prints or, assumed they did have them there, had no way of checking up and proving by comparison that they were his prints. And the description of him that was broadcast was a description to which about every tenth man you met essentially might answer; small, dark, smooth-shaven, quietly dressed, Jewish-looking, apparently about twenty-five years of age, weight approximately one hundred and forty; when last seen wearing a faked-up press card in his hatband, posing as a photographer for a Bronx newspaper and carrying inside a camera-case a deadly weapon with a silencer attached to it, probably an automatic revolver.

But naturally, not even the most simple-minded citizen expected that the party sought for would go on wearing a bogus press card or posing as a photographer for a Bronx newspaper or, most unlikely prospect of all, toting about with him a muted pistol concealed in a camera-box.

Constant Reader or Regular Subscriber or even old Vox Populi does not know this trade secret:

To every big crime mystery that breaks, there are two distinct

231

angles – the angle which is printed in the public press and the angle embodying what technically is known as the "inside story" or the "real low-down." Now, this latter angle, although familiar to the police and to the reporters and usually to the deskmen in the city-rooms, is rarely or never presented in the public press. For this there are reasons which we won't go into now – it would only confuse the Rollo Boys all the more.

For instance, as figuring in this Slats Horan case was, first: the interview which Chief Inspector Fay, speaking for the Commissioner, gave out for publication on the day of the killing, and second, the entirely private statement which he made to a couple of Headquarters reporters in whom he had special confidence. These two were his trusted and valued friends – they'd helped to make him what he was to-day. So to them he spoke freely, if somewhat bitterly, and before them exhibited an air of chagrined defeatism vastly different from the air of jaunty confidence he had worn an hour earlier in his official audience for the assembled pressmen.

"Oh, I get your slant, all right," said the harried chief inspector. "To you fellows this here Slats is a heap bigger man dead than he ever was alive and kicking. And yet, lova Mike, how you did swell him up out of all reason when he was alive! That was his ruination – the way you swelled him up. You made him think he was the top of the pack when he was never anything more, first, last, or any time, than a dirty deuce.

"Listen, I'll prove it to you: He gets all swelled up until he takes it in his cheap head to try to muscle in, single-handed, on a real racket. And while he's muscling-in, he feels called on to prove how important he is by bumping off some little guy. And then all of a sudden he wakes up to what any guy with brains would have known before – that he's bumped off a connection of somebody that's about ten thousand times as powerful as he'll ever be. So the yellow crawls up his neck and he takes a running jump right into the bosom of the Federal court with a plea of guilty to that old indictment against him. It was a rap he could 'a' beaten but he takes it quick, and so to-day, thinking he's out in the clear, he comes out of stir, grinning all over.

"And then what? Why, a real face-card, an ace that probably was imported for this special job from Chi' or St. Louis or Detroit or points west, wipes that grin off his map with a slug out of a

232

dead-and-dumb gun rigged up in a phony camera, whilst a couple of other smart lads on the roof of a tenement house a block away are cutting loose in the air to cover up for him. What's more, by working that trick they give the operator plenty of time for making his get-away while my boys are running circles around the neighborhood following after the false lead. Now, between us, who was it framed up that swell plant right under the noses of a dozen cops? I give you fellows one guess and it'll be the right one – the only performer in this town that's slick enough to have thought it out, that's who. And my private bet is we'll not be able to pin it on him any more than we could pin that lovely Lex. Avenoo job on him last month when Sammy The Suet got his. Here's one Wop that when he sucks eggs he sure hides the shells."

"But you're going after him all the same," said one of his confidants. "What for?"

"What for, but a stall?" admitted Inspector Fay. "Only you'll keep that part under your hats, you two. You saw the head-line the *Star* had on its second extra after the shooting – 'Dragnet Out for King of Gunmen in "Slats" Assassination.' 'Dragnet' – get that? When he'd already telephoned these Headquarters he'd be right down to answer any questions as soon as he could get here. And he'll be here any minute now, looking like a smooth-faced Santa Claus and handing out that regular line of hooey of his about being just a quiet business man trying to do the best he can and why is it the cops don't leave him alone instead of trying to hang it on him every time somebody gets sneezed off in this town?

"It's a laugh, fellows, all the way through, only you'll excuse me for not laughing much."

THE JOKER

"Smooth-faced Santa Claus" was good. It was very good. It was better than Inspector Fay dreamed when he coined it.

Because, forty-eight hours later, the Ten Spot, at his luxurious apartment on upper Fifth Avenue, was playing that identical rôle for his adored son and heir, Master Angelo Romano, aged three and a half.

For Master Angelo and for his doting father, not to mention

his small fat mother, it was indeed a grand Christmas. The spirit of the festival even extended to the attendant gorillas on guard fore and aft of the building. A share of the Yuletide joy, of the Yuletide peace on earth was theirs.

And why shouldn't all three members of the Romano household be happy? Mama Romano had the new mink coat and the new ermine coat and the new diamond bracelet she wanted. Baby Romano had a tall and lovely tree and half a carload of expensive gifts. Papa Romano had within him the beautiful glow of satisfaction which comes to a creative genius when he knows that the work of his hands has been good and that on it the world – or at least his world – has put the stamp of its approval.

Still, Fate certainly moves in a mysterious way its blunders to perform, doesn't it? Here was the Romano family all filled with contentment and joy on Christmas Day in the morning and yet within a week Papa Romano would be engaged in dying, after considerable suffering, of acute blood-poisoning.

There was nothing sinister about this tragedy. No subtle enemy laced the wassail cup with venomed drug or put some deadly essence in ye olde minced pie – absolutely nothing of the sort.

What happened, and all that happened, was this: Childlike, Master Romano toddled past a thousand dollars' worth of mechanical toys to fix his juvenile fancy on a small, cheap, gaudily-painted Noah's Ark which some humble friend and well-wisher of the father had bought at the five-and-ten and had sent along. And presently, under baby's rude handling, the head of the spotted wooden lamb came unglued from its whittled neckpiece. So the baby carried the lamb to his father for mending; and the father moistened the socket with his tongue and stuck the head back on. And some trace of a most unbenignant acid in the glue or some corrosive foreign substance in the dye – the physicians had both notions but no positive evidence either way – got into Papa Romano's person by way of a tiny canker sore on his lower lip and set up in his system so malignant a chemistry that neither nature nor the best science which money might buy could save him.

All of which would seem to establish, if indeed it establishes anything at all, that once in a while Destiny deals unobserved from a marked deck to take the winning trick.

Or maybe the reader has a better theory of his own?

BALM OF GILEAD

Where old man Jethro Tallbee was, he was as much out of place as a bald-headed eagle would be in a pet store. Where he was, was one of those unbeautiful Chicago suburbs which sprawl under the lower flanges of Chicago like so many unweaned pigs nuzzling along the belly of the mother pig. Where he came from was a cleft fenced in by two bony-looking mountains, and this mountain here on this side a Virginia mountain and that mountain over on yonder side a Kentucky mountain, so that the clove between them straddled the state line like a saddle-blanket on a sway-backed mare.

For his present declining years, old man Tallbee lived on the upper floor of a square-faced, tin-roofed, two-story, two-family house made of cheap wood and once painted over with cheap paints. It was a typical one of those houses which look so disagreeably new when some jerry-builder of a contractor throws them up in long sad rows, and so incredibly old as soon as they quit looking new, which nearly always is quite soon. He lived there with his daughter, Myrtle Ellie, and she had nimble fingers and did piece-work for a mass-productionist of artificial flowers for the hat trades and the decorative trades. In your time, you must have seen, on the fake indoor trellises of cheap tearooms or on the trick indoor fences of midget golf courses, those sprays of woodbine or those clumps of grape leaves, all arson red and arsenic green, dangling from the ceilings of the same, great pendent garlands of wisteria blooms the likes of which, even by Nature's most careless gesture, never yet were suffered to sprout on land or sea? Oh, you must've! Mr. Tallbee's daughter fabricated such, but since she did so with honest intent thereby to earn her daily bread, much must be forgiven her. To Myrtle Ellie, life here in the North was full to an abundance. But if home is where the heart is, then her father's home still was away off yonder on the ancestral steadings of his own people in a certain shut-in cove that dipped across the gaunt and knuckly *chine* of a certain spur.

They say that uprooting them from their native crannies

236

takes your born-and-bred mountaineers like that, and, for proof, point to the chronic melancholia of transplanted Swiss and to a suicidal nostalgia said to be common among expatriated Montenegrins. It surely was true of this elderly Tallbee person. Homesickness afflicted him like gripes in the stomach – with almost a physical gnawing, almost an actual pain.

Consider his case: Bodily, with the aching tentacles of his being unearthed and dangling, he had been torn away from the spot which had given his family nutriment of a sort since before the Revolution. Those slopes of the Cumberlands had been the first frontier of the young nation and practically to this day have endured as the last frontier of a nation grown up. He came, you know, of a breed who began as pioneersmen and, by virtue of the fact that the newer American civilization flowed on by and around them, remained pioneersmen. So now he was an unreconstructed pioneer in exile. He was all of that and he was more than that: He was a big-game hunter lamentably imprisoned, so to speak, in a stranger's poultry-yard. The game he persistently had hunted from his early youth on, was the shrewdest, the most formidable and the most dangerous game known – human beings. For forty-odd years, until they ripped him loose from where he followed the perilous sport of gunning for his fellowman, he had been the titular head of the Tallbee clan in the famous Tallbee-Zachary clan war.

The Tallbee-Zachary war was so old that no living survivor of it knew exactly how old it might be or even knew for sure what started it. One story was that a quarrel between a Tallbee and a Zachary concerning overlapping land-grants led to the first shedding of blood. And another was that so trifling a matter as the disputed ownership of a yearling shote – just a slab-sided, dirty-nosed little razorback – had been the original cause. And yet a third version had it that back in the ancient time of the wilderness invasion, while Kentucky still was a domain of Virginia, a son of the Zachary flock wronged a virgin of the Tallbees and thus began the beginnings of it there where twin ridges spread apart, like a forking of a spinal column, to make a narrowed valley behind the spraddled inner ranges.

That valley, for going on four generations, had been a funnel for trouble. At sixteen, Jethro Tallbee, by ambushing a Zachary twice his age, qualified himself to carry on the serious affairs of

237

manhood. At twenty-four, when his father was wiped out in a courtroom duel, he succeeded to the leadership of his faction, becoming commander of a force which through the ramifications of marriage and intermarriage, by now included dozens of families. He had two brothers killed in the intermittent but desperate fighting, and he lost divers uncles and sundry cousins. Had he bred a son, he might also have lost that one. As nearly as might be though, he and his partisans kept the score evened: an eye for an eye, a tooth for a tooth, a life for a life – at least one life for every life of theirs violently taken. The feud was as much a part of him as the marrows of his bones were. The run of us pray for peace and security with our neighbors; this was a nook of the world where pious men and women – for most all here were strict church-members and strict church-goers – prayed for strength to go on hating their neighbors, prayed for better opportunity to stretch their neighbors dead upon the earth.

If this feud was the oldest of the feuds in the hind-country of the mountains, likewise it lived the longest. Wherever the railroad went nosing into a feud district, bringing in its trail such marks of modern improvement as long-distance telephones, radio-sets and northern investors, there you had a district whose feud was found to languish and wither away. New blood coming in meant bad blood fading out. Now it came to pass that finally capital came knocking at the doors of the Tallbees, their kith, and of the Zacharys, their kin. Capital had heard of the timber on the soil of this border-county, and capital suspected coal and maybe oil but certainly gas down in the ground, and capital dreamed nourishing dreams of harnessing up much and large water powers from tumbling swift streams. By such legal processes as prevailed upon the flanking lowlands, there was no hope whatsoever of pacifying the disputants over a terrain which for outsiders had the nickname of "Satan's Stamping Ground." How might the law operate according to the law's orderly procedures where practically every local officeholder owed his election to the faction in political ascendancy for the moment, where every other potential grand-juror was related by blood or marriage or clannish ties to some household actively embroiled; where prudence or prejudice sealed up the mouth of every witness to this brisk mêlée or that stark homicide?

Faced by a condition and not by theories, the harassed

governor of a forward-looking commonwealth appealed personally to the leaders. He pleaded with them for a temporary truce while unbiased plenipotentiaries of his choosing sat on the battle-field and heard evidence and, at the end, proposed such remedies as seemed to these mediators feasible and just. The proposition appeared reasonable. Speaking for his henchmen, old Jethro Tallbee said all right, and speaking for his, old Zach Zachary made a solemn pledge that there shouldn't be no hostilities for a given season. Both belonged to a race which, when it passes its word, keeps it.

From various strongholds at the head of the gap, the Tallbees sent down their chosen representatives and from their natural fortresses at the foot of the gap, the Zacharys sent up theirs. No delegate came openly bearing arms; it was a rule. It was the first time in all their adult lives that these men while journeying anywhere – to the little corn-fields and the little tobacco patches to work, to the log barns to feed their stock, to the dooryards to milk scrub cows, to the court-house or meeting-house, still-house or school-house; to weddings or funerals, to infairs or to quiltings – had failed to fetch their weapons along.

Proceeding cautiously, His Excellency's legates sounded for suppressed opinion and at length by deft and diplomatic probing they arrived at it. On the surface, the old bale-fires burned as hotly as ever, but underneath it seemed there was a hidden sentiment for something else than everlasting vendetta. Barring a few embittered old crones who by violence had been orphaned in their youth, widowed in their prime and shorn of sons in their age, the shy, silent mountain women, so it was revealed, favored no more shootings on the public square, no more "laywayin's" on the highroads, no more tight shutters for lighted windows at night. Some of the younger generation were more articulate in their craving for an enduring treaty. For some of them had been eastward toward Tidewater Virginia, or westward toward Blue Glass Kentucky, and had seen how much securer was every-day existence among the "furriners" of the "settlemints." They spoke out openly and boldly.

So the upshot was that the governor's ambassadors drew up a report making a recommendation that the head of either faction and a specified equal number of the members of either faction should bind themselves to remove from the state and stay

239

removed for a given period. As between the ringleaders, Jethro Tallbee and Zach Zachary, both implacable, both baptized in the red dye pots of a perpetual enmity, there could never be harmony or even the semblance of harmony; that was freely conceded. Therefore Tallbee should go entirely away, and also three of Tallbee's chief lieutenants, two being nephews of his and one a cousin, likewise should depart taking their immediate families with them; while, for their part, the Zacharys must send forth to voluntary exile old Zach Zachary and his remaining three sons of the seven he had begotten, with their wives and all their get.

And the strangest part of the thing was that the proposed plan actually prevailed.

It was his daughter, Myrtle Ellie, who took him by the hand and steered old man Tallbee's bewildered footsteps onward north by nor'west, to the Chicagoan outskirts. Nor was it chance alone which halted the pilgrimage of these two émigrés where the city, like a fecund and prodigal great sow of a city, had farrowed this huddled little of communal sucklings, one touching against another and each one snuggled up to the long teats of some far-reaching boulevard stretching outward across the prairie. From a former roommate at a school for technical training near Lexington, which for two terms she attended, Myrtle Ellie already had the promise of hire in a factory, the ex-roommate being established there as an assistant forewoman of one of its departments. The wages scale was good but you had to speed up to make the grade. Two partners named Glaum & Rofalsky, saw to that.

So, having concluded the first trip by rail he ever had made, and having, with mingled amazement and distaste, looked his first intimate looks upon the packed environs of a metropolis, old man Tallbee at length was guided to the flat spot where thereafter he would abide. Wearily then and with a lack-luster eye, he stared about him and to the exhilarated, excited girl he said:

"Daughter, you have tolled me one fur and toilsome piece to a sorry and a dauncy prospect. To you, this here may be like unto the land of Gilead but there'll everly be no ba'm in it fur me – not nary smidgin'. This minute I'm pinin' and honin' fur the knees of them high-up rocks that cradled me. Myrtle Ellie, it's a cravin' within me that I ain't never goin' to be able to 'swage all the long-lonesome time I'm penned up here."

He talked like that – with the tongue of the isolated southern hillsman whose Elizabethan words and phrases, obsolete everywhere else except in those Appalachian back-washes, often are intermingled with twistified Old Testamental metaphors.

"Oh, pappy," she told him, "you'll like it – soon as ever you get used to it. It's different, that's all. I like it fine. I know I'm going to like it better, once I get acquainted and all."

He shook his head with long swinging motions, like a yoke-chafed steer,

"It mout mebbe do fur you, child, you bein' in your mind more souple-like. Besides which, you air a woman-person and young, whilst I air a man-person and doddered with age and main-fast set in my ways."

About herself, she being an adaptable little body, she was quite right, but about him she was all wrong; things turned out so. For the freed Myrtle Ellie, each succeeding day now was an emancipation and a carnival. She shortened up her skirts and bobbed off her hair. She acquired a lipstick and a Lithuanian lover. She attained to complete social independence and to promotion at the place where she worked. She became a patron of movie-theaters and of beauty-parlors, a sophisticated attendant of Saturday night dances. She learned the difficult art – at least she learned the basic rudiments of it – of slyly flirting with other girls' sweethearts and yet keeping her own sweetheart docile and faithful although racked with the pangs of a dumb jealousy. She found out how to browse without buying in big department stores and how to find bargains in cheap shops run by shrewd copy-cats on obscure side-streets. In the Loop she shortly was at home, on the Lake Front likewise. As her horizons expanded, so likewise her cultural and her professional ambitions grew. In short, Myrtle Ellie with marvelous speed became naturalized, acclimatized, citified, and, to her way of thinking, civilized.

With her father it was a very different story. By all the elements of his nature, as by all the memories of his environment and his upbringing, it had to be a different story with him. Those sweet clean winds of the upper heights; he had traded them off for a mixture of monoxide gas, coal soot, street dust and second-hand air. For the sightly view which during all his sixty-seven years had been, or so he regarded it, practically his own private view – Spicebush Mountain on the left, Powder Smoke Mountain on the right, and down the middle the diminishing panorama of the walled-in valley – he now commanded from his bedroom window a chopped-off vista essentially composed of wooden porches, fire-escapes, clothes-poles, garbage cans and ash cans and foraging alley-cats. Instead of the musky smells of the woods and the reeky smells of his still by a spring in a thicket behind his rear brush fence, he had his share, when the wind blew south, of the wafted breath of the stockyards. In time you may get used to the wafted breath of the stockyards but you never really learn to care for it. Old man Tallbee couldn't even get used to it.

His waking hours largely were spent in making comparisons. He compared the present crowded, noisy, mussified and messified neighborhood to the brooding quiet of sparsely settled uplands, always to the disparagement of the first-named. The alien chatterings of the polyglot multitude that hived about him here in this dingy vestibule of a civic House of All Nations he compared to the quaint Chaucerian periods and the sonorous Biblical misquotations of his own kind. To be sure, he never had heard of any one named Chaucer and it never had occurred to him that his language might have quaintness, but he did most woefully and constantly miss that speech which seemed to him the only proper speech for rational creatures to use. That had been talk, understandable talk, human talk. This was just so much gabble when it wasn't just so much gibberish.

Most of all, though, the highlander missed his chief employment of the past – the absorbing, uplifting, tremendously important, fearfully precarious business which had concerned him from the time of his 'prentice days on to this dreary time of a fierce and utter boredom. For excitement, he had now an occasional traffic accident to watch or a quarrel to overhear among children who seemed always to be quarreling, or once a taste of rescue work during a fire in a hat-cleaning shop across the way. Such trivialities he had for his spiritual uplifting these days – he who had known the vasty lure of stalking armed men; the pitting of his woodcraft and his skill and his trigger-wisdom against theirs; the listening in ambuscade for the footsteps of the victim; the surprise attack; the shock of the counter-attack coming suddenly and unexpectedly. He missed his friends and he missed his enemies. If anything, he missed the enemies more than he missed the friends, for the friends had been his followers and his enemies had been the big game he painstakingly but blithely had hunted. If only once in a while he could shoot at somebody and be shot at by somebody, he would almost feel reconciled to the edges of Chicago. He told himself so often. He told himself he was rusting out; was getting to be a sluggardly old heifer. But when he called himself a heifer, he didn't mean what you, on using the same word, would mean. He meant what Marlowe or Spenser might have meant.

He had a job that engaged him for twelve hours out of the twenty-four, which helped. A house-wrecking contractor paid him to watch buildings in process of being torn down or sometimes heaps of salvaged building materials. His spells of duty ran from six in the evenings until six in the mornings. This meant he returned to the upper flat in the double-flat house about the time Myrtle Ellie was dressing to be off for her daily rendezvous with a time o'clock. They would have breakfast together and then he would go to sleep in the darkened rear room and she would go forth, stylishly teetering on high heels and pinched-in toes, to make her artificial flowers.

Along toward the middle of the afternoon the father would awake and get himself a meal of sorts and pack a lunch in a basket to be eaten at midnight. Then invariably he followed a certain ritual. He would take up his heavy repeating rifle, the favored weapon which he had brought with him as his most precious possession when he moved North. It was old-looking and battered and scarred upon its walnut stock but always its metal parts dripped oil and always it had a dull sheen on it for proof of frequent polishings with an oiled rag.

He would take it up from where it stood in a corner by the head of his bed, and briskly he would operate the unloading mechanism so that the tallowed cartridges vomited from the magazine, each emerging with a smooth and lubric little clucking sound, and tiny globules of grease spattered on his hands and his shirt-front. Doing this, he would be sitting on a chair indoors if the weather were very cold or very rainy, but in pleasant weather he would squat for the ceremonial rite on a camp-stool upon a very small outer porch which filled the V-space below the tuck of the sharply gabled roof. This porch, being enclosed on three sides, and snugged back beneath and behind the jut of an overhanging tin cornice that was like a wen on a lowbrow's brow, made a congenial retreat for old man Tallbee while he practised the intricacies of a once-invaluable but now useless accomplishment. For, having emptied the rifle, he next would make expert play with it. With swift darting motions he would point it here and there, pulling the trigger each time, and between pulls jerk the lever bolt down and up again as though each pretended discharge he were pumping in a fresh shell for firing. At each time of aiming, he recreated a treasured brain picture. Sometimes, by a familiar trick of the imagination, the repeater would become an ancient squirrel rifle with brass mountings on its butt and brass scrollings on its lock; and squinting down its octagonal long barrel, he drew a fine bead on that earlier Zachary whom he, a boy of sixteen then, had dropped. Or perhaps he sighted once more at a certain bulky foeman who, having shot at him with an old-fashioned derringer and missed, jumped behind a tree to reload; but the tree was slim through the bole and only partly sheltered the other man so that with two quick snap-shots Tallbee shattered one leg and one arm for him and forever after made a mutilated fractional joke out of him. A man who became only a hobbling two-thirds of a man was no longer an asset but just a liability in a clan war. That certainly had been smart gunnery.

And so on, through repetitious performances of the performer's share in a dozen or more individual affrays and his share in at least one pitched fight by appointment where clan in force met clan in force and they shot it out, man to man, bullet for bullet. It served somewhat to ease that besetting homesickness of his.

The pleasant reminiscent routine being concluded, Jethro Tallbee would gather up the spilled cartridges from the floor about him and refill the magazine and start off to report for service. He was the only night guard on the housewrecker's pay-roll who stood watch with a rifle beside him. His predecessors had carried clubs and some of them, under permit, had carried revolvers.

By now, the many-tongued neighborhood had grown accustomed to his armed passage along the sidewalks. To casual onlookers, though, beholding him for the first time against the jumbled-up background across which he strode twice daily, the old warlock made a fascinating and a daunting show, what with his rifle at the trail or else caught up in the notch of an elbow, and what with his longish hair and his thick grizzly beard; and that loping gait of his and the weather-tanned puckered-up face and those vigilant squinty eyes of his. To such spectators as these he seemed almost as an apparition from another planet might have seemed. Moving on past, silent and contemptuous and brooding, the shaggy ex-clansman paid no heed to their staring. Mentally he brushed them from his path, abolishing them, one and all, with a psychic gesture. By his standards their sort, and not his sort, were the universe's weirdest and most curious folk.

There was, up in the city itself, an inner division of a larger division which, generally, went by the name of the Christy Bannon mob. Once these affiliated young gentlemen – for all of them were young or youngish – would have been called gangsters. Later they commonly had been referred to as gunmen. Now the title of "racketeers" increasingly was used in this connection.

Of this lesser coterie of affiliates the acknowledged captain was a youth of the mercurial Sicilian blood with a nervous mannerism of shooting people. He was about twenty-one years old, and at that he was the senior of the particular sub-group who largely looked up to him for authority. Indeed, their junior member, a Polish lad, dapper and trim, had just passed his seventeenth birthday. But any naturalist will tell you that a newly hatched baby cobra is just as deadly and frequently more irritable than either mother cobra or father cobra. In all, there were four of these high-spirited juveniles, and of the four, one was an expert driver of motor-vehicles and had a forged chauffeur's license, which came in very handy sometimes.

In their regular lines of specialized endeavor, things were dull, due to the summertime off-season. So, boy-like, these boys decided to rob a bank. Upon a muggy Saturday in mid-August, this blithesome quartet got in a camouflaged private taxi which had extra fast engines concealed within its frame, and they drove a few miles down-state until they reached a prospering industrial purlieu. Perhaps it was the humidity or perhaps, on the other hand, it was some private pique which made their temperamental chieftain even more touchy than usual. At any rate, in the forepart of the ensuing coup he petulantly killed a frightened and perfectly inoffensive paying-teller.

Under the slanted eaves of the sun-warmed tin roof, the air on the back bedroom was so smotheringly close that old man Tallbee, who generally slept well, slept restlessly. On this day he was up by noon, mopping at his skinny wrinkled red neck. In the kitchen he ate a cold bite – it was too blisteringly-hot for hot food – and then, in his undershirt and trousers and bare-footed, he went out on the little front porch and perched on his camp-stool behind the guard-railing. Such being his habit, as previously described, he mechanically took his repeating rifle with him and rested it across his sweaty knees and bit off a chew of tobacco from a plug, and for a little while sat listlessly chewing and listlessly watching the huddle of vicinity life stirring in the by-street beneath him. It being Saturday, there was, despite the heat, a large out-turning hereabouts of the residents, shopping for over Sunday. "A lavishmint of belongers" Mr. Tallbee would have called the assembled populace at the open-air market below him had he been sufficiently interested in the populace to call it anything at all.

All at once, from a distance of perhaps three cross-town blocks, there came a sharp harsh series of explosions – one bang, then a second bang, then a heavy booming noise, then a whole rat-tat-tat-tat of reports pitched on a crackling key. Among the swarms elbowing one another about the pavement stands and the push-carts, the volley of sounds led to no more than a momentary lifting and turning of heads. But old man Tallbee now; he had the trained ear. Old man Tallbee was one to know the difference between the backfiring of a balky automobile and a superimposed medley of shots from lethal tools of varying types and distinctive calibers.

It happened then that of all in this teeming area, he alone was poised and prepared for what immediately followed; and that was this: A taxicab, moving at terrific speed, careened on two wheels around the nearest corner south and, heading toward him, sped right into and through the milling mass on beyond where he stood tautly waiting. There arose a shrieking, as the suddenly terrorized jam of people scrambled and tumbled every-which-way, and cowered and crouched, trying to escape from the swerving, onrushing car. There was from somewhere in its roaring wake a panicky tumult of shouts and cries and screeches and next, spinning into view behind it, appeared a policeman on a motorcycle, and this policeman had his service revolver in one hand as he steered his throbbing machine with the other.

From a window of the fleeing cab, a marksman's arm came out and a sleek young head, and, to a staccato blast from an automatic, the lone pursuer went down in the roadway, and his motorcycle went slithering along with him and, with two holes in him, he probably was dead before his body quit sliding and bouncing. Also, from the interior of the car, a sawed-off shotgun was let off. It was let off seemingly in pure wantonness since no one menaced the flight of the fugitives from the quarter toward which the slanted barrels were turned; and at their bellowing outburst of buckshot, a push-cart pedler flopped on his face, wriggling and heaving, and a woman who was scrooged up against a show-window screamed in a mortal frenzy to see what had befallen her baby in its riddled baby-carriage.

Now, all of this, you'll understand, took place in less time than the time required to read about it, and within the length of less than half of a city block. What thereafter took place, likewise was over and substantially done within a whisk of minutes – maybe a minute and a half, maybe two minutes. To tell about such matters takes longer than to do them, if the operator be both practised and prompt, as in this case was the case.

With his sparse frame craned outward across the wooden railing of his overhead vantage, the old clansman entered into the above proceedings by firing twice, firing so rapidly that the two shots sounded almost like one shot which had stammered slightly. He sent the first shot at a whirling forewheel and, things considered, it was rather a hard wheel to hit; but he hit it and ripped its tire wide open, which was his intent; and he poured the second shot into the considerably less difficult target of the driver's lap, whereupon that grievously surprised individual collapsed behind his wheel and remained there in a slumped heap even after the uncontrolled car angled off wildly and crashed to a halt against the curb of the opposite sidewalk; in fact, remained there until the coroner an hour or so later gave orders for dislodging his wedged-in remains.

In the jump-seat just back of the chauffeur, facing aft so that, with a midget machine-gun which was balanced upon his knees, he might defensively cover their retreat, the junior murderer of this disrupted partnership of murderers had been riding. By the jolt of the smash when the skewing taxi struck the curbing, the door alongside him was jerked open and he was dumped out upon his hands and knees. Shaken and partly stunned, he still was on all fours, groggily lifting himself when a soft-nosed slug took him obliquely between the shoulders and flattened him. Although perforated from back to front and with one lung punctured, this adolescent lived to be tried.

Still unaccounted for, were the remaining two in the rear seat of the damaged car – the volatile but peevish leader of the party and he with his automatic gripped in that impulsive right hand of his; and beside him, that irritable confrère who toted the abbreviated scatter-gun, the twin tubes of the latter weapon being for the moment empty. They must have figured that, shut in as they were, with their vision interrupted and their movements hampered, they had no proper chance against the still-unseen enemy so unexpectedly loosed at them and so frightfully fatal. For, after a pause to be measured by seconds, out the pair popped, one to the right and the other to the left. But hardly had their feet touched the earth when, from diagonally above them, there descended a fresh slat of hot lead. On that, the young Latin-American emotionalist very slowly dropped his automatic and bent himself double and clasped both hands against his abdomen, very much in the posture of one who has just been taken with a quite severe cramp colic; and he took several jerky deliberate steps forward and then he sat down on the concrete. Probably he did have a colicky sensation seeing that he was drilled through and through. He held the affected pose for a brief space before he gently rolled over on his side, still with that 'midships curl in him.

While this was going on, the fourth youthful raider was fumbling to slide fresh cartridges in at the open breach of his converted blunderbus. But a shot came and raked the thing right out of his hands and took with it two of his fingers and a thumb.

248

Nursing the maimed hand, he turned to run for the shelter of the taxi, not ten feet away. He couldn't quite make it because, with one final shot, the painstaking and thorough Mr. Tallbee bored his skull for him.

Behind so many shattering, echoing concussions, the succeeding quiet – with everybody in sight for the moment stricken dumb and that wailing mother over there dropped in a merciful faint across her baby's baby-carriage – made a great void, an almost unendurable silence which was more deafening than claps of reverberant thunder would have been. So Mr. Tallbee, like the veteran big-game hunter that he was, took advantage of the hush to tot up his totals, firstly considering item by item his sprawled handiwork just yonder, and secondly making a swift tally of the sowing of ejected shellcases on the porch floor at his naked feet. He counted the scattered little brass capsules, each smeared by powder staining and each streaked and dulled with molten wax; and then the lingering lust for slaughtering died out of his lean face and instead appeared a look of deep chagrin; vehemently he spat out his quid and he said:

"Jis to ponder it – them four fine-pretty boys all vouchsafed to come within clost and easyful range and yit me a missin' one shoot complete! I am fur true a dotaged old trifler and must be turnin' blind, moreover!"

Comparative calm had descended upon the Tallbee domicile and high time, too, the head of that fluttered establishment thought. Until to-morrow, the last civic dignitaries – mayor and common councilmen coming, and the chief of police and the county prosecutor coming together with joint congratulations – had departed. Until to-morrow the last of the citizens at large seeking handshakes, and the last of the staff cameramen seeking photographs, and the last of the reporters seeking human-interest stories, and the last of the descriptive writers seeking character studies and interviews, and the last of the Sunday editors calling up to arrange for special articles and special sittings, were through with their botherments. It was well after midnight.

249

"Pappy," the proudly important Myrtle Ellie was saying, "pappy, listen: With the reward that the bank people already have promised, and the fund that they're going to take up by popular subscription – anyhow they're talking about it now – and the money those newspapers are going to pay you besides, just for you signing some pieces that they'll write 'em out themselves, there'll be a whole lot of money coming in. Why don't you take that money and go on back down home – the time that you were to stay away is almost up anyway – and buy back the old home place and finish out your lifetime the way you always wanted to? I can make out all right by myself."

"Daughter," said he, "harken unto me and give due heed ez befittin' a woman-person. You air goin' to take all them pusses of money and buy that there head-gearin place – whut's that furrin' name of your'n fur it?"

"Millinery shop. Oh, pappy, darling!

"– that there whuttever-'tis you've been honin' fur to follow after runnin'. You buy it. And you git yoreself married to a genteel man-person and start in a-multiplyin' and replenishin' the yearth, like the Book says."

"But, pappy," Myrtle Ellie, all tremulous with joy, was striving to be unselfish about it; "but, pappy, you've been so miserable here; you've hated the change so – and everything!"

"Mebbe I mout find it some changeful in the mountings," he told her. "Sence the word come of Zach Zachary's dyin' in that fur-off settlemint of California, seems like I ain't been feelin' so overly zestful to git back ez once't I wuz. Moreover," Mr. Tallbee put forth a gnarled hand and tenderly caressed his recharged rifle where conveniently it was propped against the center table; "moreover, frum whut tidin's they fotched me this evenin', them spiteful boys that got themselves massacreed out yan to-day has got friends and kinnery that air both survigrous and uppy-tempered. It's possible some amongst 'em mout feel it 'cumbent upon 'em fur to cherish the gredge and come round a-purpose to pick fusses with me. It's only politeful I sh'd wait."

FAITH, HOPE AND CHARITY

Just outside a sizable New Mexico town the second section of the fast through train coming from the Coast made a short halt. Entering the stretch leading into the yards, the engineer found the signal set against him, indicating the track on ahead was temporarily blocked.

It was a small delay though. Almost at once the semaphore, like the finger of a mechanical wizard, made the warning red light to vanish and a green light to appear instead; so, at that, the Limited got under way and rolled on into the station for her regular stop.

But before she started up, four travelers quitted her. They got out on the off side, the side farthest away from the town, and that probably explains why none of the crew and none of the other passengers saw them getting out. It helps also to explain why they were not missed until quite some time later.

Their manner of leaving her was decidedly unusual. First, one of the vestibule doors between the third sleeping car and the fourth sleeping car opened and the trap in the floor flipped up briskly under the pressure of an impatient foot on the operating lever. A brace of the departing ones came swiftly into view, one behind the other. True, there was nothing unusual about that. But as they stepped down on the earth they faced about and received the figure of a third person whose limbs dangled and whose head lolled back as they took the dead weight of him into their arms. Next there emerged the fourth and last member of the group, he being the one who had eased the limp figure of Number Three down the car steps into the grasp of his associates.

For a fractional space their shapes made a little huddle in the lee of the vestibule. Looking on, you might have guessed that among them there was a momentary period of indecision touching on the next step to be taken.

However, this muddle – if that was what it was – right away straightened itself out. Acting with movements which somehow seemed a bit difficult and awkward, as though their very haste hampered them, the two burden-bearers carried their unconscious load down the short embankment and deposited it on the cindery under-footing close against the flank of the slightly built-up right of way.

Number Four bent over the sprawled form and fumbled at it, shoving their hands into first one pocket and then another. In half a minute or less he straightened up and spoke to the remaining pair, at the same time using both hands to shove some article inside the vent of his waistcoat.

"I have got them," he said, speaking in English with a foreign accent.

They pressed toward him, their hands extended.

"Not here and not yet, Señors," he said sharply. "First we make sure of the rest. First you do, please, as I do."

Thereupon he hopped nimbly up the shoulder of the road-bed and headed toward the rear of the halted train, slinking well in under the overhang of the Pullmans; in fact, brushing against them as he went. His mates obeyed his example. They kept on until they had passed the tail coach, which was a combination coach, and then they stepped inward between the rails and continued on westward, still maintaining their single-file formation.

Immediately the dusk swallowed them up. It was only for a space of instants that their diminishing outlines against the paling afterglow of the sunset were revealed to anybody who might be sitting or standing on the observation end of the club car. So far as could be learned afterward, nobody there took note of them.

Yet there was something peculiar about the way each one of these three plodding pedestrians bore himself. The peculiarity was this: He bore himself like a person engaged in prayer – in a silent perambulating act of piety. His head was tucked in, his face turning neither to the right nor left; his eyes were set steadfastly forward as though upon some invisible goal, his hands clasped primly in front of him.

Thus and so the marching three plodded on until the train, having got in motion, was out of sight beyond a curve in the approach to the station. Then they checked and came together in a clump, and then, had you been there, you would have understood the reason for their devotional pose. All three of them were wearing handcuffs.

The man who had spoken before unpalmed a key ring which he was carrying. Working swiftly even in the half-darkness, he made tests of the keys on the ring until he found the proper keys. He freed the wrists of his two fellows. Then one of them took the keys and unlocked his set of bracelets for him.

He, it would seem, was the most forethoughted of the trio. With his heel he kicked shallow gouges in the gritty soil beside the track and buried the handcuffs therein. After that they briefly confabbed together, and the upshot of the confab was that, having matched for the possession of some object evidently held to be of great value, they separated forces.

One man set off alone on a detour to the southeast, which would carry him around the town. His late companions kept on in a general westerly direction, heading toward the desert which all that day they had been traversing. They footed it fast, as men might foot it who were fleeing for their lives and yet must conserve their strength. As a matter of fact, they were fleeing for their lives. So likewise the one from whom they had just parted was fleeing for his life.

It was partly by chance that these three had been making the transcontinental journey in company. Two of them, Lafitte the Frenchman, and Verdi the Italian who had Anglicized his name and called himself Green, met while lying in jail at San Francisco awaiting deportation to their respective countries. Within a space of a month each had been arrested as a refugee from justice; within the space of one week the formalities for extraditing the pair of them were completed.

So, to save trouble and expense: to kill, as it were, two birds with one stone, the authorities decided to send them together across to the Eastern seaboard where, according to arrangements made by cable, they would be surrendered over to police representatives coming from abroad to receive them and transport them back overseas. For the long trip to New York a couple of city detectives had them in custody.

When the train bearing the officers and their charges reached the junction in lower California where the main line connected with a branch line running south to the Mexican border, there came aboard a special agent of the Department of Justice who had with him a prisoner.

This prisoner was one Manuel Gaza, a Spaniard. He also recently had been captured and identified; and he also was destined for return to his own land. It was not by prior agreement that he had been retransferred at this junction point to the same train which carried the Italian and the Frenchman. It just happened so.

It having happened so, the man who had Gaza in tow lost no time in getting acquainted with his San Francisco brethren. For a number of reasons it seemed expedient to all the officers that from here on they should travel as a unit. Accordingly the special agent talked with the Pullman conductor and exchanged the reservations he previously had booked getting instead a compartment adjoining the drawing-room in which the four from the city were riding.

It was on a Friday afternoon that the parties united. Friday evening, at the first call for dinner, the three officers herded their three prisoners forward to the dining car, the passage of the sextet through the aisles of the intervening sleepers causing some small commotion. Their advent into the diner created another little sensation.

Since it was difficult for the handcuffed aliens to handle knife and fork, they were given such food as might readily be eaten with a spoon or with the fingers – soups and omelets and soft vegetables and pie or rice pudding. The detectives ate fish. They shared between them a double order of imported kippers – a dish not on the typewritten menu for this meal but selected from the printed list of staple edibles.

Presumably they were the only persons on the train who that day had chosen the kippered herrings. Shortly, the special agent was giving private thanks that his church prescribed no dietetic regulations for Friday, because within an hour or two after leaving the table, the San Francisco men were suffering from acute and violent cramps – ptomaine poison had them helpless.

One seemed to be dangerously ill. That night at a town near the border between California and Arizona, he was taken off the train and carried to a hospital. During the wait at the station, a local physician dosed the second and lesser sufferer, whose name was McAvoy, and when he had been somewhat relieved of what ailed him, the doctor gave him a shot of something in the arm and said he ought to be up and about within twenty-four hours or some much matter.

During the night McAvoy slept in the lower berth of the compartment and the secret agent sat up, with the communicating door open, to guard the aliens, who were bedded in the so-called drawing-room.

Their irons stayed on their wrists; their lone warden was accepting no foolish odds against him. He had taken the precaution to transfer the keys of the Frenchman's handcuffs and the Italian's handcuffs from McAvoy's keeping to his own, slipping them on his key ring, but this had been done in case McAvoy should become seriously ill en route and it should devolve upon him to make at least a lap of the journey single-handed.

Next morning McAvoy's tortured stomach was much easier but he felt weak, he said, and drowsy. Given a full twelve hours of rest, though, he thought he would be able to go on guard when the nightfall came.

So through the day while the Limited rocked across the desert he lay in his berth, and the special agent occupied the camp stool or an end of the drawing-room sofa. The trapped fugitives sat in the drawing-room seats, smoking cigarettes and when the officer was not too near, talking among themselves.

Mainly they talked in English, a language which Gaza the Spaniard and Lafitte the Frenchman spoke fairly well. Verdi or Green, as the case might be, had little English at his command but Gaza, who had spent three years in Naples, spoke Italian; and so when Verdi used his own tongue, Gaza could interpret for the Frenchman's benefit. They were allowed to quit the drawing-room only for meals.

When dinner hour came on that second evening of their trip, McAvoy was in a doze. So the Department of Justice man did not disturb him.

"Come on, boys," he said to the three aliens; "time to eat again."

He lined them up in front of him in the corridor and they started the regular processional. It was just at that moment that the train broke its rhythmic refrain and began to clack and creak and slow for that unscheduled stop outside that New Mexico town. By the time they had reached the second car on ahead, she'd almost stopped and was lurching and jerking.

In the vestibule beyond that second car the special agent was in the act of stepping across the iron floor lip of the connection when a particularly brisk joggle caused him to lose his hat. He gave a small exclamation and bent to recover it. Doing so, he jostled against Gaza, the third man in the line, and therefore the next and nearmost man to him.

The agile Spaniard was quick to seize on his chance. He half turned and, bringing his chained wrists aloft, sent them down with all his might on the poll of the officer's unprotected skull. The victim of the assault never made a sound – just spraddled on his face and was dead to the world.

No outsider had been witness to the assault. No outsider came along during the few seconds which were required by the late prisoners to open an off-side car door and make their escape after the fashion which already has been described for you. Nobody missed them – for quite a while nobody did.

It wasn't until nearly nine o'clock, when McAvoy had roused up and got uneasy and rung for the porter and begun to ask questions, that a search was made and an alarm was raised.

Penned up together through that day, the aliens had matched stories, one story against another. A common plight made them communicative; a common peril caused each to turn with morbid reiteration to his own fatal predicament. It was as though he took a melancholy pride in painting his prospect as the most desperate.

There was no doubt that each looked upon the penalty which awaited him on the farther side of the Atlantic Ocean as a more dreadful thing than the things which these, his brother murderers, would suffer. He shrank from the frightful prospect of it but nevertheless kept dwelling upon it.

Said the Frenchman to the Spaniard: "He" – indicating his recent cell-mate, the Italian – "he knows how with me it stands. With him, I have talked. He speaks not so well the English but sometimes he understands it. Now you shall hear and judge for yourself how bad my situation is."

Rapidly, graphically, with working features, with foreshortened gestures of his linked hands, this criminal sketched his past. He had been a Marseilles dock hand. He had killed a woman. She deserved killing, so he killed her. He had been caught, tried, convicted, condemned. While lying in prison, with execution day only a few weeks distant, he had made a getaway.

In disguise he had reached America and here had stayed three years. Then another woman, in a fit of jealousy, betrayed him to the police. He had been living with that woman. She also was French. To her he had given his confidence. It would appear that women had been his undoing. He went on:

"Me, I am as good as dead already. And what a death!" A spasm of shuddering possessed him. "For me the guillotine is waiting. The devil invented it. It is so they go at you with that machine: They strap you flat upon a board. Face downward you are, but you can look up, you can see – that is the worst part. They fit your throat into a grooved shutter; they make it fast. You crane your neck; you bring your head back; your eyes are drawn upward, fascinated. Above you, waiting, ready, poised, your eyes see the – the knife."

"But only for a moment do you see it, my friend," said the Spaniard, in a tone of one offering comfort. "Only a moment and then – *pouff* – all over!"

"A moment! I tell you it is an eternity. It must be an eternity. Lying there, you must live a hundred lives, you must die a hundred deaths. And then to have your head taken off your body, to be all at once in two pieces. Me, I am not frightened of most deaths. But that death by the guillotine – ah-h!"

The Spaniard bent forward. He was sitting alone facing the other two, who shared a seat.

"Listen, Señor," he stated. "Compared with me, you are the lucky one. True, I have not yet been tried – before they could try me I fled away out of that many-times accursed Spain of mine."

"Not tried, eh?" broke in the Frenchman. "Then you have yet a loophole – a chance for escape; and I have none. My trial, as I told you, is behind me."

"You do not know the Spanish courts. It is plain you do not, since you say that," declared the Spaniard. "Those courts – they are greedy for blood. With them, to my kind, there is not mercy; there is only punishment.

"And such a punishment! Wait until you hear. To me when

257

they get me before them they will say: 'The proof is clear against you; the evidence has been thus and so. You are adjudged guilty. You took a life, so your life must be taken. It is the law.'

"Perhaps I say: 'Yes, but that life I took swiftly and in passion and for cause. For that one the end came in an instant, without pain, without lingering, yes, without warning. Since I must pay for it, why can not I also be made to die very quickly without pain?'

"Will they listen? No, they send me to the garrote. To a great strong chair they tie you – your hands, your feet, your trunk. Your head is against a post, an upright. In that post is a collar – an iron band. They fit that collar about your neck. Then from behind you the executioner – may he forever fry in hell! – he turns a screw.

"If he chooses he turns it slowly. The collar tightens, tightens; a knob presses into you behind. You begin to strangle. Your tongue comes forth from your mouth and swells. Your eyes pop from their sockets. Your face turns black. Oh, I have seen it myself! I know. You expire by inches! I am a brave man, Señors. When one's time comes, one dies. But oh, Señors, if it were any death but that! Better the guillotine than that! Better anything than that!"

He slumped back against the cushions, and rigors passed through him.

It was the Italian's turn. "I was tried in my absence," he explained to the Spaniard. "I was not even there to make my defense – I had thought it expedient to depart. Such is the custom of the courts in my country. They try you behind your back when you perhaps are thousands of miles away, as I was.

"They found me guilty, those judges. In Italy there is no capital punishment, so they sentenced me to life imprisonment. It is to that – that – I now return."

The Spaniard lifted his shoulders; the lifting was eloquent of his meaning.

"Not so fast," said the Italian. "You tell me you lived once in Italy. Have you forgotten what life imprisonment for certain acts means in Italy? It means solitary confinement. It means you are buried alive. They shut you away from every one in a tight cell. It is a tomb, that is all. You see no one ever, you hear no voice ever. If you cry out, no one answers. Silence, darkness, darkness, silence, until you go mad or until you die.

"Can you picture what that means to one of my race, to an Italian, who must have music, sunshine, talk with his fellows, sight of his fellows? It is in his nature – he must have these things or he is in torture, in constant and everlasting torment. Every hour becomes to him a year, every day a century, until his brain bursts asunder inside his skull.

"Oh, they knew – those fiends who devised this thing – what to an Italian is a million times worse than death – any death. I am the most unfortunate one of the three of us. My penalty is the most dreadful by far."

The others would not have it so. They argued the point with him and with each other. It was a strange triangular debate that they carried on. They renewed it at intervals all through the day, and twilight found their beliefs all unshaken.

Then, under the Spaniard's leadership, came their deliverance out of captivity. It was he who, on the toss-up, won the revolver which they had taken from the person of the senseless special agent. Also it was he who suggested to the Italian that for the time being, at least, they stick together. To this the Italian had agreed, the Marseilles man Lafitte already having elected to go on his own.

After the latter, heading east by south, had left them, the Spaniard said reflectively:

"Did you hear what he said at the last? He is optimistic, that one, for all that he seemed so gloomy and down-hearted to-day when speaking of that guillotine of his. He said he now had faith that he would yet dodge his fate. Five minutes after he is off that train he speaks of faith!"

"I can not go quite that far," answered the Italian. "We are free, but for us there will be still a thousand dangers. So I have not much faith, but I have hope. And you, my friend?"

The Spaniard shrugged his shoulders. His shrug might mean yes or it might mean no. Perhaps he needed his breath. He was going at a jog-trot down the tracks, the Italian alongside him.

Take the man who had faith. Set down as he was in a country utterly strange to him, this one of the fugitives nevertheless made steady and unmolested progress. He got safely around and by the New Mexico town. He hid in the chaparral until daybreak, then took to a highway running parallel with the railroad.

A "tin-canner," which is what they were beginning to call an itinerant motor tourist in those parts, overtook him soon after sun-up and gave him a lift to a small way station some forty miles down the line. There he boarded a local train – he had some money on him; not much money but enough – and undetected and, so far as he might judge, unsuspected, he rode that train clear on through to its destination a hundred miles or so farther along.

Other local trains carried him across a corner of Colorado and clear across Kansas. Forty-eight hours later or thereabouts, he was a guest in a third-rate hotel on a back street in Kansas City, Missouri.

He stayed in that hotel for two days and two nights, biding most of the time in his room on the top floor of the six-story building, going down only for his meals and for newspapers. The food he had to have; the newspapers gave him information, of a sort, of the hunt which the authorities in several interior states were supposed to be making for the three fugitives. It was repeatedly stated that all three were believed to be fleeing together. That cheered Lafitte very much. It strengthened his faith of ultimately escaping.

But on the morning of his third day in that cheap hotel, when he came out of his room and went down the hall to ring for the elevator – there was only one passenger elevator in this hotel – he saw something. Passing the head of the stairs, which ended approximately midway of the stretch between the door of his room and the wattled iron door opening on the elevator well, he saw, out of the corner of one watchful eye, two men in civilian garb on the steps below him, their faces being just about at the level of the floor.

They had halted there. Whether they were coming up or going down there was no way of telling. It seemed to him that at sight of him they ducked slightly and made as if to flatten themselves back against the side wall. That, though, might have been only his imagination playing him a little trick. There was just one quick flash for him and then he was past them.

He gave no sign of having seen them. He stilled an impulse to make a dash for it. Where was he to dash for, with the stairs cut off? He followed the only course open to him. Anyhow he told himself he might be wrong. Perhaps his nerves were misbehaving. Perhaps those two who seemed to be lurking just there behind him on those steps were not interested in him at all. He kept telling himself that, while he was ringing the bell, while he was waiting for the car to come up for him.

The car did come up and, for a wonder, promptly; an old-fashioned car, creaky, musty. Except for its shirt-sleeved attendant, it was empty. As Lafitte stepped in, he glanced sidewise over his shoulder, making the movement casual – no sight of those two fellows.

He rode down, the only passenger for that trip so there were no stops on the descent. They reached the ground floor, which was the office floor. The elevator came to a standstill, then moved up a foot or so, then joltingly down six inches or so, as the attendant, who was not expert, being an early-morning substitute for the regular elevator man, maneuvered to bring the sill of the car flush with the tiling of the lobby.

The delay was sufficiently prolonged for Lafitte to realize, all in a flash, he had not been wrong. Through the intervening grille of the shaft door he saw two more men who pressed close up to that door, who stared in at him, whose looks and poses were watchful, eager, prepared. Besides, Lafitte, having spent three years in this country in intimacy with members of the resident criminal class, knew plain-clothes men when he saw them.

Up above and here below, he was cut off. There still was a chance for him, a poor one but the only one. If he could shoot the elevator aloft quickly enough, check it at the third floor or the fourth, say, and hop out, he might make a successful dart for the fire escape at the rear of the hotel – provided the fire escape was not guarded. In the space of time that the elevator boy was jockeying the car, he thought of this, and having thought it, acted on it.

Swinging his fist from behind with all his might, he hit that helpless substitute on the point of the jaw and deposited him, stunned and temporarily helpless, on his knees in a corner of the cage. Lafitte grabbed the lever, shoved it over hard, and up the shaft shot the car. Before he could get control of it, being unfamiliar with such mechanism and in a panic besides, it was at the top of the house. But then he mastered it and made it reverse its course, and returning downward he pulled the lever, bringing it toward him.

That was the proper notion, that gentler manipulation, for now the car, more obedient, was crawling abreast of the third-floor level. It crept earthward, inch by inch, and without bringing it to a dead stop he jerked up the latch of the collapsible safety gate, telescoped the metal outer door back into its folded-up self, and stooping low, because the gap was diminishing all the while, he lunged forward.

Now that elevator boy was a quick-witted, a high-tempered Irish boy. He might be half-dazed but his instincts of belligerency were not asleep. He told afterward how, automatically and indignantly functioning, he grabbed at the departing assailant and caught him by one leg and for a fleeting moment, before the other kicked free, detained or at least retarded him.

But by all that was good and holy he swore he did not touch the lever. Being down on all-fours at the rear side of the slowly sinking car, how could he touch it? Why, just at that precise fraction of a second, the elevator should pick up full speed was a mystery to him – to everybody else, for that matter.

But pick up full speed it did. And the Irish boy cowered down and screamed an echo to a still louder scream than his, and hid his eyes from the sight of Lafitte with his head outside and his body inside the elevator, being decapitated as completely and almost as neatly – if you could use the latter word in such connection – as though a great weighted knife had sheared him off at the neck.

Take the Spaniard and the Italian: Steadily they traveled westward for nearly all of that night which followed their evacuation from the Limited. It put desirable distance between them and the spot where they had dumped the special agent down. Also it kept them warm. This was summertime but on the desert even summer nights are chilly and sometimes they are downright cold. Before dawn, they came on a freight train waiting in a siding for more important traffic to pass. Its locomotive faced west. That suited their book.

They climbed nimbly aboard a flat and snuggled themselves down behind a barrier of farm implements. Here, breakfastless but otherwise comfortable, they rode until nearly midday. Then a brakeman appeared, swinging himself from car to car, and found them. He harshly ordered them to get themselves up out of there and off of there.

Immediately though, looking at them where they squatted half-hidden, his tone softened, taking on a more friendly note, and he told them he'd changed his mind about it and they could stay aboard as long as they pleased. On top of this, he hurried forward as though he might have important news for the engine crew or somebody. He kept glancing back toward where they were crowded.

They chose to get off. They had noted the quick start as of recognition which the brakeman had given. They figured – and figured rightly – that by now the chase for them was on and that their descriptions had been telegraphed back and forth along the line. The train was traveling at least twenty miles an hour but as soon as the brakeman was out of sight, they jumped for it, tumbling like shot rabbits down the slope of the right of way and bringing up all jarred and shaken in the dry ditch at the bottom.

Barring bruises and scratches, Green had taken no hurt, but Gaza landed with a badly sprained ankle. He gathered himself up, and with Green to give him a helping arm, hobbled away from the railroad.

To get away from the railroad was their prime aim now. Choosing a course at random, they went north over the undulating waste lands and through the shimmering heat, toward a range of mottled high buttes rising on beyond.

It took them until deep into the afternoon to cover a matter roughly of five miles. By now, Gaza's lower left leg was elephantine in its proportions and every forced step he took meant a fresh stab of agony. He knew he could not go much farther. Green knew it too, and in his brain began shaping tentative plans. The law of self-preservation was one of the few laws for which he had respect. They panted from heat and from thirst and from weariness.

At the end of those five miles, having toiled laboriously up over a fold in the land, they saw close at hand and almost directly below them, a 'dobe hut, and not quite so near at hand, a big flock of sheep looking like woolly white larvæ against the slope where they grazed on the scanty and astringent herbage.

At the door of the cabin, a man in overalls was stripping the hide from a swollen dead cow.

Before they could dodge back below the sky-line, he straightened his back and looked and saw them and stood expectantly. There was nothing for them to do except to go toward him. At their slow approach, an expression of curiosity crept over his brown face and stayed there. He looked like a Mexican or possibly a half-breed Indian. He wore no beard, which would be a rare thing for a sheep herder, but not so rare a thing if he were part Indian.

When Gaza, stumbling nearer, hailed him in English, he merely shook his head dumbly. Then Gaza tried him in Spanish and to that he replied volubly. For minutes they palavered back and forth, then the stranger served them with deep drafts from a water-bottle swinging in the doorway with a damp sack over it. The water was lukewarm and bitterish-tasting but it was grateful to their parched throats. Then he withdrew inside the little house and Gaza, for Green's benefit, translated into Italian what talk had passed.

"He says he is quite alone here, which is the better for us," explained the Spaniard, speaking swiftly. "He says that a week ago he came up from Old Mexico, seeking work. A gringo – a white man – gave him work. The white man is a sheep man. His home ranch is miles away. In a sheep wagon he brought this Mexican here and left him here in charge of that flock yonder, with provisions for a month.

"It will be three weeks then before the white man, his employer, comes again. Except for that white man he knows nobody hereabouts. Until we came just now, he had seen no one at all. So he is glad to see us."

"And accounting for ourselves you told him what?" asked Green.

"I told him we were traveling across country in a car and that going down a steepness last night the car overturned and was wrecked and I crippled myself. I told him that, traveling light because of my leg, we started out to find some town, some house, and that, hoping to make a short-cut, we left the road, but that since morning and until we blundered upon this camp we had been quite lost in this ugly country. He believes me. He is simple, that one, an ignorant credulous peon.

"But kind-hearted, that also is plain. For proof of it observe this." He pointed to the bloated, half-flayed carcass. "He says three days ago just over that red hill behind us, he found this beast – a stray from somewhere he knows not where. So far as he knows there are no cattle droves in these parts – only sheep.

"She was sick, she staggered, she was dizzy and turned in circles as if blind, and froth ran from her mouth. There is a weed that does that to animals which eat it, he says. So, hoping to make her well again, he put a scrap of rope on her horns and led her here. But last night she died. So to-day, with his big sharp knife, he has been peeling her.

"Now he goes to make ready some food for us. He is very hospitable, also, that one."

"And when we have eaten, then what? We can't linger here."

"Wait, please, Señor. To my mind already an idea comes." His tone was authoritative, confident, and under his heavy moustache a smile showed. "First we fill our empty stomachs to give us strength, and then we smoke a cigarette, and while we smoke, I think. And then – we see."

On *frijoles* and rancid bacon and thin corn cakes and bad coffee, which the herder brought them on tin platters and in tin cups, they did fill their empty stomachs, squatting meanwhile in the skimpy shade of an improvised arbor of thin brush set on poles, which fronted the 'dobe. Then they smoked together, all three of them, smoking cigarettes rolled in corn-husk wrappers.

The Mexican was hunkered on his heels, making smoke rings in the still hot air, when Gaza, getting on his feet with difficulty, limped toward the doorway, gesturing to show that he craved another swig from the water-bottle. When he was behind the other two, almost touching them, he drew the special agent's pistol and fired once and their host tumbled forward on his face and spraddled his limbs and quivered a bit and was still, with a bullet hole in the back of his head. There was very little blood; there was only a slight oozing from the wound.

This killing gave the Italian, seasoned killer as he was, a profound shock. It seemed so unnecessary unless –? He started up, his features twitching, and backed away, fearing the next bullet would be for him.

"Remain tranquil, Señor," said the Spaniard, almost gaily. "For you, my comrade, there is no danger. There is for you hope of deliverance, you, who professed last night to have hope in your soul.

"Now me, I have charity in my soul – charity for you, charity for myself, charity also for this one lying here. Behold, he is now out of his troubles. He was a dolt, a clod of the earth, a creature of no refinement. He lived a hermit's life, lonely, miserable, in filth. He knew only sheep – and sheep are poor company even for a clod. Now he has been dispatched to a better and brighter world. That was but kindness." With his foot he touched the sprawled corpse.

"But in dispatching him I had thought also for you – for both of us. I elucidate: First we bury him under the dirt floor of this house, taking care to leave no telltale traces of our work. Then you make a pack for your back of the food that is here. You take also the water-bottle, filled. Furthermore you take with you this pistol which is mine and which I give to you.

"Then, stepping lightly on rocky ground or on hard ground so that you make no tracks, you go swiftly hence and hide yourself in those mountains until – who can tell? – until those who will come presently here have ceased to search for you. With me along, lamed as I am, me to hamper you, to hold you back, there would be no chance for either of us. But you, going alone – you armed, provisioned, quick on foot – you have a hope."

"But – but you? What then becomes of you? You – you sacrifice yourself?" In his bewilderment the Italian stammered over the words.

"Me, I stay here to greet the pursuers. It is quite simple. In peaceful solitude I await their coming. It can not be long until they come. That man of the freight train will be guiding them back to pick up our trail. By to-night at latest, and probably sooner, I expect them."

At sight of the Italian's more deeply mystified face he broke now into a laugh.

"Still you are puzzled, eh? You think that I am magnanimous, that I am generous? Well, all that I am. But you think me also a fool and there you err. I save you perhaps but likewise perhaps I save myself. Observe, Señor."

He stooped and lifted the dead face of his victim. "See now what I myself saw the moment I beheld this herder of ours: This man is much my shape, my height, my coloring. He spoke a corrupt Spanish such as I can speak. Put upon me the clothes which he wears and remove from my lip this mustache which I wear, and I would pass for him even before the very eyes of that white man who hired him.

"Well, very soon I shall be wearing his clothes, my own being hidden in the same grave with him. Within ten minutes I shall be removing this mustache. He being newly shaven, as you see for yourself, it must be that in this hovel we will find a razor. I shall pass for him. I shall be this mongrel dull-wit."

A light broke on the Italian. He ran and kissed the Spaniard, on both cheeks and on the mouth.

"Ah, my brother!" he cried out delightfully. "Forgive me that for a moment I thought you hard-hearted for having in seeming wantonness killed the man who fed us. I see you are brilliant – a great thinker, a great genius. But, my beloved" – and here doubt once more assailed him – "what explanation do you make when they do come?"

"That is the best of all," said Gaza. "Before you leave me you take a cord and you bind me most securely – my hands crossed behind my back – so; my feet fastened together – so. It will not be for very long that I remain so. I can endure it. Coming then, they find me thus. That I am bound makes more plausible, more convincing the tale I shall tell them.

"And this is the tale that I shall tell them: To them I shall say that as I sat under this shelter skinning my dead cow, there appeared suddenly two men who fell upon me without warning; that in the struggle they hurt my poor leg most grievously, then, having choked me into quietude, they tied my limbs, despoiled me of my provender, and hurriedly departed, leaving me helpless. I shall describe these two brutal men – oh, most minutely I shall describe them. And my description will be accurate, for you I shall be describing as you stand now; myself I shall describe as I now am.

"The man from the train will say: 'Yes, yes, that is true; those are surely the two I saw.' He will believe me at once; that will help. Then they will inquire to know in which direction fled this pair of scoundrels and I will tell them they went that way yonder to the south across the desert, and they will set off in that direction, seeking two who flee together, when all the while you will be gone this way, north into those mountains which will shelter you. And that, Señor, will be a rich part of the whole joke.

"Perhaps, though, they question me further. Then I say: 'Take me before this gringo who within a week hired me to watch his sheep. Confront me with him. He will identify me, he will confirm my story.' And if they do that and he does that – as most surely he will – why, then they must turn me loose to go about my business and that, Señor, will be the very crown and peak of the joke."

In the excess of his admiration and his gratitude, the Italian just naturally had to kiss him again.

They worked fast and they worked scientifically, carefully, overlooking nothing, providing against every contingency. But at the last minute, when the Italian was ready to resume his flight and the Spaniard, smoothly shaven and effectually disguised in the soiled shirt and messy overalls of the dead man, had turned around and submitted his wrists to be pinioned, it was discovered that there was no rope available with which to bind his legs. The one short scrap of rope about the spot had been used for tying his hands.

The Spaniard said this was just as well. Any binding that was drawn snugly enough to fetter his feet securely would certainly increase the pain in the inflamed and grossly swollen ankle joint.

However, it was apparent that he must be securely anchored, lest suspicion arise in the minds of his rescuers when they arrived. Here the Italian made a contribution to the plot. He was proud of his inspiration.

With the Mexican's butcher knife he cut long narrow strips from the fresh slick cowhide. Then the Spaniard sat down on the earth with his back against one of the slim tree trunks supporting the arbor, and the Italian took numerous turns about his waist and his arms and the upper part of his body, and tightly knotted the various ends of the skin ribbons behind the post. Unaided, no human being could escape out of that mesh. To the pressure and the wriggle of the prisoner's trunk, the moist, pliant lashings would give slightly but it was certain they neither would work loose not snap apart.

So he settled himself in his bonds, and the Italian, having

shouldered his pack, put a lighted cigarette between his benefactor's lips and once more fervently kissed him in token of gratitude and wished him success and made off with many wavings of the arm and shouted farewells.

So far as this empty country was concerned, the Italian was a greenhorn, a tenderfoot. Nevertheless, and considering his fatigue and everything, he made excellent progress. He marched northward until dark, lay that night under a murdered man's smelly blanket behind a many-colored butte and next morning struck deeper into the broken lands. He entered what he hoped might be a gap through the mountains, treading cautiously along a narrow natural trail half-way up the face of a dauntingly steep cliff side.

He was well into it when his foot dislodged a scrap of shaly rock which in sliding over the verge set other rocks to cascading down the slope. From above, yet larger boulders began toppling over into the scoured-out passageway thus provided, and during the next five minutes the walled-in declivity was alive and roaring with tumbling huge stones, with dislodged earth running fluid like a stream, with uprooted stunty piñons, with choking acrid dust clouds.

The Italian ran for dear life; he managed to get out of the avalanche's path. When at length he reached a safe place and looked back, he saw behind him how the landslide had choked the gorge almost to its brim. No human being – no, not even a goat, could from his side scale that jagged and overhanging parapet. It was reasonable to presume that it could not be mounted from the other side. Between him and pursuit was a perfect barrier.

Well content, he went on. But presently he made a discovery, a distressing discovery, which took the good cheer right out of him. This was no gateway into which he had entered. It was a dead-end leading nowhere – what westerners call a box canyon. On three sides of him, right, left and on ahead, rose tremendously high walls, sheer and unclimbable. They threatened him; they seemed to be closing in on him to pinch him flat. And, of course, back of him retreat was cut off. There he was, bottled up like a fly in a corked jug, like a frog at the bottom of a well.

Frantically he explored as best he could the confines of this vast prison cell of his. He stumbled upon a spring and its waters, while tainted lightly with alkali, were drinkable. So he had water and he had food, some food. By paring his daily portions down almost to starvation point, he might make these rations last for months. But then, what? And in the meantime, what? Why, until hunger destroyed him, he was faced with that doom which he so dreaded – the doom of solitary confinement.

He thought it all out and then he knelt down and took out his pistol and he killed himself.

In one of his calculations that smart malefactor, the Spaniard, had been wrong. By his system of deduction, the searchers should reach the 'dobe hut where he was tethered within four hours or, at most, five. But it was nearer thirty hours before they appeared.

The trouble had been that the brakeman wasn't quite sure of the particular stretch where he had seen the fugitives nestled beneath a reaping machine on that flat car. Besides, it took time to spread the word; to summon county officials; to organize an armed searching party. When at length the posse did strike the five-mile trail leading from the railroad tracks to the camp of the late sheep herder, considerably more than a day had elapsed.

The track was fairly plain – two sets of heavy footprints bearing north and only lacking where rocky outcrops broke through the surface of the desert. Having found it, they followed it fast, and when they mounted the fold in the earth above the cabin, they saw the figure of a man seated in front of it, bound snugly to one of the supports of the meager arbor.

Hurrying toward him they saw that he was dead – that his face was blackened and horribly distorted; that his glazed eyes goggled at them and his tongue protruded; that his stiffened legs were drawn up in sharp angles of agony.

They looked closer and they saw the manner of his death and were very sorry for him. He had been bound with strands of fresh rawhide, and all through that day he had been sitting there exposed to the baking heat of the sun, and heat, operating on damp new rawhide, has an immediate effect. Heat causes certain substances to expand but green rawhide it causes to contract very fast to an ironlike stiffness and rigidity.

So in this case the sun glare had drawn tighter and tighter the lashings about this poor devil's body, squeezing him in at the stomach and the breast and the shoulders, pressing his arms tighter and tighter and yet tighter against his sides. That for him would have been a highly unpleasant procedure – impeding his circulation, hampering his breathing, bruising his flesh – but it would not have killed him.

Something else had done that. One loop of the rawhide had been twisted about his neck and made fast at the back of the post. At first it might have been no more than a loosely fitting circlet but hour by hour it had hardened and shrunken into a choking collar, a diminishing noose, a terribly deadly yoke. Veritably it had garroted him by inches.

Parallel Universe Publications

OTHER VISIONS OF HEAVEN AND HELL by Jessica Palmer
ISBN: 978-0-9935742-1-4

A SAUCERFUL OF SECRETS by Andrew Darlington
ISBN: 978-0-9935742-0-7

THE WINTER HUNT AND OTHER STORIES
by Steve Lockley & Paul Lewis
ISBN: 978-0-9932888-9-0

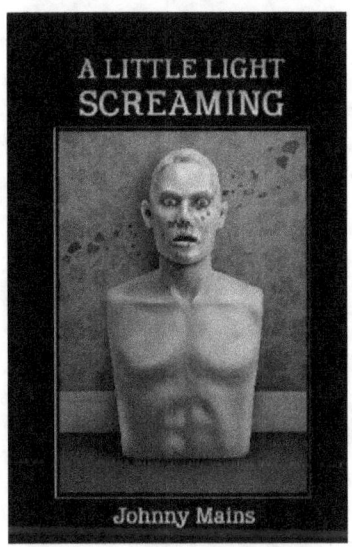

A LITTLE LIGHT SCREAMING by Johnny Mains
ISBN: 978-0-9932888-5-2

ENGLAND 'B': 90 MINUTES OF HELL by Richard Staines
ISBN: 978-0-9932888-7-6

AND NOBODY LIVED HAPPILY EVER AFTER by Kate Farrell
ISBN: 978-0-9932888-8-3

KITCHEN SINK GOTHIC: Selected by David and Linden Riley
ISBN: 978-0-9932888-3-8

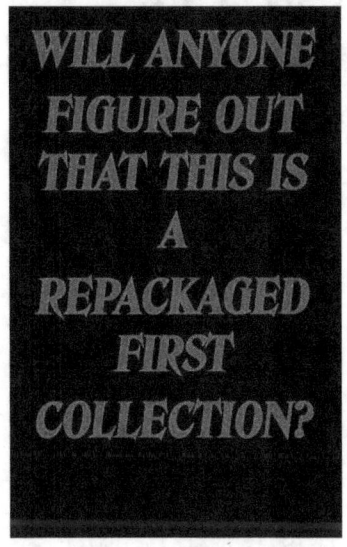

WILL ANYONE FIGURE OUT THAT THIS IS A REPACKAGED FIRST
COLLECTION? by Johnny Mains
ISBN: 978-0-9574535-7-9

BLACK CEREMONIES by Charles Black
ISBN: 978-0-9574535-5-5

HIS OWN MAD DEMONS:
DARK TALES FROM DAVID A. RILEY
ISBN: 978-0-9574535-8-6

THEIR CRAMPED DARK WORLD by David A. Riley
ISBN: 978-0-9574535-9-3

THE HEAVEN MAKER AND OTHER GRUESOME TALES
by Craig Herbertson
ISBN: 978-0-9932888-2-1

GOBLIN MIRE by David A. Riley
ISBN: 978-0-9574535-4-8

THINGS THAT GO BUMP IN THE NIGHT
selected by Douglas Draa and David A. Riley
ISBN: 978-0-9574535-6-2

CLASSIC WEIRD selected David A. Riley
ISBN: 978-0-9574535-3-1

MOLOCH'S CHILDREN by David A. Riley
ISBN: 978-0-9932888-1-4

Check our website:

http://paralleluniversepublications.blogspot.co.uk/